mulengro

by Charles de Lint
from Tom Doherty Associates

mulengro

Charles de Lint

A Tom Doherty Associates Book New York

Grateful acknowledgment is made to Robin Williamson for permission to use a portion of "The Road the Gypsies Go" from the album *A Glint at the Kindling,* copyright © 1979 by Robin Williamson. For further information on Robin Williamson, write: Pig's Whisker Music Press, P.O. Box 27522, Los Angeles, CA 90027; or Pig's Whisker Music Press, BCM 4797, London WCIN 3XX, England.

Also thanks to Ewan MacColl for the use of the following: "The Moving-On Song," "Goodbye to the Thirty-Foot Trailer," and "The Travelling People." Words and music by Ewan MacColl, copyright © 1964, 1967 by Stormking Music Inc. All rights reserved. Used by permission.

MULENGRO

Originally published in October 1985 by Ace Fantasy Books

An Orb Edition
Published by Tom Doherty Associates, LLC
175 Fifth Avenue
New York, NY 10010

www.tor.com

ISBN 0-312-87399-9

First Orb Edition: December 2003

Printed in the United States of America

0 9 8 7 6 5 4 3 2 1

for

Charles R. Saunders
who got the ball rolling

Andrew J. Offutt
who pushed it
a little further

and for those folks
who bounced it back and forth
a few times:

Barry Blair
Roger Camm
John Charette
Larry Dickison
Ronald Grossey
Loay Hall
Richard Hall
Gordon Linzner

Contents

Introduction

When *Mulengro* first appeared in 1985, readers picked it up expecting the usual de Lint novel. But sometimes the darkness calls, and I find myself approaching it, to try to understand it. The Otherworld contains as much darkness as it does ambiguity and light, and to ignore it entirely strikes me as only telling half the story.

While *Mulengro* has many of the elements that readers have come to expect in my work, it also contains graphic descriptions of violence and its aftereffects. It also portrays hope, love, humor, loyalty, and personal growth. Almost twenty years have passed, and I remain proud of this story about modern Romany culture.

I can well understand that some people prefer not to read horror fiction, and in subsequent work where I explored the dark, I used the pseudonym Samuel M. Key. No secret was made of the fact that the pseudonym was mine, since it was merely a device to let readers know in advance that they could expect a darker story between the covers. As fate (or actually, my publisher) would have it, the Sam Key books are now being published under my own name, with Forewords similar to this. I suppose this indicates a measure of success in my career, and certainly I've received plenty of mail from people who enjoy these books as much as my others, but I still wanted to give a cautionary heads-up, in case this story might cause anyone discomfort.

"Far and near as fool's fire,
  they come glittering through the gloom.
  Their tongues as strong and nimble,
  as would bind the looms of luck. . . ."
              —from "The Road the Gypsies Go"
                 by Robin Williamson

"The boshom engro kils, he kils,
  The tawnie juva gils, she gils,
  A puro Romano gillie,
  Now shoon the Romano gillie."
              —traditional Lowara Romany refrain

[The fellow with fiddle plays, he plays,
 The little lassie sings, she sings
 An ancient Gypsy ditty,
 Now hear the Gypsy ditty.]

Part One

Patteran

With every light another color.
   —Romany description of themselves

Wagon, tent, or trailer born,
last month, last year, in far-off days;
born here or a thousand miles away,
there's always men nearby who'll say:
You better get born in someplace else,
So move along, get along, move along, get along!
   Go! Move! Shift!
         —from "The Moving-On Song"
            by Ewan MacColl

one

Janfri Yayal watched his house burn down without expression.

The two-story, wood-frame structure was beyond rescue. Flames leapt half its height into the night skies. Smoke erupted from windows and eaves, roiling upward like a ghost escaping the doomed flesh of its host body. A gasp came from the watching crowd as a section of roof collapsed in a shower of sparks. The firemen pulled back, all too aware of how ineffectual their efforts were at this point. Janfri's only response was a nerve that twitched in his cheek.

The red light of the flames and the glare of the rotating beacons on the police cars and fire trucks flickered across his dark skin, highlighting the strong features set in their mask of indifference. He was oblivious to the growing crowd of thrill-seekers who jostled for position against the hastily-erected barricades that the police had set up. He watched the home he'd known for three years burning and remembered other fires. Not the cook and camp fires of his childhood, nor the pleasant crack and spit of seasoned wood burning in a stone hearth. Instead his mind thrust up memories of a man set afire and the crowd around him, jeering and laying wagers as to how long he would live. Of the wagons of his parents and grandparents and others of their *kumpania* burning in the night. Of the men who wore the four-armed symbol of the swastika and set countries alight with the same single-minded purpose with which they burned Gypsy wagons.

But there were no swastikas here. It was another symbol that had erased the expression from Janfri's features. He had seen it on the

wall of his home before the flames and smoke took it from his
sight—a scrawl of black paint that was meaningless to the *Gaje,* the
non-Gypsies, but that he understood with a bleak emptiness. It
meant *marhime.* Ceremonially defiled. Unclean. It was a message
from another Rom to him that there was no welcome among the
Gypsies for a Rom who had become too *Gaje.* And yet, though he
understood, he could not believe that one of his people could have
done such a thing. Such a display of violence was not the way of the
Rom. One who was *marhime* was not tolerated in the company of *o
phral,* the true Rom. He was ostracized from every facet of Rom
society, but he was not treated with violence. Or fire.

And yet . . . He had seen the symbol, the black paint with the
excess liquid dripping from its lines like drops of blood; and who else
but a Rom knew that he was one of their own? Who else but a Rom
would know the secret *patrin* and defile the wall of his home with it?

"Jesus, John," a voice said in hushed tones at his side. "You've lost
everything."

Janfri's companion knew him as John Owczarek—one of Janfri's
Gaje names. Like all Gypsies, Janfri used and discarded names as a
Gajo might a suit of clothes. Only the other Rom of his *kumpania*
knew him as Janfri la Yayal—Janfri son of Yayal—and they were
most likely to call him by his nickname, *o* Boshbaro, "the Big Fiddle," for his skill on the instrument that was at this moment tucked
under his arm, forgotten. To Rom who didn't know him as well he
was simply Boshengro, "the fellow who plays the fiddle."

"I sure as hell hope you've got enough insurance to cover it,"
Tom Shaw added. He glanced at Janfri's face, puzzled by his friend's
lack of emotion. It had to be shock, he decided, because the stiff
lack of response he saw in Janfri's features simply didn't jibe with
the man Tom knew him to be. The John Owczarek that Tom knew
was expansive in his moods, apt to gigantic joys and sorrows.

Tom stood a half head taller than his friend. He was a burly six-
two, barrel-chested and meaty. Amongst the Gypsies, his size would
label him as an important man, for they judged importance by size as
well as other attributes. He was forty-seven this summer, which
made him Janfri's elder by two years.

"John . . ." he tried again, touching his friend's arm. The wiry muscles were stiff under the light cloth of Janfri's coat.

The Gypsy turned slowly to regard him. *"Yekka buliasa nashti beshes pe done grastende,"* he said softly. Forgetting himself, he spoke Romany. With one behind you cannot sit on two horses. He saw the puzzlement rise in Tom's eyes, but made no attempt to explain. Let Tom think he spoke Hungarian. But the old saying rang all too true in his own mind. One was either Rom or *Gajo*. There was no in between.

"Listen, John," Tom said. "If you want a place to stay . . . ?"

Janfri shook his head. His dark features were pained now. A fire smoldered in the depths of his eyes that were such a dark brown they were almost black.

"There is no John Owczarek," he said. He turned and, before Tom could stop him, disappeared into the crowd.

For a long moment Tom stood in shock. The noise of the crowd seemed to grow louder. The roar of the flames and the pushing, jostling bodies around him combined to throw off his sense of the here and now. The night was abruptly surreal, filled with strangeness and menace. A chill traveled up his spine. He stared into the crowd, trying to see what had become of his friend.

"John!" he cried. "John!"

But the night had swallowed up the man he knew as John Owczarek as completely as though he had never existed.

two

The body lay at the back of the alley and, looking at it, Detective-Sergeant Patrick Briggs of the Ottawa Police Force bit down hard on the well-chewed stem of his unlit briar. He thought he might be sick. Under the bright glare of the police photographer's lights, there was no avoiding the gruesome sight. The body lay in a sprawl. The head, half severed from the neck, was on its side, facing Briggs, its glazed eyes holding his gaze with a vacant stare. A gory trail of abruptly disjoined muscle, esophagus, trachea, spinal cord, jugular veins and carotid arteries trailed from below the jaw. It looked, Briggs thought, as though something had chewed right through the neck.

The body itself had sustained wounds as well. The right hand and forearm had been opened to the bone—defense wounds caused by the victim's unsuccessful attempt to fend off his attacker. The flesh and muscle hung in ribbons from the arm. The left shoulder was no prettier. The cloth of the man's jacket hung in tatters, matted with blood, and clung wetly to the corpse and the ground around it. Briggs looked away, hoping his stomach would settle down.

He was a veteran of twenty-four years on the Force—the last fifteen of them in General Assignment. To some extent he was inured to the inevitable results of violence that his work brought him into contact with—more so than a civilian confronted with the same situation might be. But at the same time, that familiarity, the sheer volume of man's brutality against his fellow man that he was forced to be witness to, fueled an anger in him that sometimes frightened him with its intensity. This . . . thing lying in the alley had once been a man. Someone had worked real hard to make it look like he'd been torn apart by some kind of animal, but Briggs wasn't buying it.

"Paddy?"

Briggs looked up at his partner's call. Will Sandler was a tall, sharp-featured black man who went through life in a constant state of suppressed tension. It showed in the taut pull of the skin at his temples, around his eyes and the corners of his mouth, in the birdlike darting of his gaze. He contrasted sharply with the unimposing figure that Briggs cut—five-eight with a perpetual slouch that made him appear shorter, dark hair that was prematurely gray at the temples, sorrowful eyes. His suit was rumpled, tie loose, shoes scuffed. Will, on the other hand, always looked like he'd just left his tailor's. But the two men made an effective pair, for their strengths augmented each other's weak points. Briggs was a slow mover, a deliberate collector of details with little imagination, while Will's mind moved in intuitive lunges. Since they'd been paired, their success on cases had reached a departmental high of sixty-seven percent.

Briggs removed his pipe and thrust it into the breast pocket of his suit coat, stem down, as he moved closer to his partner. "What do you think?" he asked.

"Well, it sure as hell wasn't a mugging. There was over fifty bucks in his wallet."

"Animal or man?" Briggs asked, wanting his own feelings confirmed.

Will shook his head. "A doberman might leave a mess like that . . . but I don't know. We're going to have to wait to see what Cooper comes up with once he's done the autopsy. Thing is," he nodded to the ground, "there's enough dirt here to hold a track, but Alec didn't come up with anything we could even pretend was an animal's." Alec MacDonald was with forensics and was standing at the mouth of the alley waiting for the body to be removed so that he could finish up. "I think we've got us a psycho on our hands. That, or a case of spontaneous mutilation." Will glanced at his partner, but Briggs didn't smile. "Bad juju, Paddy," he added softly. "All the way."

Briggs nodded and studied the body again.

"Hodgins wants to know if we're finished with it," Will said.

Briggs glanced to where Al Hodgins waited with the medics. A pale green body-bag lay on the stretcher. Briggs imagined them moving the body and the head coming loose, bouncing down the alleyway with a wet sound. . . . He grimaced.

"Stan got all the shots we need?" he asked.

Will nodded.

"What about that?" Briggs pointed to a symbol that had been scratched into the dirt near the victim's head. It was a circular shape, cut with three slashing lines. Two of them were so close together that the topmost line ran into the one below it.

Will called the photographer over. "Did you get a shot of that, Stan?"

Stan Miller nodded. "A nice close-up," he said. He was chewing on a pencil stub and talked around it rather than removing it.

"What the hell's it supposed to mean?" Will muttered.

Briggs motioned to the medics that they could collect the body and watched his partner. He could see the cogs turning under Will's short Afro, but his face mirrored the bewilderment Briggs knew was on his own. He and Will moved aside as the medics took the body away. All that remained now were the chalk outlines of where it had lain and the thickening pools of blood. It never failed to shock Briggs as to how much blood there was in one human being. There were only about ten pints in a full-grown man, but when you saw it all spilled out in some alleyway like this, it looked like about ten gallons.

"Hey! Is one of you Briggs?"

Both men turned to see a patrolman standing at the mouth of the alley.

"Yeah?"

"I've found you a witness."

The man's name was Ralph Cleary and he was a wino. He was in bad shape tonight, hands shaking like he had palsy, shuffling his feet, staring at the detectives with scared rheumy eyes. He wore a baggy suit that even the Sally Ann wouldn't have accepted on a bet. It hung from his sloped shoulders and slender frame in loose, oversized folds. His face was flushed with alcohol poisoning, blue veins prominent.

"Where'd you find him?" Briggs asked the patrolman.

"Down the street in the park. He was sitting on a bench, just shaking and talking to himself. When I asked if he'd seen anything, he just started telling me that he 'didn't hurt no one.'"

Briggs nodded. "Okay. Thanks. Stick around, would you? I want to talk to you after we've had a word with him."

"He's all yours," the patrolman said, turning Cleary over to them with obvious relief.

Briggs led the frightened man to the unmarked car that he and Will had arrived in. He helped him into the back seat, then climbed in beside him. Will got into the front and leaned over the seat to look at them.

"I didn't do nothing," Cleary mumbled.

"No one said you did," Briggs explained gently. "We just want to ask you what you saw tonight, that's all. Think you can do that, Ralph?"

The wino nodded. "They call me Red-eye on the street," he offered, "on account of the way my eyes get, you know?"

"Would you prefer to be called that?"

"No. I like being called Ralph better." He shot a quick glance at Will, then returned his watery gaze to Briggs. "I used to be a mid-shipman, you know—out of Halifax. I wasn't always . . . you know. Like this."

Briggs nodded sympathetically. "Times are getting tough again," he said. "All we can do is just hang in there the best we can."

"Yeah. We just gotta hang in there. . . ." His voice trailed off. Briggs let the silence hang for a few moments before he spoke again.

"So what did you see, Ralph?"

Cleary shrugged. "I was just minding my own business, you know, sitting on the stoop over there, resting my feet." He nodded to the front of the indoor parking lot across the street from the mouth of the alleyway. "I was just sitting there, when this guy comes by. I thought I might hit him up for some change, but when he got into the light and I could see him better, I saw he didn't look a whole lot better off than me. I thought maybe I'd call him over, offer him a swig, you know, just to be sociable. I had about a third of a bottle left and I was feeling pretty good, but then . . ."

He'd been looking at what he could see of his feet between his legs while he spoke. As his voice trailed off for a second time, his gaze flicked to Briggs' face, then back to his shoes.

"What happened then, Ralph?" Briggs prompted him. For a long moment Cleary didn't say anything. When he finally spoke, his voice was strained. Scared.

"Did you ever stand in a harbor and . . . and watch the way the fog comes rolling in?" he asked. "The way it licks up the streets at first, you know, hanging real low?"

"Yeah, sure." Briggs wasn't sure what Cleary was on about, but he wanted to keep him talking.

"Well, that's what it was like . . . like a little patch of fog that
came rolling up the street, only there was this guy in the middle of
it and the fog just sort of hung around his feet like it was . . . I don't
know . . . following him. The first guy, he stopped in front of the
alley when the guy with the fog called out to him, and then he just
sort of faded back into the alley, like he was scared of him, maybe.
The other guy followed and the fog . . . it . . ." He looked up at
Briggs. "You're going to say I was drunk, and maybe I was, but there
was something in that fog, mister. It was up to the guy's knees now,
maybe, and there was . . . things moving in it. It didn't look like no
fog I ever saw and I've seen a lot. I used to be a midshipman, you
know—out of Halifax. I worked hard, real hard, but old Red-eye
likes his bottle, you know, and I guess they just had to let me go. . . ."

"Then what happened, Ralph?"

Cleary looked back at his shoes. "Then the other guy—the first
guy—screamed. . . . But it wasn't loud or anything, you know? It
was this long whispering . . . wet sound. Well, I just took off, mister.
I dropped my bottle and I ran, but I just didn't get too far. I made it
to the park and I just sort of couldn't go no more. I sat down on a
bench and I been there ever since.

"I saw you boys all pulling up with your lights flashing and I
knew I should tell you what I saw, but I couldn't get up. And I
thought . . . maybe . . . you'd think I done it, you know? Whatever
happened to that guy in the alley . . . I thought you'd think it was
me that done it. But I never hurt no one, mister." His gaze fastened
onto Briggs, searching for confirmation, needing to know that the
detective believed him.

"No one thinks you did," Briggs assured him.

"That first guy . . . he's dead, isn't he?"

Briggs nodded.

"Jesus. . . ."

"Did you see the second man come out of the alley?" Will asked.

Cleary shook his head. "I just took off."

"Was he ever in the light?" Briggs asked. "Would you recognize
him if you saw him again?"

Cleary shivered. "I . . . I think so. He had these scars under his eyes. . . ." He lifted a trembling hand and touched his upper cheeks. ". . . right around here, but maybe . . . maybe it was just the way the light fell on his face. He was dark-skinned—not as dark as you," he added, looking at Will, "but dark. His clothes looked all black and so did his hair. And his eyes . . . his eyes were like the fog . . . all sort of pale and smoky. . . ."

"You've been a big help, Ralph," Briggs said as the man's voice trailed off once more. "I want you to know that." He nodded to Will and the two detectives got out of the car. "What do you think?" Briggs asked Will as his partner came around the car to stand by him.

"A defense lawyer would tear his story apart in about ten seconds."

"Yeah. But what do *you* think?"

Will sighed. "I don't know, Paddy. All this weird stuff about a fog doesn't make a whole lot of sense."

Briggs nodded. "But he saw something and it scared the shit out of him. And I don't think it was just the booze."

"No. It wasn't just the booze. . . ."

"What I can't figure," Briggs said, "is why the murderer would take the time to make it look like it was the work of an animal, but then leave that symbol scratched in the dirt like some kind of calling card. Anyone with half a brain—"

"Psychos only have about half a brain."

"Yeah."

The two men stood silently by the car. At length, Briggs headed over to where the patrolman was still waiting.

"I want you to run Cleary downtown," he said. He pulled out his wallet and took out a twenty-dollar bill. "But get some food into him first."

"Sure. What's the charge?"

"No charge. Let's call it protective custody. He's all we've got right now and I don't want to lose him. And I don't want the press to get wind of the fact that we've got him and I don't want anybody—and I mean *anybody*—asking him questions. Now before you go, this is your beat, right? Where were you when it happened?"

"I had a disturbance up on Dalhousie—a couple of hookers got into a tussle over this John and . . ."

The coroner's initial report, combined with the story Ralph Cleary had given them, brought Will's offhand remark about juju a little too close to home. Juju was Will's catchall word for anything inexplicable or spooky. And this alley murder, Briggs thought, was shaping up to fit both categories perfectly.

"Look, Briggs," Cooper had said when the two detectives stopped off in his office, "at this point I can't rule out the possibility that some kind of animal *didn't* do it."

"What about the symbol scratched in the dirt?" Briggs asked.

"*And* there were no tracks," MacDonald said from his desk across the room.

The two men shared the office, Alec MacDonald a hulking figure behind his desk, while Peter Cooper was almost lost behind the clutter on his own. Cooper was a waspish, balding man who moved his hands in broad gestures as he talked. He pointed a finger towards MacDonald, but Alec spoke first.

"No tracks, no traces of fur, claws or saliva in or around the wounds." He ticked off the items on his fingers as he listed them. "And most importantly, we've got nothing in this city capable of inflicting that kind of damage. If we're talking animals, we're talking panthers, maybe. Or tigers. With," he added, grinning at Briggs, "some artistic ability."

"Then what kind of weapon could it have been?" Will asked.

"There was no trace of metal in the wounds," Cooper said firmly. "Nor were there the usual sort of lacerations one could expect if a weapon had been used."

"Do you think we could come to some kind of a consensus?" Briggs asked. "Was there a weapon involved or not?"

"The wounds weren't caused by a knife or any other sharp implement that I can think of," Cooper replied. "Something tore into the victim, that's all I can say. I'm still waiting for a few final tissue samples to come back from the lab. Meanwhile, what you've got there," he indicated the report that Briggs was holding, "is all I can give you."

"You want a weapon that could have done it?" MacDonald asked. He was rummaging around in the bottom drawer of his desk and finally came up with an object that he deposited on his blotter. It looked like a metal bracelet, with a narrow oval opening rather than a round one and four wicked-looking metal spikes protruding from one side like the lumps on a set of brass knuckles. "Here you go," he said.

Briggs laid the report down and picked up the object, turning it over in his hands.

"What the hell is it?" Will asked as Briggs passed it over to him. He fit his hand inside and brandished it, the spikes jutting up from his knuckles.

"You've got it on backwards," MacDonald told him. "The spikes should protrude from the palm of your hand. It's called a *shuko*—a Japanese climbing spike. We picked it up from some guy who thought he was going to be the next Bruce Lee and I've been hanging on to it ever since. Mean-looking little sucker, isn't it? Can you imagine getting swiped by that?"

"It's still metal," Cooper said, "and there was no trace of metal in the wounds."

"So maybe he used a plastic one."

Cooper nodded grudgingly. "It would be less likely to leave any traces," he admitted.

"So there you go," MacDonald said. "Or maybe he had one of those clubs the leopard cults in Africa use." He glanced at Will.

"Hey, don't look at me. The closest I've been to Africa was a *National Geographic Special* that I watched from my sofa, thanks all the same."

"What kind of clubs are these?" Briggs asked.

"What they'd do," MacDonald explained, "is mount a stuffed leopard's paw on the end of a club and use it to mimic the blows of a leopard in ritual killings."

"Are you serious?"

"Sure."

"You saw the body," Briggs said. "Could something like that have been used on it?"

MacDonald shrugged. "Who knows? Maybe it *was* a leopard or a panther. Maybe you should check around to see if a circus is in town. You know, Zabu van Gogh—the Amazing Drawing Panther."

"Everybody's a comedian," Briggs muttered.

Cooper cleared his throat and began to straighten the papers on his desk. "I'll be in touch with you as soon as I get those final samples back from the lab. It might have been one of those fancy knuckle-dusters, it might have been an animal. We'll see."

"No fur, no saliva, no claws. . . ." MacDonald was ticking the items off on his fingers again. He looked up at Briggs. "But maybe you'll get lucky and someone'll step forward like a good citizen to tell you that he's got a panther sleeping under his porch and would you please come to remove it."

"Maybe I'll get even luckier and you'll get transferred out to the West End." Briggs smiled sweetly and MacDonald laughed.

"Better watch it, Paddy," he warned. "Next thing you know, you might start developing a sense of humor."

"I hate waiting to get lucky," Briggs complained to Will later that morning.

They were sitting at Will's desk in the new police station on Elgin Street, one floor above the Morgue and the office where they'd left Cooper and MacDonald. The final construction on the new station had been completed this past spring and everybody had been happy to move out of the crowded confines of the old building on Waller. The new five-story structure was the pride of the city's police department. It was five times the size of the old station and cost fifteen times the price tag of the Waller Street station that had been built in the late fifties for a modest $1.4 million. Everything in it was still shiny, with a smell of new paint about it. Briggs figured the glow would last another month, tops. The Morgue already had its own peculiar odor, as though it had never been moved.

"I know what you mean," Will said. "If we go by Cooper's report and what the rubbie told us, we should be out looking for a guy with a panther that can sometimes change itself into fog. Unless, of course, our boy in black is like one of those people in *Cat People*. You ever see that?"

Briggs nodded wearily. "It was bullshit. And so's what we've got so far. But they're not the same kind."

He glanced at his partner's lanky frame. Will's feet were draped across the top of his desk, head tilted back against the headrest of his chair as he went through Miller's photographs. One by one, Will tossed the B&W glossies over to Briggs. The detective frowned down at them. They were Stan's usual excellent work and didn't look any prettier this morning than the real thing had looked last night. But at least they had a name to go with them now. Cooper had managed to pull the victim's prints—from the hand that hadn't been chewed up or whatever had happened to it—and, once they'd run them through Ceepik, they'd come up with a prior's sheet as long as the desk. Ceepik was an abbreviation for the Canadian Police Information Computer—a teletype information-sharing computer serving all police departments in Canada and, in some cases, the United States.

The victim had been one Romano Wood, aka John Yera, aka Kalia Winter. . . . In fact, he had as many names as he had arrests. Thirty-seven of them, ranging from vagrancy to fraud, with fourteen convictions. All told, Wood or whatever his real name was, had served a total of six years, ten months and three days in various county, provincial and federal jails. But the most interesting snippet of information, to Briggs' way of thinking, was the fact that Wood was a Gypsy. No fixed address. No occupation. They weren't even sure what nationality he was. He'd been picked up with everything from Canadian ID to a Brazilian passport.

Gypsies weren't the same problem now as they had been when Briggs had had to deal with them on a continual basis back in his days as a patrolman in the late sixties. They had a much higher profile then. He could even recall a fortune-telling joint on Wellington Street—right across from Parliament Hill. These days you hardly

heard a peep out of them, though he knew his counterparts in Hull,
just across the river, still had to deal with them. Harassment charges.
Vagrancy. Welfare, check and insurance frauds. Squabbles between
the extended families that seemed to operate on the same principles
that the Mob did. He'd have to check with Castleman in the Fraud
and Commercial Crimes Unit to see if there were still any in
Ottawa.

They were a weird people, no doubt about that. It wasn't so
much that they were lawless, as that they didn't believe that non-
Gypsy laws applied to them. They were asocial—except within their
own communities. Briggs wasn't sure that he cared all that much for
them. They were always causing trouble of one kind or another. A
headache, more than a serious problem—though he'd heard some
ugly stories about the families in Montreal, Toronto and Vancouver.

Briggs shrugged. His own feelings were irrelevant. What he had
to deal with was the fact that someone had killed a Gypsy on his turf
and he had the uncomfortable feeling that it had been a premedi-
tated ritual killing. There was the symbol scratched in the dirt beside
the victim's head, and the way he'd been killed. . . . Bad juju.

"You think Wood being a Gypsy had something to do with the
way he died?" Will asked suddenly, surprising Briggs at how close
his partner's thoughts paralleled his own. Maybe some of Will's
intuition was rubbing off on him. "It doesn't make a whole lot of
sense otherwise," Will continued, answering himself. "Shit. If we're
going to have a repeat of what went down in Van last year . . ."

Briggs nodded. He remembered now. Gypsies were rarely
involved with serious crimes of a violent nature, but last year something had set off a rampage of infighting between two Vancouver
families that had ended in a minor riot in Gastown, leaving three
men dead and another half-dozen or so in the hospital. If he
remembered correctly, by the time it all blew over, the Vancouver
police never did piece any of it together. The Gypsies issued dozens
of conflicting statements and none of the parties involved were willing to lay charges against each other. Without one piece of hard
evidence, even concerning the deaths, the police had been helpless to
bring anything more serious to court than creating a nuisance and

disorderly public conduct. He could just imagine how the detective in charge of that case must have felt.

"There's another possibility," Will said.

"What's that?"

"Could be these Gypsies are horning in on some of the Syndicate's rackets. Or maybe the Mob's pushing them out of Montreal or Toronto and they're looking for a new base. We should check into that."

Briggs regarded his partner with interest. "Are you just whatifing still," he asked, "or've you heard some noises in that direction?"

"Whatifing. I'm going to phone Gaston over in Hull. Maybe try a few contacts in T.O."

"You might try Montreal, too," Briggs added. "Dan Sullivan's still working the Main and he owes us one for the connection we made with Coletti's people last winter. He built himself a nice little case out of what we gave him."

"Will do. You going to give me a hand?"

Briggs indicated the thick stack of unsolved cases that they were still working on. "I'm going to take a stab at a few of these," he said. "But call me if you need me."

He carried the files over to his own desk and sat down. Filling his pipe, he drew out the photograph of the symbol scratched into the dirt beside Wood's head and stared at it, troubled. Ritual. Murder. Just what kind of rituals did Gypsies have? He thought about fog and panthers and a man in black and frowned. Sighing, he shoved the photo back into its file and tried to concentrate on one of the other cases.

three

The Ottawa River neatly separates the Nation's Capital from Hull, its Quebec neighbor, with an average width of about a third of a mile. By 1820, when Ottawa was still dense bushland, Hull was already a thriving village. At the time Hull was first settled by the

Boston farmer Philemon Wright in 1800, there was not even a landing on the Ontario side of the river. Parliament Hill was merely an
impressive limestone cliff, and the remainder of the future Capital
was composed of marshland and beaver ponds. The first structure
on the Ottawa side wasn't raised until 1809 when a Vermont Loyal-
ist named Jehiel Collins built a shanty tavern and store at the canoe
landing below Chaudière Falls and the shoreline now called Nepean
Point came to be known as Collins' Landing.

Today Ottawa is an urban sprawl of highrises and neatly laid-out
residential areas, while Hull is relegated to the position of a poor
cousin where the bars are open two hours later per night and general housing is anywhere from 30 to 50% cheaper. It wasn't given a
facelift until the mid-1970's when the Federal Government began
moving some of its offices to the Quebec side of the river. Every
few years talk arises of turning the area into a Federal Region
encompassing both sides of the river—legislation that is as vehe-
mently fought by the Quebec government as it is supported by
many of the residents who are tired of that same provincial government's heavy taxing and bizarre Language Bills.

Five bridges, four auto and one railway, connect downtown
Ottawa with Hull. In the early morning following the loss of his
home, Janfri Yayal was crossing one of these bridges. He had
removed his tie, replacing it with a burgundy and yellow *diklo,* a traditional Rom scarf that he carried in his violin case. Small gold earrings, stored in the same case, were now in each lobe. His shoes were
tied together by their laces and slung over his shoulder, the socks
thrust into their toes. His bare feet slapped the cool pavement as he
passed the E. B. Eddy Mill and headed northwest on Taché Boulevard. When he reached Front Street, he turned off the road and followed the CPR Railway tracks into the narrow stretch of woodland
that followed the contours of the river.

The few simple changes in his appearance were symbolic of a far
more profound reawakening inside himself. The *diklo* he always carried because it was the one he'd worn on his wedding night. The
earrings had been given to him by his late wife. He had never asked
where she had acquired them. And while the Rom were normally

indifferent to the acquisition and holding of physical goods, he was greedy in his possession of these for they were all he had to remember her by.

As he moved through the trees he walked with a quick silent grace that Tom Shaw and his other *Gaje* friends would never have recognized. It was far harder for Janfri to move unnoticed in the *Gaje* world than for him to forget the ways of the Rom, and that was what made the notice of *marhime* so unfair. He was scrupulous in his adherence to the laws of *marhime* for all that he'd chosen to live in a house that he owned, away from the *tsera* of his *kumpania*. There were the separate soaps in his bathroom—the one for the upper body, the other for the lower—the food he ate, the hospitality in his home for any Rom who cared to drop by. He was quick with the wedding gift or to share the grief at a *pomana* when the kin of one of the *kumpania* died. Was it his fault that the *Gaje* gave him money to record the music of his violin? It wasn't as though he gave them Rom music for their money.

And yet . . . and yet . . .

With the burning of his home, Janfri felt as though a great weight had been lifted from his shoulders. He had thought it important to rise in the world, the *Gaje* world, to take their money and smile behind his hand with the knowledge of his secret that they gave it to a Gypsy. He hid his heritage, not through shame—for were the Rom not expected to be musicians and great lovers as well as thieves?—but because he would not have them trade on that heritage to make a profit. They did not, could not understand what it was to be a Rom. Only a Gypsy could. And perhaps . . . just perhaps he had forgotten a little himself. But not in such a way that deserved a notice of *marhime*.

Janfri sighed. For every good luck, *o Beng* the devil handed out an equal share of *prikaza*. He had been too clever by far and now he reaped the bad luck that *o Beng* would charge was his due. It would have been different if Pesha was still alive, but her *muli* had long since fled this world into the land of shadows. She was dead and he was too clever by far.

And so, he thought. What now? *Bi kashtesko merel i yag,* his Uncle

Nonka would have said. Without wood the fire would die. Dwelling on sorrow and *prikaza* merely made them grow. But there was no return for him to the charred ruin of his home and the *Gaje* with their hands held out, filled with money, waiting for him to play. Not until he dealt with this matter of *marhime*. But who could he return to? Would Big George even speak to him when he was *marhime?* When merely to speak to Janfri meant risking the stigma of being outcast himself? And if Big George, who was the leader of his *kumpania,* its *rom baro,* if he would not, then who would?

Janfri imagined trying to explain this concept to a *Gajo* like Tom Shaw. It was so simple, a keystone to the Romany way of life, yet at the same time it was so complex. He had tried to explain it to other *Gaje* with predictable results. They either responded with disbelief, or that certain look that meant they were assimilating it as a curious anthropological quirk—the same way they responded to the customs of Native Americans or African tribesmen, with the superior air of an adult listening to a child describing the fairies that lived at the bottom of the garden. *Che chorobia*. What vagaries. How odd.

And yet, Janfri realized, the *Gaje* were not so different themselves. They had only one crime amongst them and that was theft. Theft of goods. Murder, which was the theft of life. Rape, which was the theft of a woman's privacy and dignity. All they cared about was their possessions. All their laws were devoted to protecting their property. It was as simple and complex as *marhime* and, from an outsider's point of view looking in, just as bewildering. *Che chorobia,* indeed.

The woods gave way to a small subdivision that Janfri skirted by hugging the riverbank, then opened up into Parc Moussette. He could see the filtration plant just beyond the park in the growing light. The traffic was sporadic on Taché Boulevard which had swept in closer to the river at this point so that he heard the sound of a familiar engine long before he saw it. He paused in the middle of the park and turned towards the road to watch the beat-up black Lincoln pull up on the shoulder. The engine of the touring car died with a rumbling cough and a tall heavy-set man disembarked from the driver's side. When he caught sight of Janfri, he started across the road. Janfri sat down on the dewy grass, with his back to the approaching man, and laid his violin case down beside him. He placed his shoes on the case and waited patiently. He would not speak first, nor welcome his friend who was as close to him as a brother. Not when he was *marhime*.

The big man made his way slowly across the park. He had an unruly thatch of black hair and a well-groomed walrus mustache that neatly cut his face into two disproportionate halves. Below the mustache, his lips were thick, his jaw square. Above it was a large nose and a pair of warm brown eyes overshadowed by black bushy eyebrows that joined across the top of his nose. His complexion was dark, though not as dark as Janfri's who could pass as a mulatto. His name was Yojo la Kore. He and Janfri had both married into the Pataloeshti *kumpania* whose *rom baro* was Big George Luluvo. Yojo's wife Sizma was still alive and they had seven children.

Yojo said nothing as he sat down beside Janfri. He took the makings for a cigarette from his pocket and rolled himself one with quick deft movements of his big fingers. Sticking it in his mouth, he flicked the tip of a wooden match. The flame flared and he lit the cigarette, inhaling deeply. Not until he'd replaced the tobacco in his pocket did he greet Janfri.

"*Sarishan, prala.*" How do you do, brother?

Janfri gave him a quick sidelong glance. He was not surprised that Yojo had found him. The bond between them ran too strongly for either of them to be long from the other, or for one not to know where the other was. That Yojo had sought him out meant he knew of Janfri's problem, but Janfri still felt obliged to spell it out.

"I am *marhime* now," he said flatly.

Yojo smoked in silence for a long moment. The morning light was growing steadily stronger about them. The dawn bird chorus was in full swing. Janfri waited. Yojo had something to say, but he would only say it in his own time, so Janfri looked to the river. He let the flow of the water and the growing warmth of the morning fill him. Slowly the tension eased in his shoulders.

"The son of Big George's cousin Punka died last night," Yojo said finally.

Janfri looked at him, surprised. "Romano?"

Yojo nodded. "It was a *prikaza* killing, Janfri—very bad luck. There was a *patrin* found on or near his body—I'm not sure which. But someone thought he was *marhime,* too."

Patrin were a part of the *patteran,* the information that the Rom left for any of their companions who might follow the same route that they had taken. There was a circular *patrin* that meant friend and was carved on the wooden door of a house where Gypsies might find a welcome. Janfri had had one on his door. There were others that told of unclean water at a stream or well, of Rom that were *marhime* who were traveling nearby, of good campsites with grazing for the horses. Some even told of the mood of the countryside— whether the constabulary was friendly, whether a village should be avoided.

Janfri and Yojo were both Lowara Rom and therefore more attuned to such signs than might the North American *kumpaniyi* who were mostly Kalderash. In Europe, where they had both origi- nated and spent their formative years, the Rom still traveled by horse-drawn wagons in many areas. According to the Rom, there were four *natsiyi* or tribes of Gypsies. They were, in order of impor- tance: the Machwaya, or people of Machwa; the Lowara or Horse- dealers who were primarily from Hungary or England; the Kalderash or Coppersmiths who claimed most of continental Euro- pe and were the first to go *perdal l paya,* beyond the waters, to Amer- ica; and the Churara or Kuneshti who were the Knife-makers. This didn't include sedentary tribes such as the Gitanos who lived in Spain, or the Sinti of the Low Countries. In Rom myth, the Lowara were symbolized by the moon, while the Kalderash, by their very numbers, were the stars.

"What does Big George say?" Janfri asked. He turned so that he was facing Yojo now. Yojo offered him his tobacco and, though Janfri didn't normally smoke, he accepted it and rolled a cigarette. The offer was meant to show that so far as Yojo was concerned, Janfri was not an outcast. To refuse would have been an insult—even between brothers.

"He wants to talk with you," Yojo said.

"Because of the *patrin* on my wall?"

"And the burning of your *tsera.*" Strictly speaking, *tsera* meant tent in Romany, but time had evolved the word to mean anywhere that a Rom had his household.

The two men finished their cigarettes and ground them into the dirt when they were done.

"Let's go see what Big George has to say," Janfri said, collecting his shoes and violin case.

"*Bater,*" Yojo agreed, seriously. So be it. Then he grinned. "But I claim you as my guest, o Boshbaro. Keja still has eyes for you."

Yojo had been trying to marry Janfri to his widowed eldest daughter ever since the one year's mourning period for her husband had been over three months ago. "You will need children to support you when you are old and your fingers don't work so well anymore, *prala,*" he insisted whenever the subject arose—usually at his instigation. Remembering all the arguments Yojo could produce—from claims of grave insult to outright weeping—Janfri prudently kept silent and merely rolled his eyes. It wasn't that he disliked Keja. Rather he couldn't face the idea of having Yojo for his father-in-law. The big man would be insufferable.

"She's still a virgin, you know," Yojo confided as they started back to his car.

"A married virgin?"

"In her heart, *prala,* in her heart. As God is my witness."

Janfri let his shoulders lift and fall despondently. "I'd been thinking very seriously about it, you know, but now . . . I have nothing to offer her. I couldn't even afford the bridal price."

"I have a very low bridal price in mind," Yojo said. "Not because she is worth so little, but because you have so little."

Janfri smiled. Yojo had an answer for everything.

"Do you want to be a *vadni ratsa*—a wild goose for the rest of your life?" the big man asked. The conversation continued along the same lines all the way to Big George's *tsera* without being resolved.

Everything about Big George Luluvo was larger than life. He weighed 350 lbs. and his mustache was twice the size of Yojo's—an impressive sweep of thick hair that touched the tops of his massive shoulders. It was as much for his sheer bulk as his shrewdness in dealing with the *Gaje* that he was the *rom baro* of the Pataloeshti Kalderash in Ottawa. Janfri always felt like a child when he was around the big Gypsy leader and even Yojo knew the rare sensation of having another tower over him when he was in Big George's presence.

The *rom baro's tsera* was a wood frame bungalow in Mechanicsville—a low-rent tenement district east of a grouping of Federal Government buildings known as Tunney's Pasture. A number of the Pataloeshti *kumpania* lived in and around Mechanicsville, to be close to the *baXt,* or luck, of Big George that they all knew to be very strong. A Cadillac sat in the driveway on a makeshift block constructed of two-by-fours and cinder blocks and a dark-green Lincoln was parked in front of the bungalow. The Rom in North America had a preference for touring cars which had become the modern equivalent of their horse-drawn *vurdon,* or wagons. The vehicles were usually in poor repair—great hulking gas-guzzlers that appeared to be held together only by their rust.

Inside the *tsera* itself, all the walls had been removed, leaving only the bare wooden pillars of the support beams from which hung a motley collection of sacks, cloth bags, wineskins and tools. There were a number of shabby couches lining the walls and threadbare Oriental carpets on the floor. The atmosphere inside was oppressive when Janfri and Yojo entered. They were offered guests' tea, but neither Big George nor his wife partook of it themselves. Because Romano had been the son of Big George's cousin Punka, and because Big George was the *rom baro,* his family would share Punka's grief. They would not wash, nor eat, nor partake of any drink but water until the first three days of mourning were over.

Big George nodded gravely to them when they had taken their first sip of tea. He wore a large tweed cap and a 1930's style large-lapelled suit that was patched in places and shiny at the elbows. His wife Tshaya wore a traditional long pleated skirt and a sleeveless blouse that offered a generous view of her heavy breasts. She sat beside Big George and smoked a meerschaum pipe. Its white clay was heavily discolored with yellow tobacco stains.

"Droboy tune Romale," Big George said when Janfri set his tea cup on the floor. *"Devlesa avilan."* Greetings, Gypsy. It is God who brought you.

"Devlesa araklam tume," Janfri replied. It is with God that we found you. *"Rom baro,* we share your grief."

Big George sighed. "Who could do such a thing? Romano was *phral*—a true Rom. He was like a son to me."

This wasn't entirely true, Janfri knew. Romano's continual run-ins with the law had necessitated Big George's sending him away from the *kumpania* more than once—just long enough for the immediacy of his transgressions to be forgotten—but amongst the Rom one did not speak ill of the dead.

"And your *tsera,*" Big George added. "You were meant to die last night as well, o Boshbaro." A dark anger brewed in his eyes. Not one, but two of his *kumpania* had been attacked. "The ones who have done this . . . these pigs . . . *Te xal o rako lengo gortiano!*" May the cancer eat their gullets.

Janfri and Yojo nodded in agreement. Yojo rolled a cigarette, after first offering the tobacco to Big George. This time Janfri shook his head when it was offered to him. The *rom baro*'s comment that he'd been meant to die last night shocked him. He hadn't considered the destruction of his house as anything more than that. But if he'd been meant to burn inside it . . . For a moment he was five years old again. The cold dark night around him was lit by the burning wagons, the screams of the dying. The big brutal hands of the soldier who held him bit into his neck as he was forced to watch . . . He shivered, feeling a chill sheet of perspiration upon his chest and back, then the moment was gone.

"Do you know who is responsible?" he asked softly.

"Who *can* be responsible?" Big George replied. "Do you know how Romano died? His head was half torn from his body! Only the *urme* or a demon would kill a man in such a way." The *urme* were faeries or evil spirits that the Rom believed decided the fates of men.

Janfri shifted uneasily and shot a glance at Yojo. His friend was regarding the *rom baro* with widening eyes. Janfri sighed. He might tell himself that *o Beng* was responsible for his troubles, but he did not mean it literally. Men were far more capable of evil and cruelty than any creature out of legend. Unfortunately, many of the Rom took what should be left as superstition all too seriously.

"You think it was some . . . animal?" Janfri asked halfheartedly.

Big George shook his head. "He was slain by *draba*—by magic. The same *draba* that burned down your *tsera,* o Boshbaro."

Janfri frowned. "You and I," he said. "We do not believe in magic, do we? We know that men kill other men. Men set fires."

Big George was silent for a long moment. He glanced at Tshaya who smoked her pipe in stony silence.

"I was never a man to jump at signs and omens," Big George said finally.

Janfri said nothing, waiting for the *rom baro* to continue. He gave a nod to show Big George that he was prepared to hear him out. The Gypsy leader sighed.

"This morning," he said, "Joji Anako was collecting scrap behind the repair shop just up on Scott Street—do you know the place?"

Janfri shrugged.

"He was taking a load to his car," Big George continued, "when he saw two men approaching him from downtown. It was perhaps three hours after midnight and dark, so he did not know them for Rom until they were very close to him. One was Romano Yera— Punka's son. The other was a stranger—a Rom as well, but dressed all in black."

Janfri's eyebrows lifted quizzically. It was odd that a Rom would wear black for it was considered a very *prikaza* color. Very unlucky. Except for *drabarne*—those who professed to be magicians. It was also curious that the Rom was a stranger. It was an accepted tradition that any Rom entering an area already claimed by a *kumpania* reported his presence to its *rom baro* as soon as he arrived. But times were changing, for the Rom as well as for the *Gaje*. Matters of tradition were not always so judiciously adhered to as they had been in the old days.

"A stranger in black," he said, "does not necessarily have anything to do with *draba*."

Big George leaned ponderously forward, a grim expression on his face. "Romano Yera died yesterday evening. His body was found by the *shangle* before midnight and they took it away to their police building downtown. What Joji saw was Romano's *mulo*, o Boshbaro. Romano's ghost walked last night in the company of a man wearing black."

Black. Like the paint of the *patrin* on the wall of his house before it burned down. Beside him, Yojo drew in a sharp breath. The skin prickled at the nape of Janfri's neck.

"Did . . . did Joji speak to them?" he asked finally.

Big George nodded. "But they passed him in silence. The stranger was a Rom—Joji is sure of that—a scarred Rom with eyes like smoke, o Boshbaro. There was death in his eyes."

"Joji . . . ?"

"Told me this before he left town," Big George said. "Now tell me. You know both worlds, o Boshbaro—ours and that of the *Gaje*. What does this mean?"

"*Prikaza*," Janfri said softly. "Very bad *prikaza*, Big George."

The *rom baro* nodded. "So tonight I will call a meeting of the *kris* and we will discuss this thing. You will come?"

"Of course."

"Then think on this, o Boshbaro, before you speak to the elders tonight: What is it that makes you and Romano like two beads on the same necklace?"

The prickling of Janfri's skin changed to a stab of fear that traveled down his spine. He knew what Big George spoke of. The *marhime patrin*. The *rom baro* would not speak of it aloud because he knew of no reason that Janfri should be outcast. But someone thought there was good reason and Big George was emphasizing that Janfri should have an answer as to why he and Romano had been singled out before the *kris* met tonight.

"I will do that," he said, rising from his chair. Yojo followed suit.

"Go with God," Big George said.

Janfri nodded wearily. "Stay with God," he replied.

Together he and Yojo left Big George's *tsera* and returned to Yojo's car. The black Lincoln was a twin to the *rom baro*'s dark green vehicle, though in slightly better shape. It, at least, still had both rear quarter panels.

"So," Janfri said as he leaned his head back against the seat. "Do you still want to see me married to your daughter?"

"Why not?" Yojo replied. The thin smile that touched his lips was real, but there was still a subdued air about him. "You have done nothing wrong. Someone is working magic against you, *prala*—is this then your fault?"

Janfri sighed. "I don't even believe in *draba*," he said.

The smile left Yojo's face. "Then you had better learn to," he said grimly, "or it will be your *mulo* that some poor Rom will see in the company of this man in black."

four

Rideau Ferry is a small collection of houses clustered on either side of the narrows that separates the Lower Rideau Lake from the Big Rideau. The village was originally called Oliver's Landing, after Captain Oliver who ran the ferry service across the lake during the early 1800's. Captain Oliver and his wife lived very well, the ferry service proving to be quite lucrative even if the good Captain did refuse to make night crossings. Travelers arriving too late to cross the lake were boarded in the Olivers' cabin. Curiously enough, although the Captain said he took them over at first light the following morning, overnight guests were never seen again. It wasn't until years later that workmen demolishing the old cabin discovered the grisly remains of numerous human skeletons buried under the cabin's earthen floor and the true source of the Olivers' wealth was explained. The residents of the village, needless to say, were quick to change the landing's name to the one it presently bears.

The village lies about midway between Perth and Lombardy, approximately an hour's drive southwest of Ottawa, and boasts little more than a small general store, two marinas, a motel and the Rideau Ferry Inn by way of commercial amenities. A highway now crosses the lake where in earlier time wagons and travelers—or at least those that arrived when there was still plenty of daylight—were ferried across. Most of the properties along the shorefront are houses or winterized cottages, the latter insulated as an afterthought and usually heated electrically.

The house that Ola Faher was renting was one of those. It had the look of a red-brick English cottage, with broad lawns, front and back, and a long pier going out into the lake. A tall cedar hedge was sufficient to cut down the noise of the highway that ran along the embankment to the east side of the property and, while the sound that traveled across the water from boaters in summer could be irritating, it was generally a quiet retreat, perfect for Ola's purposes. The odd strains of the jazz bands that played in the Inn across the highway on Saturday night were more soothing than disturbing, though she could have lived without the rock bands that played there most of the week.

On the day following the murder of Romano Yera, Ola was drowsing in a deck chair on the pier. The afternoon was drawing to a close and when a sweep of heavy stratocumulus clouds moved across the sky to hide the westering sun, she packed up her chair and carried it back to the house. Though the air was still warm, something about the cloud covering as it put to bed the sun reminded her of the uneasy premonitions and visions that had been troubling her for the past few days. She leaned the deck chair against the side of the immense glassed-in porch that took up the whole south side of the house facing the lake, and went inside. There she wandered from room to room in the tiny cottage, trailing her hand along the mantelpiece and the back of the couch. She was restless and couldn't relax. At length she returned to the porch and stared off across the lake.

She was a striking woman in her mid-thirties, with light brown skin and very dark eyes. She had taken to wearing her hair in beaded braids and at first glance most people decided that she was a black of African descent. It as a misconception that she tended to promote because it was still easier to be a black in Canadian society than it was to be a Gypsy. Especially for one of her vocation.

The Rom are rarely a solitary people. Though they value their privacy, even in the middle of a crowded *tsera,* they do not like to be far from their own people. But Ola was like Janfri Yayal in some ways—caught between maintaining her self-image as a Gypsy, but needing the *Gaje* world for the freedom it gave her. There was nothing romantic, to her way of thinking, about the poverty that most Gypsies were forced to live in because they could not adjust their lifestyle to that of the *marhime Gaje* from whom all Rom were forced to make their living. That was why the *Gaje* were on this world—to support the Rom.

There is an old Gypsy folktale that the Rom like to tell. It dates from when they first entered Europe in the late 1300's and pretended that they were Egyptians on a pilgrimage to the holy places of Europe. It goes like this:

When Jesus was going to be crucified, a Rom blacksmith who was a slave was ordered by the Roman soldiers to make four nails. There was to be one nail for each hand, one for the feet, and one for the condemned man's heart. The Rom stalled and stalled until the soldiers whipped him. Then he made the four nails. He called to God and asked Him to help the Rom, but God's only reply was tears and the Rom cried with him. When he was to deliver the nails, he swallowed one of them and told the soldiers he had lost it. God, when he saw that the Rom had swallowed the nail meant for Jesus' heart, said: "Rom, you are free to go and travel anywhere. You can steal your food and take what you need to live." And that, the old Rom relating the tale would say with satisfaction, is why Gypsies travel and why they steal.

Still, the Rom stole less than the *Gaje* believed they did, and never for a profit. A chicken running loose might end up in a Rom stew-pot. Firewood was there for the taking, as was grazing. This was not theft, the Rom averred, for how could anyone claim they owned a forest or a field? But while they might have survived so in the old days, augmenting their incomes with metalwork, horse-trading, basketry, fortune-telling and even begging, those options were no longer open to them. Even the Rom no longer kept horses, but drove in cars like they were *Gaje*. Baskets made in the Far East were far cheaper to import and sell in North America than buying them from a Gypsy would be. There were shops that had the equipment to do automobile work far more cheaply and efficiently than ever a Rom could. *Dukkerin,* or fortune-telling, was outlawed in most places—at least when practiced by Gypsies.

So the Rom lived in poverty, subsisting by begging and welfare and the odd petty fraud or theft. They could not work at a *Gaje* job, nine to five, because that would put them into too much contact with *Gaje* and therefore label them *marhime*. But Ola could not countenance the poverty. She had seen her mother waste away, impoverished and alone except for her, and had vowed that it would not happen to her. She didn't want wealth, nor worldly possessions. Merely the freedom to live in a clean environment, without harassment.

Her trade was *dukkerin,* but fortune-telling on a far different scale than that traditionally practiced by Gypsy women when they could. Ola's *dukkerin* reached the *Gaje* public by way of books that were a synthesis of practicalities and old Gypsy lore. She never sold the secrets of her people, not the *true* secrets, only the common-sense cures such as honey or honeysuckle berries for a canker in the mouth, or linseed tea to give an expectant mother an easy birth. The books were couched in a plainspoken, but mystical voice that was a combination of her own natural speech and the input of her collaborator Jeff Owen, who actually put the material on paper for her.

The Rom tell no fortunes for each other. They maintain their mystique as a defense against the *Gaje*—such as in tales of Gypsy magic and curses—but do not believe in magic themselves, or at least will rarely claim to. But in the paradoxical way of the Rom,

they still knew it existed. That it was real. And that was Ola's greatest barrier between her own people and herself. It ran deeper than
her aversion to the poverty that her people allowed themselves to
live in. Ola was a true *drabarni*—a woman who worked magic as
well as medicine. Wherever she lived for some time, she gained control over her environment. It took time to learn the true names—
even of inanimate objects—but once she did, they were hers to
command. Even *Gaje* objects. Having lived in this cottage for the
better part of a year, she could turn the lights on and off with a
thought. The television could show her images as disparate as her
own mind was capable of conceiving, even events that were actually
transpiring a great distance from where she lived. Animals found
human voices and conversed with her.

Such a person was not welcome in the *tsera* of the Rom. Nor
accepted by the *Gaje* unless one was clever. Unless one spoke of the
"potential within us all which I have realized" and other such
phrases that Jeff was so capable of composing. But even Jeff was
uncomfortable in her presence—for all that he knew nothing of
what she truly was. So she lived in retreats such as this cottage in
Rideau Ferry, lived here until the talk began again and she must
move on. But at least no one knew her for a Rom. She was "that
pretty black lady"—a curiosity still in such out-of-the-way places in
the Ottawa Valley, but a known quantity. Not a Gypsy who the
country folk thought they knew all too well from the stories their
parents and grand-parents had handed down of when the *kumpaniyi*
still traveled by wagon from town to town.

She knew there had to be another way to live, a way that harmo-
nized her straddling of the two worlds, but to this date she hadn't
found it—at least not to her satisfaction. Instead she lived day by day,
as a Rom will, while Jeff and their agent planned their career with
this next book, and those appearances to promote the last one. Nothing to put her too much in the public eye—she was adamant on that
count—but enough so that she was known to those who needed
books such as the ones she and Jeff produced. Enough so that Kerio
Rouge, whose mother was a tribeswoman from Gabon and whose
father was a Parisian chemist, was looked to for advice and comfort.

Perhaps she truly helped some. She hoped so. The fan mail said as much, though sometimes there were other letters, filled with so much hate that she wondered how a man, *Gaje* or Rom, could exist with such an emotion festering inside of him. Such people who needed help the most were never the ones who sought it. But the ones she did help . . . they could be kind with their letters of thanks. For while she never told the true Romany secrets, she never lied either.

So here she was, she thought as she looked out over the darkening lake. Troubled, and alone. With foreknowledge, but unable to offer it to those who needed it this time. She had seen, in dreams and visions, Rom in danger. She knew where they were and who it touched most gravely. What it was that stalked them was not so clear. She only knew that . . . something did.

"Go to them," a low-pitched gravelly voice said from behind her.

She turned to see the calico tomcat she called Boboko watching her with his impenetrable gaze. She had inherited him with the cottage and knew his true name, but it was never spoken between them. She wasn't even sure if Boboko actually spoke—she'd warned him never to speak when *anyone* else was present—or if she merely heard the sounds that issued from his mouth as words. If she had been a *Gaji,* she would have gone into analysis by now.

"I can't," she said.

Boboko licked nonchalantly at a fat paw before replying. "Not can't," he said. "Won't."

The timbre of his voice was a pleasant tickle in her ear. Once she'd come to puberty and understood that animals would gain speech around her, she soon learned which voices she could abide and which she couldn't. Both a budgie and a small lapdog she'd tried to keep as companions had maddened her with the shrill pitch of their voices. A big lab had almost deafened her. Boboko was infinitely superior, even if he tended to play on his own Gypsylike mystique and philosophize too much.

"You know," she said, turning back to the window, "that for a Rom to share her *dook* with another Rom is almost *marhime.*"

Boboko grinned like the cat in a *Gaje* storybook that Jeff had loaned her once telling of a young girl's adventures after she fell down a rabbithole.

"*Almost* is not quite the same as certain," the cat replied.

"They must come to me. Then, if there is *marhime* to be laid, it will be with them, not with me."

"You might as well be *marhime* as it is—considering the way you're living now. By yourself. Alone."

"I have you," Ola said. She had to smile at his infernal logic. Then the seriousness of what they were discussing returned to her and the gentle look that the smile had brought to her features was erased by a thoughtful frown.

"Can you stop any further deaths?" the cat asked.

"Only if they listen to me."

"And will they listen to you?"

Ola shook her head slowly.

"*Bater*," Boboko purred. So be it. He enjoyed using Romany words with her, sometimes pretending he knew them long before she'd taught them to him.

Ola nodded. "They must come to me," she repeated. But the truth of the statement did nothing to ease her pain. At length she turned from the window and went into the kitchen to begin their supper. Though she wasn't hungry herself, she knew that Boboko never lost his appetite. To him, human concerns were almost as indecipherable as *Gaje* ones were to her.

five

Try as he might, Tom Shaw couldn't shake his memories of the previous night. By the time he finally got home, after spending the better part of an hour trying to track down the man he knew as John Owczarek, his wife Gillian was already asleep. He had put away his guitar—he and John had been on their way home from a rehearsal at

Doug Martin's when they'd spotted the fire—and undressed down to his boxer shorts before he realized that he wasn't going to be able to sleep tonight. At least not right away. Not with what he had on his mind. He could understand John's shock at the loss of his home, but what baffled him was the sheer strangeness he'd sensed in his friend—a distancing from the event, a withdrawal into himself, a change in him until the man looking back at Tom was a complete stranger who merely happened to bear a very strong resemblance to the man he'd known.

There is no John Owczarek.

What the hell was that supposed to mean? And why had John just taken off like that? He'd been stunned—that was natural. But he hadn't even approached the police and identified himself as the owner of the house. He'd just stood there staring at the fire as though the building that the flames were devouring belonged to someone else. It had been spooky and that feeling merely intensified when Tom woke the next morning and tried calling around to find John.

Doug had heard about the fire but had not known it was John's house. Phillip Baker, who was producing the new album that they'd been rehearsing for last night, hadn't heard the news and asked Tom to call him back once he'd gotten in touch with John. Angie Kelly, John's agent, was out of town until the weekend. With his finger poised on the rotary dial to make his fourth call, Tom suddenly realized that he didn't know who else to try. He'd known John for three years, become rather good friends with him during the past eight months or so, but it occurred to him now that he really didn't know very much about the man at all. The blank wall he'd abruptly run up against brought the knowledge home like the slam of a door closing in his face. It was as though—

There is no John Owczarek.

Jesus, he thought as John's words came back to haunt him. He ticked off what he did know. John was a brilliant musician—especially when performing the folk music of his native Hungary. Or at least Tom assumed he was of Hungarian descent. John had never said where he was from and now that Tom thought of it, there was a darker cast to his complexion than you might normally find in someone originating in one of the Slavic countries. He had an almost mid-Eastern set to his features as well. Tom shook his head. John had kept his distance in some ways, but not so you'd think he was standoffish. His humors were broad and sudden. His sorrows vast—especially when he played pianissimo, with his violin tucked under his chin, his eyes shut tight, head cocked to one side, the whole of his body as still as an inheld breath except for the slow graceful sweep of his bow arm. He never talked politics or religion, liked spicy foods . . .

Tom cradled the receiver slowly. And with his house burned to the foundation, there was absolutely no way he was going to get in touch with John unless John called here.

"Do you have another rehearsal tonight?"

He turned to find Gillian in the doorway of the kitchen. She was dressed casually in an old sweatshirt and jeans, which meant she was planning to spend the day in the studio working on her new canvas.

"I . . . I'm not sure."

Gillian nodded. "The fire. I forgot. Have you managed to get in touch with John? You know he's welcome to stay with us for as long as he wants." She moved across the kitchen and poured herself a cup of coffee. Holding the pot towards him, she lifted her brows quizzically.

Tom nodded and brought his cup over. "It's strange," he said, "but without his home number to reach him at, I don't know how to get in touch with him."

"Well, he must have said *something* to you last night." She sat down in the kitchen nook with her coffee and brushed a spill of blonde hair back from her shoulders. Some of that color came from a bottle of Miss Clairol—but only enough to touch up the gray hairs that were invading, each year a few more than there had been the year before. As far as Tom was concerned, she needed nothing to remain attractive to him. She looked just as good in an evening gown as when he caught her in the studio, dressed as she was now, with paint smeared on her cheek or brow where she'd rubbed her face, forgetting the paint on her hands. There was something to be said about growing old together. He knew he loved her more now than he had the first year they'd met.

"He didn't say much of anything," Tom said as he sat down across from her. "Just up and ran off—like that." He snapped his fingers.

"I'm sure he just needs some time to himself," Gillian said. "Lord knows, *I*'d want some time to myself if it happened to us."

"I suppose you're right."

"He'll call, Tom. If not today, then tomorrow for certain." Gillian smiled, trying to cheer him up. Tom dredged up a weak response that merely touched the corners of his mouth. "In the meantime, I hate to sound callous, but about tonight . . . If you've nothing planned, Diana's asked us over this evening for a few drinks."

"Fine."

Gillian regarded him worriedly for a long moment, then sighed. She stood up and kissed the top of his head, then went upstairs to her studio, coffee in hand. Tom sat for a long while, his own drink going cold. When he closed his eyes, he saw only flames. He tried to work during the day, but found he couldn't concentrate. The music he was preparing for his own new recording sounded flat no matter how often he tuned his guitar, and he couldn't work on the material for John's new album because that just started the whole train of thoughts over again, a repetitive run-through from the fire to the somewhat disquieting feeling that perhaps—

There is no John Owczarek.

Why would he have said that—phrased it in such a way? Tom didn't like puzzles. He hated crosswords, Trivial Pursuit and mystery novels. His mind didn't work that way. He tended to just bull through problems. Thinking things through merely gave him a headache—like the one he had now. The only thing he had patience for was his music, and today even that wasn't doing any good. At length he left his guitar in the music room and took a couple of painkillers, then went out for a walk, studiously avoiding the route that would take him by the burned-out shell of John's house.

There is no John Owczarek.

The phrase left him with an eerie sense of dislocation—as pronounced now as it had been last night. He could remember reading a book once about a man who woke up one morning and found that he didn't exist anymore. The concept had frightened him far more than any of the horror movies his son Matt had taken him to before he moved out west last year. Today there was no John Owczarek. What if he woke up tomorrow and there was no Gillian? Or Gillian was there, but she didn't know who *he* was? Irritated by the turn of thought his mind had taken, he stepped up his pace, determined to outwalk the confusion inside him. He concentrated on going over to the Mitchells' place tonight and hoped that Ed had laid in a good supply of his office jokes, because he knew he needed something to lighten his day.

John would call before he and Gillian went out, he decided. Or tomorrow morning for sure. Why shouldn't he? He couldn't just up and disappear forever. They had a recording date set, material to arrange, a friendship to maintain.

There is no John Owczarek.

God, he hated those words.

six

"You know that guy we picked up this morning?" Will moved forward in his chair and leaned his elbows on Briggs' desk. "Mr. I'll-shove-this-broomstick-up-your-ass?"

Briggs nodded. They'd been lucky to find him in the basement when they followed a tip to pick him up, instead of upstairs in his apartment. The last time Briggs had seen a collection of weapons like Yves Chenier had was when he'd been involved in a raid on the West End chapter of the Devil's Dragon biker gang at the beginning of the summer. They'd found enough arms in Chenier's apartment to start a small war. A sawed-off shotgun. A .45, two .38's, a .22 target pistol. Six rifles, including one with an infrared scope. A grenade launcher. He shook his head, remembering. A grenade launcher, for Christ's sake!

"What about him?"

"I just got word from Jean that he's out on the street. Bail was set at a lousy two grand."

Briggs understood Will's frustration. Sometimes it all just seemed so pointless. The punks were being put back on the street faster than they could bust them.

"And I *know* he was in on that Caisse Populaire heist last month," Will added. "It was just his kind of gig. This guy's sheet reads like an index to the Criminal Code, and he's back on the street already. I'd like to catch him in a dark alley doing *anything*—even littering—and maybe fire a couple of warning shots through his head."

"Tell me about it." Briggs gathered up the reports and file folders on his desk and made a neat stack out of them. He knew Will had been busting his ass on the Chenier case. They'd both figured that they'd come up with a real break with this morning's tip, but now the owner of the Mac's Milk claimed he couldn't pick Chenier out of the lineup—more like wouldn't—and the judge had been forced to turn him loose on bail. He was still going to go up on the weapons charges, but it wasn't going to be the same.

"What did you think of MacLean?" Briggs asked to change the subject. Andrew MacLean was the man who'd found Wood's corpse in the alley last night and—surprise, surprise—actually called it in. They'd interviewed him again this morning after they'd double-checked the statement he'd made last night.

Will sat back in his chair and shook his head. "Sometimes I think you're like a hound dog, you know? You just don't let go."

"He lives in Alta Vista. You don't go clear downtown for a walk in the evening—not in that area."

"No. But it's the right place to have a few drinks with the boys after working late and maybe getting a blow-job in an alleyway—if you're not too particular about what kind of diseases your old wanger's going to come in contact with. Ten-to-one he was going in there with a hooker, but there's no way he's going to tell *us* that. Let's just be happy he took the time to call it in. What we found wasn't pretty. Just imagine what it would've looked like if a few rats had been gnawing away at it for half the night."

"I suppose . . ."

Will laughed. "You don't fool me, Paddy. It wouldn't surprise me if you found out that he was once given a kick in the ass by a Gypsy when he was five years old and now he's decided to pay them back. Just dig back far enough. Me, I'm packing it in for today. Sharon's got the night off and we're going to have a nice quiet dinner at home—together for a change. You want a lift?"

Briggs patted his stomach and shook his head. "Think I'll actually walk and shock some weight off the old system."

Will grinned. "Hey. Just say the word and I'll see what I can do about having the Inspector put you back on a beat for a month or so—just to get in shape, you know what I mean?"

"Do the words 'fuck off' mean anything to you?"

"I don't know. I'll look 'em up when I get home." He stood up to return to his own desk. "Take it easy, Paddy."

"Yeah. You, too."

Briggs headed for the stairs with a wave of his hand. He mounted one step at a time, thinking of the appropriateness of keeping the General Assignment Unit tucked away downstairs with Morality Control, the holding cells and the Morgue. It reflected the attitude of the public, if not that of the Chief of Police. Sweep it away and pretend it doesn't exist—except for the juicy bits you can slap on the front pages of the daily paper and the tube. Here one day, relegated to limbo the next. Because of the residential outcry when the location for the new police headquarters was announced, four-fifths of the new building was underground so that it wouldn't "overpower the site." The General Assignment offices were too close to the holding cells for Briggs' liking. Everything might smell clean now—except for the Morgue downstairs which was maybe too clean-smelling like a hospital—but give it a couple of months and you wouldn't be able to mistake the stink of the winos' vomit as it drifted down towards their offices. Not that the guys upstairs had it much better. They didn't have windows either. But at least they *knew* they were above ground.

When he reached the street, Briggs stood a moment, adjusting to the change of temperature. That was the worst thing about working in air conditioning—the moment you stepped outside and the heat hit you. Your body was still attuned to the cool, if somewhat stale air, and was saying, "Nope. I don't *want* to be out here." And just to make the point absolutely clear, it'd turn on the sweat like a kid playing with a new faucet. Lovely. At least it was supposed to cool down again tonight.

Turning south on Elgin, he crossed under the Queensway to walk the ten blocks to Fifth Avenue. Another three blocks west brought him to Rupert Street where he rented the middle apartment of a three-story red-brick building. He was sweating profusely by the time he got home, but hadn't wanted to take off his jacket because he was still wearing his shoulder holster. The Chief wasn't big on his plainclothes officers sporting their pieces in public. Didn't do a whole lot for the image.

It was quiet inside his apartment, and too warm. He took off his jacket, hung it by the door and removed his holster. Carrying it into the living room, he sat down and laid it on the battered coffee table that still had last night's dinner dishes on it. Briggs sighed as he leaned back on the sofa. He was tired. Not because of the lack of sleep from getting called out last night. Rather it was a deeper, more disturbing weariness. The endless parade of victims and perpetrators, like the almost headless stiff last night and this morning's punk with his arsenal, wouldn't leave him. Their faces and the knowledge of the crimes they'd either committed or were victims to left him alternating between anger and exhaustion. They were like ghosts that lived inside him and never stopped their haunting. And their number count never let up. A day, Christ, an hour didn't go by without someone getting it. A purse snatched, some little five-and-dime getting hit. A gas bar. A hit and run. A knife job. Something like last night. Or Chenier being out on bail already. . . .

He turned on the TV and went into the kitchen, wishing he'd

picked up a pizza on the way home. He pulled a frozen dinner out of the freezer without even looking to see what kind it was and thrust it into the oven. A second trip to the fridge got him a beer. Popping the tab, he went back into the living room and stretched out on the sofa. One of those "real-honest-to-God-people-do-these-things" shows was on and the announcer's eager voice was an irritating buzz even at low volume. He got up, turned the channels until he found a documentary, then returned to his seat, watching the screen with the sound off. The beer was just what he'd needed. After dinner he'd take a shower, but right now he just didn't want to move.

Part of the reason things got to him so much was that, outside of work, he really didn't have much else. Most men his age were married, had a couple of kids, were living out in the suburbs like Kanata, or Alta Vista, or *somewhere* by now. Working around the house, in the garden, when they got home from work. Puttering. He glanced around his shabby apartment. Maybe he should get into puttering. The place could certainly use it.

Oh, he'd had plans . . . once. He was going to get married, have kids, go the whole route. Her name was Francine Gillard—a pretty French Canadian from the Hull side. He still had a picture of her on the fake mantelpiece across from the couch. A five-by-seven that was dusty and didn't look right anymore. He couldn't imagine the young woman in the photograph as a lover or wife now. He was old enough to have daughters her age. . . .

It was his own fault that things hadn't worked out. She'd been a waitress when he was still a rookie patrolman—no taller, but in a hell of a lot better shape. They'd talked about marriage. She wanted it right away, but he wanted to wait until he was making enough to support her properly. No wife of his was going to work, by God! And no family of his was going to be raised in anything even close to the poverty he'd been raised in.

Briggs sighed. He didn't need to be thinking like this. What he ought to do was put Francine's picture away and get on with his life—even if it was twenty years too late. She sure as hell wasn't coming back. Not that he was waiting for her to. He didn't know what he was waiting for anymore. He wondered if she was happy with her car salesman. If they had a house in the suburbs and children. If her husband puttered around the place on the weekend. . . . He stared at the picture. He really should get rid of it. Instead he went into the kitchen and took his dinner out of the oven.

He was in bed by ten-thirty and bleary with sleep when the ringing of the phone finally roused him. He stared at the luminous dial of his alarm clock. Five to twelve. His hand found the receiver and blessed silence cut across the room as he lifted it from its cradle. He grunted into the mouthpiece.

"Paddy? Will here. We've got another one."

Briggs sat up. The room was dark—a perfect backdrop for the image that flashed through his mind. He didn't think he could face another body with its head half-severed from its neck. Not tonight. Not ever again if he could help it.

"Where?"

"In the Market again. They called me when they got an ID. Cooper ran the victim's prints and came up with another Gypsy so he gave me a call. You coming down?"

They didn't need this, Briggs thought. He could see the headlines if the media connected tonight's victim with last night's. "GYPSY KILLER ON THE LOOSE!" From time to time you'd get a string of four or five of these before the maniac got scared or, less often, got caught. It was the kind of thing the newspapers loved. The kind of thing that brought the pressure from the brass upstairs down hard on the men trying to deal with the case. Not to mention the poor fucking victims. . . .

"Was it the same as last night?" he asked into the receiver.

"Yeah. Happened in another alleyway about two blocks from the first. Cooper's still working on the autopsy. He says it's shaping up like the other one."

"Great."

"Got a couple of witnesses this time."

"They saw it happen?"

"Not exactly."

"I'll be down in fifteen minutes," Briggs said and hung up.

• • •

The operating room was brightly lit and stank of chemical soap. Briggs stared at the body on the surgical table, at the sheer damage of the corpse's neck and forearms highlit under the merciless lights. The room itself was neat and orderly. Sterile. The corpse had brought its own horror into the room with it. One of Cooper's assistants was preparing slides at a side table. Cooper had nothing to add to the quick briefing that he'd given when Briggs had arrived.

"Did you find anything we can use?" he asked.

Cooper shook his head. He indicated the defense wounds on the victim's forearms. "He put up a better fight—better than the other fellow did last night—but it didn't help him much in the long run."

"And you still say there wasn't a weapon involved?"

"I don't know, Briggs. As soon as I get anything . . ."

"Yeah," Briggs replied wearily. He stared at the corpse for a long moment, then looked away. "Well, I've seen enough. You coming, Will?"

Briggs' adrenaline was working overtime and he wanted to get upstairs to follow what leads the victim's arrest sheet might give them and to talk to the witnesses. There was nothing they could do down here. He hoped that the witnesses could give them something, because he knew that anything they got from the victim's sheet would eventually run them up against a dead-end. Tonight's Gypsy wasn't going to give them anything more than last night's had. They just didn't exist on paper the way a normal man did. No credit cards. No anything that wasn't registered under an alias. But they had to give it a try.

"What did you say the victim's name was?" he asked as they entered the stairwell.

"The driver's license he was carrying was in the name of Arnold Smith," Will said, "but ceepik matched his prints with one Ingo Shandor. At least that was the name at the top of the list."

Briggs sighed. Come morning they'd have to round up someone in Fraud to see if they could come up with the names and addresses of some Gypsies who were still alive.

"What about the address on his license?" he asked. "Did anybody check it out?"

"It was an empty lot."

"How come I'm not surprised?" Briggs muttered. He held the door open for Will and followed him into the General Assignment offices. "About these witnesses . . . ?" he continued, then paused as Will stopped in front of a bench where two women were sitting. Will grinned at his partner.

"Ladies," he said. "This is Detective-Sergeant Briggs, who's working on this case with me."

The older of the pair looked to be in her late twenties. She was well-built and tastelessly dressed in a purple leather miniskirt, knee-high beige boots and a flimsy red blouse unbuttoned halfway down her chest. She wasn't wearing a bra. Her hair was a silver blonde, straight out of a bottle of dye, and her makeup appeared to have been laid on with a trowel. Her companion was younger and slimmer, brown hair cut in a shag style, the makeup not quite so heavy. She was wearing a summer print minidress and high-heeled sandals, and clutched a small purse on her lap. She looked scared. She also looked, Briggs realized uncomfortably, like Francine. Or the daughter he and Francine might have had. If she wore her hair differently . . . He shook his head irritably. It was getting bad when he started seeing Francine's face in the features of a hooker. Especially one this young. She couldn't be much more than sixteen.

"Names?" he asked Will.

"The lady on the left is Carol Wesley." The platinum blonde looked up at the sound of her name. "The kid hasn't got any ID, but she claims her name's Tracy Hilborn and that she's eighteen, though personally—"

"I want to see a lawyer," the blonde demanded. "You got no right to arrest us."

"I told you earlier," Will said. "You're not under arrest. We just want to ask you some questions."

"I don't have to answer nothing." She stood up and glanced at her companion. "I'm walking. You coming, honey?"

"I . . ."

"Sit," Briggs said firmly. Wesley sat, glowering at him. He turned to Will. "Who brought them in?"

"Constable Porter—you were talking to him last night. He picked them up when they were running down Dalhousie. Said he was kind of jumpy after last night and he hung onto them while his partner checked the alleys further on up. They found Shandor's body in the second one near the corner of Murray and called it in."

Briggs nodded, regarding the two women, trying to decide how to play it. If it was just the kid—Christ, he couldn't get it out of his head how much she looked like Francine—it'd be easy. But the older woman was going to play it hard.

"We'll take their statements separately," he said.

"Sure. Okay, Wesley. On your feet."

Briggs glanced at the younger girl as Wesley stood up and sauntered between the desks to Will's. She watched them go, then lifted her gaze nervously to look at Briggs. The detective sighed.

"If you'll come with me, Tracy," he said.

She rose, clutching nervously at her purse, and followed him to his desk.

"How long you been in this line of work?" he asked as he rolled a fresh sheet into his typewriter.

"I . . . I don't know what you mean."

Briggs glanced at her, then over to Will's desk where the other hooker was lounging in a chair. When he looked back, Tracy dropped her gaze to her lap. "Look," he said softly. "I'm going to level with you. All we want is some information on what you saw tonight. I'm going to type it up and you're going to sign it, and then you're out on the street again. What you do to make a living is none of my business, okay?"

Tracy looked up. "I can't tell you anything," she said in a small voice. "They'll kill me if they think I've told you . . . whatever. . . ."

"Who will? Your pimp? Wesley over there?"

She shrugged. Her fingers were tight around her purse, knuckles going white.

"If you don't talk," Briggs said, "I'm going to have to hold you overnight. I might have to turn you over to Morality or Juvenile in the morning if you don't cooperate."

"I *am* eighteen."

"So you're eighteen." He waited for her to go on, but she remained silent, lips trembling. He shook his head. "You're just making it harder on yourself."

"What . . . what do you care?"

"I care. I don't like seeing people hurt—especially not when they're doing it to themselves. Maybe you think that's weird, me being a cop, but we're people too, you know. Right now I need a little information. Give it to me, and you're walking out that door in an hour or so—no strings."

"Really?"

Briggs nodded. He was willing to wait her out now. She was scared under that street-tough veneer. She'd talk. He just wished it'd be as easy to get her out of the Life.

"Okay," Tracy said softly. She had to repeat herself before Briggs realized that she'd spoken. "There . . . there's this guy named André Fedun. Carol and I were waiting for him to . . . to collect his money, you know? He doesn't like us carrying too much in case . . . well, in case something happens to us. So he comes by every couple of hours or so.

"We were standing beside the church near the corner—the church on Murray, you know? Andy was late. Carol says it happens. He's got a deal going down or something and he takes his time getting around to us. So anyway, we saw this guy coming down the street and Carol figures maybe he'd go for . . . you know." She wouldn't look at Briggs as she spoke, staring instead at the purse on her lap, hands clenched into small fists now. Either she was really green, Briggs thought, or one hell of an actress.

"What'd he look like?" he asked.

Her gaze lifted momentarily, then dropped. "Just ordinary. Nothing special. Anyway, Carol says this to me and she's about to go across the street when we see this other guy coming from Rideau. He's walking tall, all in black, and there was something—I don't know. Not *right* about him. He spooked me. Spooked Carol too, because she just sort of froze up and we both stood there watching him get near the first guy."

"Could you see his face?"

Tracy shook her head. "Not really. And I don't even know if he was wearing black clothes. It just seemed like he was."

Briggs nodded encouragingly. He was taking notes by hand instead of using the typewriter so as not to intimidate her further. "Was there any . . . fog around?" he asked. He glanced at her face to gauge what reaction the question would get. She only looked confused.

"Fog?"

"Yeah, you know. Like mist. Maybe hanging around his feet."

She shook her head. "Not then. But after . . ." Her voice trailed off and the frightened look returned to her eyes. Briggs was beginning to realize now that she hadn't just been scared about getting busted.

"Let's get back to this guy coming down the street. He was approaching the first man. Did he look your way—did he see either you or Carol?"

"No. But the first guy didn't look too happy to see him coming. I figured maybe he owes this guy some money or something and wasn't paying up, you know? He backed into the alley and the second man went in there after him. . . ."

It was a replay of the story that Cleary had given them—minus the fog. That suited Briggs just fine. He didn't need the fog. Just like he didn't need Cooper and MacDonald's smart-ass comments about panthers or leopards prowling the streets.

"What happened then?" he prompted.

"We . . . we didn't see anything," she said in a small voice. "But we heard . . . it was like someone screaming, but it wasn't loud. Just this wheezing sort of gurgle, but it . . . it sounded desperate. . . ." Briggs could see the goose bumps lifting on her arms and she shivered.

"Is that when the two of you took off?"

She shook her head. "We were too scared to even move. We just

stood there shaking and . . . and watching the mouth of the alley. I
didn't know what was going down in there, but I didn't want to be
any part of it, you know? So I just stood there, holding onto Carol's
arm, and she's hanging onto mine, and then we saw this—I thought
it was smoke—coming out of the alley and the second guy walked
out through it. He didn't look left or right then, but just headed on
up Dalhousie towards the river. We waited until he was a couple of
blocks away and we could hardly see him and then we just took off
the other way. That's when we got busted."

"What about the fog? The smoke?"

"I wasn't looking for it. Maybe he set the guy on fire or something, I don't know. I was just watching his back until I thought he
was far enough away from us to split without him seeing us." She
was still for a long moment, then asked: "What . . . what happened
in the alley?"

"A man was murdered."

Tracy glanced nervously to where Wesley was sitting, smoking a
cigarette while Will typed up her statement. "Look," she said. "We
didn't have *anything* to do with it. I *swear* we didn't."

"No one's saying you did. Would you recognize the second man
if you saw him again?"

"It was pretty dark."

"But would you recognize him?"

"Maybe . . . if I saw him walking. He was real stiff-backed and
had a funny sort of—I don't know. A determined way of walking."

Briggs nodded. "What about scarring? Did you see any scars on
his face? Under his eyes maybe?"

She shook her head. Briggs tapped his pencil against his lip,
studying his notes. It wasn't a whole hell of a lot to go on. Not
much better than what they'd got from Cleary last night. He sure
hoped Will had had better luck with Wesley, but he wasn't putting
any bets on it.

"What happens now?" Tracy asked.

"I'm going to talk to my partner—compare your statement with
the one he took from your friend."

"But what about after?"

Briggs stood up. "After we get your statement typed up, you'll be free to go."

"Yeah. Sure." She sounded tired, her voice empty.

Briggs sighed. He started to say something else, then decided to leave things lie. Next thing you knew he'd be trying to get her off the street—because she looked like Francine, because she was just so fucking young looking—but it wouldn't work. Never did. He moved away, motioning to Will. His partner joined him by an empty desk.

"Looks like you put the fear of God into her," Will remarked.

Briggs frowned. "I'd like to help her, but . . ."

Will shook his head. "Wouldn't work, Paddy, and you know it. What did she do, give you the 'poor, pitiful me' song-and-dance? 'Please, sir, if you'll just give me the busfare to get back home, I'll quit the Life—I swear I will.' So you fork over the fare and she hands it over to her pimp and she's back on the street and it starts up all over again."

"Just full of sympathy and the milk of human kindness tonight, aren't we?"

Will sighed. "I just spent a half hour with Ms. Spread-'em over there, Paddy, and I'm right out of sympathy. I could be home with my wife right now. Instead, I'm exchanging bullshit with some cheap hooker. You should take a look at her rap sheet. I mean this lady's been around."

"What about the kid? Anything on her?"

"If that's her real name—nope. Her prints came up clean as well."

"Well, that's good to know."

"Paddy, don't get involved. She's lowlife. Once they're out there peddling their buns, there's no more hope for them. There's just no such thing as the good-hearted whore. Or the innocent young hooker."

Briggs frowned. Will was right. He'd told himself the same thing about five minutes ago. And if she didn't look like Francine and if the ghosts of all those victims through the years weren't playing a tap dance in his head right now . . .

"What did you get out of Wesley?" he asked.

"Pretty much the same story Cleary gave us. Not a whole lot we can use. What did yours tell you?"

"The same."

"So are we going to turn them loose?"

"Might as well. We've already got Cleary in a holding cell, and we're sure as hell not running a hotel here. Just give me a chance to type up Tracy's statement and get her to sign it and we'll drop the pair of them off."

Will sighed. "Okay." He shot a glance at Wesley. "Guess I'll go find out a few more interesting things that you can do with a night-stick. This lady's got an imagination like you wouldn't believe."

"Will! What's Sharon going to say?"

"I don't know, Paddy. One of these days I figure I'll come home and there won't be anybody there to say anything to me anymore. We've *gotta* do something about these hours."

"Wearing you out?"

"Paddy, I'm too tired to get worn out."

7
seven

The *kris* of the Ottawa area Romanies had a fluctuating member-ship composed of whichever of the more important Rom happened to be in town at the time. They gathered only when necessary and then wherever it was convenient. It might be in a vacant lot or the backfield of a sympathetic farmer's property. Tonight they met in the yard behind the house of Marko Lazlo, the *rom baro* of the Kore-shti Kalderash in Vanier. Marko was a tall, heavy-set man, dressed to-night in a splendid dark-blue suit that was a size too small for him. Consequently, when he sat, he sat carefully, leaving the jacket open at his chest. A purple and yellow *diklo* was knotted at his throat, clash-ing with the suit. His wife Yula and his unmarried daughters bustled amongst the talking guests, serving *chao*—tea brewed with sugar and served over fruit. When all the guests had been looked after, the daughters withdrew and Yula took her place beside her husband.

Present this evening were the *rom bari* of all the *kumpaniyi* in and around Ottawa, as well as other respected adults of the Rom community. Stevo Gry, the head of the Hull *kumpania,* sat with his two brothers, his grandfather, and Old Lyuba, a wizened aunt in her seventies. The Deschenes *kumpania* was represented by white-haired Paul Vakako and his wife Boti. Big George had arrived with Tshaya, Yojo, Janfri, the Yoska sisters Tinka and Rosie, and old man Petulengro. Tibo Lee had come up from the trailer park outside of Perth with his widowed sister Ursula, the Wells brothers had come down from Gatineau, and there were perhaps a dozen others, including Melalo Wanko, the son-in-law of Prince Bakro Columbus, the *rom baro* of the Tomoeshti Kalderash in Montreal.

The *kris,* or collected will of the Rom, is only as effective as the acceptance of its decision by the majority of Rom. Gypsies have no police force, no jails, no executioners. There is no direct element of coercion to enforce the rule of their laws. A claim brought before them leads only to a judgment. For its actual enforcement, the Rom have to rely on their own strength and the strength of their kinsmen. In the case of the problem being discussed this evening, there was not so much a judgment being sought, as an attempt to understand what might prove to be yet another incident to add to a long history of harassment. The potential danger to the Gypsy community as a whole needed to be weighed. If the brutal murder of Romano Yera and the burning of Janfri's *tsera* were agreed by all to be isolated incidents, the *kris* would offer its condolences to the victims and allow their kin to mourn in private. But if this was seen as another campaign against the Rom, an uprising of new anti-Gypsy sentiment, then measures would have to be taken to protect the community as a whole, either by confronting the menace, if this was possible, or by withdrawing all the *kumpaniyi* and declaring the area *marhime.*

When the guests had finished their *chao*—all save Big George and his wife, neither of whom had accepted the tea because they were still in mourning—Marko, as host, arose and surveyed them. They were seated in lawn chairs mended with burlap and twine, wooden crates, a tattered sofa, and the back-seat and rims of a dismantled station wagon that took up most of the driveway. The street in front of the house was lined with battered Caddys, Lincolns and Tibo Lee's old Volkswagen bus. In the center of the yard, a small fire crackled, throwing light onto the faces of the gathered Rom. The scent of its smoke, mingled with spices, was in the air.

To an outsider, the *kris* holding their council in Marko's backyard might be an object of amusement. Many wore ragged or ill-fitting clothes. All had an almost wild look about them with their bright eyes and shocks of blue-black hair. They ranged in size from the frail-limbed Old Lyuba, seated on a wheel rim and pillow as though they were a throne, to the elephantine stature of Big George, ensconced in a lawn chair that creaked ominously whenever he moved. But an astute observer could not fail to see their quiet dignity and the seriousness with which they awaited the matter at hand.

When he was certain that he had everyone's attention, and the quiet gossiping that had accompanied the drinking of the *chao* had died away, Marko turned to where Janfri was sitting with Yojo and Big George.

"Boshengro," he said, using the name by which Janfri was known amongst the Rom not a part of Big George's *kumpania*. "Who named you *marhime*—and why?"

Janfri stood when his name was called. The dark faces turned toward him were sympathetic and curious. The yard fell utterly silent. Standing alone, with the weight of their patient gazes upon him, Janfri knew what he must say, but he hesitated. He'd thought on the reasons this afternoon and, with what he knew of Romano, it hadn't been difficult to decide what connected the two of them with the *marhime patrin*. It was the world of the *Gaje*. And that afternoon, for the first time since he'd watched his house burn down, he'd grown angry. "There is not to love, nor to hate," his uncle Nonoka had told him once. "Only to understand." That might be true. But until he understood, he would let his anger run its course. He took a steadying breath.

"I don't like to speak ill of the dead," he said, "but Romano's *mulo* will understand why I must—may he go quickly to the land of shadows." Romano's father Punka wasn't present, but Big George nodded with understanding when Janfri glanced at him. "Romano spent many years in *Gaje* jails, isolated from other Rom, just as I have lived amongst the *Gaje* myself. Neither of us was named *marhime* because of this, but someone has still decided that we were no longer *phral*—no longer true Rom. I am not Romano; I can't speak for him. But . . ." He looked slowly around the circle of faces. "*Te merav*—may I die if I have forsaken the laws of the Rom.

"I have lived amongst the *Gaje,* but in my heart I was always Rom. My *tsera* was open to any of my people. My home was open, and undefiled. You that have been my guests know this. Yet some unknown accuser has brought violence against my *kumpania* and myself. This coward murders and sets fires from the shadows and will not stand forth to face me with his accusations. If he is present tonight, I demand that he step forth. Who will speak against me? Who will speak against Romano?"

Janfri folded his arms against his chest and glared at the *kris,* his eyes black with emotion. "Stand and speak now," he added softly, "or I will speak such a curse against you that *o Beng* himself will not abide your company."

A long silence greeted his words. There was not one man or woman present, not even Prince Bakro's son-in-law Melalo, who had not tasted his hospitality and seen that though he lived amongst the *Gaje,* he lived as a true Rom. He took *Gaje* money, consorted with them too much perhaps, but that was a matter of poor taste, not *marhime.* At last Big George lumbered to his feet.

"You all know me," he said. Here and there a flash of white teeth grinned in reply. "I say that o Boshbaro might be somewhat of a wild goose—there's more than one here tonight who has a daughter Janfri should think seriously of marrying—but I have no reason to believe that he has ever done anything that he should be named *marhime.* And even Romano, whom I have had to instruct from time to time, was never an evil man. To Janfri's curse, I add my own: Step forth now, or forever be outcast in the eyes of Rom and God!"

The *kris* shifted uneasily under this pronouncement, staring at the fire, not willing to meet their neighbors' faces. Not until Marko stood once more did the tension ease somewhat.

"No one accuses Boshengro or Romano," he said. "If they are *marhime* in their dealings with the *Gaje,* then so are we all." A murmur of nervous agreement arose in reply. "What we must do now is discover who is responsible and what we can do to deal with him."

"Pardon my advice," Melalo said from the corner of the sofa where he sat with Paul and Boti Vakako. "But as to what you must do with him, that is simple: destroy him."

"We aren't mobsters," Stevo Gry said. "Not like the Montreal Rom."

Big George nodded in agreement. "The last time I was on the Main I was hard put to tell the Rom from the gangsters."

"We do what we must to survive," Melalo replied.

"You give us all a bad name," Stevo said.

Melalo scowled. His suit was new and, unlike those of the other men, well-tailored. "Would you have us run from every little problem?" he demanded. "As our fathers did? And where did it get them? The Rom can learn a thing or two from the *Gaje,* and one thing that we have learned is that we must stand and fight when trouble comes."

Old Lyuba cleared her throat and the argument died. When she saw she had everyone's attention, she nodded to Melalo. "And when the trouble that comes is *draba* trouble," she asked quietly, "what advice does Prince Bakro give you then?"

Around the fire heads nodded. All had heard the story of Romano's *mulo* and the man in black. Melalo had heard it as well.

"Most respectfully, *phuri dai,*" he said, "*draba* tales are for the *Gaje.* You know as well as I the art of sleight of hand. *Draba* is but the tricks you women play on the *Gaje.*" He smiled. "From the tales my mother told me of you, there's not a Rom alive could match you for the *bozur,* except perhaps Pivli Gozzle."

Old Lyuba snorted at being called a wise woman. "We don't play the money-switching game anymore," she said. "And if that's all the magic that your mother knew enough to tell you about, she didn't raise you very well."

"What I meant," Melalo said, "was that there's a trick behind every supposed magic. Only the *Gaje* are gullible enough to fall for them now. What happened here is a misfortune—but if you believe it to be the work of a *drabarno,* you will never catch the one that is truly responsible. While you look for demons and magic-workers, he will only strike again."

"What then would *you* suggest?" Big George asked. "That we beat up a few *Gaje* until we find one willing to confess?"

"No. Only—"

"It seems to me," Stevo said, breaking in, "that there was trouble in Montreal last winter. Rom died then as well—was it five or six *phral* that died?"

Melalo nodded. "We had trouble, *uva.*" Yes.

"And if I also remember," Stevo continued, "you hushed it up pretty damn quick, too."

"It was bad for business," Melalo said. "We had to keep it quiet."

Old Lyuba spat on the ground. "Rom dying should have nothing to do with business."

"You don't understand. We were having trouble with the Mob. The men who died—"

"*I* heard that the first to die was Lisa Vosho, a Romany *chi,*" Old Lyuba said. "And that she died because she married a *Gaje*. Because she was *marhime.*"

Around the fire, heads turned to look at the old woman, surprise in their features. None of them had heard that.

"Lisa Vosho was married to Marcel Pellier," Melalo said. "The Pelliers are . . . business partners of my father-in-law. She died because some business rivals wished to make a statement as to what would happen to any of Prince Bakro's people who sided with the Pelliers. When her death changed nothing . . . other statements were made. This was not a matter of *marhime*. It was terrible. A misfortune. But it was a matter of business."

Old Lyuba shook her head sadly. "To think that I would live to hear a Rom speak as you do, Melalo Wanko."

"Better to live in poverty than as thieves," Big George added.

Melalo frowned. "You speak of what you don't know, as though poverty were something to be embraced with glad smiles. Do you smile when your children are starving and you can't even beg the price of a loaf of bread? When you have nowhere to sleep but the backseat of your car—a car that no longer runs and the winter winds are howling outside? If that is how you wish to live, do it, but don't begrudge others taking what they can, when they can and how they can. The only one of you here who has any sense is Boshengro—and that is because he has the courage to be more than a poor homeless Rom, waiting for the *Gaje* to give him a handout."

Janfri shifted uncomfortably, for all that the words were true. But they had only been true for him since Pesha had died. If his wife were still alive, he didn't doubt that he would have lived as the rest of his *kumpania* did. But she had died because he could not afford the medicine she'd needed on a winter's night as foul as Melalo's example. Had he been able to, he would have gladly stolen the medicine, or the money to buy it, but Pesha had died before he could do either. Never again, he had vowed. Never again would the lack of money kill one that he loved. He lifted his head as Old Lyuba spoke.

"But *how* did they die, these Rom?" she asked Melalo.

"*Not* by *draba*."

"By the gun then? Such as your 'business partners' carry? Or by a knife? Or were they slain as Romano was—butchered in an alleyway?"

Before Melalo could answer, the sound of squealing tires cut across the night. A car screeched to a halt in front of Marko's house. The *kris* remained silent, listening to the slap of bare feet on the driveway. Janfri glanced at Old Lyuba and saw her nodding sadly to herself. When Marko's eldest son Kore ran into the backyard, all gazes save hers turned in his direction.

"Father!" he cried. He paused near the fire, catching his breath. "Ingo Shandor was found murdered in the Market not half an hour ago!"

Silence fell across the yard, then dozens of voices erupted in a babble. Janfri sat down beside Yojo, his shoulders slumped.

"It's just beginning," he said with a catch in his voice. "I thought it was over, but it's just beginning."

Yojo started to answer when a shadow fell across his face. The two men looked up to find old Lyuba standing over them.

"We'll all go soon," she said. "The city will empty, like a leaking keg on the back of one of our old *vurdon*. *Tsera* by *tsera* we'll go and *o Beng* will rule where we raised our tents."

Janfri nodded, struck by the weird tone in the old woman's voice. There was a light in her eyes that made them seem almost luminous.

"And there's nothing we can do," he said.

"Not we," Old Lyuba agreed. "Not Big George who must see to his *kumpania,* nor Yojo here who must look after his family, nor an old woman like myself who's good for nothing but sitting in a corner and telling old stories. But you could do something, Janfri la Yayal. The bad luck touched you with its hand. It *knows* you. The next time it comes, it won't just take your tent. Instead it will swallow you up, just as it did Romano and Ingo—swallow up your soul until nothing remains but your bones and the skin holding them together."

A cold shiver danced down Janfri's spine. He glanced at Yojo, remembering the big man's warning. *You'd better learn to believe in* draba *or it will be your* mulo *that some poor Rom'll see in the company of the man in black. . . .*

"What do you mean?" he asked. "What could *I* do?"

"Find this man who walks with ghosts . . . this Mulengro. Find him and destroy him. I have *seen* him, Boshengro. My *dook,* what little I have left of it, has shown this demon to me. He stalks the night like Martiya and he feeds on the ghosts of the Rom he kills." Martiya was the night spirit, the Gypsy Angel of Death who stalked the land between sundown and sunup, seeking unwary Rom. "The *mule* of the dead Rom become his to command, Boshengro. They feed him. They are his eyes and ears. They are his strength. He swallows them before they can flee to the land of shadows and makes them his own."

"Stories," Janfri protested hoarsely. "Martiya and demons . . . they are just stories to tell around the campfire. Like the ones of the little *kesali* that haunt the forests . . ."

Old Lyuba crouched down, facing him eye to eye. "What do you have in your pocket, o Romany *chal* who does not believe in *mule?*"

"In my . . . pocket?" Janfri's hand touched the knotted cloth that was hidden from sight in his pocket. It was what the Lowara Rom called a *mulengi dori*—a dead man's string. It was the cloth that was used to measure the size of a dead man for his coffin. Afterwards it was cut up into short strips and knotted. It was very good luck to carry one, but had another use as well. When you were in dire need of help, you undid a knot and called out the name of the dead man and said: "Sweet dead one, let the noose about to be tied around my neck be undone." Then the *mulo* was supposed to help you. Once it was used, and it could only be used once, you had to throw it into running water as soon as possible afterwards—to keep the luck good. The one in Janfri's pocket had been used to measure his uncle Nonoka for his coffin. He carried it . . . just because he carried it. If he had believed in its *draba,* he would have used it that night Pesha died.

"*Mule* are restless when first they are freed from their bodies," the old woman said. "Most find their way quickly to the land of shadows. But some lose their way—like the *mule* of *Gaje* slain by a Rom. Or like a murdered Rom whose *mulo* a *drabarno* controls with his magic."

"I don't believe . . ."

"And yet you carry a dead man's string in your pocket."

"As a keepsake. A memento. Nothing more."

Old Lyuba shook her head. "Inside, you know," she said. "You have a touch of the *dook* about you, Boshengro. It puts the heart into your fiddle's music, and the cleverness in your eye. But now you must lay aside your fiddle awhile and hunt this magician down. You must kill him, before he kills you. Before more Rom die at his hand."

"But . . ."

"I know," Old Lyuba said. "That isn't the way of the Rom—except perhaps in Montreal. Better to pack up and move away from trouble. I believe that. But the man in black has touched you and, like *o Beng,* once he knows the smell of your soul, he won't let go. More Rom will die, Boshengro. I have *seen* that. And though I don't like to share the *dook* with another Rom—I have *seen* you die, too. Unless you destroy this devil Mulengro."

Mulengro. The word the old woman had coined to describe the man in black sent a shiver up his spine. It was ridiculous to take her seriously and he knew it. This was the twentieth century and neither *Gaje* nor Rom truly believed in demons and ghosts. Except . . . there was the weird light in Old Lyuba's eyes. He remembered Big George discussing the possibility of magic so seriously this afternoon. And Yojo—sitting stiff with shock beside him now—he too believed. Janfri told himself that he'd be insane to seriously be considering any of this, but to his own surprise he found himself asking:

"What can I do, Lyuba? I don't know any magic."

"Men rarely do," she replied. "Why do think you leave the *dukkerin* to us?"

"But that's just—"

"Tricks. I know. Like wise young Melalo was bragging about. But I'll tell you a secret, Boshengro. Sometimes a woman comes along to the Rom and the true *draba* is in her. She will live alone because we Rom don't like such folk living amongst us any more than the *Gaje* do. *I* know. When I was young I had a bit too much of the *dook* in me, too. Not as much as some, but I had enough to force me to live apart until Stevo took me in. I hide it well, but sometimes I still *see* things, *hear* things. . . ."

Her voice trailed off and Janfri exchanged a glance with Yojo. His friend's eyes were as round as saucers and his hand was in his pocket—clutching his lucky rabbit's paw, Janfri knew. Janfri shivered himself, found his own hand inching towards the knotted cloth in his pocket, and forced himself to keep his hands on his knees. But there was something about the old woman that had him believing too. Almost.

"Come see me tomorrow," Old Lyuba said. She glanced meaningfully at the *kris* who were still discussing the news of the latest killing. The talk was dying down now and it was obvious to Janfri that whatever the old woman was telling him, she didn't want it talked around. Why? Because if Stevo knew she had used her *dook* for a Rom he would send her away from his *kumpania?* "Come and see me before

Stevo packs us all up and we leave," she added. "Old Pika Faher had a daughter and the *dook* was very strong in her. I'll see if I can find where she is. She might help you—if you ask her nicely."

"Phuri da," Janfri said. Old Lyuba smiled, accepting the name from his lips. "How . . . how can this be true?"

"Tshatshimo Romano," she replied. The truth is expressed in Romany. "Where did you think the Rom's reputation for spells came from, my little *chal?*"

Janfri sighed. *"Bater,"* he said. So be it. "I will see you tomorrow then." As Old Lyuba arose to go, Janfri called softly after her: "What does this . . . this Mulengro want with us?"

The old woman shook her head. "You'll have to ask him that yourself—when he catches up with you."

Janfri turned to Yojo when she was gone. Around them, new arguments had broken out and the Rom were competing for attention with loud voices.

"Prala," Janfri said. "What should I do?"

Yojo swallowed thickly. "See her tomorrow, brother."

"But, Yojo. How can such things even be possible?"

His big friend regarded him sadly, then reached over and embraced him. "Go to her," he said. "The world would be an empty place without you."

The cold shiver that had touched Janfri grew stronger. Was it his own *dook* that the old woman said he had, warning him of peril? He remembered a *Gaje* expression of Tom's: *Someone's just stepped on my grave.* He wished he hadn't thought of it just now.

eight

Jeff Owen was sitting alone at the bar in Tinkers—a small restaurant/bar on Foster Street in Perth. The lights were low and a tape of The Motels was playing on the cassette machine. The song was from their first album, but neither the staccato guitar work nor Martha

Davis' throaty vocals as she worked her way through "Anticipating" was doing a blessed thing for his mood. What did he have to anticipate but more of the same? He still couldn't believe it. He'd put two years of work into the book, in between collaborating with Ola on her herb and old wives' tales collections, but the editor wouldn't consider it. The manuscript had come back with a short note tagged onto it: "Interesting, but we're looking for the new Rouge & Owen, Jeff." *Interesting?* At least it had something meaningful to say. At least it was based on reality—not some collection of mumbo jumbo that read as though it was lifted straight from the pages of *The Enquirer*. To cure cankers, merely suck on honey. Maybe it paid the bills, but it sure as hell wasn't literature.

Jeff was a big blond Valley boy—born and bred on a farm just outside of Smith Falls. He'd worked his ass off trying to establish himself as a writer, all to no avail until he'd finally hooked up with Ola Drake—or as their public knew her, Kerio Rouge. But the foot in the door that he'd thought he'd found wasn't really panning out when it came down to the nitty-gritty. Their publisher was real nice to him—so long as he stuck to transcribing and rewriting Ola's work. But let him just try to submit something serious, something that actually *said* something, and the door slammed in his face faster than you could say lickety-split.

It wasn't that he didn't like Ola herself or blamed any of this on her. She was quite supportive and, if the truth be told, he was more than a little enamored of her. But he just didn't want to be known as the man who put her recipes and little folk philosophies down on paper for the rest of his life. There was more to him than just being a glorified copyeditor—but did you think anybody else could see that?

Oh, Owen, he told himself as he took a pull from his draft. You're burning your own torch a little too bright. What he should be doing instead of crying into his beer was sending the manuscript around to a couple of other publishers—maybe even use another name like Ola did. He could almost hear his father's voice in his ear: "Papa Owen ain't raisin' no crybabies. You just get up offen your lazy ass, Jeff-boy, an' give 'em hell." He grinned. Maybe he should drop by Ola's and have her mix him up a happy-potion. Berries picked only under the full moon and kept under the pillow of a virgin for three nights. Mix with powdered bats' wings and a healthy dose of morning dew. Hey-ho. Drink while standing on one foot and facing west. Or maybe she had some spell he could slip their editor so that he'd buy anything he sent in.

It was a nice idea. Too bad it wouldn't work. And he knew he really wasn't being fair to Ola. Whatever he might say jokingly about what went into their books, he knew that there was no bullshit in them. Not really. Weird stuff—oh, yeah. By the bucket. But then Ola could be a little spooky herself. When you came right down to it.

Drinking another half-inch of his beer, he turned on his stool and looked around the room to see if there was anyone he knew that he could pass a couple of hours with, just to get the sour taste of the rejection letter out of his mouth. Most of the regulars were in, but nobody he knew well enough to foist his somewhat grumpy company on except for Jackie, but she was working tonight and the customers were keeping her too busy for them to exchange more than just a couple of words. He saw a couple from Brooke Valley sitting at a table with another of the waitresses who was off duty. There were three tourists or cottagers at one of the window tables, old John Danning who had a regular column in *The Perth Courier* was at the far end of the bar, and the girl who ran the craft shop on Wilson—he never could remember her name— was with her boyfriend near the back. There were a few others that he knew only to nod to on the street. Maybe he should just go home, type up a new submission letter, get up bright and early and mail the whole shebang out again in the morning. Or he could get drunk.

The door opened from the street and he turned to see Bob and Stan Gourlay come in. They were a couple of good ol' boys who usually spent their time across the street in the Revere Hotel, known locally as The Zoo. They matched Jeff in height—he stood six-one without his boots—but were meatier around the chest and arms. Stan was the one with the big mouth. His brother wasn't considered to be all that bright, but he was the one who liked to get things down to a fist and toe level.

Trouble with a capital T, Jeff thought. He started to turn back to the bar, but Stan's gaze had already fallen on him.

"Say-hey. How's it goin', Owen? Still writing that fag shit?"

Jesus, Jeff thought. This he didn't need. He glanced at Jackie behind the bar. She was looking a little nervous, fingers playing with the tie-strings of her Indian print skirt as she glanced at the closed door of the kitchen, probably hoping that Mike would come out. Jeff was hoping Mike would come out too. This wasn't the kind of place to start anything, but he just wasn't in the mood to put up with any shit from the Gourlay brothers. Not tonight. Tinkers was a quiet bar with a sort of Whole Earth sixties atmosphere. In the old days it had been an Irish drink-and-slug-it-out hole, but not anymore.

Stan settled on the stool beside Jeff while Bob leaned up against a pillar looking bored. "You still got that little black nooky stashed away up at the Ferry?" Stan asked with an exaggerated wink. There was no humor in that broad stupid face.

Jeff sighed. He set his half-finished beer down on the bartop and laid a two-dollar bill beside it. Without taking his gaze from the brothers, he slipped off his seat, turned and headed for the door. He didn't know what had gotten into the Gourlays tonight, but he sure as hell wasn't sticking around to find out. The alcohol on Stan's breath was strong enough to knock a horse down at ten paces.

He reached the street without incident, but before he could get into his car, he heard the door to Tinkers open behind him.

"Hey, Owen! I was talking to you!"

Jeff started to turn, but he'd misjudged the distance between himself and the pair. Bob's fist caught him square in the gut and he buckled over. He didn't know who booted him in the head. Stars exploded behind his eyes and the sidewalk came rushing up to him.

"We were just bein' sociable, you know?" he heard Stan say. The voice seemed to come from a long distance away. As he began to lift his head, Bob kicked him in the side. What breath remained in him went out with a whoosh and he found himself curling up into a fetal position. His throat filled with puke. He wanted to get up, but his muscles didn't seem to work anymore.

"We just wanted to have a drink with our old pal, Owen the Boneman." Stan punctuated every few words with a kick. "You got a bone big enough to fit that black pussy, Owen? Whadaya think, brother Bob?"

Bob picked at his ear and looked down at Jeff. "He sure as hell won't be pluggin' her tonight."

"You got a point there, brother Bob. You surely do. And I think it's our duty, as Owen's pals, to see that she don't miss out on any fun just because Jeffy here's feelin' too poorly to go out and pay her a visit."

"I don't know, Stan. I don't think I could get it up for no black pussy."

"Shit. We'll just keep the lights off. All pussy's black in the dark, brother Bob."

Jeff could hear their footsteps retreating, then the roar of their pickup starting up. Dimly he was aware of someone bent over him, but his left eye was already swelling shut and the face swam before him. He knew he had to say something so that Ola could be warned to get out of the house, or at least call the cops, but the words wouldn't take shape on his lips. All that came out was a moan. Darkness rushed up to swallow him.

nine

Ola was asleep before ten o'clock that night. She had been reading on the porch, trying to shut out the whining of the mosquitos on the other side of the screen, when she began to drift off. Her hands went limp and the hardcover she was reading closed with a slow flip of pages and a final quiet *twap* as the book shut. It slipped between her legs onto the sofa cushions. Her chin rested against her chest. A loon called out on the lake—a long low sound that she didn't hear.

In the living room, Boboko watched the lights dim around him as Ola's breathing evened out and deepened. When she was finally asleep, it was as dark on his side of the windows as it was outside. Rising slowly to his feet, he padded out onto the porch and settled on her lap, ears twitching until he too was sleeping.

When the Gourlay brothers walked into Tinkers in Perth, Ola's *dook* stirred, but she didn't waken. Boboko cocked open an eye and regarded the shift of expressions on her face. He could see the movement of her eyes behind her closed lids. Her breathing quickened. Just as he was about to wake her, he heard the television set go on in the other room. He continued to study her for a long moment, then hopped down from her lap and went into the cottage proper. The TV threw a flickering light across the living room, awakening weird shadows that chased each other across the mantel and into the kitchen, but the cat ignored them. He sat on his haunches in front of the set and watched Ola's dreams take shape on the screen through the power of her *dook*.

The picture was in black and white, grainy and soundless. Two men were kicking another man who lay at their feet on a sidewalk. Their mouths worked and eyes sneered, bringing a low grumble to Boboko's chest. He recognized the man who was being beaten and shot a quick glance to the doorway of the porch. Was this the future, or was it happening now? Either way it didn't bode well for Jeff. He thought again of waking Ola, but then the picture on the screen flickered and dissolved into a meaningless dotted pattern. For a long moment Boboko stared at the pulsating dots. The hair along his spine began to prickle and rise.

There was something about the two men who had been beating Jeff . . . the way that they had left him lying on the pavement . . . a look in their eyes. . . . He knew enough about Ola's *dook* to know it wouldn't show her anything in her own future. But those men . . . Boboko's own *dook,* a curious combination of a feline's sixth sense and the something more than sentience that Ola had awoken in him, buzzed a warning. It was past midnight and the darkness outside had taken on a witchy quality. Events were shaping, moving in the ether, drawing closer to fruition. Those men meant her harm.

He *knew* that. He had to wake her, to warn her that—But then the dot pattern on the screen cleared enough so that new images could take shape there. It was another of Ola's farseeings. Her *dook* was bringing her another vision. . . .

While her body slept, Ola's spirit was drawn out into the night. Swift as a thought it sped over darkened fields and lonesome highways until the dull glow of Ottawa's skyline beckoned on the horizon. In moments she was above the city, passing it by. She crossed the river, hovered above Hull. Here there were more people on the streets. The bars were still open—they would be open until three. Taxis and police cars took turns cruising the side streets and main thoroughfares. Her *dook* prickled the hair of her scalp back in Rideau Ferry as it drew her spirit down into a low-rent district, down to quieter streets grimy with refuse and to front yards littered with car parts and other less-recognizable junk. On a run-down porch she saw an old woman in a wicker rocking chair, an old Gypsy woman with an air of expectancy about her. She didn't appear aware of Ola's presence, or if she was, she gave no sign of it. She seemed to be waiting for something else.

Ola turned at the sound of footsteps on the quiet street. Though she was present only in spirit and invisible to sight, she drew back into the shadows of the porch when the approaching man came under the glare of the one streetlight still working on the street. He was dressed all in black and she knew him from her visions. She wanted to shout a warning to the old woman, but had no throat to speak the words. She could only watch the man come near. Wisps of fog clung to his lower legs. They were present one moment, like a tatter of corpse-veil fluttering as he moved, gone the next. And his eyes . . .

"Mulengro," the old woman hissed, naming him.

In Rideau Ferry, goose bumps lifted on the arms of Ola's sleeping body.

• • •

The pickup truck passed the Rideau Ferry Inn and crossed the bridge beyond it, pulling off to the left on a small side road that led to Frost Point. Bob Gourlay killed the truck's engine and joined his brother who'd stepped out of the cab as soon as they'd come to a halt.

"Nice night," Bob said.

Stan grinned. "Beauty. No doubt about it."

They started back for the highway on foot, turned right and crossed the bridge.

Old Lyuba rocked back and forth, bird-bright eyes fixed on the approaching stranger. His leather shoe soles clicked softly on the pavement. The sound died as he turned into the yard. Lyuba continued to rock. The rattle of her chair's slats on the uneven boarding of the porch seemed to grow in volume. When the stranger reached the top of the stairs and finally stood in front of her, she stopped the movement of the rocker and faced him silently.

He was a dark Rom, tall and slender, with abruptly chiseled features and thin lips. His eyes were ghostly pale-blue against the deep tan of his complexion. A web-work of fine scar tissue atop each cheek drew attention to the eyes and gave him a wolfish look, as though he wore a mask. Determined though she'd been not to let him frighten her, Lyuba couldn't suppress a shiver. Her old heart began to work overtime, pumping the thin blood through her body. She had seen eyes like his before. They were a fanatic's eyes. In his *prikaza* black and with that face, it was as though Martiya the night spirit, the Angel of Death himself had come for her.

"What do you want of me, murderer?" she demanded suddenly. His very silence made her speak. "Is this old woman *marhime*, too?"

The thin lips pulled back into a tight humorless smile, almost a grimace. "An old *phuri dai* such as you should know better than to fill the heads of Rom with nonsense," he said finally. His voice was cold, like a draft issuing from the grave. "You should not point out roads . . . or tell secrets. Not to those who are *marhime*. Did no one tell you? *Na may kharunde kai tshi khal tut.*" Not to scratch where it did not itch.

"I spit on you!" the old woman began. "I call down a plague of—"

The man in black slowly shook his head and the words died in Lyuba's throat. Mist arose from between the floorboards of the porch like whorls of smoke. As the frightened woman watched, shapes formed in the mist. Two . . . three of them. They were like dogs at first, then rose on their ghostly hind legs to take the appearance of men. A smell of rot came from them and hung heavy in the air. Lyuba thought she would gag. They had no features, only shape, and as she watched, their paleness darkened until they were as black as the ebony *diklo* that hung at the stranger's neck. They were *mule,* Lyuba knew with dread. Ghosts of the dead.

"When you speak with those who are *marhime,*" the stranger said, "you only dirty yourself. And now you have become an itch that *I* must scratch."

The *mule* moved closer as he spoke.

Boboko stared at the television in fascinated dread, his calico features weirdly lit from the play of light and dark that spilled from the screen. It was so quiet in the cottage that his own breathing was raspy in his ears. He heard Ola stirring on the sofa in the porch. The images on the screen flickered but didn't die, so he knew she wasn't awake yet. Best he called her now, he thought. Then he heard a sound from outside, a sound that didn't belong.

"You see that, brother Bob? A fuckin' cat watchin' TV!" Stan drew back from the window when the animal's head turned towards it. "Weird shit. Weird movie."

Bob shrugged. "Maybe it's one of those vid-ee-os."

"Could be," Stan agreed. "But who really gives a horse's ass? So long as she's in there with her legs spread—waitin' for little Jeffy Owen who's pullin' a no-show. . . ." He moved around the building as he spoke, towards the front door. Bob followed.

• • •

Lyuba couldn't move. She watched the *mule* approach, saw her own death reflected in the stranger's mad pale eyes. A hand of shadow reached for her, entered her body like icy smoke passing right through the pores of her skin. Inside her body, the shadow grew solid and gripped her heart like a vise, smoky fingers tightening. Her back arched. A scream rose up in her throat but died before it could pass her lips. The hand on her heart squeezed harder. A cold wind whistled through her, whined in her ears, froze the blood in her veins. Then her heart burst and she slumped back in the chair.

The *mulo* withdrew its hand once more. It passed immaterially through her flesh and the fabric of her blouse. There wasn't even a bruise on the skin to leave evidence of its passage. The man in black smiled his tight-lipped smile and nodded. The *mule* lost their dark hue, drifted apart like smoke before a wind, and were gone.

"I gave you a clean death, old woman," the stranger said to the corpse, "for you meant well. But the *marhime* must die and nothing may stop me. God gave me this task, as he gave me my *mule* to complete it. Mulengro you named me and it is a good name. I might keep it."

In her hiding place, Ola was numb with shock. The casual brutality of the murder skittered through her like a trapped bat. The natural inclination of a Rom to best a foe by wits rather than force was swept away by a piercing red anger. She wanted to hurt the murderer as a *Gaji* would, to strike him with a club and feel the bones break under her blows. But her body was miles from her. She was nothing more than a wraith—as insubstantial as Mulengro's *mule* had been. No, less so, for they could kill while she was no more than an observer. Helpless. Only able to watch, with the anger burning inside her. . . .

She moved a half step out of the shadows, then paused, eyes flaring wide. Out of the dead woman's body a dark shadow was wreathing, taking shape in the air between the man in black and the corpse.

Boboko turned as the door to the cottage was kicked open. He recognized the two men from Ola's earlier farseeing. They stood in the doorway for a long moment, then one of them crossed over to the phone and ripped the line from the wall.

"Say-hey," Stan said as he dropped the phone on the floor. "Guess the little lady'll know we're here now." He turned to grin at his brother, then cursed as a calico shape hurled itself at him. The cat landed on his upper thigh, claws digging in. It bit at his crotch, but all it got was a mouthful of jean and zipper.

"Jesusfuckgetitoffame!" Stan roared. He swept his arms down, succeeded in dislodging the spitting, clawing animal. He aimed a kick at its head, but Boboko moved out of range too quickly. Holding onto his thigh, feeling his own blood wet on his hand, Stan tried to back the cat into a corner. "I'm gonna kill you, you little fucker," he told it. "You're worm-food!"

Bob moved in from the other side. He picked up a heavy book that was lying on a side table near the door and hefted it in his hand.

"Christ!" he said. "What if it's rabid?"

"I don't give a fuck if it's got cancer," Stan said. "I'm gonna rip its guts out."

Boboko backed up slowly. "Just try," he said.

The two men stared at the animal, their jaws going slack.

It was the old woman's *muli,* Ola realized as the new shadow stood before the man in black. It was thinner than the other *mule* had been and not quite so black.

"Now you are free," the stranger said. "Free of what *marhime* you had, free of that worn-out body you wore beyond its time. Join me in my work. Help me make the Rom clean once more in the eyes of God."

Never. The disembodied voice seemed to come from all parts of the porch. *I will never join you in your* dilo *ways. You are mad, Mulengro. You are a monster.*

"Perhaps," the stranger said. "But if I am mad, then God gave me this madness to see where others are blind. The strength to complete the work He has given me. And you will join me."

No.

"Now you are close to your life, to what you were," Mulengro explained. "But soon the memories will grow dim. You will shed them as a tree does its leaves. You will forget life and know only what I will teach you."

Never. NEVER!

The old woman's *muli* drifted apart and fled to the sound of the stranger's laughter. Ola watched until the *muli* had completely dissolved, then realized that the man in black was looking in her direction.

"Stan. Did you hear—"

"Shut up, Bob." Stan stared stupidly at the tomcat, a finger of fear clawing up his spine. Animals just didn't talk. It had to be a trick. Little Jeffy's black pussy was tryin' to pull one over on them, but it wasn't gonna work.

"Come on, boys," Boboko said, taking his words from the dozens of late-night western and detective movies he'd watched. "One at a time, or all together." The last words ended in a hissing spit.

"The bitch," Stan said. "Where the fuck's the stupid bitch? *She's* doin' this!"

While Bob held the cat at bay, he shot a quick glance at the bedroom. Empty. At least it looked empty. It was hard to tell with only the light of the TV to go by. The stupid movie was still playing on it—some kind of horror flick. Shitty reception. He looked back at the cat, then at his brother. He started to move towards the porch and Boboko leapt for him. Bob flung the book, catching the cat on the side of the head with a glancing blow.

"In here!" Stan cried, running for the porch.

Book and cat landed hard against the floor as Bob ran to join his brother. He looked back into the living room to see the cat trying to stand on wobbly legs. It was shaking its head.

"Bingo!" Stan said. "B–I–N–G–fuckin'–O!"

He crossed the porch in a few quick strides and dragged Ola up from the sofa by the front of her dress. Her head hung slack.

"I don't know what you've got that cat on, little lady, but you just better call it off. You hear me?" He punctuated the question with a rough shake. "What's the fucker doin' out there, brother Bob?"

"It's tryin' to stand. Stan, it was talkin'. . . ."

Stan shook his head. "No way. The little lady here's just like one of those ventro guys—the kind that can throw their voice around, you know? Go finish off that cat, Bob."

"I don't know." Bob looked at the cat. It still appeared to be stunned. "Little fucker's got me spooked. . . ."

Stan gripped Ola's throat with his free hand, then sat down on the couch, pulling her upper torso across his knees. Taking a firmer grip of the material at her bodice, he ripped it down.

"Cunt's not gonna throw her voice, Bob. Just kill the cat, would ya? Have I gotta do everything?"

There was only starlight coming through the windows, but Bob's eyes had adjusted to the dark enough for him to make out the brown curves of Ola's breasts.

"Just you wait for me, Stan," he said as he turned back to the living room.

Mulengro knew she was here. He could *see* her spirit by the porch as surely as her *dook* let her *see* beyond the veils of the here and now. Ola pulled back into the shadows, uncertain. Should she flee or hide? If she fled, would he be able to follow the trail of her spirit back to Rideau Ferry? She took a half step back, deeper into the shadows, but something gripped her by the throat. She was choking. Mulengro? Did he—No! Something had attacked her body.

She fled back to where she'd left her sleeping body. On the

porch, the stranger watched the shadows where she had been hiding for a long moment, then shrugged and returned to the street, where he retraced his steps until the corner of a building at the far end of the block hid him from sight.

Bob stepped into the living room and looked for something he could kill the cat with. He didn't want cat guts all over his boots, nossir. He kept a wary eye on the animal as he edged towards the fireplace and grabbed a hefty piece of firewood.

"Okay, you little fucker," he said, holding the makeshift club between himself and the cat. "Here's where you get yours. Got any last words?" He chuckled to himself, glad that Stan had explained how it had seemed that the cat could've talked. He'd been spooked bad there for a minute and was looking forward to giving the little creep the old one-two for doing that to him. He'd splatter its brains all over that nice carpet and—

Just then the television went off and the room plunged into darkness.

Ola returned to her body to feel the weight of a hairy arm across her stomach, fingers at her breast, a hand at her throat, choking her. . . . She could feel the man's grin as she went stiff in his arms.

"Say-hey, 'bout time you woke up, honey. Jeffy-boy couldn't show, you see, so we thought we'd do the neighborly thing and poke you for him."

Ola blinked, stilling the fear that went through her like a January wind, biting and lean. The man's breath was strong in her face, reeking of alcohol. His arms were like thick cables—all corded muscle. Panic reared in her until a sudden unfamiliar rage gripped her for the second time that night. But this time she wasn't helpless as she'd been when she'd had to watch the old woman being murdered. This was her home. Here she knew the names—and they didn't need to be spoken aloud.

From the same stack of firewood by the hearth that Bob had fetched his club, a two-foot length of hardwood rose and came whistling through the air. Before Stan was even aware that something was wrong, it struck him in the side of the head, dislocating his jaw and making a pulp of the bones and cartilage where it hit. He made a sound halfway between a howl and a gurgle and let go of her. The wood rose again and smashed into his face with enough force to drive straight through the front part of his skull and into his brain. A shower of wetness splattered over Ola as she lunged to her feet. Stan's body flopped onto its side, then rolled off the sofa to land on the floor with a soft wet thump. A moment later the log was dislodged and clumped onto the floor beside him.

Ola stared at the body, breathing heavily. She could see as well in the dark as she could by day. What she saw made her stomach churn with an acidic rawness. There was no sense of victory in her—only outrage that she had been forced to do what she had done. She hadn't even thought about it—just struck out blindly. It had all happened so quickly. Seeing the old woman die, her own helplessness in wanting to stop Mulengro, finding her body in the grip of this *Gaje* pig. . . . Who was he? What in God's name was he doing here? He'd said something about Jeff—

A sound in the doorway leading to the living room made her turn. A second man, as big as the one she'd just killed, stood there, blinking, trying to see.

"Stan?" he said. "Stan, what's goin' on in there?"

So. The dead man had a name. And he wasn't alone.

Ola called up a name and the lights came on at her command, catching the second man by surprise and momentarily blinding him. Ola's pupils were already contracted in anticipation of the sudden glare. She regarded the stranger, anger swelling in her again.

"Oh, Jesusfuck," Bob mumbled, horror-struck by the ruin of his brother's head. His shocked gaze shifted to the woman. Any desire that had woken in him at the sight of the bared breasts died. She was wild-eyed, splattered with blood and brain-matter, the tatters of her bodice hanging at her waist like a gruesome parody of an apron.

She . . . He blinked again as the truth hit home. Stan was dead. The whore had killed him. Stan was dead! The makeshift club lifted in his fist and he lunged for her.

Ola's thoughts gripped the log and spun it from his hands. The rug moved under him, spilling him to the floor. The log hovered above him, ready to strike, but then Ola shook her head, forcing the anger down. She wouldn't allow it to make her kill a second man— monster though he was. The air in the porch gathered at her command, lifting the man to his feet and propelling him back into the living room. His eyes rolled in his head, stark fear etched in every line of his face. His bowels went weak and his jeans filled with excrement. Ola followed him into the living room, eyes burning. The air held him like a fist and threw him out the front door of the cottage, across the lawn. Twigs and stones lifted from the ground, pelting him, forcing him to keep to his feet. He stumbled to the street, tears streaming down his face, excrement seeping wetly down the legs of his jeans, arms lifted to protect his head from the storm of debris. He clawed his way up the steep embankment that led to the highway and lurched along the side of the road, sobbing.

The pelting stones and debris thinned out as he was crossing the bridge, dying fully by the time he turned off the highway and staggered up to the parked pickup. He collapsed beside the vehicle, shoving his face against its metal door, the blood thundering in his veins. His body heaved with great wracking sobs. The utter panic that had filled him was a long time in dying. What had happened tonight was his worst nightmare become real. Stan was dead and he was alone. And that whore . . . that stupid fucking black whore . . . she was going to pay for it.

Slowly he got to his feet, still sniffling. His jeans were soiled clear down to his boots and he reeked. He looked back towards the Ferry, numbly trying to understand what had happened—*how* it could have happened. How could Stan be dead? How could everything just . . . come alive like it had? And that, whore . . . He didn't know how she'd done whatever it was that she'd done, but he was goin' to make her pay for it, yessir. He'd make her pay in spades—like the spade she was. He didn't know how, but he was goin' to hurt her until she begged him to kill her.

He rubbed a meaty fist against his eyes. Wouldn't bring Stan back, though. Goddamn her! Nothing was goin' to bring him back! The tears erupted again as he climbed into the cab of the pickup.

Ola stood in the doorway of the cottage, leaning weakly against the doorjamb. The adrenaline rush was fading but the blood still roared in her ears. She followed the man's progress up the road, read his fear and his hate. . . . The hate. It was like a dead black coal lodged in his chest, slowly being fanned to life. Wearily she turned back inside. She couldn't stay here anymore. The man would be back once he regained his courage. And there was the body on the porch. There would be police, questions. . . . She trembled, sick with what she had been forced to do. No, that wasn't true. She hadn't been forced to kill him. It had been a combination of frustration and sheer unadulterated panic at returning to her body and finding this Stan abusing her that had brought on the killing frenzy.

Her gaze fell on Boboko. His head lifted weakly from the floor. He was no longer trying to stand. She moved quickly to his side, stroking him with one hand while she gently probed his injuries with the other.

"Can't . . . can't seem to get up. . . ." he mumbled in a low hurt voice.

"There, love, there. It's over now. Lie still a moment."

There was so much to do. Would the man who had escaped go directly to the police? How much time did she have before they arrived? Or would he be too afraid? After all, they had assaulted her. But she couldn't stay. She frowned, trying to think, but the presence of the corpse in the other room intruded too much on her thoughts for her to think anything clearly through.

At last she lifted Boboko in her arms and rocked with him on her lap, her fingers trailing through his fur where he'd been hurt. She sang softly, making a song of his secret name, his true name, and concentrated on healing the wounded tissue, knitting the fractured bones. His name was like a blueprint as to what he should be when he was healthy and unhurt. By singing it and pouring her own energy into him, it allowed her *dook* to repair the damage that had been done to him. When she was finally satisfied that she'd done all that she could, she laid him on the carpet once more and let him sleep. He would awake healed.

She rose tiredly to her feet. She was expending too much of herself, too rapidly, but she knew there was still work to do. The corpse. . . . Steeling herself, she went into the porch and stared at it for a long moment. She didn't want to touch it, but forced herself to work his wallet free of his back pocket. Flipping it open, she found his name on his driver's license. Stan Gourlay. In case of emergency, one was to call Bob Gourlay. Well, this was an emergency, Ola thought, but she decided that Bob Gourlay already knew about it. He must have been the one that fled. And now that she thought of it, she could remember Jeff telling her about these men. They were troublemakers and not well liked. And now one of them was dead. . . .

She shook her head, irritated at the way her thoughts were going. First she had to get rid of the body. Knitting her brows, she awoke the carpet to movement. It wrapped around the body and lifted slowly into the air. Perspiration beaded on her forehead as she concentrated. Catching up a bathrobe, she followed the tubular bundle out into the night.

They crossed the yard and the dirt road leading to the highway. At the highway, she took to the ditch, still following the rolled carpet and its gruesome load. The veins stood out at her temples and she was perspiring freely by the time she reached the fields beyond the last houses. This was an area she knew well, having walked it summer and winter since she'd first arrived. The trees and other vegetation were almost friends; the earth knew the feel of her weight, the sound of her voice. Allowing the carpet to settle on the ground, she leaned against a tall elm, fighting back the pain in her head. After a few precious minutes of rest, she stood straighter and fixed her attention on the ground by her feet.

For a long moment, nothing happened. Then with a sound almost like a groan, a section of earth three feet deep rose slowly in the air. Small clumps of dirt fell from its edges and she murmured apologies to the hundreds of tiny roots that had been severed by her need. When there was enough room, she physically pushed the rolled carpet into the hole. She tossed the wallet in after, then quickly stripping off her dress, stuffed it in on top of the carpet. With a gasp of relief, she let the earth settle down once more. At first there was a gravelike mound, but as she exerted pressure, she heard the dim sound of the corpse's ribcage collapsing and the ground settled until all that remained was a slight rise. Stupid with weariness, she collapsed to her knees and pressed her face against the dirt.

She knew there was more she should do than simply cover the corpse with dirt. But she was too spent to reach out and see if her victim's *mulo* had flown free of its dead shell. She wasn't even sure what shape a *Gaje*'s *mulo* would take—if she would even recognize it. Among her own people, when a Rom died, some part of the dead one's spirit remained behind. Usually it took a few days for the *mulo* to forget what it meant to be alive and find its way to the land of shadows. But when a Rom died violently, the *mulo* couldn't accept that it was dead, or sometimes the *mulo* was simply too strong and refused to release its grip on life, becoming more potent rather than fading.

As a *drabarni,* Ola was able to see these spirits and was responsible for keeping her tribe—if she had had one—away from areas haunted by such a spirit. At the same time, she was obliged to do what she could to send the creature along its way to the land of shadows. She must convince it that it was, indeed, dead. Sometimes, the *mulo* required forgiveness for wrongs it had done when it was living. Most *Gaje* refused to believe in *mule* and Ola wasn't sure how they dealt with the spirits of their dead. But she knew one thing. She lifted her head and stared at the low rise of earth that hid the corpse.

"I cannot forgive you," she said. "You are dead. Go to your God, if you have one. But I cannot forgive you."

She continued to study the grave, but could sense nothing stirring at her words. She knew from experience that the Rom and *Gaje* had very different spirits. There was a presence in the soul of a Rom that called out to her as never a *Gaje* spirit would. Were their *mule* different as well, then? She had met gifted non-Gypsies who were born with the *sight,* as well as others who acquired it through a traumatic experience or even by sustaining a head injury, but the natural reticence of a Rom kept her from comparing notes with them. Gypsies kept their secrets as precisely as *Gaje* did their possessions. Yet whatever *sight Gaje* had, it was not like a Romany *dook.*

So she studied the grave, but she was too weary to concentrate properly. There was little enough that she knew about *Gaje mule* and there was still so much—too much—to do. She didn't feel she had the strength left in her to go, but she knew she must. Her body glistened with perspiration as she stood, and she was too tired to brush away the swarming mosquitos that buzzed around her in droves. It was all she could do to stay conscious, but at length she tugged on the bathrobe she'd brought with her and stumbled back to the cottage.

The return journey seemed endless. The monotony of it was only broken once when a late-night driver sped by on the highway and she was forced to crouch low in the ditch, hiding her face so that the whites of her eyes wouldn't catch in the headbeams. She rose to her feet after the scare with only the greatest effort. There was still . . . so much . . . to do. . . .

It was almost first light by the time she'd finished scrubbing the cottage clean and had bathed. She sat outside when she was done, a large backpack beside her. Her beaded braids were gone, replaced by a ponytail that pulled the hair tightly back from her face and gave her a somewhat Latin look. Jeans, a sweatshirt and a pair of sturdy walking shoes added to the illusion. Kerio Rouge—the half French, half Gabonese writer—was no more.

She stared dully up at the lightening sky and knew she should be on her way, but wasn't sure where that way would lead her. It was frightening just to think of leaving the cottage. It had been a refuge, become safer with every month she stayed. Her control of the environment had grown steadily—as witness how she'd dealt with the intruders last night. Once she left the cottage behind, her *dook* would only charm what she brought with her. Had she been in a strange place when the attack came last night, she would probably not have survived.

She turned slightly as Boboko stepped gingerly from the cottage. He came to where she sat and settled on her lap. The dawn chorus was beginning and they listened to it in silence, smelling the pungent thyme that grew in amongst the flowers beside the house.

"Thanks," Boboko purred after a time.

Ola smiled wanly and laid her hand on his head.

"We're going now?" he added.

She nodded. "I let the second man go. Perhaps I shouldn't have. Perhaps I should have killed him too because I know he'll be back. I read the need in him to strike back at me."

"They deserved to die," Boboko said. There was a bitterness in Ola's voice that he wanted to quell. He killed easily, but he knew they were different in that respect.

"Perhaps," she replied. "But I don't need the guilt of even one of their deaths on my conscience."

"Where will we go?"

Ola stroked his head. "You needn't come with me, love."

The head moved under her hand. "I won't stay without you."

"Bater," Ola sighed. So be it.

"We won't be so well . . . protected once we leave, will we?"

"We'll have what I can bring with me," she said, "and pray that the need doesn't arise that we must be protected against anything."

"But the man in your vision," Boboko said. "The one who killed the old woman . . . ?"

"Mulengro," Ola said softly. "I haven't forgotten him."

"If you must face him, it should be here—where you are strong."

Ola shivered, remembering the *mule* and the man who ruled them. His eyes . . . If she closed her own, she could almost see them, watching her.

"Ola?"

"If we stay," she said, "we chance a meeting with the *shangle* as well as the dead man's brother."

"There is nothing here for the police to find."

"And the brother?"

Boboko made no reply. A few minutes later, Ola stood and hefted the pack, grimacing at its weight, at her own watery muscles. It would have been easier if she'd had a car, but she'd never felt the need for one, even living out here. Jeff had driven her into Perth for her weekly grocery shopping and also to whatever appearances they had scheduled. She felt a twinge of guilt at just packing up without saying good-bye to him. She would have called, but one of the pigs last night had pulled the phone cord from the wall. She didn't think it wise to leave a note. What would she say in it? Dear Jeff, I've just killed a man so I can't stay any longer. . . . What if the police *did* arrive and found it first? Or this Bob Gourlay came back? She'd call Jeff later.

"Where are we going?" Boboko asked.

"For now, cross-country. I don't want to be seen and remembered on the highway."

"We could go wild—start up a band of outlaws in the forest."

Ola had to smile. *The Adventures of Robin Hood* had been on the late movie last weekend and Boboko had been utterly fascinated by it.

"I think we'll just keep a low profile for now," she said.

"Bater," the cat replied, but she could see the schemes taking shape behind his eyes. "If you should change your mind . . . ?"

"I'll definitely let you know," Ola assured him.

She looked back from the road and regarded the cottage, thinking of the man she had killed, how perhaps his soul was trapped, needing her forgiveness before it could travel on to the land of shadows. Then she shook her head. He had been a brute. A *Gaje* pig. He was nothing to her. Not her responsibility. The dawn was pink in the east when they crossed the bridge at Rideau Ferry. The woods southwest of the Lower Rideau Lake swallowed them.

ten

"Hey, Paddy. How's it going?"

Briggs looked up as Will dumped a stack of books on his desk. The spines were facing Briggs and he could see the library stickers with their numbering on them. Most of the titles had the word "Gypsy" or "Romany" in them.

"What are these for?" he asked, waving the stem of his pipe at the books.

Will grinned and pulled up a chair. "Research. 'Know thy enemy' and that sort of thing. Except this time, we're going to have to know our victims."

"Just knowing they're Gypsies says it all. They're like Indians, Will, and that means they're trouble."

"I don't like that kind of talk, Paddy."

Briggs sighed. They'd been through this before. "Look," he said. "When it comes to Indians, I *know*. I've booked enough of them to start my own reservation."

"Well, what the hell do you expect from them, Paddy? We took everything from them and just dumped them on the reserves. You ever read the stats on their suicide rates? Kids thirteen-years-old blowing themselves away because they just haven't got anything—I mean *anything*—in their future. What the hell kind of life is that?"

"They don't have to stay on the reserves. They can leave anytime they want."

"And go where? Or be what? They've got all the strikes against them and maybe they just don't want to *be* white men."

"Maybe my granddad didn't want to leave Ireland either, but there was nothing for him there, so he packed up and made a new life for himself here. The world changes, Will, and there's fuck-all we can do about it except try to fit in. They don't try."

"I've been there, Paddy, and it's not that easy."

Will remembered his own childhood all too clearly—the kids at school, the cops stopping him when he was out cruising like any teenager. It always came down to the color of your skin. And every time he caught himself prejudging some punk, he got the feeling like there was a rock in the pit of his stomach and a slow burning sensation crawled up his throat. He couldn't stop the mad anger from coming on.

"When you're different," Will told his partner, "when you're black, or Indian, or even a Gypsy, you're starting off with a couple of strikes against you. Some compensate by overachieving. Some just give up. When you're on this side of the fence, Paddy, there doesn't seem to be a whole lot of middle ground."

"You're right," Briggs replied. "But you've still got to deal with the gut feeling that hits you when you see so many of this kind of person or so many of that coming across your desk. Christ, it's not like you're innocent of it either, Will. Or are you forgetting the ladies last night?"

"No. But they were just . . ." His voice trailed off and he looked at Briggs. There was no triumph in his partner's face at having caught him out. Just a weariness.

"You were going to talk to Cooper," Briggs said to change the subject.

Will nodded, happy to get back on neutral ground. "Right. He's backing off on the wild animal theory, but only because something like a big cat or a dog would've used its teeth to make the kill. The wounds on the necks and arms of the victims match—and neither were made by teeth."

"So what does that leave us?"

"With theories that are still too far off the wall. That *shuko* that MacDonald showed us is used by practitioners of *ninjitsu,* which is a sort of combination of martial arts and black magic from what I could find out. The ninjas died out a long time ago, but like anything weird, there are still supposed to be holdovers, not to mention all the buffs of chop suey movies that have been taking to things like this with a vengeance."

Briggs nodded. "I've seen a couple of those flicks. These ninjoos dress all in black, don't they?" He was thinking of Cleary and Tracy's description of a man in black.

"Ninjas," Will corrected him. "But you're right. I've got a book on them in that pile if you want to go through it. Anyway, I've done some checking around the martial arts studios around town, but so far I've come up with nothing."

"What about those other guys MacDonald was telling us about?"

"I was getting to them. The Leopard Men or Lion Men. Again, it's all mixed up with black magic, assassinations, stealth. These are secret societies and we could have them in town, but no one's talking and they've never surfaced before."

Briggs shook his head wearily. "Christ, there's just too much weirdness in the world, you know? So do either these nin*jas*—" he pronounced the word carefully this time"—or cat people have a thing for Gypsies?"

"No. But I've come up with a couple of interesting things in these books."

Will had discovered a certain empathy in himself for the Gypsies from what he'd read. Talk about your oppressed peoples. From the time they first left northern India around 1000 A.D., they'd known nothing but grief. Enslaved in Hungary and Transylvania by the Magyars—he'd always thought Transylvania was something Stoker had made up for his vampire novel. Butchered by the Nazis in the Second World War. Five hundred thousand of them died in the camps. It was little wonder they kept so much to themselves. What was amazing was how they'd managed to remain insular for so long. They never integrated with whatever society was on top—not even in this present day and age.

As a member of a minority himself, he could understand that. But not just because he was black. It was also because he was a cop. It was hard to mingle with civilians when you were off-duty. Nobody trusted you. They always had that look in their eyes. And when you went to a party, it was worse than being a doctor. Why the hell *are* you a cop, anyway? Say, could you fix this ticket? Are you carrying a gun *right now?* In their own way, policemen were almost as insular as Gypsies. You stuck with your own because it was the only way you could let your hair down without getting burned. Will used that analogy as he explained what little he'd learned about the Gypsy concept of *marhime* to his partner.

Briggs chewed on the stem of his pipe and stared up at the ceiling. "So they become ostracized, is that it? When they're guilty of this *marhime* thing?"

"From all aspects of Gypsy society."

"Do they ever try to ostracize someone a little more permanently than just cutting them off from the rest of the—what? Family? Tribe?"

"*Kumpania.*"

"Right. Company. When they're blackballing someone, it never gets violent—is that what your books say?"

Will nodded. "A person labeled *marhime* effectively doesn't exist anymore. They just ignore him."

"Well, that fits in with my own experiences with them. They'd lie, cheat, steal you blind, but I rarely got an assault complaint against a Gypsy." He tapped his pipe stem against his teeth, thinking. "So what makes them outcast? What do they have to do?"

"That's where it gets complicated. I think only a Gypsy could tell you that. It's everything from cheating a fellow member of your *kumpania,* or any Gypsy for that matter, to using the wrong kind of soap on the wrong part of your body."

"You're kidding. They'd kill someone for something like that?"

"Not kill. Outcast them. And it doesn't always last that long. Usually you just go away for awhile and then when you come back, everything's died down and the elders get together and take the stigma from you. At least if it wasn't over something too serious in the first place."

"So it's not permanent? Ever?"

"I don't know, Paddy. I suppose if you did something really bad . . ."

Briggs nodded. He tapped his pipe against a report sitting on his desk that Will had ordered last night. Ceepik had put a list together for them and it didn't look good. Twenty-seven Gypsies had died in Canada over the past eleven months—all violently. And who knew how many others weren't even accounted for? The places of death were spread out across the country, from Vancouver, through Edmonton, Winnipeg, Toronto, Montreal and Halifax. And now on their own turf. The two in Vancouver had been a part of the trouble in Gastown. Will had contacted Dan Sullivan of the Montreal Police this morning. Sullivan had told him that the six Gypsies that died on the Main had been part of a Mob struggle, so there was no big mystery there either. The case files were still open, but nobody was expecting anything to come of the investigation. Not unless they broke one of the Mob's gunmen. But that still left nineteen unaccounted for—twenty-one when you added the latest two here in Ottawa to the tally.

"What I can't figure," Briggs said, "is why no one put these all together before. Twenty-one deaths over an eleven month period—someone's got a real hard-on for Gypsies."

"Bad juju."

Briggs nodded. "You're telling me. So, what do you think? What the hell are we dealing with? Assassination cults?"

"I can't buy that. Sure we've got an international profile in this city, but that kind of theory just doesn't work. There's no motive—not when you look at the victims. My guess is we're dealing with a basket case—or some Gypsy that's gone loco."

"I can run with the fruitcake," Briggs said, "but why the killer Gypsy?"

"Because of this *marhime* concept."

Briggs let that settle in his mind. He filled his pipe, tamping it carefully, lit it, exhaled a wreath of blue-gray smoke. "Okay," he said. "It's time we talked to some Gypsies."

It was night and the streets were dark. Tall unfamiliar buildings reared on all sides of her. She wasn't sure where in the city she was, or even what city. All she knew was that she was alone and the night was stalking her. At the far end of the block one lonely streetlamp cast a dull glow on the intersection. Fog wreathed there, where it did nowhere else. It hung low to the ground as it drifted towards her, moved without a wind. She backed slowly away, shivering. There was something . . . some *things* moving in the fog. She could see their eyes, watching her. Hungry eyes. Pale-blue and cold as frost. She wanted to scream, but her throat was too thick with fear. She backed up another few steps, then heard something rustle behind her. She turned, her eyes frozen wide with fear, and saw him, the man in black. His eyes were the eyes in the fog. It roiled all around them, plucked at her with wispy ethereal talons. Then suddenly there was a sharp pain in her side. She looked down to see a four-clawed paw tearing at her flesh, blood streaming over the smoky claws . . . *her* blood . . . spurting like a fountain and she finally found her voice and—

Screamed herself awake.

Tracy Hilborn sat bolt upright in the familiar bed of her familiar apartment, clutching her nightshirt tightly around her, but everything seemed wrong. Then slowly the surreal gauze that lay across the room faded. It had been a dream. Sweet Jesus, just a dream. Except . . . those eyes. Slowly she calmed the wild pounding of her heart, regulated her breathing. A dream. She got out of bed and padded barefoot into her closet-sized kitchen and put on a kettle. Her stove clock told her it was after ten.

Those eyes . . . She should have told the cops about the eyes. She'd seen them in the smoke or mist or whatever it had been that had come out of the alleyway just before the man had. Just remembering made her legs start to tremble. She went into the living room and sat down on the couch, pulling her knees up to her chin. Everything had happened so fast last night that it still didn't seem real. The man in the alley, Carol and her running, both of them scared shitless, and then getting pulled in for questioning by the cops. But those eyes . . . she'd seen them last night. And now she was dreaming about them.

The kettle was boiling, so she got up to get it. The day was hers, she could do what she wanted. But tonight. Andy'd have them out on the street again and she didn't know if she could face it, not when she knew that the man with those eyes was still loose out there. Because tonight, maybe it wouldn't be a dream. Tonight, maybe those eyes would be out there again, only this time they'd be looking for her.

"Thing you've got to understand," Castleman said, "is you can ask ten Gypsies a question about some aspect of their culture and get ten different answers. To be honest, you can ask the same Gypsy the same question ten times and *still* get ten different answers."

Briggs and Will were at Theo Castleman's desk in the Fraud and Commercial Crimes Unit. Castleman was a lean, brown-haired man who lived on a steady diet of junk food and never put on a pound. Briggs thought he might actually hate Theo for that, considering the way he was putting on weight himself. They'd brought him a Coke and Castleman kept tapping the red and white can on the top of his desk while he spoke.

"So what have you got on this Luluvo?" Briggs asked.

"Big George? Not a whole lot. He's the *rom baro* of Ottawa—at least for the west side. Marko Lazlo runs the east right out past Vanier. We just like to keep our eye on Big George. When his people start to get out of hand—passing too many bum checks, or we get a complaint from Welfare or something—we pass the word to him and he usually has the problem cleared up in a couple of days."

Briggs nodded. "So he's sort of like a Mob chief, then?"

"Gypsies don't work that way, Paddy. We get very few standard complaints on them—no violent stuff. At least not in Ottawa. I'd love to know what went down in Van last year—just to make sure we don't ever get a repeat of it here."

Briggs nodded and laid Luluvo's file back on the desk.

"Think he'll talk to us?" Will asked.

"Sure." Castleman took a swig from his Coke. "Talking to you two will boost his importance in the community. No matter what you've got to say to him, the word'll get around that you were there to ask him for his advice and he, big man that he is—" Castleman smiled privately at the double entendre "—he was more than happy to help you out. But just remember—that doesn't mean he'll tell you anything useful."

"Great," Briggs muttered.

Castleman laughed. "Bring him a case of 24 and he'll tell you anything."

"I can just see writing up an expense claim for that," Will said. "The Inspector'll think we were trying to buy *you* off."

Castleman laughed again. "He *knows* I don't come that cheap."

Wrinkling his nose, Briggs led the way through the car parts, welding equipment and litter that made an obstacle course of Big George's driveway. They hadn't even tried the front door. There was an engine block sitting at the top of the stairs, dripping oil from stair to stair that finally puddled at the bottom of the walk. A taillight snapped under his heel and he jerked guiltily at the sudden sharp noise. He glanced at Will who smiled back at him.

"The other half," Will said.

"Yeah. Right. I don't *need* to see how they live."

God, Briggs thought, what a dump. When they reached the backyard they saw a pair of raggedly-dressed children watching their approach with big dark eyes. There was a circle of dead coals in the center of the yard that looked as though a small bonfire had been burned there a week or so ago. Beer cans were littered everywhere. Briggs wondered why the fire marshal wasn't down on these people for having an open fire inside city limits. And this place . . . But then he thought of his own apartment. It wasn't exactly the Taj Mahal either.

"You got a quarter, mister?" one of the children asked, stepping up close. "Maybe a dollar? My mother's sick and I need the money to—"

Briggs cut him off with an abrupt motion of his hand. The boy looked expectantly at Will who quickly shook his head. Grinning, the boy said something in Romany that made his companion laugh. Then the pair of them ran off, vaulting over the fence at the back of the yard and disappearing between the buildings on the far side. The two men turned back to look at the house to find a middle-aged Gypsy woman studying them. She stood by the back door in a low-cut blouse and long pleated skirt. Smoke curled up from the pipe she was smoking.

"Why are you men here and not Detective Castleman?" she demanded before either of the detectives could speak.

"Ma'am?" Briggs began.

"You are police, yes? When the police have a problem, it is Detective Castleman who comes to see us. We know him, he knows us. It is better to deal with those you know, heh?"

"We're with a different department," Briggs said. "My name is Patrick Briggs and this is my partner Will Sandler. We're here to see a Mr. George Luluvo." He dug out his wallet and flipped it open so that she could see his badge. "Is Mr. Luluvo in?"

"Big George is sleeping."

"Could you wake him please?"

"No. He is not sleeping. He is gone away for the day."

Briggs sighed. "Look, ma'am. We can play this two ways. The nice way is for you to let us have a word with Mr. Luluvo and then we'll be on our way. The not-so-nice way is for us to go back downtown, get a warrant, and then take Mr. Luluvo away with us. Which way do you want it?"

"What do you want with Big George? Are you here to arrest him?"

"We just want to talk to him, Mrs . . . ?" Will said persuasively.

"My name is Tshaya Luluvo and we don't have anything to tell you. Ask Detective Castleman. Ask our World's Fair worker. We are innocent of all crimes, but poverty. As God is my witness, we have done nothing."

Briggs sighed. The woman's broad features were impassive, but there was no give in her eyes. She matched him, stare for stare.

"We're not here to arrest anyone," Will said. "We just need to talk to Mr. Luluvo about a case we're working on."

"I think you had better go now," Tshaya said.

"You're just making it hard on yourselves by refusing to cooperate," Briggs told her. "We can be back here in less than an hour with a warrant, Mrs. Luluvo."

Tshaya looked off across the yard, studiously ignoring them. She

puffed on her pipe and hummed to herself. Briggs shifted from foot
to foot, trying to wait her out. Finally Will touched his arm.

"Let's go," he said.

Briggs nodded. "Okay. We'll play it the hard way." He looked at
Tshaya but she continued to ignore them.

They picked their way back down the driveway and settled heavily in the front seat of their unmarked Dodge.

"Looks like nothing's going to be easy about this case," Will
remarked.

"You said it."

Briggs stared at the house for a few minutes longer, then started
the car and pulled away from the curb, giving the car a little more
gas than was necessary. The rear tires squealed and left a rubber burn
on the street behind them.

"You see?" Tshaya said as she watched the policemen leave. "This
whole city becomes *prikaza* for us. Last night Ingo is murdered, and
this morning Stevo finds Old Lyuba dead in her rocking chair on
the porch. Now the *shangle* come to trouble us. There is no more
luck for us here. Must we wait until we too die?"

Big George shook his head, the decision made. "We will leave.
Now."

"Good. You and I—we have both been too tired. A little traveling
will let us rest. And if God will it, the bad luck will stay here and not
follow us."

"Bater," Big George said.

By the time that Briggs and Will, over Castleman's protests,
returned with a warrant, Big George and most of his *kumpania* were
on back roads leading to Kingston in a caravan of eight touring cars
and stationwagons filled with Rom and their belongings.

eleven
11

The black Lincoln made its way slowly down the street and pulled up in front of Stevo Gry's house, disrupting a sidewalk baseball game. The young players good-naturedly hurled a few well-chosen French epithets at the occupants of the car, moving on down the street in a laughing cluster when Yojo gave them the finger. Turning off the Lincoln's engine, he glanced at Janfri and the momentary humor died in him. Janfri was staring at the porch where Old Lyuba had died. The house looked empty, but her rocker still stood patiently in the morning sunlight, as though waiting for her to return.

"At least she died peacefully, *prala*," Yojo said. "Not like the others."

Janfri couldn't disagree with that. But he still couldn't shake the feeling that it was too appropriate the way Lyuba had died, just when she was going to put him in touch with a *drabarni* whom she thought could help him. This Pika Faher's daughter that none of the other Rom seemed to be familiar with. He knew Lyuba's death was yet a further indication that Ottawa had become too *prikaza* for the Rom, but at the same time her dying had effectively cut off his only starting point. His search was ending before he'd even taken the first step.

He tried to tell himself that this was a sign from *o Beng* that the pursuit of this Mulengro was not his affair, but at the same time he knew he'd accepted an obligation from the old woman last night and it must be fulfilled. Not simply because the hand of this enemy had struck him personally, but because she'd told him it was his duty to stop Mulengro and he had accepted it. Not in so many words, perhaps, but the knowledge had passed between the old woman and himself all the same. And now she was dead and he was left with . . . what? He sighed. Old Lyuba's death was simply too convenient. He could sense Mulengro's hand in it—already he gave his enemy the same name that Lyuba had—but he didn't know where to turn now.

"There is nothing for us here," Yojo said.

"I know."

"Only *prikaza.*"

Janfri turned to his friend. "I have to go up on the porch, *prala*. Just to . . . I don't know. Stand there."

Yojo nodded, somewhat nervously. With all that had happened of late, the possibility of *mule* making their presence felt seemed more probable than it ever had—except perhaps for when he and Janfri were boys and traveling with the Lowara Rom through Europe. The old men of their uncle's *kumpania* would tell the *swatura* around the campfires to chronicle the history of the Rom and to keep it alive. But sometimes the old men told other stories and then they had listened to tales of *o Beng* and *mule* with wide eyes and hearts beating fast.

Glancing at the porch, Yojo was sure that the old woman's *muli* was still present, guarding the place of her death. They had brought no *baXt* foods with them as an offering, nothing of luck. The ghost might be displeased or would not remember who they were because of that oversight. It was nearing noon as well. Traditionally the *mule* were said to walk from sundown to sunrise and for half an hour at noon. There was no luck to be gained by turning the *muli*'s attention to them. But that was what Janfri felt they must do, so . . .

"You can wait here," Janfri said as Yojo reached for his door handle. "I won't be long."

He was out of the car before Yojo could argue. Yojo thought of following, then weighed his nervousness against Janfri's wishes and decided he would simply keep watch from the car. He pulled out his tobacco and began to roll a cigarette as Janfri made his way up the walk and onto the porch.

Janfri paused at the top of the stairs, not really certain what he was doing here. He knew that Stevo was gone. Most of the *kumpaniyi* in the area were packing up and leaving. It was the sensible thing to do. They'd return when the luck changed. He supposed the real reason he was here was because he'd promised Lyuba that he would come today. Even though she was dead, it seemed the respectful thing for him to do. He moved slowly across the porch, the uneven boards creaking under his weight. When he reached the rocking chair, he stared down at it for long moments, then sat down. The chair moved under him, back and forth, until he stopped the motion with his foot.

What had Old Lyuba been doing out here on the porch last night? Trying to remember the name of Pika Faher's daughter, or to understand what it was that moved against the Ottawa Rom? Or had she simply been remembering her life as the old will, searching for a pattern in amongst the spill of years that made her what she'd been? Had she felt her heart stopping and known that she was dying? Or had she seen him coming, this Mulengro of hers, with his ghosts in tow and the toadlike features of *o Beng* where his face should be? If legends could be real, perhaps it was Martiya who had come to claim her, or the third son of Moshto, the god of life. He was the son who destroyed any part of the world that was beyond repair and rendered it into the raw material that his eldest brother would use to make new life.

Janfri placed his hands on the arms of the chair, disturbed at the turn his thoughts had taken. His mind was filled with thoughts of *mule* and death and magic, for all that he'd never considered himself a superstitious man. He looked across the porch. *Che chorobia.* How strange indeed. He sat a moment longer, then as he started to rise, his gaze fell on a crumpled piece of paper that lay against the support post by the porch's stairs. He picked it up, unfolding it carefully, and looked at the roughly scrawled pencil marks on it. They were *patteran*. There was the *patrin* for *drabarni,* followed by symbols indicating distance and direction. If this was a message from Lyuba to him, it said that the magic worker could be found about an hour southwest of Ottawa. An hour by car or walking? What lay southwest of Ottawa? He closed his eyes, trying to think, the scrap of paper a heavy weight in his hand.

" 'Allo, *monsieur Gitan!*"

He looked up at the sound of the boy's voice to find one of the street urchins who'd been playing baseball regarding him from the lawn.

"Ils sont tous parti, monsieur Gitan." They are all gone, Mister Gypsy.

"All but the ghosts," Janfri said. The boy regarded him without comprehension, so he repeated the words in French. The boy made a quick sign of the cross in the air between them and ran off down the street. "All but the ghosts," Janfri repeated. He shoved the *patteran* message into his pocket and made his way back to the car. He needed to look at a map of southern Ontario. When he reached the Lincoln, he glanced back at the house and the empty rocker on its porch.

"Ashen Devlesa, Lyuba," he said softly. *"Te aves yertime mander tai te yertil tut o Del."* May you remain with God, Lyuba. I forgive you and may God forgive you too.

She needed no forgiveness that Janfri knew of. He merely spoke the benediction to help speed her *muli* on to the land of shadows. A small gust of wind stirred some litter at the bottom of the stairs as he watched. It was just a quick rustle that was gone almost before he noticed it. He knew it was a little past noon and took the movement as an omen of Lyuba's approval. He was not a superstitious man, nor did he believe in magic. But he could learn. *Feri ando payi sitsholpe le nayuas,* Uncle Nonoka used to say. It was in the water that one learned to swim. If Mulengro was truly one who had mastery over *mule* as Lyuba claimed he did, and if he *was* after Janfri, the Rom knew he was in water so deep that he could only hope that he wouldn't drown before he *did* learn how to swim.

The Lincoln's seat cover was hot against his shoulder blades when he got back into the car. Yojo regarded him curiously.

"Did you find what you came for, *prala?"* he asked.

Janfri took the scrap of paper from his pocket and showed it to Yojo. "I found something," he said.

Yojo looked from the *patteran* on the paper to the porch of Stevo Gry's *tsera* and a shiver of—not so much dread as otherworldliness—touched his spine. Old Lyuba, like most Rom, was illiterate. But the older Gypsies, and those brought up on the roads of Europe as he and Janfri had been, knew other ways of communicating. With tufts of grass twisted in a certain way, or bits of cloth hung on the trail above normal eye level. And with symbols that could be scratched in wood, in dirt, on stone. Or scrawled in pencil on a scrap of paper such as the one Janfri held in his hand. Lyuba had made her *patteran* and died, but her message went on, as though she spoke from beyond the grave.

"Perhaps," Yojo said, "all the luck's not gone yet."

Janfri nodded. "When all our luck's gone, *prala,* the blood no longer moves in our bodies. That is something the *Gaje* have never understood."

"Gaje si dilo," Yojo replied. The non-Gypsy is a fool.

Janfri smiled without humor. Unfortunately, if Mulengro was the man in black that Joji Anako had seen walking down Scott Street with the *mulo* of Romano Yera, he was neither *Gaje* nor a fool.

twelve

"Look, Tom," Phillip Baker said. "If I hear anything—anything at all—I'll call you right away. You know that."

Tom sighed. He had the phone receiver propped between his shoulder and ear and was sitting on the long beige couch that took up one length of his living room. Across from him, two of Gillian's oil paintings hung on the wall. One was an expressionistic rendering of the Rideau Canal in winter—a view from the MacKenzie King Bridge downtown that was a swirl of jagged colors against an almost-realized backdrop of the canal, with the Laurier Street Bridge rearing up behind it. The other was a realistic study of a ballerina on a street corner in the Market that somehow turned the incongruous background into a perfect setting.

"Yeah," Tom said into the phone. "I know."

"It's only been a day or two," Baker continued. "He's probably found himself a retreat in the Gatineaus and is planning to stay there until he comes to grips with the shock of the situation."

"Maybe. Did you try Angie again?"

Her answering service said that John's agent was still out of town. Tom had tried it twice this morning anyway, and the message was still the same as the one he'd gotten yesterday. Doug hadn't heard anything either. That was why Tom was on the phone with Baker again. They were supposed to start recording soon and Baker was the producer this time out.

"I can understand your being worried," Baker said, "but I think the man deserves his privacy if he wants it. If he wanted our condolences, we would have heard from him. Why don't you just let it lie, Tom? If he hasn't been in touch with either of us by the end of the week, *then* we can start to worry. But by that time Angie will be back and we'll have somewhere to begin looking for him."

"Okay. I guess you're right. It's just . . ." Tom sighed again, cutting the sentence off. The bad feeling that was building up inside him just didn't make any real sense. "I'll talk to you later in the week."

"Do that. How's your own work going? Are you still planning to use that Cimarosa Concerto?"

"I'm working on it."

"Good, good. I've a few ideas I'd like to bounce off of you on that one, but right now the other line's on hold and I've got to run. Don't worry about John, Tom. I've known him for a couple of years and he seems to have a pretty good head on his shoulders. It would take more than a fire to twist him around."

"I suppose."

"Don't worry, Tom. Talk to you later."

"Yeah. Right."

Baker cut the line at his end and Tom slowly brought the receiver from his ear and cradled it. He wondered if Baker would still think that John had a good head on his shoulders if Tom told him what John had said before he disappeared into the crowd that night. Brow furrowed, Tom reached for an album jacket that lay on the coffee table and studied it. John Owczarek looked back from the jacket photo. He was standing in an open field, holding his violin the way the old time fiddlers held theirs for photos—in the crook of his arm with the bow dangling from his index finger. The title was at the bottom of the jacket. *Until We Meet Again.* Tom wondered when that would be, as he laid the album back down on the table.

The party last night had done nothing for the restlessness that was prowling through him, except that he'd woken up with a mild hangover this morning. He knew he wasn't being good company by the way that Gillian had avoided him at the breakfast table—a late breakfast. She'd already been at work for an hour or so by the time he got up. He knew that if he could pinpoint what it was that was bothering him so much, he'd be able to get on with his day-to-day life. But it wasn't just the cryptic statement that John had tossed to him before he'd vanished that night. It was more a sense of impermanence that those few words had made him aware of; the simple fact that everything changed. Sometimes people changed so that you could hardly recognize them anymore. He'd seen that happen when he ran into people he'd gone to high school with. But other times . . . other times you discovered that you'd never really known the person in the first place, and that left you wondering how much you really knew about anybody. Even yourself.

Was that it? At forty-seven he was just beginning to realize that he wasn't really sure who he was or what he wanted out of life. Music had been so important for so many years. And of course his family— Gillian and Matt. But he was one person when he played, another with his family, still another at gatherings like last night's little party. . . . So many faces. Everybody had their masks. Was it because John's mask had been so perfect that this was all bothering him so much, or because he wasn't sure when he was wearing one himself? He rubbed at his temples. He didn't need an identity crisis right now.

He stood abruptly, called to Gillian that he was going out, and left the house for another walk.

The charred ruin of John's home looked bleak and desolate in the afternoon sun. Tom stood across the street from it, staring at the blackened timbers that had fallen in on themselves like some oversize grotesque game of Pick-Up-Sticks. The smell of the fire still lingered in the air—a smell something like a wet ashtray—and he wrinkled his nose.

"Can't say I'll miss him," a voice said from behind him.

Tom turned to find an old woman watching the ruin with him, sitting on a worn wicker chair on the porch of a red-brick two-story house directly across from where John's house had stood. Her thighs were tight in her lime green shorts, her waistline hidden by the folds of the pale-yellow blouse with a pattern of mauve and orange flowers, the height of Woolworth fashion.

"What did you say?" Tom asked.

"Fellow who owned that place—can't say I'll miss him. You should've seen it burn."

"I was here."

"Oh?" The woman peered at him, obviously trying to place him.

"Why did you say that?" Tom asked.

"Say what?"

"That you wouldn't miss him—the man who lived there."

The woman sniffed. "Wrong sort. Day and night, the place would be filled with all sorts of odd folks. Gypsies, you know? They'd park their beat-up old cars any old place and carouse in there until all hours of the night."

Tom looked from the ruins of the house to the woman, not sure that she was talking about the same man that he knew.

"Gypsies?" he said.

"You know. We don't see so much of them as we used to—not like when I was a girl, I can tell you—but I remember them. Worse than any kind of folk I can think of. Dirt poor and always out begging. Loud-mouthed brats running wild. Women showing as much cleavage as the law'll let them without so much as a blush. And those handsome men!" She nodded towards the ruin. "He wasn't so bad—not like the kind I knew when I was a girl. I lived down on Murray Street then—in the Old Market—and we had enough Gypsies and other riffraff down there to choke a dog. Not that things've changed so much. The Market might look better now, but come the night and I'll give you ten to one that the whores and their pimps are still crawling all over it."

"Yes, but——"

"But the Gypsies were the worst," the woman continued, warming up to her subject. "My mother used to threaten us—my sister who was two years older and little Timmy—said they'd steal us away if we weren't good. There was some that lived down the street from us. I can remember sneaking up to the fence to watch them drinking and throwing knives into an old elm tree for a whole afternoon. Of course that tree's gone now. Diseased, you know? Took some of the prettiest trees we had in this city."

"You're saying that the man who lived there was a . . . Gypsy?" Tom asked. Stereotypical images came to his mind—old canvas-covered wagons traveling down picturesque English country lanes pulled by plodding old horses, women with the dark good looks of Spanish dancers and men with bright scarves around their necks and gold hoops in their ears.

"Well, if *he* wasn't, his friends sure were. They had a few parties there and I swear there was every Gypsy in the Valley come to them. Not every night, mind, but enough times so that I wouldn't miss it happening."

"A Gypsy," Tom said more to himself than the woman. He could almost picture John with a bright red scarf around his neck as he played some lively Gypsy tune on his violin. But did Gypsies even exist outside of turn-of-the-century novels? If the woman was right, it opened up a whole new spin of questions.

" 'Course, even with him gone, we've still got two row houses of Pakistanis to contend with down the block. I swear, if it's not one damn thing, it's another. They must live twenty to a room. I've seen so many coming or going from that place that——"

"This is all very interesting," Tom said, breaking in, "but I really can't stay to listen."

The woman peered at him, mouth puckering with disapproval. "Yes, well," she said. "I suppose you must have more important things to do than listen to an old pensioner shoot off her mouth. Not that I expect any respect these days. Check's always late anyway and those new tellers at the bank wouldn't know a smile if it fell from the sky and lay gasping in front of them. And what with . . ."

Tom walked away with a curt nod, no longer listening.

"Bloody liberal!" the woman called after him. "It's because of people like you that this country's in the poor shape that it is. Always crying about . . ."

Tom stepped up his pace until the woman's voice was lost in the distance. He was thinking about Gypsies and what the possibility of John being one might mean. The woman obviously didn't have much good to say about them—but then she didn't appear to have much good to say about anyone. A Gypsy. If John *was* a Gypsy, why hadn't he used that obvious sales gimmick to promote his records? If he'd never thought of it, then surely Angie would have. Unless John didn't want anyone to know. It had never come up in his own conversations with John.

Frowning, Tom retraced his footsteps home. What was wrong with being a Gypsy? Why was it important to keep it a secret? He had the feeling that if he understood that, he'd be a lot closer to understanding what had happened to John and why he had simply vanished. The curious prickling of a bad feeling grew stronger in him. The possibility that he wasn't going to like what he found out, that the information would be more disturbing than John's disappearance itself, was just beginning to make itself felt.

thirteen

The Lincoln was packed and idling by the curb. Yojo's wife Simza sat in the front passenger's seat with her youngest, Jasper, suckling at her breast. Twelve-year-old Lala sat beside her. The two older boys, Georjo and Young Jan, were in the back seat with Racki and Carolina. Keja stood by the curbside, looking back at the house where Janfri and Yojo sat on the stone stoop. Her pleated skirt came to just below her knees and her brown skin was dark against the creamy white of her blouse. The mid-afternoon sun awoke shining highlights in her black hair.

"I feel wrong leaving you behind," Yojo said.

Janfri shrugged, his gaze on Keja. "She's very beautiful," he said. "You must be proud of her."

Yojo followed his gaze. "She loves you, *prala*. Let her stay with you. Jump the broom with her. Simza and I will be your witnesses in the eyes of God."

"You would send her into danger?"

Yojo looked shocked. "What danger can there be to the wife of my brother?"

Janfri smiled wryly. In Yojo's eyes, he and Keja were already married. "Perhaps," he said, "when this business is done, you'll find me at the door of your *tsera* with the bridal brandy in my hand."

"You see?" Yojo said. "You show your very responsibility by not taking her into danger. I would be honored to be your *khanamik*, Janfri. And to drink your *pliashka*. Don't make me wait until I am old and gray—do you hear me?"

"*Bater.*" Janfri sighed. "Remember the first time *nano* Nonoka brought us to Royal Town?"

Yojo nodded. "Such a place, London! Our eyes held everything at once. And the time we fought those farmer boys in the Siebenge-birge. Hey, *prala?*"

Their uncle Nonoka had taken them back and forth across Europe, from the British Isles to Turkey; through the Siebenge-birge, the mountain range that separated Hungary from Rumania; to the Right Bank where the Rom gathered in Paris; down through the Pyrenees to where the Spanish Gitanos lived on Sacro Monte under the watchful eye of Alhambra. They roamed where they would in the traditional horse-drawn wagons, sometimes one or two together, other times in the rare caravan of fifteen or twenty wagons. And always there was tall, strong Nonoka Kejako to teach them horsing and smithing; the way to skin a hedgehog by cutting a hole in the skin near its foot, then blowing it up like a balloon and hanging it from a line; fishing and hunting and trading. Nonoka, who took the two fosterlings into his *kumpania* in Nazi-occupied France, who took them into his own *vurdon* when they escaped the burning of their parents' wagons and the ravages of the old glassworks in

La Pierre that the Germans had turned into a camp for Gypsy prisoners.

The good times held Janfri and Yojo together far more than the bad, but the horrors of the camp could never be forgotten—they were something that they shared with no other in Big George's *kumpania*. They had stayed on with Nonoka's people, even after the old man died, but eventually cousins took Aunt Magda, and the two young men crossed the Atlantic by working on a freighter to New York. There, in what the Gypsies called Rommeville, they vanished, without papers or money, into the lower half of Manhattan where the Rom have carved a hundred *tsera* from that famed concrete jungle.

"We did it all," Janfri said.

Yojo grinned. "And the world's so big still, *prala*. There is much that we have not yet seen."

"And much that we will never see. *Bater*. We do what we can." Janfri touched Yojo's shoulder. "God go with you, brother."

Yojo embraced him. "And with you. You will call me if you need help?"

"Surely."

"And find us when you are done with this little task?"

"I know you too well for you to hide long from me, *prala*."

Yojo nodded, blinking in the sunlight. "I have something in my eye," he muttered.

Janfri regarded him through his own thin film of tears. "As do I. There's too much dirt in this city, *prala*—in all cities. It's long past time we were on the road once more."

They embraced a last time, then Yojo slowly made his way down to the curb where his family was waiting for him. Keja's gaze lingered on Janfri for a long moment before she squeezed into the backseat. She lifted her hand and Janfri returned the wave. He watched the Lincoln pull away, following it until it turned the corner. Sighing, he picked up the map that Yojo had left him and studied it with blurring vision. He wiped his eyes, concentrating on the task at hand as though it would ease the emptiness inside.

He spread the map on his knee, tracing the roads leading south-west from Ottawa. There was a lot of country lying approximately an hour in that direction. It was cottage country, with dozens of small villages and lakes. The towns of Smith Falls, Perth, Mer-rickville, Lanark . . . Where was he supposed to begin? All he had was thirty-two dollars and change, the '73 Chevrolet that Yojo had found for him, and his violin. The money would cover his gas, but it left nothing for living expenses. So the first thing he had to do was clean up and go to his bank. He hadn't changed in three days and couldn't even remember where he'd left his shoes, so he was wear-ing a pair of unclaimed running shoes that he'd found in Yojo's house. He could just imagine the raised eyebrows of the bank teller if he went in to close his account looking like this. He wouldn't even have a bank account if he hadn't needed one to cash the checks he earned from the income his violin brought him. Removing his *diklo* and earrings, he put them in his pocket. There was going to be enough time spent producing ID, explaining why he was withdraw-ing all his money. The *Gaje* were always eager to take one's money, but retrieving it from them was never such an easy matter.

He started to get up from the stoop when he saw a Dodge sedan pull into the spot that Yojo's car had so recently vacated. He identi-fied the two men inside as plainclothes policemen before they even stepped out of the car. One was short and somewhat out of shape. The other was a tall black. Janfri's eyes narrowed slightly as they came up the walk, then he eased a vacant look onto his face. He folded the map and thrust it casually into his pocket.

"Nice afternoon," the white policeman said to him.

Janfri shrugged.

"We're looking for a man named Yojo Kore who's supposed to live here," the policeman continued. "Are you him?"

Janfri shook his head.

"Do you know if he's in?"

"No one is home," Janfri replied in a deliberately heavy Slavic accent. "I come for the money he owes me, you know? But no one is home. So I wait. Maybe he will come back soon and pay me, yes?"

The two men exchanged glances. "Could we see some identifica-tion, please?" the white policeman asked. When Janfri regarded him blankly, the detective pulled out his wallet and showed his badge. "I'm Detective-Sergeant Briggs and this is Detective Sandler. We're police officers."

"How's it going?" Will added, flashing a smile.

Janfri chose to answer the second officer. "Not so good," he said. "I need money to fix my car, you know? Not this one—it is my brother's—but the one I have at home. So I come, all across town, but Yojo is not home. So what can I do, you are telling me?"

"Do you have a driver's license?" Briggs asked. "Or maybe a credit card?" As if *that* was likely.

Janfri let his eyes go wide with shock. "You are here to arrest *me?*" he asked, fumbling in his pocket. He produced a billfold and started to hand it over, but Briggs shook his head.

"Just the identification, please," he said.

Janfri tugged the worn driver's license identifying him as Jim Cerinek out of its plastic protective covering and laid it onto Briggs' outstretched hand.

"Thanks," Briggs said. He passed the license over to Will who took it back to the car. "How long have you been waiting here, Mr. Cerinek?"

"Too long, you know? An hour, maybe—maybe longer."

Janfri met Briggs' gaze with a slightly off-focus stare. He wasn't worried about the ID. Yojo had promised him it was good.

"And you've seen no one in that time?"

"Some people walk by on the street," Janfri explained. "I saw them. And there were cars, too, you know? So what is it that Yojo has done? Will you be throwing him in jail? Then I will never get my money and the car, she needs the work, you know? I do deliver-ies sometimes—pick up food for the old people, sometimes beer. They will give me a little money, you know? Or a beer. Once a man gave me ten dollars just to pick up a case of beer! I was a happy man that day, I tell you. I bought almost a whole tank of gas. But that was a long time ago—when the car was working. Now she is not so good, you know?"

"He's clean," Will said, returning from the car.

Briggs nodded. This was a very patient man, Janfri realized, and therefore, potentially a very dangerous one.

"Have you seen anyone—anyone at all—coming in or out of the house, Mr. Cerinek?" Briggs asked, handing Janfri back his license.

"No one at all. But I am still waiting. Unless Yojo is going to jail. And then I will never get my money, and the car won't run. . . ." Janfri let his shoulders rise and fall despondently.

"To the best of our knowledge," Briggs said, "Mr. Kore has done nothing that would warrant criminal charges. We just want to talk to him in connection with a case that we're working on."

"Heh?"

Briggs regarded the man's confused face and slowly shook his head. He was still trying to decide if Cerinek was really stupid or just putting them on.

"Never mind," he said. "Do you know a Big George Luluvo?"

"Oh, sure," Janfri said. "He is a very important man with the Gypsies, you know? Once I helped his son haul some scrap metal. We worked for the whole afternoon and Big George was there the whole time, showing us what to do. He's a *very* important man. Everybody knows him. I knew some Gypsies in the old country, but none were such good men as Big George."

Briggs nodded, his irritation showing only in a small tick at the corner of his mouth. "Yeah, well thanks for your help, Mr. Cerinek."

"Did I help you? That is good." Janfri started to scratch under his arm and grinned. "I like to be helping people, you know?"

"I'm sure." Briggs regarded him with growing distaste. "You're probably wasting your time waiting here for Mr. Kore. I have a feeling he won't be back."

"You think so?" Janfri asked slowly. "But my money . . . ?"

"You win some and you lose some. See you later, Mr. Cerinek."

Briggs started back for the car. Will remained a moment longer, then tipped his finger against his forehead and followed his partner. Janfri continued to sit on the stoop, occasionally scratching himself, until they pulled away. Once they were out of sight, he remained where he was, counting slowly to himself. He smiled inwardly when the Dodge came around the corner again and cruised by at a slow pace. When it passed out of sight for a second time, he went over to the Chevy that Yojo had acquired for him and got in, laying his violin on the seat beside him. He started the car up and backed out of the driveway. It was too late to go to the bank now. If the police were looking for Yojo and Big George, it was a good time for all Rom to leave the city. He didn't need trouble with the law on top of having to deal with Mulengro. He decided to drive down to the trailer park outside of Perth where Tibo Lee was staying. He'd start with Tibo and his sister, see what they knew, and work his way on from there. He could also check out a few spots on his way down to Perth.

"Did you get a make on the Chevy parked in the lane?" Briggs asked.

"Yeah. It's registered to one Tonio Cerinek, no outstanding violations. Tonio's clean—just like his brother."

"What did you think of him?"

Will grinned. "Mr. Scratch-where-it-itches? He's either just what he seems to be or one hell of a good actor."

"Maybe we should've pulled him in anyway. We're coming up with a lot of dead ends."

"That's the way the game plays sometimes."

Briggs nodded. "We should've gone down to Luluvo's with a warrant in the first place. They're starting to take off like rats deserting a sinking ship.

"Can you blame them? They probably think that any one of them could be next."

"I suppose. Who's next on the list?"

Will studied his notebook for a moment. "Joji Anako. He's another of Big George's lieutenants—if you can call them that."

But Joji's house was empty as well when they reached it. The next door neighbor told them that he'd packed up and left a couple of days ago.

"Cerinek was a Gypsy, wasn't he?" Will asked as they pulled away from the deserted bungalow.

"Probably. Slavic anyway. Way our luck's been running we really should've picked him up."

"Want me to put an APB out on him?"

Briggs shook his head. "Gypsy or not, he wasn't playing with a full deck. I doubt we would've got much more out of him except for a bad case of fleas."

Will laughed. "You want to take a break and have some lunch?"

"You buying?"

"How come whenever a case is going nowhere, I have to pay for the lunches?"

"Because I get too depressed to spend money," Briggs replied, pulling in to the curb in front of a bar and grill on Wellington Street.

"At least you picked a class joint," Will said as he regarded the restaurant's dirty windows.

Briggs led the way in. "Don't complain," he said over his shoulder. "It's your money I'm trying to save."

"How come I don't feel grateful?" Will asked, not expecting an answer. Briggs didn't disappoint him.

14
fourteen

Jeff awoke to a complete sense of disorientation. He was lying in a bed—neither his own nor a hospital's—and looking up at a mobile of glass unicorns that glinted in the sunlight coming in from a window to his left. The effort to sit up exhausted him. His head throbbed from a dull headache that wasn't helped by the room doing a slow spin before it settled down. He ached from head to foot. When the vertigo eased, he could make out a flowered wallpaper on one wall, a windowsill overhung with plants, and a dresser, the top of which barely contained a spill of knickknacks, makeup, a small hand-held hair dryer and a stack of magazines.

He caught a glimpse of his face in the mirror above the dresser and winced. The left side of his face was swollen and discolored with an ugly blue-black bruise. His left eye had a neat circle of bruising around it as well. By the feel of his body under the sheets, he didn't have to pull them back to know that it didn't look any better. Jes*us*. Where was he? The last thing he could remember clearly was the two Gourlay brothers beating on him.

The bedroom door opened and Jackie Sim, who'd been waitressing last night at Tinkers, stood in the doorway for a moment, regarding him sympathetically. Her long brown hair was still uncombed and fell to her waist in a tangle. She was barefoot and wearing a cream flannel nightie with a pattern of forget-me-nots on it.

"Hi," she said. "Do you feel as bad as you look?"

"Worse. Jackie, what am I doing here? And where is here?"

"Here's my place. Don't you remember us bringing you here last night?"

"The last thing I remember is the Gourlays declaring open season on me."

Jackie frowned. "Those animals. Mike and I took you up to the hospital. It was wild there for a moment. Nobody was on the street when the Gourlays were beating you up, but by the time Mike and I got outside there were people everywhere. Anyway we drove you up to the hospital and they were going to keep you—at least for overnight—but you got all excited so in the end we brought you here to my place. It must've been around three by then. You passed out again in the car coming home and Mike and I had to drag you up the stairs—so you can probably blame us for a few of those bruises."

"You should've just taken me home instead of putting me up like this."

Jackie shook her head. "We figured it'd be better for you to be here where I could look in on you—just in case, you know?" She moved from the doorway and perched on the end of the bed. "And here you are. You look terrible."

"Thanks. Have you got any aspirin?"

"The doctor gave you some painkillers. I'll go get them."

While she was out of the room, Jeff closed his eyes, trying to remember. The lost hours nagged at him. Once Jackie had mentioned taking him to the Perth Great War Memorial Hospital, vague memories of being there and the doctor examining him returned, but everything else was a blur. There was just the pain, the memory of the boots coming at him. . . . Jesus! Ola! The Gourlays were planning to go after Ola when they'd finished with him. He was half out of bed when Jackie returned with a glass of water and the pills.

"Uh-uh," she said. "Maybe you could talk the doctor out of keeping you overnight, but he gave me orders and you're not getting by me."

The movement had set Jeff's head spinning again. "Ola," he said. "They were going to go after Ola."

"Who was . . . ?" Jackie began, then her face went white. "Oh, my God!" Her head filled with an image of the two hulking Gourlays attacking the slim black woman that came into Tinkers just about every Saturday afternoon with Jeff.

"I've got to phone her," Jeff said.

Jackie nodded numbly. Leaving the water and pills on the nightstand, she left the room again, returning with the phone. She plugged it in by the bed and looked at Jeff.

"What's her number?"

She punched it out as Jeff told it to her, held the receiver to her ear. There was nothing. No ringing. No busy signal. Her fingers trembled as she cut the silence off, got the dial tone and punched in the number again.

"There's nothing," she said. "I can't get through."

"Oh, Jesus! Try the operator."

As she cut the connection again, Jeff started to get out of bed once more. "You can't get up, Jeff," she said as she punched O.

"I've got to go there."

"You're in no condition to go anywh—Hello? Operator? I'm having trouble reaching this number. Yes. It's . . ."

The room was spinning for Jeff again. He fumbled with the pills, managed to get two between his lips. His mouth felt fuzzy, like it was full of dry mold. The water he used to wash down the pills helped only marginally.

"She says there's something wrong with the line," Jackie said as she set the receiver down. "Maybe I'd better call the cops."

"No police," Jeff said. What little he knew of Ola included the fact that she wasn't big on authority figures of any kind. It was almost a phobia with her. First he'd go down to the cottage, then he'd worry about calling the cops. Maybe she'd just unplugged the phone or something. Jesus, his head hurt. He leaned on the end of the bed once he'd stood and looked down. All he had on were his boxer shorts.

"Jeff, you're not supposed—"

"Where are my clothes?"

"But—"

"I can't just lie here and not *know!*" He winced as he shouted the last word. Jackie looked like she was going to bolt. "Jesus! I'm sorry, Jackie. I didn't mean to yell at you. You've been a real sweetheart and I love you for it, but I've got to get out there."

Jackie studied him for a moment, then nodded. "Okay. But *I'm* driving."

"You don't have to do that."

"Do you think that you could even get down to the end of the block on your own, let alone all the way out to Rideau Ferry?"

Jeff shook his head. "Okay. I give up. You're hired."

"Wait'll you see my bill." She smiled, but the tension showed around her eyes.

"Thanks, Jackie." He grabbed his jeans and shirt from the chair by the dresser and made his way into the living room. There was a pillow on the sofa and a couple of sheets twisted together lying half on it and half on the floor to show him where Jackie'd slept while he'd taken her bed. It just showed you, he thought. For every asshole like Stan Gourlay there was someone like Jackie just to keep the balance. He tugged on his jeans and got both arms into his shirt, then sat down on the sofa to button it up. He started when Jackie called his name.

"Are you still up for this?" she asked.

Jeff blinked. He'd almost dozed off there. Jackie's hair was pulled back into a long braid and she was wearing a pair of beige cotton pants and a print blouse. She hadn't bothered with her makeup and Jeff decided he liked her better without it.

"Let's go," he said, rising wearily to his feet. Jackie shook her head and took his arm, helping him down the stairs.

The utter tranquility of Ola's cottage when they pulled into her driveway did wonders for Jeff's mood. The broad neatly trimmed lawns—Tom Kerr's boy mowed them once a week through the summer—lay inviting in the sunshine. Bees hummed around the flower beds. On the lake there were sailboats and someone was waterskiing. But peaceful though everything appeared, Jeff wasn't going to feel relaxed until he'd talked to Ola and seen for himself that she was all right.

"Looks like the biggest shock here is going to be when Ola sees how the Gourlays did a dance on your face."

Jeff didn't answer. He was still going to have to deal with the Gourlays at some point, but he didn't want to think about that right now. He got out of the car and waited for Jackie to join him before going down to the cottage. He started to knock on the door, then saw that it was slightly ajar. A new pinprickle of fear knifed up his spine. He pushed lightly on the door and it opened wider.

"Ola?" he called. "Ola!"

There was no reply. Jeff stepped inside and looked around. The place looked as tidy as usual, but something bothered him. There was no sign of a struggle or anything, so why was he worried?

"Jeff?"

Jackie pointed at the phone. It sat in its place on a table by the kitchen door. For a moment he didn't know what she meant, then he saw the end of the cord. It was shredded—as though someone had ripped it from the wall. His pulse quickened.

"Ola? It's Jeff!"

He walked further into the room, looking around. There was no one in the kitchen, or the bedroom. The bathroom was empty. He paused in its doorway, suddenly understanding the reason why he'd been bothered. The shelf below the bathroom mirror was empty. The toothpaste, hairbrush, makeup . . . it was all gone. He turned quickly and surveyed the living room. All Ola's personal belong- ings—few though they'd been—were missing.

"She's gone," he said. "Just packed up and left."

"What do you mean?"

Jeff waved his hand at the furniture. "All this stuff came with the place. But her own things . . . There was a picture on the mantel of an old woman, dark as Ola, but without her kinky hair—it's gone. And she had a couple of books there, this fetish thing hanging from the end of the mantel . . ." He turned slowly, taking it all in. "Even Boboko."

"Bobo-who?"

"Boboko. Her cat."

His headache, pushed to the back of his head by the pills, came throbbing to the fore again.

"They took her away. They . . ." His bruised face went ugly with anger. "Those bastards! If they've hurt her . . ."

Jackie touched his arm. "Maybe she left on her own, Jeff. The place isn't wrecked or anything. Surely she'd put up a fight if those two bruisers showed up at her door in the middle of the night?"

Jeff's gaze went to the shredded end of the telephone cord. "Maybe they just cleaned the place up. Oh, Jesus . . . I don't know."

Jackie didn't know what to do. Jeff looked utterly lost. She knew he had a bit of a thing for Ola and also knew that he'd never gotten it together to do anything about it. They'd talked about it once or twice after-hours in the restaurant with Marion and Mike, on those nights when everyone was feeling a little worn-out and down and that kind of thing came up. Like Marion's husband leaving her, or Jeff and Mike, who was also aspiring to be a writer, talking about how hard it was to get published, or her own frustrations at trying to find something she cared enough about to put some direction in her life.

"Jeff?" she said softly, but he didn't hear her.

He moved slowly into the porch and stood there for a long moment, staring out at the lake. The phone had been pulled out of the wall and the Gourlays had talked about coming out here to get her—but how often didn't those assholes just shoot off their mouths? There were a hundred things they were going to do and people they were going to get. And sometimes they did. But more often they didn't. What if Ola *had* just packed up and taken off? He'd thought they were friends, but there was always something unapproachable in her. Maybe she didn't feel she owed him any-thing. They were only collaborators. They didn't even have to *see* each other to do that.

"Shit," he muttered. He didn't know what to think now and his head was aching like there was a little demon with a jackhammer in it having a go at his skull.

"Jeff? Are you okay?"

He turned to look at Jackie. No, he wasn't okay, he wanted to shout at her, but he held it back. It wasn't her fault any of this was happening.

"Yeah," he said. "I just . . . I don't know. I don't know what to do. I mean we can't really call the cops—the place hardly looks lived in, little say it being the scene of a kidnapping or whatever. But if the Gourlays did come up here last night and grabbed her . . ."

The floor of the porch felt odd under his shoes. He looked down, trying to figure out what it was. Then he realized the carpet was gone. It had been an Oriental weave—a real nice one, all deep reds and blues and golds. And it hadn't been Ola's. Now why would she take that—

The jackhammer devil turned on a buzz saw in his head. For a moment all he saw was a flare of white burning light. He stared at the floor, thought he saw the carpet still lying there, and on it . . . Stan Gourlay lay in a sprawl of limbs, his beer-belly hanging out of his belt and his T-shirt riding up his chest. But the only way he knew it was Stan was because of the eyes and by the top of the head. Half of his face looked like it had been torn away and there was a big hunk of firewood sticking right out of the lower half of his face like a bizarre parody of a nose.

Cold sweat seeped out of Jeff's pores. He tried to blink the sight away but it was as though his eyes had been riveted open. His stomach churned with acid. There was a hungry sound in the air like the buzzing of flies. He had the insane thought that Stan had been a closet Pinocchio—hiding the fact from the world until he told one too many lies and his nose just grew and grew until it ripped out of his head and looked like a log. Stuck there.

"Oh, Jesus!" he cried.

The eyes blinked open and stared at him. Brain matter and blood gathered in their corners, dribbling down the sides of his head where they pooled on the carpet. The hands opened and closed, slowly, and all Jeff could think of was a hundred B-horror movies he'd taken in at the drive-in, drinking beer and laughing his ass off because it was just so damn hokey. But this . . . this wasn't hokey. This was—

Something touched his arm and he turned, swinging a fist. Jackie danced out of his way and he stumbled, pulled by the force of his swing. He lost his balance and went falling. The thing on the floor lifted its arms to embrace him, eyes grinning. Jeff howled as he fell, clawing at the air to get away. He just wanted to . . . get . . . away. . . .

He hit the floor with a thud that knocked the breath out of him. He could almost feel the wet blood on him, the hands all puffy, but still strong. Flies roared in his ears, thousands of wings beating the air like a storm. Then he realized there was only linoleum pressed up against his cheek. And what his hand was pushing him away from was the couch. And there was no dead . . . thing . . . waiting for him.

He sat up very slowly, touching the floor with a trembling hand. When he lifted his head, Jackie was watching him with a scared look on her face.

"I'm cracking up," he said in a hollow voice. The sound of flies was only the drumming of his headache as it tried to batter its way out of his skull. "I'm seeing . . . things like you wouldn't believe."

Jackie approached him cautiously. "Jeff, what's going on?"

"I had . . . this hallucination. I thought I saw Stan Gourlay lying here . . . with his head all smashed in by a log. I'm going crazy, Jackie."

She shook her head. Going into the kitchen, she fetched a glass of water and sat down on the floor beside Jeff. "I brought these," she said, taking the pills the doctor had given her last night out of her purse. She shook two of them into her palm and fed them to him. "The doctor said that head injuries can do weird things to you. That's why you weren't supposed to get up out of bed." She held the glass to his lips and tilted it slowly, letting him drink it all.

"Did . . . did he say how long they were going to last?"

"No. He wasn't even sure you'd have them. But you'd better go back and have them run some tests on you, Jeff. A concussion's no laughing matter."

Jeff shuddered, remembering what he'd thought he'd seen. "I'm not laughing," he said. He looked again at the floor, but there was nothing there. What he'd just experienced frightened him in a way that the few hours he'd lost last night couldn't begin to. It had been so real. And that was the horror of it. If his mind could call up a vision like that and make it so real . . .

"Think you can stand?" Jackie asked.

"Yeah. Sure." The pills hadn't kicked in yet, but he wanted to get out of here so bad he could taste it. "I'll be okay."

Jackie helped him to his feet and they made their way slowly through the cottage and across the lawn to where they'd left Jackie's Honda Civic. It was just turning twelve thirty-five when they pulled back onto the highway. Jeff sat silently in the passenger's seat, staring out the window. Jackie drove worriedly, anxious for Jeff, frightened that he might turn around at any minute and lash out again as he had before. Behind in the cottage, the thing that Jeff had thought a figment of his head injuries settled down to wait patiently once more. It hadn't known that it could manifest itself like that. Now it waited eagerly for the night to come.

Superstitious *Gaje* worry about midnight and call it the witching hour. The Gypsy worries about all the hours between sunset and dawn, as well as the half hour that follows noon. With good cause, for they know about such things.

• • •

When the Honda reached the transformer station that marked the turnoff to Highway 2 that runs northeast to Port Elmsley, Jeff spoke softly.

"Turn here."

"What?"

Jackie put on the brakes, but they'd already passed the turnoff. She pulled over to the side of the road and set the car in neutral with the handbrake on.

"Jeff, if you're going weird on me again . . ."

He shook his head, wincing at the movement. "Look, Jackie. I'm really sorry about what happened back there. I just didn't know what was going on. When you touched me, I thought it was . . . that thing . . . or I don't know what. Please don't be scared of me."

"I'm not scared of you. Not really. It's just . . ."

"It's okay. I'd be freaking too."

Jackie held the steering wheel with whitening fingers and looked straight ahead. She took a deep breath and managed to dredge up a smile. She knew it wasn't his fault what had happened back there. The Jeff she knew rarely raised his voice, little say got physical. Not that he wasn't capable of it. She'd heard about a time or two at a couple of high school dances when some of the boys just pushed him too far. He'd been dating a Perth girl, but still went to school in Smiths Falls, a fact that didn't endear him much to the local yahoos at the time. But mostly she knew him to be a real pussycat. She turned to face him again and pushed the fear down.

"Why do you want to go to Port Elmsley?"

"It's not that," he said. "It's just—"

"No," she said before he could finish. She'd just remembered that the Gourlays lived in an old farmhouse about halfway to the locks. "Now that *is* acting crazy."

"If they've got Ola, that's where they'd take her."

"They'll kill you this time, Jeff. And me."

"We'll just go look. Drive by slowly, if you like, without stopping."

"Jeff, you should be going back to the hospital."

"I will. I promise. Just as soon as we drive by their place. Deal?"

"That's a lousy bargain."

"How about if I throw in dinner at my place?"

"Now you're bribing me. Besides, you're in no condition to be offering anyone dinner. You'd probably collapse across the stove while you're making it."

"C'mon, Jackie. Just this one favor."

She looked at him, reading the pain and worry plain in his face and her eyes softened. "Okay," she said. "But we just drive by, right?"

"Right."

"Here it is."

Jackie slowed down as the Gourlay house came up on their right. It was a two-story wood-frame in bad need of a paint job. The barn behind it had fallen down years ago in a storm. A couple of supports reared into the air, like the ribs of some fallen behemoth, but the rest of the building was nothing more than a flattened heap of boards. To the left of the house was a small storage shed. Its door hung ajar, only the top hinge still keeping it in place. The yard was overgrown. And the driveway was empty.

When she saw there was no one there, Jackie pulled the Honda over to the side of the road and stopped in front of the house.

"They're still unemployed, right?" Jeff said.

"Last I heard."

"So where are they?"

Jackie stared at the house. The place gave her a creepy feeling. She wanted to turn around and get back to Perth as quickly as possible, but a vision of Ola held captive somewhere in that place crept into her mind and she couldn't shake it. For a long moment she held her breath, then she put the car into reverse and backed into the driveway.

"We don't have to go in," Jeff said. "Maybe just one of them's gone."

She hadn't thought of that. She looked at the house again, goose bumps crawling up her arms. Before she could lose her nerve, she killed the engine. "Now . . . now that we're here," she said, trying to keep the quiver from her voice, "we might as well have a look. Besides, did you ever see the Gourlays when they *weren't* together?"

Before Jeff could answer, she got out and went around to her trunk. She had the hatch lifted by the time Jeff joined her and tugged a tire iron free from the tangle of rope, jumper cables and odds and ends that just seemed to end up in there.

"Let's go," she said.

She led the way to the house. When they reached the porch, Jeff moved past her and tried the door. It was unlocked, so he pushed it open and listened for a long while.

"Hey!" he called into the silent house. "Anybody here?"

He waited a moment or two, then repeated the call. When there was still no response, he glanced at Jackie, shrugged and limped across the threshold. The hallway was in worse repair than the outside of the house. Faded wallpaper was peeling and the floor was lined with boots and mud-stained work shoes. There was a heap of coats and checkered flannel shirts behind the door. In the living room a faded sofa stood across from a fancy new Sony Trinatron perched incongruously on an old orange crate. A couple of kitchen chairs completed the furnishings.

Jackie wrinkled her nose when she stepped into the kitchen behind Jeff. Cases of empty beer bottles piled floor to ceiling along one wall. The fridge and stove had once been white; they were now an off-gray and stained. The sink was full of pots. A table stood near the window that looked out onto the backyard and it was littered with dishes and beer bottles. A stack of pizza boxes was on the counter beside the sink.

"The lap of luxury," Jeff murmured. "Do these boys know how to live or what?"

A nervous smile flitted across Jackie's features, then died as they heard a creak. For the first time she understood the expression of someone's heart being in their throat. She could hardly breathe, she was so scared.

"Just the house settling," Jeff whispered.

Jackie nodded hopefully. The tire iron was a dead weight in her hand. Her muscles felt so watery that she didn't think she had the strength to lift it even if Dracula himself came lunging down the stairs at them.

"Do you want to go?" Jeff asked.

Jackie bit at her lip, but shook her head. They'd come this far, they might as well see it through.

They went up the stairs, Jeff first, Jackie following. She tried not to touch the walls. God knew what they had growing on them. First thing she was going to do when she got home was take a long soak in the bath. Just the air in this place made her feel soiled.

Jeff paused at the top of the stairs, listening carefully. There were four doors, all of them open. The first they peered into was a bathroom. It was so filthy that they both felt like gagging. The next two rooms were empty—no furnishings, nothing. Only some litter piled in the corners. The last room, at the front end of the house, had a couple of mattresses on the floor and a pile of soiled clothes between them. The walls were lined with nude pinups. There was a stack of girlie magazines underneath the window. A couple of them were open and lying beside one of the beds. A rifle leaned up against the wall in one corner, with a box of shells beside it. Jeff looked into the closet, then turned back to the center of the room.

"Let's get out of here," he said.

Jackie nodded. The sooner the better. When they were finally back outside, she stood beside the car for a long moment, drawing clean air into her lungs. Then she glanced at Jeff and saw how pale he was. She tossed the tire iron into the back seat and started up the car. Jeff settled in his seat and stared out the window.

"Now we're going to the hospital," Jackie said. "Any argument?"

Jeff shook his head wearily. Jackie looked worriedly at him, knowing what was going through his mind. Just because Ola wasn't there, didn't mean the Gourlays had nothing to do with her disappearance. But the likelihood of them taking her anywhere else seemed remote. In fact, she thought, as she pulled out onto the highway and headed towards Perth, it was unlikely that the Gourlays would ever go that far in the first place. They were animals and they got away with a lot, but even they couldn't be that stupid. They might be able to bully their way out of assault charges, but rape was a whole other thing. The hardest thing for Jeff to accept right now, but accept it he must, was that Ola had simply packed up and gone.

Dr. Mulley wasn't at all happy to see Jeff up and about. When he heard about the hallucination, his thin lips had pursed and his eyes narrowed.

"It happens," was all he would say until the X rays came back from the lab. Jeff tried to convince Jackie to leave him there, but she shook her head firmly.

"Nope," she told him. "You're my patient now as much as Mulley's and besides that, you owe me a dinner."

They didn't get out of the hospital until past four and then only with Jeff's firm promise to stay in bed for the next few days. The X rays had come back negative. There was no fracture, but Jeff was told in no uncertain terms that if the hallucinations persisted, he was to return immediately. When that was also duly agreed to, Dr. Mulley let them go.

They paused on the sidewalk in front of the hospital.

"You can stay with me for a couple of days," Jackie said.

Jeff shook his head. "I've taken up enough of your time as it is."

"Guess I didn't make myself clear in there, did I? I want you somewhere where I can keep an eye on you."

"You're a beautiful person, did anyone ever tell you that?"

Jackie grinned. "Lots of times—only not in the last twenty-four hours or so. C'mon, patient o' mine. Dr. Sim says its time to hit the sack."

"Yes, ma'am," Jeff replied. He tried to match her smile, but it didn't reach the hurt in his eyes.

"She'll get in touch with you," Jackie told him. "She probably just got called away, you know? But when she does show up again, you'd better let her know how you feel about her. I don't think mooning over something ever got anybody anything, Jeff. It's the doing that counts."

Jeff started to agree with her, then froze. Jackie followed his gaze and gripped his arm when she saw the pickup truck go by. Bob Gourlay was alone at the wheel. He looked neither left nor right, just drove down Drummond, heading south.

"Jackie," Jeff said softly, remembering the thing he'd seen in Ola's cottage. "Where's Stan? Those bastards never go anywhere by themselves." The ache in his head quickened its tempo again.

Jackie swallowed with difficulty. Her throat was too dry all of a sudden. "Don't even think about it," she said.

"I've got to go after him."

Jackie glanced at him. A fine sheen of sweat had broken out on his brow and the arm under her hand was trembling. "Ola's okay," she said. "If they had her, she'd've been at their house. Now get in the car, Jeff. Please."

Jeff stood stiff and unmoving, watching the disappearing truck. But the only thing he saw was a ruined face with a hunk of wood sticking out of it. . . .

"Jackie. Where the hell is Stan?"

She pulled at his arm, talking soothingly, and got him to the car. By the time they reached the vehicle, he was easier to manage. She went around to her own side of the car, wondering how she'd managed to get herself mixed up in this whole mess. Well, that was easy enough to work out, she thought as she shot a look at Jeff. He was a friend and he'd needed somebody and she'd just happened to be there. But the rest of it. . . . She hoped Ola was safely on a bus, going God knows where, but safe. For Ola's sake as well as for Jeff's peace of mind. But Stan . . . She remembered the brief glimpse she'd had of Bob's face as he drove by. He was so . . . intense. Disturbed. And the two of them were inseparable. So where *was* Stan? As she started the car, Jackie wasn't sure that she really wanted to know the answer to that question.

fifteen

The longer she walked, the less tired Ola became. Like all Gypsies, simply being on the move was invigorating. So, as the morning drifted into afternoon and her step grew lighter, the immediacy of the previous night's events faded. She found herself smiling more and teasing Boboko when he lagged. After leaving Rideau Ferry, they had walked through fields, following the contour line of the highway as far as Lombardy where it joined Route 15. Still keeping to the fields, they crossed 15 a mile or so north of the village and headed due east until they reached the marshy ground on the far side of Otter Creek. Ola carried Boboko over the wet ground, her own shoes squelching uncomfortably each time she lifted her feet and set them down again.

"You're not planning to live *here?*" Boboko asked when she stopped on a bit of higher ground for a rest.

Ola laughed. "Why not?" she teased. "Who'd look for us here?"

"We don't even know if anyone's looking for us in the first place."

"Bob Gourlay," Ola said, repeating the name she'd read in the dead man's wallet.

"I suppose," Boboko sighed. "He's probably the only one stupid enough to think of looking for us here." He twitched a mosquito away from his whiskers that was immediately replaced by a half-dozen others. "It's not exactly the Hilton, you know," he added, not knowing what the reference meant exactly, but knowing from the TV show that he'd heard it on that it had something to do with comfortable lodgings. The Hilton, he assumed, was a dry cozy place with thick carpets to scratch, pillows to curl up on and a good stretch of dirt nearby to relieve oneself on.

"You wouldn't like the Hilton," Ola informed him. "The only cats allowed in there arrive in carrying cases."

Boboko sniffed disdainfully. "Barbaric," he muttered. He watched a tuft of grass stirring with an interest that lasted only as long as the grasshopper hidden in it remained out of sight. When it hopped into view, he turned back to Ola and gazed hopefully at her backpack. "What *are* we going to do?" he asked. "After we've eaten, of course."

"Walk some more." Ola stretched out on the grass and stared up at the sky, ignoring the sulky look on Boboko's face. She knew it was put on just for effect. If she didn't pay any attention to it, he'd forget it soon enough himself. Clouds were drifting sleepily across the sky and she followed their movement, trying to make out features and shapes in them. When one looked too much like the man she'd killed last night, she took a quick breath and sat up. What *were* they going to do?

She started to think about the countryside around Perth, glad now that she'd let Jeff talk her into letting him take her for drives through it from time to time. It was too bad that the cottagers were still out in full force or she could have commandeered one of their places for a week or two. As it was . . . How long should she drop out of sight? Should she stay in the area or go on to a big city where she could lose herself in its maze of streets and buildings? Toronto, perhaps. Or Rommeville—New York. That might be safer, but there was still the man in black to consider. Mulengro, the old woman had named him. Go or stay? Her *dook* told her that she would have some part in stopping Mulengro if he was to be stopped at all. She didn't understand what part—her *dook* was never clear when it came to herself. But if she stayed . . .

The dead man's brother would be looking for her and she didn't want to put herself in a position where she might have to deal with Bob Gourlay as she had with his brother. But was Bob Gourlay all she had to fear? What if he'd gone to the police? She'd cleaned up the cottage as best she could, but that wouldn't stop a forensic team from coming up with evidence of the murder. And once it was found out that she was a Gypsy, what hope would there be for a fair trial? Never trust a *Gaje,* her mother had been fond of telling her. At least not with anything important.

It wasn't always the easiest advice to follow. Ola knew the *Gaje* were *marhime* and on the whole held no good will towards her people, but there were exceptions, weren't there? Like Jeff. She hadn't trusted him with everything—he didn't know she was a Rom, for one thing—but on the other hand, what trust she had put in him had never been betrayed. He was attractive, too, in a big boyish way, and sometimes when she felt him watching her, when he thought she wasn't looking . . .

Ola sighed. Her mother had died in poverty in Toronto—a widow, with no one to look after her but the gangly teenager that Ola had been at the time. Those were not the easy years, especially as Ola had been forced to deal with both puberty and the arrival of her *dook* by herself. Her mother had been sick, broken by her husband's death and the weight of the city's indifference. Too proud to seek help from other Rom, she'd deteriorated rapidly. Ola, confused at the double changes in her body, had been too scared to go to other Rom herself and *Gaje* were out of the question. She was sure that her *dook* was a madness that had lodged in her and her monthly period was God's curse for some unfathomable sin that she wasn't even aware of having committed. It wasn't until after her mother's death, when she met the *drabarni* known as Pivli Gozzle—the Widow of Goose Hill—that she learned to come to terms with what she was: a woman and a *drabarni* herself.

"Loneliness and responsibility—those are the burdens of a *drabarni*," Pivli had told her once. "Our *dook* has few rewards, child, but in time you'll come to understand, as I did, that you would sooner give up life itself than to lose it."

She lived with the old woman for only a month, but that month was long enough to set her on the road to acquiring knowledge that she still followed. She met other Rom then and spent long evenings and afternoons talking to the old men and women, learning the old skills and stories. A chance meeting with an editor who was preparing a book on herbal lore and legends gave her an outlet for her knowledge, as well as a means of living that didn't include the poverty that had killed her mother.

Those years of trying to survive in Toronto's slums were never far from Ola's thoughts. Remembering them was what kept her balancing between the worlds of the *Gaje* and the Rom as she did. Before her father had died, life had been different. They'd traveled in the old *vurdon* from country to country in Europe and Asia, and if her mother had nothing else when she died, she had at least the memories of those times and the good man who'd been her husband. While Ola . . . She met few Gypsies because her gift set a distance between her and them that was almost as wide as the one that lay between the *Gaje* and herself. She knew the loneliness that Pivli had spoken of all too well.

A few years ago she had met the old woman again, in Rommeville, while she and Jeff were on a promotional tour for their newest book. Ola had slipped away and shared an afternoon of tea in a small restaurant on the Lower East Side with the old *drabarni,* an afternoon of talk and understanding that flew by all too quickly. "We are Moshto's last defense against the evils of *o Beng,*" Pivli told her as they left the restaurant. "Let that knowledge sustain you against the loneliness, sister. For in the end, it is all we have."

She hadn't seen the old woman since that day, but Pivli's advice stayed with her. It helped to balance the confusion she felt as she weighed the world of the *Gaje* and her own people and tried to understand where she fit in. And it was what would keep her in this area as well. Her *dook* told her that Mulengro would come for her. From what she had seen of him, he could well be *o Beng* himself, but whatever he was, it was the responsibility of one such as her to stand against him. How she would do that, her *dook* hadn't troubled to show her. She only knew it must be done. The Rom had not come to her, and she could not go to them. But Mulengro would come. She need only wait and be prepared for him.

She stood up and swung her pack onto her back, wearing a sense of determination that was almost as much put on as Boboko's sulking had been. Talk was easy. When she thought of Mulengro, of the power she saw that he could wield . . . Boboko regarded her with a suspicious look in his eyes.

"You were serious, weren't you?" he asked.

"About what?"

"The walking—*and* on an empty stomach."

Ola smiled and some of her misgivings drained away. Trust Boboko to bring everything down to the most basic levels.

"As I recall," she said, "you invited yourself along."

"Yes, well that was before I understood just how much walking was involved. And there was *never* any discussion about fasting."

Ola picked him up and started off. "I think I liked you better when you were mysterious and profound—and quiet," she told him. "If the Egyptians had had to listen to your complaining, I doubt very much that they would have worshipped cats."

"It's hard to be mysterious and profound on an empty stomach," Boboko replied. He squirmed into a more comfortable position. "Where are we going now? Deeper into the marsh? Maybe we could live at the bottom of a lake—*no one* would look for us there."

"I could just let you wade along behind me."

Boboko peered down from her arms to study the soggy ground. "It's the water that does it, you know," he said. "It affects my kind differently than it does yours. Sucks away our vitality, our . . . our . . ."

"Dignity?"

"Well, that too. *Have* we got a course planned, or are we just going to wander aimlessly until the winter comes?"

"I thought we could try the bush south of Bass Lake. There's a fairly large section of land down that way that's hardly built up at all."

"Bass Lake?" Boboko repeated, liking the fishy sound of the name. He had very little conception of distances, having lived the whole of his short life around Rideau Ferry. Ola had inherited him from the cottage's previous tenant. "What's it like there?"

"Dry, for one thing."

"Already I like it."

The afternoon was half gone by the time they reached the area that Ola had been thinking of. They were perhaps a half mile east of Canton Lake—a tiny piece of water due east of Murphy's Point on the Big Rideau. The stretch of countryside they were traveling through rose and fell gently in long slopes of cedar and pine, birch and trembling aspen. Boboko was faring under his own steam a few paces ahead of Ola, his calico coloring blending into the riot of ground cover, striped tail lifting from the grass and weeds like a periscope, complete with a kink in its end. Suddenly the tail went stiff and he stopped to peer ahead, one forepaw lifted in the air and his neck craned to see above the grass.

"Ola, what was—" he began.

"Did you hear that?" she asked at the same time.

Before they could think of hiding, a man came out of the forest at the far side of the field and saw them. He paused as well, then started over to where they were. Boboko glanced back at Ola to see what she thought they should do, but she simply shrugged and decided to wait it out. To run off now would only attract more attention than they might if they stood their ground. She was a hiker, nothing more. As the man came nearer, she began to wonder at her own wisdom.

He was a tall gangly individual, all arms and legs, wearing a pair of faded jeans that were patched with a motley assortment of different pieces of patterned cloth and frayed at the cuffs. His feet were bare and all that covered his chest was a fringed buckskin vest with a small button on it that read in fading letters: "Make love, not war." A thin scraggly beard hung halfway down his chest, his waist-length hair was tied in a ponytail at the nape of his neck and a bright red and yellow scarf was tied around his forehead. Perched on the end of his nose was a pair of square-rimmed glasses—the kind that were called Granny glasses, popular in the sixties. He nodded in a friendly way to Ola, then saw Boboko and a big smile formed, half-hidden by his beard.

"O wow," he said. "Nice cat." He bent down to pat Boboko who backed up a few steps until he was almost on top of Ola's shoes. The man glanced at Ola. "What do you call him?"

"I call myself Boboko," Boboko said, forgetting Ola's continual warnings that he wasn't supposed to speak around other people.

Ola held her breath and glared at Boboko. This wasn't the way to pass by unnoticed, her angry look told him. But she needn't have worried. The man's smile grew wider as he stood up.

"Far out! He can talk."

Ola nodded, not knowing what to make of this strange leftover from the sixties who'd appeared out of nowhere. "He . . . he does that sometimes," she said lamely.

"No shit? Did you teach him?"

"You could say that. Do you live around here?"

"What? Oh, sure. I'm Dr. Rainbow," he said, as though that explained everything. When Ola regarded him blankly, he added: "You know, like in Dr. Rainbow's Magic Dulcimers."

"Oh." Ola looked down at Boboko, who rolled his eyes at her. "You make instruments, then?"

"Sure do. You want to see 'em?"

"Well . . ."

"It's not, like, far or anything." He bent down to eye Boboko from a closer vantage once more. "What do you think, kid? Think you could go for a saucer of milk or something?"

Boboko regarded the man as though he was a lunatic.

"Do you live by yourself?" Ola asked.

"What? Oh, yeah. I've got a place on a lake back there." He stood up and negligently waved his hand back in the direction he'd come from. When Ola remained silent, a worried look came into his eyes. "Like, it'd be nothing heavy or anything. I know what you're think-ing: Who's this guy tripping around the woods like some spaced-out elf—right? But, hey, it's nice out here. I like to hang out and catch some forest vibes, that's all. World's a crazy place, so you gotta catch what sanity you can. Place like this, it's long on the real—a natural high, you know? Used to be like this everywhere till we went crazy with the concrete." He grinned ruefully. "Guess I'm babbling. I don't see many folks around and it gets a little lonely sometimes. It's just that you seemed like a nice person, you know, and . . ." His voice trailed off and he shrugged.

Ola smiled. Her *dook* told her there was nothing to fear from this man who seemed so gentle, even if he was out-of-synch with the rest of the world. "My name's Ola," she said, "and I'd love to see your place."

"No shit?" His whole face, or at least what wasn't hidden by his beard, beamed. "Wow. That's great."

At Ola's feet, Boboko sighed. Ola reached down and hoisted him into her arms, deliberately ignoring the pained look in his features.

"Does everyone call you Dr. Rainbow?" she asked.

"No. That's just, like, a name I made up." Really? Boboko thought. What a surprise. "My real name's Zachary Acheson—but my friends just call me Zach. I used to be in a band, you know. We played this sort of medieval music but on American instruments. Anyway, we all took these nicknames that had a kind of Englishy feel to them and mine was Nobb then. But I like Zach best myself. What do you think of it?"

"I think I like it, Zach."

"It's Hebrew, you know. Means 'God has remembered.' Say, are you an Aquarius?"

Ola shook her head.

Zach grinned. "Neither am I. Come on, I'll show you my place." He set off and Ola fell in step beside him. "Is Ola, like, a nickname?" he asked.

"No. It's the one my parents gave me."

"Really? That's far out. What kind of nationality is it? Italian?"

"Sort of."

Zach nodded to himself as he digested that. "When I saw you in the middle of the field, you know what I flashed on? That song about the Gypsies in the greenwood-o. Don't know why."

Ola regarded him from the corner of her eye, surprised. There was an air about him, she realized, that gave her the impression that he might have something like the *dook* himself.

"What do you think of Gypsies?" she asked.

"Well, like, I've never met one or anything, but I think they're pretty neat. What about you? Do you know any?"

"One or two."

"No shit? Wow. What're they like?"

She smiled, wondering where to begin and how much to tell him. In her arms, Boboko settled mournfully, certain he was going to regret ever having left Rideau Ferry.

"It's not far now," Zach said as he led them out of the forest onto a narrow dirt road. It twisted through the woods, tire tracks deeply gouged into its uneven surface. They followed the road until it gave way to a grassy track that led straight through long rows of planted spruce trees. Looking ahead, Ola could see that the track disappeared down a rise. With the straight lines of the spruce on either side of them, it felt like walking down a corridor. When they reached the spot where the track dipped, Ola let out a little cry of pleasure. Below her was a small cottage, white-walled with green trim and a dark shingled roof. To its left was a smaller one-room building, on the right a set of swings and a tipi. Beyond the cottage, the land dropped quickly, but through the trees, there was a breathtaking view of the lake. She could see no other buildings on the shore from where she stood, just the greens of the forested hills beyond the lake, and the mottled browns of the reeds and bulrushes on the far shore.

"It's called Mill Pond," Zach said. "There's only six other cottages on it, over that way—" he waved to the right "—and all the rest is a Conservation Area so, like, there'll never be anybody else building here. What do you think?"

"It's beautiful," Ola said. "So private."

"Oh, yes," Boboko murmured. He squirmed in her arms until she let him down. "Far out," he added, mimicking Zach's voice.

Zach glanced at him, missing the sarcasm, and grinned. "For sure. I'm glad you like it."

Boboko sighed and headed on down the steep incline that led to the cottage below. Ola stood drinking in the view for a moment longer, then she and Zach followed the cat. She'd been surprised at her first view of the cottage and its property. It hadn't been nearly as hippy-dippy as she'd expected it to be—considering its owner. But as she made her way down the slope, details she'd missed earlier came into focus. There was a beat-up old Volkswagen bug parked beside what she supposed was the tool shed. Hanging on the side of the shed was a great wooden mask, easily four feet high, brightly painted, with woven reeds for hair that hung like a Rastaman's dreadlocks to either side of the mask's primitive features. Beyond the tipi was a large vegetable garden. Painted on the side of the cottage facing the garden was a huge yellow sun, complete with facial features and rays that streaked to the edges of the walls. Carved into the front door was a peace symbol. It reminded Ola of the welcoming *patrin* of her own people. Once they stepped inside, she had no more doubts that her new friend was a holdover from the days of flower power and be-ins.

The walls were decorated with posters from that bygone era advertising appearances by the Grateful Dead, Jefferson Airplane, the Lovin' Spoonful, Donovan. A gray fishnet hung from the ceiling in sweeping dips and folds. There were shells in its netting, dried flowers and the skeleton of a starfish. The furnishings were comprised of a sofa near the cast-iron stove, a worktable with a scatter of woodworking tools and some half-finished instruments upon it, and a wooden kitchen table with three chairs. Above the worktable hung a half-dozen completed dulcimers. A macrame owl hung on the door leading to the porch overlooking the lake.

"Want some tea?" Zach asked. He watched her reaction to his home with pleasure.

She nodded. "I'd love some. This place is incredible. It's like the sixties never ended."

"Well, in a way they didn't—for me anyway. There were some good things went down then, you know, and maybe other folks changed, but I couldn't. I never found anything better, you see?"

He went to the kitchen that was just off the long main room. A corridor ran along it, leading to a bathroom and a couple of bedrooms. There were posters here as well—psychedelic art that spoke of love-ins, The Fillmore East, The Riverboat in Toronto's old Yorkville. While Zach put on the water, Ola wandered into the living room. There was a small stereo perched on a couple of apple crates and a collection of records that took up three plastic milk crates. Ola smiled as she glanced at the albums. Jimi Hendrix. The

Doors. The Nazgul. The Incredible String Band. Dr. Strangely Strange. The Electric Prunes. She'd been aware of much of this in a peripheral sense. It was something that teenaged *Gaje* went through, but it had still fascinated her when it was all happening. Beside the sofa, she discovered a bookcase made of wooden planks laid on stacked bricks. Tolkien's *Lord of the Rings* was there. Kahlil Gibran's *The Prophet*. Books on instrument building and gardening. Orwell's *Animal Farm*. A book of poetry by Dylan Thomas. Another by Bob Dylan. Then she had to laugh.

"What's so funny?" Zach asked her.

Ola plucked a book from the case and held it up so he could see the cover. It was called *A Herbal Garden* by Kerio Rouge and Jeff Owen.

"Hey, that's a good book," Zach said. "I got the recipe for this tea out of it, I'll have you know. Did you ever read it?"

"Often," Ola told him, her eyes sparkling with humor.

"A friend of mine told me that Jeff Owen was born up around Smiths Falls—did you know that? And he lives just outside of Perth now. Far out, eh?"

Boboko wandered in from his exploration of the bedrooms and looked from Zach to Ola. "Oh, no," he said when he saw the book Ola was holding. "Another fan."

Zach pushed his glasses up higher on his nose. "What do you mean?" he asked.

"She wrote it," Boboko explained in a bored voice and proceeded to clean his shoulder.

Zach's eyes went wide. "No shit? *You're* Kerio Rouge?"

Ola nodded. "It's the name I write under—like you use Dr. Rainbow for your dulcimers."

"Far out. Hey, would you autograph it for me?"

Ola smiled. "I think the water's boiling."

"What? Oh, yeah. Don't move. I'll be right back."

Ola laid the book down on top of the makeshift bookshelf and went into the kitchen to see if she could give him a hand. She knew it was nothing more than coincidence that had him serving her tea immediately. It was a Gypsy custom and he was a *Gajo,* even if he did use as many names as a Rom would, so it had to be a coincidence, but she couldn't help feeling more comfortable because of it. It was just possible, she realized, that she might have found the haven she'd been looking for.

sixteen

The Lees lived in a trailer camp off Highway 4, about a mile or so east of Perth. Janfri's Chevy bounced in the ruts of the long laneway as he left the highway and drove the half mile to the camp. It was close to seven o'clock and he was tired, having spent the better part of the afternoon cruising the back roads of Lanark County, not really sure what he was looking for, just driving and thinking. He'd been waiting for an inspiration, stopping at a few general stores in Franktown, Munster and the like, asking circumspect questions that led him nowhere. A young girl in one had thought he was trying to pick her up and called her dad out from the storerooms to have him thrown out. An old geezer in another was sure that Janfri was trying to sell him some insurance and kept telling him that it "didn't make no never mind—no one to leave the money to anyway, son." Most of the time, people simply regarded him blankly, not sure what he meant by a "gifted" woman or a card reader. One man in Armstrongs Corners gave him the address of a woman named Lucy in Harper who turned out to be willing to give him a few favors for "two twenties and a five—but nothing kinky, you understand?"

He parked the Chevy in between the Lees' VW van and an old Dodge Sedan. Tibo and Ursula were sitting on the steps of their trailer. Tibo was a thin wiry man whose walrus mustache looked big enough to throw him off balance when he stood up. He wore a white shirt that had seen better days and baggy flannel pants that were rolled up at the cuffs so they wouldn't drag. His sister was bigger than him by a good four inches and thirty pounds. She wore the traditional low-cut blouse of a Gypsy woman but eschewed the pleated skirt in favor of trousers as baggy as her brother's and smoked a meerschaum pipe.

"*Sarishan,* Boshengro," Tibo said when Janfri stepped out of his car and approached the steps. Ursula smiled around her pipe and stood to fetch a cup of tea from a pot that was warming on a Coleman stove set up on a card table beside the trailer.

"*Sarishan,*" Janfri replied. He tugged a rickety lawn chair over to the steps and sat down.

There was no further conversation until Ursula had served Janfri his tea. He drank it slowly, savoring the sweet dark taste of it. When he finally set the empty cup down by the legs of his chair, Tibo cleared his throat.

"You'll be eating with us?" he asked.

"With pleasure."

"Good, good." The small man's head bobbed. "We don't get many guests out this way."

Janfri looked around the camp. "It's very peaceful here," he said.

Tibo shrugged. "Too quiet, sometimes. But today I'm glad of it. They're all gone now?"

"Stevo left this morning. Marko and Big George this afternoon. I think you'll have to dig hard to find a Rom closer to Ottawa than Deschenes or Gatineau now."

"*Prikaza* times," Ursula said. "It must make *o Beng* smile to see this lack of Gypsy luck."

Janfri nodded. Tibo tugged at his mustache.

"And you?" he asked. "You're traveling, too? I thought you'd be with Yojo."

"No. I've business here."

"Ah." There was a moment's silence. "Shall we play a hand or two of cards before dinner?" Tibo asked.

Janfri smiled. "And lose what little money I have?" Throughout the Gypsy communities, Tibo Lee was a man known to have too much luck with cards.

"But you are a guest!" Tibo said with a shocked look on his face. "We will not play for money."

"A hand or two then."

After dinner they sat drinking black *kafa,* heavily sweetened with honey. It was almost dark now and Ursula lit a small kerosene lamp that she placed on the hood of the Dodge. Mosquitos hummed in the night air and pale moths threw themselves against the glass sides of the lamp.

"How can we help you?" Tibo asked, referring to Janfri's business for the first time since he'd arrived.

"I'm not sure if you can," Janfri replied and proceeded to tell them of his talk with Old Lyuba the previous night. They all shifted uncomfortably when the talk turned to the being she'd named Mulengro and ghosts. The night seemed to draw closer around them and the chorusing crickets and bullfrogs in the fields around the camp no longer seemed as loud. Martiya the night spirit might be near them now, overhearing their talk, a grin stretching his toadlike face wide and a clawed hand opening and closing at his side. Ursula shivered though the night wasn't that cool and drew her shawl closer around her. Tibo shifted the position of his feet more than once. When he was finished, Janfri showed them the scrap of paper he'd found on Lyuba's porch with the *patteran* penciled on it. Tibo and Ursula exchanged uneasy glances.

"Do you know who it could be?" Janfri asked. "Is it the daughter of this Pika Faher?"

Ursula shook her head. "It's your story itself that makes us uneasy, Boshengro."

"I know," Janfri replied. "The more I drove around this afternoon, the stupider it seemed to me. But now, with the night around us . . ."

A long silence followed that Ursula filled by topping their *kafa* mugs once more. When she was done, she sat down beside her brother and filled her pipe. She tamped the tobacco with her finger and stared out into the night, not turning her attention to Janfri again until she had the pipe lit. Blue-gray smoke wreathed around her head when she finally spoke.

"This is not woman's *draba,"* she said.

"I know nothing of magic," Janfri replied. "I'm not sure I even believe in it."

"It is the times." Ursula sighed. "And you have lived with the *Gaje* a great deal, Boshengro. But some things I remember and others remember. There is a great deal in the world that no one can explain. A great deal. But a man who can call the *mule* to his bidding . . . such a thing I have never heard of."

"And there is no one you can think of—no *drabarni* in the area such as the one Lyuba wanted to send me to?"

"No one," Ursula said.

"No Rom," Tibo offered. He glanced at his sister. "But there's that boy . . . Jeff Owen. The writer."

"A man?" Janfri asked.

Ursula was nodding her head. "The Owen boy writes books on herbal cures and lore and they contain some Gypsy remedies and the like. He writes them with a black woman—an African, I heard. But I have never met her."

"Does she live nearby?"

"In the Ferry—Rideau Ferry."

"What's her name?"

"Something French—Rouge, I think." Ursula frowned. "But why would Lyuba send you to her?"

"Perhaps because she knows Gypsy lore," Janfri said.

Ursula's frown deepened. "Only the Rom can know that."

"I should still talk to her."

"Perhaps."

"But not tonight," Tibo said. "I'll take you into Perth tomorrow. The people at Tinkers Restaurant know Jeff Owen and can introduce you to him, and he in turn can introduce you to this woman. It would be better that way."

Janfri nodded. "Rouge," he repeated. "What's her first name?"

"I don't know," Ursula said. "But I don't see how she could help you. A *Gaji* can pretend at *draba* enough to fool her own people, but what can she truly know?"

Janfri looked away into the darkness surrounding the pool of light that the kerosene lamp threw. "I suppose I'll find out tomorrow," he said.

"*Bater,*" Ursula replied with a faint smile.

seventeen

Memories and ghosts followed Briggs home that night. Victims, he thought. We're all victims. Some of us just hang in a little longer. But the others . . . the ghost of a dead Gypsy rose in his mind's eye . . . an eighty-year-old woman, beaten and raped by muggers . . . a shopkeeper, machettied because he tried to hang onto the lousy forty bucks or so he had in his till . . . a four-year-old kid lured into some stranger's car, found weeks later in a ditch. The ghosts followed him into his apartment building and up the stairs, ugly ghosts that haunted him, that wouldn't stop their demands for justice, a justice he couldn't give them. For every one man the courts put behind bars, at least four others walked free. Guilty as hell, but they walked free all the same. Inadmissible evidence. Insufficient evidence. There was always some legal double-talk that let them walk.

Briggs balanced the pizza he'd brought with him in one hand as he got his key in the lock, turned it and pushed the door open with his foot. His ghosts crowded by him, filling the room. Sighing, Briggs laid the pizza down on the kitchen table, no longer hungry. Instead, he got a beer from the fridge. Going into the living room, he switched on the TV and sat watching it without the sound on. He thought about Cleary, still in a holding cell. About the hookers, especially the kid. She might be all of eighteen, but it was still one hell of a stupid career choice. And then there was this thing with the Gypsies. It was starting to get to him as well. They were gone now, all of them. Ottawa's invisible Gypsy community had just packed up and disappeared, and no one, not even he, would have known the difference if he hadn't been out there looking for them himself.

"Historically," Will had told him before they left the station to-night, "that's how they've always reacted to a stressful situation. They withdraw from it. All the books say the same thing—and so does Castleman. Seems a Gypsy prefers to use his wits instead of his fists. They've got a memory that goes back a long time. If they've been wronged, they get back. But not physically."

Briggs had nodded, remembering his own limited experience with them in the sixties. They weren't anything like the braves fresh from the reserves who were just spoiling for a fight, looking to prove something. No, the Gypsies just talked smooth and backed away, and then came back and hit you in the pocketbook or in your pride. Not that there hadn't been a knifing or two back in those days. There just hadn't ever been a Gypsy they could pin it on.

So they were gone. But what about whoever had killed two of them here and God knows how many more across the country? All they had to go on was that it was a man who wore black, who maybe had scars, or maybe a mask. And fog that seemed to follow him. Right. And their only witnesses so far were an old wino and a couple of hookers. Great. Which left them basically pissing in the wind. Except that his and Will's caseload was backing up and nothing was getting done. There'd been the bank job downtown on Monday, and a couple of Johns roughed up by pimps in the Market. Didn't matter how pretty they made the renovations in that area, it was going to be a long time before the Market got cleaned up. A woman hitchhiker who was raped and robbed before being dumped on Baseline. The Inspector had made it plain to both Will and himself before they'd left the station tonight that he wanted the Gypsy case filed away because he had taxpayers to look after, and who really gave a shit about what happened to a couple of transients anyway? Yeah. Right.

He was into his second beer when the phone rang. He jumped, staring at it for a long moment before he answered it. It was going to be bad news, he knew. His ghosts stirred, making him uneasy. It was always bad news when his phone rang. It could've been differ-ent if he'd been a car salesman like the guy Francine married. Then maybe it would be one of his neighbors inviting them over for a barbecue, or one of the girls looking for a ride home from ballet class or something. A third ring jarred him out of his reverie and he hooked the receiver up and under his ear.

"Yeah?"

"Paddy? This is Chris. I think you'd better get down here."

Briggs' pulse quickened. "What happened?" he demanded. The police officer hesitated on the other end of the line and a hundred ugly images went through his head. Will. Something had happened to Will. . . .

"It's Cleary," Officer Provost said. "Your pet wino. He's dead, Paddy."

"Who turned him loose?"

"No one did. He just keeled over in his cell about fifteen minutes ago."

Briggs took half a moment to digest that. Then he said, "I'll be right down," and hung up. He was out the door before Provost had a chance to cradle his receiver on the other end of the line.

In death, Cleary looked more pathetic than he had alive, Briggs thought as he looked down at the wino's emaciated corpse. The coroner drew a sheet over the body and Briggs blinked, finally looking away. He moved from the operating table and dug his pipe out of his pocket. Chewing on the stem, he turned to Cooper.

"Run it by me again," he said.

Cooper sighed. "His heart collapsed, Briggs."

"And this happened—how?"

"Damned if I know. The cardiac muscle of the walls is all bruised. The atria and ventricles show signs of slight bruising. The mitral and tricuspid valves were mashed shut. The superior vena cava and aorta . . ." His voice trailed off and he stared at the sheet-draped corpse. "It's like no case of cardiac arrest I've ever seen, Briggs. Death came instantaneously, but what actually caused the damage I just can't explain. It's like someone just grabbed his heart and crushed it."

"In a holding cell in the middle of headquarters?"

"I said 'like'—meaning 'as if.' He didn't have any exterior bruising except for where he hit his head when he collapsed—and I'd stake my reputation that he was already dead before he hit the floor. I'm writing 'cardiac arrest' under cause of death and I'm leaving it like that. And do me a favor, Briggs, would you? Next time you call me up in the middle of the night, make sure it's for something simple—like someone getting knifed or gunned down, okay?"

Briggs nodded. He knew Cooper didn't mean it. The just plain weirdness of the past few nights was getting to him, too.

"Thanks for coming down," Briggs said. "I didn't want to leave this to one of your assistants."

"Did he have something to do with these two Gypsies?"

Briggs nodded. "He was a witness."

"Well, if you've got any more, I'd check up on them, Briggs. Christ knows what's going on, but if I were you, I'd be worrying about *them* now—not this stiff."

"Yeah, well, thanks again, Peter."

"Anytime, Briggs."

The first thing he'd do, Briggs thought as he made his way back up to his desk, was give Will another call. He'd taken Sharon out for dinner. Briggs glanced at his watch. Going on to ten. Maybe Will would be back by now. He wasn't going to appreciate another night call, but it came with the territory. And after that, Briggs thought, he'd try the numbers he had for the two hookers, though there wasn't much chance that either of them would be in. They'd be out on the street at this time of night.

It was dark outside by the time Tracy left her apartment. She was terrified of meeting that man in black, of thinking that he might be out there, waiting for her. If only they could have played it cool last night—not taking off like a couple of kids who'd got caught shoplifting or something. Then the cops wouldn't have picked them up and nobody, *nobody*'d know what they'd seen or hadn't seen last night. The word had probably gone up and down the street by now, about how they'd gotten picked up for questioning about the murder. If that man in black wanted to make sure that they didn't stool on him . . . Because Tracy had lied to the police last night. She'd recognize that face again. No way she wouldn't.

By the time she reached the foyer of Carol's building she was ready to just take off—to hell with her pimp, the cops, the man in black . . . to hell with everything. She just wanted to run. But there was nowhere to run to.

Carol's apartment was on the second floor. She knocked on the door a couple of times and when there was no immediate answer, tried the knob. The door swung open under her hand, but it was dark inside.

"Hey, Carol?" she called.

Carol had to be here—they'd agreed to meet at her place tonight before they went to work. Puzzled, Tracy stepped inside, fumbling along the wall for a light switch. Maybe Carol had taken off, like she wanted to herself. Her fingers found the switch and flicked it on. Light flared in the room and Tracy's purse dropped from her hand. Carol was lying sprawled on the living room floor, her mouth agape, eyes staring blindly at the ceiling. Mist was wreathing around her still body, thickening into wiry tendrils that came snaking across the floor towards Tracy.

"Oh, Jesus," she mumbled, backing away. Her throat was dry with fear, her pulse hammering. The fog continued to thicken as it neared her. Now it began to take a vague shape as it rose upward from the floor. A shape that was almost a man's. . . .

Tracy screamed and bolted out into the hall. She started for the stairwell she'd come up, skidded to a stop when she saw the tall man there, dressed in black, walking towards her with his familiar gait—stiff-backed and determined. The scarred face smiled at her. For one long frozen moment she stared at him, trapped by the mad glint in his pale eyes, then she turned and ran the other way down the hall.

● ● ●

"Hell of a thing," Will said as he settled in the chair beside Briggs' desk.

"I'm sorry to bust up your evening," Briggs said, "but I figured you'd want to be in on this."

Will nodded. "You said on the phone that Cleary died of a heart attack, but there was something weird about it?"

Briggs explained, then tapped the book he'd been reading when Will came in. "They talk about medicine murder in here—did you get that far?"

"Yeah—works like voodoo, doesn't it?" Will moved his chair closer, frowning. "But the victim had to believe that it worked. Are you trying to tell me that Cleary believed some voodoo man put a spell on him and that's why he keeled over?"

Briggs tapped the book with his pipe again. "In here it says the victim doesn't have to believe for the magic to work."

Will regarded him for a long moment. "Are you saying you believe in this stuff, Paddy?" he asked finally.

"Christ, I don't know what I think anymore. All I know is, Cleary saw our man and just maybe could've made him in a lineup. And now he's dead."

"I can't buy it, Paddy."

"I'm not saying that *I* do. But something weird's going down and I'm at the point where I'll give anything serious consideration. I'm thinking of going around to one of the African embassies to see if I can find someone who'll tell us a little more about these cat cults."

"They'll laugh you out the door."

"Maybe. Unless we happen to hit one that's involved in this."

Will shook his head. "It doesn't work, Paddy. There's no reason for them to be killing Gypsies in the first place."

"That's only because we don't know *why* they're being killed."

"I suppose." Will knew as well as his partner that once they had a motive they were often more than halfway to solving the case. "Did you get a hold of our two ladies of the night?"

"I tried calling the numbers that they left us, but there was no answer, so I've got a couple of uniforms keeping an eye out for

them. I thought I'd wait for you before I took a run down to the
Market myself."

"Okay. Let's get going."

"Just let me try calling them one more time," Briggs said.

Tracy reached the door at the far end of the hall and tore it open.
She chanced a quick look over her shoulder, hesitated when she saw
that the man in black had paused in Carol's doorway, ignoring her.
But then, as though he felt her gaze on him, he turned and those
mad eyes were burning into her again. The muscles in her legs
turned to water and she didn't think she'd be able to even take a
step, little say flee. The man's eyes held her, dominated her will,
sapped the strength from her limbs. She could feel her legs starting
to give way under her. In another moment she'd be sprawled in the
hall—like Carol had been sprawled in her apartment—and the
fog . . . the mist . . . whatever it was . . . would be upon her.

The phone rang in Carol's apartment and the man turned his
head, freeing Tracy from his spell. She turned to go through the
door, but suddenly the fog was all around her. She batted at it, a
scream frozen in her throat. The fog gave way under her hands and
she started to move, but then she saw the eyes staring at her from out
of its misty tendrils—eyes like those of the man in black, but even
less human. The scream finally made its way free of her throat, only
there was something wrong with it. It came out in a wheezing gurgle. She lifted a hand to her neck and it came away wet with her
own blood. The last thing she thought as she went tumbling into
darkness was that she hadn't even felt the blow that had torn her
throat open.

Briggs stood over the body on the landing, looking down at it. He
saw a lot of things in the young hooker's corpse. Francine's features.
The kid herself—not a bad kid, just stupid. And not just that kid, but
all the ones like her who thought they were going for an easy ride

until it all came home. Maybe not so bad as this. Maybe worse. Maybe it was easier to be dead than to go through some things.

He had a dry burning behind his eyes and his chest was tight with emotion. His hands were thrust deep in his trousers' pockets, bulging against the cloth as they shaped fists. The ghosts of all the dead and the hurt and the hopeless that he'd had to confront were stirring in him again. Will approached him from Carol Wesley's doorway and laid a hand on his shoulder.

"She never had a chance," Briggs said. "Not even to lift her hands to try to protect herself like the others did."

Will nodded. "Wesley's dead, too. She's like Cleary—not a mark on her."

Briggs turned slowly until he was facing his partner. "Still think it's garbage, Will? This medicine murder shit?"

"Jesus, Paddy. I don't know. . . ."

"Well, I know this," Briggs said. "I'm going to burn this fucker when we catch up with him."

Will took his arm. "Let's go, Paddy."

Briggs pulled his arm free and looked down at Tracy's body again. "We could've stopped this from happening. We could've held them—kept them off the street."

"We did that with Cleary, Paddy."

Briggs looked up, then nodded slowly. "Yeah, and we didn't do so shit-hot with him either, did we? Let's get out of here, Will."

He led the way down the hall and didn't look back.

eighteen

"See, sometimes I just *know* things," Zach said after dinner. "It's like the wind talks to me or something."

They were sitting in the screened-in porch overlooking the lake, with the lights all off in the cottage behind them. Zach was in an old pine rocker that creaked softly as it moved back and forth on the

hardwood floor. Ola was curled up on a beat-up sofa nearby, with
Boboko drowsing on her lap. Bullfrogs and crickets, with the occa-
sional mournful cry of a loon from the lake, provided a backdrop to
Zach's soft voice as he spoke.

"The Indians used to call the wind the voice of the manitous," he
said. "They're, like, the little mysteries. And since the wind can go
everywhere and knows everything, if you can tune into its vibes,
you end up *knowing* things too. It can get a little spooky, and it
doesn't always come when you want it, but it's still pretty far-out to
really know that there's more out there than what you can pick up
in your hand or touch—you know what I mean?"

Ola nodded, smiling in the darkness, enjoying the sound of
Zach's voice and his easy acceptance of her. She found herself liking
him with a surprising intensity. He wasn't like any *Gaje,* or even any
Rom, that she knew. Just a good man, living a simple life. An old
hippy who'd found what he wanted out of life and stuck with it
while the rest of the world rushed on. And he had the *sight.* She
wondered if he heard words in the call of the loon from the lake, if
the wood that he shaped with his tools took its lines directly from his
thoughts as much as from his hands.

"Now take yourself," Zach said. "I knew this morning when I
woke up that I'd be, like, meeting you. Well, not you personally, but
someone with your vibes. That's why I was out in the woods when
we met. And you know, I could *feel* the forest enjoying your walking
through it. It was like the trees knew you, knew that you're a . . ."

His voice trailed off. *Drabarni* hovered on the tip of Ola's tongue.
She settled for a more easily understood term that didn't require as
much explanation. It surprised her that she was volunteering the
information at all.

"A witch?" she asked.

Zach blinked and pushed his glasses up with a long finger. "Now,
I would've said someone who just *knows* a little more than most,
like, a medicine lady. Because of the books you write—but that's
knowledge after the fact." He paused before adding: "*Are* you a
witch?"

"Sort of."

"Wow."

His voice was still soft. Ola could feel his gaze on her in the darkness, the curiosity in him that he was too polite, or too understanding, to voice. She stroked Boboko's fur and looked away across the
water. There was something in the air that made her want to share
her life with someone else—to put into words what she was and
what she had been. "Where she was coming from," as Zach would
have put it.

She knew that he already knew she was a Gypsy—his own *dook*
had shown him that much. She wanted to confirm that verbally, to
add to it, to explain as she never had before—not to other Rom, not
to Jeff, not to anyone but to Boboko and Pivli Gozzle, who already
knew because she was a *drabarni* herself. Ola didn't understand where
the impulse came from. Perhaps the night had bewitched her. Or
Zach himself had with his gentle spaciness. But she found herself
talking about the Rom and her parents, about what being a *drabarni*
meant, about the gifts it gave her, but the loneliness as well. She
voiced her confusion about being unable to live with her own people, but how she couldn't let herself grow close to the *Gaje* either,
because the code of *marhime* was too ingrained in her basic makeup.

Zach listened quietly without interrupting. He rocked back and
forth in his chair, not looking at her, but listening. They both
watched the lake and it was as though she was speaking to its still
water and the moonlight and the words were reflecting back so that
he could hear them. It was only when she began to speak of her
most recent visions, of Mulengro and the old woman's death, that
the rocker went still. Zach leaned forward then, still watching the
water, but his lips tightened as he shared her pain. His hands gripped
the arms of the rocker, knuckles whitening when she spoke of
returning to her body, of the man she'd killed, of how she'd fled her
home, not really knowing where she was going or what she was
going to do, just knowing she had to get away.

When she finally ended her tale, they both sat in silence. Ola
stroked Boboko fiercely, wondering why she'd ever opened her
mouth in the first place. It was an act of pure madness. She was
embarrassed and frightened at what she had done. The whole point

in fleeing had been so that no one would *know*. But now . . . oh, now . . .

Zach started rocking again, slow and steady. "Now I know why you're here," he said finally. "There's something about this area—the lake and the land around it—that's like a haven. I'm not hiding from skyscrapers and parking lots and the craziness of the rest of the world by living here year round. I'm just, like, getting closer to the real world.

"I'm talking about things like the smell of the woods after a rain, or a peek at one of those big herons gliding down over the lake to settle in their colony. Tracking a fox for miles on snowshoes—not with a gun, but just to see what old Reynard's up to. There are vibes here like you wouldn't believe. Sitting out on a summer's night and listening to the hum of the June bugs, the bullfrogs holding parliament down by the stream that's fed by the lake—lake's spring-fed itself, you know, and that stream carries the runoff water down into Britton Bay. Or just watching the flit of bats as they go hunting skeeters and black flies.

"There's something here that we were all looking for in the sixties. And right here it's been distilled down until the vibes are so pure that, if you've got a heart, you're going to feel the real—you know?

"I've got a piece of paper that says I own my land here—but the government gave me that. The land didn't. I figure that I'm, like, just a caretaker. Looking after things. Keeping the vibes pure. Keeping the place holy.

"Now that kind of talk embarrasses a lot of people, I know. Hell, *I* embarrass a lot of people just being what I am. It's, like, they can't get into where my head's at because they're too busy hanging onto stuff—owning it and trying to get more—to get ahead. Me, I'm happy with what I've got. I sell a few instruments and that gives me all the money I need for anything I can't grow or gather in the woods. I've got a few friends that still come and see me—the kind that don't hassle me about the way I am and what I'm doing—but I'm okay on my own too, you know? Because I've got my work and, like, my work's keeping this place pure.

"Now someone like you, I guess you're made for a place like this. You're geared right into it, you know? You're the kind of person I'm keeping this place pure for. So let me just say that you're welcome to stay here for as long as you need to. No hassles. No come-ons. You can just hang out and take your time about getting your head straight again. No one's going to bother you. If anyone comes up to see me, well, we'll hear them coming long before they show up, so there'd be plenty of time for you to hide out in the woods for awhile if you didn't want to be seen."

"But after all I've told you . . ."

Zach's smile was lost in the darkness. "What did you tell me?" he asked. "You say you're a Gypsy—that's no big deal to me. I can dig your being a Gypsy. You say you're a witch, well . . . I don't know if that's so weird either. I mean, look at me. I hear things on the wind and there've been times . . . I can remember doing acid up here and watching the trees get up and dance for me. I'd hang out and talk to the water for hours and sometimes—" he gave her a quick grin "—the water'd answer me back.

"I guess we've all got a little bit of the impossible in us, Ola. You could say it was dope that made me see those things and hear those things, but sometimes I see and hear them still and I haven't dropped a tab in years. Now I can't recommend psychedelics anymore—not like I used to. Sometimes they can get you into some bad craziness. But I figure they opened a few doors in my head, you know?"

"But what about the . . . the man I killed?"

Zach sighed. "That's something you're going to have to deal with in whatever way you can. I don't believe violence solves anything, but I guess there're some times when you don't have any choice. I guess I'm just lucky that the same situation's never come up for me. I figure you'll have some karma to deal with—but nowhere near what the guy who attacked you's going to have to handle. Trouble is, his brother's still running around out there with a real mad on for you. I don't think he'd ever, like, find you here or anything, but if I was you, I'd stay clear of any place you think he might show up.

"Thing that scares me the most is this Mulengro guy. I get bad-vibed just thinking about him."

Ola nodded. "He's in my future," she said softly. "The *dook* shows me that much."

"I like that word. The *dook*. You think it's something like that that lets me hear things when the wind's talking?"

"The *dook* is something the Rom have, but it must be similar to what's in you."

"Far-out."

They were both quiet for awhile. Boboko stirred lazily in Ola's lap but didn't wake up. A loon cried from the lake and Zach sighed.

"Maybe Mulengro won't find you here either," he said finally.

Ola knew what was worrying him. If the man in black came here, it would destroy the purity of the place that Zach was trying to maintain.

"I shouldn't stay," she said.

"You can't go," he replied. "If you go, it'll make everything meaningless. This place can give you the strength you need to face up to something like him. Only way you can deal with negative vibes like he's putting out is by giving him a stronger dose of good ones, you know? What's important for you right now is to lay low awhile—let yourself soak up some of the good stuff this place can give you. Going through what you have is going to leave scars and the best thing you can do for yourself right now is to make sure they're not deep ones."

Ola nodded. It wasn't just Mulengro she had to deal with. He was the future. The specter of the man she'd killed was still with her and would be until she could forgive it and send it on to the land of shadows or wherever it was that the dead of the *Gaje* went.

"One thing you *can* do," Zach said suddenly, "is give these Gypsies in Ottawa a call. Doesn't matter if they're not going to listen to you. You've still got to try. Do you know any of them by name?"

"No. Well, not really. But there are numbers I can call—there are places in every city that my people use as . . . information centers, I suppose you could call them."

"Well," Zach said. "Like I said, you're welcome to crash here for as long as you want and, as for that phone call, if you want to make it, Gord Webster's got a phone at his place down the lake and—let's see. Tomorrow's Friday and I doubt if he'll be up before the evening, so we could head on down there in the morning and no one'll see you make your calls. I've got a key to the place—so you don't have to worry about us breaking in or anything. Sound good to you?"

"You're being very kind, Zach. I . . . well, thank you."

Zach started to answer, then cocked his head. "Hear that?" he asked.

Ola shook her head, not sure what he meant.

Zach grinned. "Wind just played a couple of riffs from the Beach Boys' 'Good Vibrations'—what do you think of that?"

"I think you're putting me on."

"Well, maybe I am," he said. "C'mon. I'll show you where you can crash."

Ola smiled and stood up with him, carrying Boboko in her arms. The cat was a dead weight, floppy as a rag doll, and didn't even open his eyes as she carried him to the bed that Zach had laid out for her in the tiny spare bedroom. There was a poster of Peter Pan above the bed and an Arthur Rackham print of leaf faeries on the other wall. The window looked out on the vegetable garden. When she'd said her good nights to Zach and gotten undressed, Ola stood for a long moment at the window, feeling the cool air on her skin and letting the stillness settle inside her. When at last the quiet inside her matched the deep silence outside, she went to bed and fell into a dreamless sleep.

It was awhile before Zach went to bed himself. He'd found that, as he got older, he just didn't seem to need as much sleep as a person was supposed to. Maybe it had something to do with his diet or his morning meditations—he really didn't know.

He went out and sat on the porch again, rocking softly and staring into the darkness, worrying about Ola and her dark visions, trying to figure out a way he could help her. After a long while he went off to his own bed, the problem still unresolved. That night he dreamed of Dory—one of the old members of Raggle Taggle, the group he'd played with in the sixties. Dory had been dead now for nine years—OD'd on speed and he just never came down.

In the dream, Dory was sitting under an oak tree playing his flute. He was dressed all in black and the music that came out of his instrument was like something Black Sabbath would play. Heavy duty music that was totally incongruous on the delicate silver instrument. Wraiths came spilling out of the end of the flute, gray manlike shapes, and they came for Zach, clawing at him with taloned fingers that were far more substantial than their bodies. And behind them, his eyes grinning, Dory just sat there and kept the music rolling. . . .

Zach awoke in a cold sweat and lay awake for a long time before sleep returned. Damn dream was too much like an omen and he didn't like omens. Not bad-vibed ones like this.

nineteen

All Wednesday night, Bob Gourlay just sat in the pickup. He'd parked it in the lane of the old farmhouse he used to share with his brother, but found he couldn't get out. He just sat staring at the dark house, remembering. His soiled pants were almost dry, but the stench of them filled the cab of the truck. His head hurt and he just couldn't move. He kept seeing the witchwoman standing over Stan's body and the log just floating in the air. He relived the terror he'd felt as she drove him out to the highway, out to the pickup. He'd managed to start it up and drive himself home, but he just couldn't do anything more.

Stan was dead. . . .

He didn't remember falling asleep, but he must have, because when he opened his eyes, the sun was shining in them. His head still hurt. The stink in the cab was worse than ever, but he still couldn't move.

Stan was dead. . . .

Didn't matter if he got out or just sat here forever or drove the fucking truck off a cliff, nothing was gonna change. His fingers tightened and loosened on the steering wheel. He could kill her— he *was* gonna kill her—but it still wouldn't change anything.

About midmorning he suddenly started the pickup and backed out of the driveway, spraying gravel as his wheels spun.

Too much gas . . . who the fuck cared. . . . Stan was dead. . . .

He ended up just cruising the back roads, going nowhere, wishing his head would stop aching, wishing someone would pull the pins out from behind his eyes that were making his head throb, wishing Stan wasn't dead. He just drove, all day, stopping at gas stations twice and not even seeing the disgusted looks on the attendants' faces when they caught a whiff of the rich Gourlay shit that was lying so thick and sweet in the cab of the pickup. He drove the back roads and even into Perth a couple of times and never saw the questioning looks of people who were wondering where Stan was because the Gourlays were always together. The light was against him on Foster and he sat in a lineup behind six cars or so, far enough down the block so he could see the stretch of pavement where he and Stan had showed that suck-faced Owen a thing or two.

Gonna kill that fucker too. . . .

He just drove and drove. And sometimes he stopped in the middle of nowhere, killed the engine and laid his head down on the steering wheel, tears burning in his eyes and his head pounding. And sometimes he'd lift his head and stare through the blur of tears at the empty seat beside him and almost think Stan was there. But—

Stan was dead . . . and he was gonna hurt her . . . fucking witch. . . . He was gonna cut her heart out and feed it to the dogs. . . .

Twice he cruised by the cottage and Rideau Ferry, hands trembling on the wheel, but he never pulled in. He was six-one and weighed two-fifteen and not a pound of that was fat. He'd been fighting since he was just knee-high to a nun's ass and he whupped 'em a hell of a lot more than he got whupped. It'd take two or three men to bring him down and even then they had to be good. Damned good. But he couldn't go in that cottage and face the witch, because just thinking about it made his head hurt twice as bad and his bowels go all loose and the terror walk knife-sharp up his spine. But the third time he drove by it was closer to midnight than it was to eleven and he cruised past it real slow, saw the lights were out—

She was hiding there in the dark . . . just waiting for him . . . sitting on Stan's chest . . . the fucking cat lickin' up Stan's blood . . . their eyes'd be glowing . . . cat's eyes . . . both of them. . . .

He got the shakes so bad he had to pull over or he'd wrap the truck around a tree. He didn't care—who cared? Who really gave a fuck? He pulled over all the same, tears stinging in his eyes. The pain came clouding up the back of his head and settled like a nest of hornets behind his eyes. He killed the engine and laid his head on the wheel.

He didn't see that he'd parked the pickup in the same place it'd been parked last night. Didn't hear the frogs' chorus die and the night go all still around him. Didn't hear the door on the passenger's side open. Didn't feel a weight settle on the seat and the springs give a little with a creak. Didn't smell the rank stench of a day-old corpse as it filled the cab with its sickly-sweet smell. He just moaned, holding his head, not understanding what was happening to him. He was falling apart and it didn't make sense. Nothing made sense anymore. Not Stan dying, not the magic of the witchwhore, not the talking cat. Nothing did.

"I loved you, Stan," he blubbered. "I swear I did!"

"Well, I know *that,* brother Bob."

The voice went through him like a cold blast of wind. He lifted his head and turned slowly to face the darkened passenger's side of the cab. He smelled it now, over his own reeking excrement, the stink of the grave and the dead. He *felt* the cold presence at his side. He saw something . . . more an outline than something real . . . and heard . . . heard Stan's voice . . . more distant, somehow, than the way he knew it . . . a wet sound. . . .

"St-t-stan . . . ?"

"Say-hey, brother Bob. How's it hangin'?"

"But you . . . you're dead. . . ."

"Well, there's dead and there's dead, little brother. I got half my face hanging in my mouth and the knowledge that my own brother didn't do dick-all to stop that black whore from ripping it off me, but otherwise things aren't so bad, you know?"

Bob could see more now. There was a big gap in his brother's face. The wet sound when he spoke came from the fact that his face was hanging in flaps of skin from his skull. Bob didn't have anything in his stomach, but a dry heave came acidly up his stomach all the same.

"Now, you don't act all that happy to see me, brother Bob. I'm not holdin' nothin' against you. Just set your little mind at ease on that score. I figure we've got ourselves a bit of black tail to finish a bit of business with, you know what I mean?"

Bob nodded. His voice was lost somewhere in the cold terror that gripped him. His head pounded.

"I've been hearin' things, you know," the apparition continued. "Learnin' stuff. There's somethin' about her bein' a witch that keeps me from just fadin' away, you know? And it's got somethin' to do with the plain fact that I ain't lettin' go neither. It's not too clear just what's goin' on, little brother. But I ain't complainin'. I figure bein' half-dead's better than bein' *all* dead."

Bob lifted his hand slowly and reached out, his mind numb. When his fingers neared the apparition, there was nothing solid to touch. His hand went right into the shape, the fingers going cold and the cold spreading up his arm, tingling, until he drew it back with a sudden movement.

"You . . . you're not there, Stan," he said in a small voice. "I can hear you and . . . I can sorta see you, but you're not *there!*"

Stan was dead . . . and the witchwhore had killed him . . . and he was gonna kill her. . . .

"I figure she took to the woods," the apparition said. "I'll bet she took her black ass into the bush, yessir, and she's just sittin' in there like a spider waitin' for you, brother Bob. Now the thing you've gotta do is get her before she gets you. It's just that simple."

If Stan was dead, then what was this . . . thing . . . sitting beside him . . . talking like Stan, but with that wet sound in its voice . . . ?

"And I'll help you, little brother, I surely will. You're gonna be my hands, you see? We're together again and we're gonna make her pay. We'll make 'em all pay. Little Jeffy Owen. And that whore waitress in the Zoo that wouldn't spread 'em for me. And Constable Finlay. And Jim-suck-my-ass-Rider who wouldn't give us the time of day, little say a job. We're gonna show 'em, brother Bob. We're gonna eye-for-an-eye 'em until there won't be no one left 'ceptin' folks that were good to us Gourlays. And you know, little brother, there weren't many of 'em, nossir. Weren't many at all."

But it didn't really matter what the thing was, did it? It talked like Stan, like it *was* Stan, and even if—

Stan was dead. . . .

—nothing really mattered anymore, anyway. Did it? His head throbbed, veins drumming in his temples. There was a burning behind his eyes.

"Now I figure the first thing you do before we go a-huntin', little brother, is you've gotta get you some rest. Now I 'preciate your mournin' me an' all—that's what a brother should do—but you can see I'm not all dead, so you've pretty well done all the mournin' that's needed. I figure you oughta go home and get some rest, yessir. And tomorrow night . . . we'll have us some fun."

Bob nodded. The hurt in his head was too intense for him to even think straight, little say speak. If Stan wanted to go huntin', well sure, he was up for that. Just let him get rid of this hurting first and he'd be up for anything. Just like old times.

"You keep it hangin', little brother. Say-hey!"

The passenger's door swung open. A weight that wasn't there lifted from the seat and the springs creaked again. The door shut and the apparition was gone, leaving behind the stink of its rotting flesh. Bob reached out again. There was nothing there. No tingle. No

cold. And it was so quiet. So quiet. The hurt in his head eased a little bit and he found he was grinning.

"Say-hey," he said softly, his voice just a hoarse whisper.

Stan was dead. But it was still going to be just like old times. He
didn't know how or why, and he didn't care.

twenty

"Are you going to be all right?"

Briggs glanced at his partner and nodded. "Yeah. I'll be okay."

As he started to get out of the car, Will leaned over and touched
his arm. "You can't blame yourself for what happened, Paddy. You
did everything you could."

"Then how come they're all dead?"

Will sighed. "I don't know how, but somehow the killer knew
they'd seen him. He was just cleaning up after himself. We've seen it
before, Paddy. There was nothing you could do."

"Yeah. Maybe I'm just getting tired of seeing it."

"You and me both."

Briggs nodded. "You'd better get back to Sharon. I'll see you
tomorrow, Will." He stepped out of the car and stayed on the sidewalk until the car turned the corner and was lost from sight. He
stood there a few minutes longer, feeling the ghosts gather around
him, then turned and entered his building. The first thing he did
when he was inside was throw out Francine's picture. Getting a beer,
he went out to sit on his balcony. He set the beer by the foot of his
chair and took out his pipe.

I want you, he said to the night. I know you're out there somewhere, and I want you.

The killer was clearer in his mind now, as though the three deaths
tonight had added details to the image he was carrying around in his
head. He had a shape that was clearly defined. All he needed was the
face. The name. It was like he was standing at the far end of a dark

street and the killer was at the other end with his back to him. Any moment now he was going to turn and then Briggs would know him.

He got his pipe lit and picked up his beer. The ghosts were worse than usual tonight. The two hookers. Red-eye Cleary. The two Gypsies. They were at the forefront of all those other ghosts, waiting for him to do something, to avenge them, to bring the killer to justice as though that would somehow make their deaths less meaningless. But dead was dead, Briggs wanted to tell those ghosts. Whether he brought the killer in or not, it still wasn't going to make any difference to the dead. But the ghosts didn't want to hear that kind of thing.

He took a swig of his beer and stared out at the night. Tonight he was going to mourn—for Red-eye, for the hookers, for all the dead and the hurt, the victims—because tomorrow it was going to be business as usual. He had a killer to run down and not the Inspector, not his lack of leads, not anything was going to keep him from it. He'd even do it on his own time, if it had to come down to that.

You hear that? he asked the night. I'm after your ass, you miserable fucker, and I don't care if you've got leopard's claws or two heads. I'm going to nail you to the floor.

Mulengro came up from the river, moving through the brush on the slopes behind Parliament Hill. He avoided the patrolling RCMP on the grounds as he made his way eastward, finally pausing at the War Memorial that lifts proudly from the traffic circle joining Wellington, Rideau and Elgin Streets. It was time to leave this city, he thought. The Rom had already fled it like vermin from a submerged dog and his work here was done. But not over. It would not be over until the last *marhime* Rom was banished to the land of shadows and the race was pure once more.

Uva. Yes. It was time to go. He felt strong tonight, filled with the pure light of God. All went well. He looked up into the sky where the brightness of the stars was dulled by the glow of the city, just as the *Gaje* dulled the brightness of the Rom and seduced them from

following the old ways. Time had reversed their natural roles. The
Rom were the chosen of God—created to be predators in a world
of *Gaje*. Sly and clever as foxes, while the *Gaje* were dogs. And does
a dog tell its master what he may do?

There was lightning in Mulengro's eyes as he studied the stars—a
pent-up storm that needed release, a cleansing fire that was looking
for a place to strike. But behind the storm, the eyes of a young boy
watched fearfully out of that gaze as well, seeing not the storm nor
the spread-out panorama of the stars, but the faces of cruel men and
other fires that burned the *vurdon* of the Rom, that slew father with
flame and spread the legs of the mother and filled her with hot *Gaje*
fire of another sort, that marched the Rom one by one into the
death camps, that had them dig their own graves before the guns spat
and toppled them down into the cold welcoming earth. . . .

The man in black closed his eyes and the memories slowly
burned away, the boy he had been once was banished with them.

"There is still work to do," he said in his cold whisper of a voice.

The horrors that had befallen the Rom at the hands of the Nazis
would never have been vented upon a pure race. He had tried to
explain that to the doctors, but they had only kept him locked up,
away from the world, away from his work, until he had found the
way to call the shades of the dead to him. His *mule* had freed him
and set him on this road, this road that led away from this city now
as before it had led him to it. *Marhime* Rom had escaped, but he
would track them down. With his *draba*. With his *mule*. No one
lived now who had seen him about his work, so he was free to go.
No one would see him depart.

He could pass unnoticed amongst the *Gaje* when he so wished.
But mostly he walked their world by night, and woe to those who
stood between him and his work, or watched him go about his duty.
Sometimes, he knew, it was necessary to show the *Gaje* that they did
not rule the world—that there was only God and his servants who
ruled. He closed his fists at his side, feeling the fire inside him. The
cleansing fire.

"Mulengro," he said softly.

It was a good name. The old woman had chosen well. Perhaps

she had escaped being numbered amongst his *mule,* but she helped him in this way. For a name was important. Someday the old men would tell *swatura* of Mulengro around the campfire, of the man in black and his *mule* who cleansed the Rom that they might be favored once more in the eyes of God. But for now . . .

He gathered his *mule* about him like a cloak and set off. No one saw him leave the city. By the time the sun rose over Ottawa, he was walking along a highway that led away, southwest of the city, to where he sensed *draba* rising against him and Rom who were *marhime.* There was still work to do.

Part Two

Mulengi dori

Le Romano shib motol o chachimos ande xoxayimos.
　　　　　　　　　　　　　—Romany saying

[The Gypsy tongue tells the truth in lies.]

The old ways are changing, you can nae deny,
the day of the traveller's over;
there's nae where tae gang
an' there's nae where tae 'bide,
so farewell tae the life o' the rover.
　　Goodbye tae the tent and the old caravan,
　　tae the tinker, the Gypsy, the travelling man,
　　and goodbye tae the thirty-foot trailer.
　　　　—from "Goodbye to the Thirty-Foot Trailer"
　　　　by Ewan MacColl

twenty-one

The ghosts stayed with Briggs all that night. They were still there when he woke up on his balcony and stumbled into his apartment, they stood behind his shoulder while he shaved, they followed him as he walked to work. But like the cursed protagonist in *The Monkey's Paw,* he was the only one to see his burden, the only one who knew the ghosts were there, because they were only in his mind. But knowing that didn't make them any less real for him.

He thought about finally throwing away Francine's picture last night and knew that so long as he had these ghosts he'd never be able to escape the past. The picture hadn't been the cause—only the outward manifestation of what was inside him. He thought of that imaginary family he daydreamed about sometimes. This time the daughter had Tracy's face. He had to wonder if this kind of thing was healthy.

To keep such questions, to keep the ghosts at bay, he threw himself into a regular routine of going through reports and wearing a mask of false jollity that only Will would see through, but he was in court this morning. One small favor, Briggs thought. Not that Will didn't mean well, but Briggs didn't really know how he could explain anything to his partner when he didn't even know what he was going through himself.

"I see they've got you working for a change, Paddy."

Briggs looked up from his desk to see Sam Robertson, also from General Assignment, pulling up a chair. He was a lean, stoop-shouldered man with a hawk's nose that would have done Caesar proud. He had a couple of coffees in hand and pushed one across the desk to Briggs.

"I'm up to my ass in paperwork," Sam complained. "If it's not file six reports on this, it's seven on that. I'm thinking of hiring myself a secretary and paying her out of my own pocket."

Briggs managed to find a smile. "Bribes that good this month? Thanks for the coffee."

"Don't mention it. Hey, you know someone handing out shut up money? Tell me where I can line up. I got mortgage payments like you wouldn't believe and the car's in the shop again—three lousy days after the warranty ran out and isn't that a pisser? Jimmy's told me he's not going to university, the cat shit all over the rug this morning, and then to top it all off I've got this fucking fire on Frank Street—arson, plain and simple, you know? Except nobody's collecting the insurance, mainly because there *was* no insurance on the place. Can't even find the fucking owner. Oh, it's going to look just dandy in the report."

Briggs shrugged and dug his pipe out of his pocket. "How'd you know it was arson?"

"Concerned citizen stepped forward—after I spent the better part of a day knocking on doors and wearing my butt off—and claims he saw a man torch the place."

"Let's hear it for hot detective work," Briggs said. His smile wasn't so forced this time. He'd needed something like this—just to get back into the swing of things and let the ghosts lie.

"Sure. Yuk it up. I might be handing the case over to you if this Owczarek who owned the place doesn't show up soon."

"I don't need it."

"Hey, go cry to the Inspector. I'll be real happy to wipe my hands of it. More headaches I don't need. I've got plenty all on my ownsome." He drew his chair up closer to Briggs' desk so that he could hook his heels on a corner of it and shook out a cigarette from a battered Export package. His narrow face was red from too much sun and the chair creaked as he tipped it back on its legs.

"So what's the story?" Briggs asked. "This Owczarek owe somebody some money and wasn't paying up?"

"Damned if I know. Guy makes plenty pumping out Hungarian fiddle music records. Got his bio from his producer yesterday when I was trying to track him down." He lit his cigarette, took a drag, then balanced it on the end of the desk beside his coffee. "There was this weird thing, though. I got to the fire before the place collapsed, and I saw this symbol painted on the wall—sort of a circle with these squiggly lines going through it, you know? I figured it was supposed to be a message, but unless it meant something to Owczarek, it sure was a waste of time. Meant shit to me.

"Anyway I wanted to get a couple of shots of it before the flames ate it up, but Stan was out shooting about fifteen rolls in that strip joint down near Sunnyside—for professional purposes, of course—and then he was working with you, and I sure as hell didn't want to go with one of the newspaper's boys. Christ knows what they'd've printed if they thought we were interested in it."

Briggs didn't crack a smile. "What kind of a symbol did you say it was?" he asked.

"I don't know. Black paint. A circle with lines. Give me a pencil and I'll try to draw it for you—though the only thing I can handle is paint-by-numbers, I'll tell you. Any artistic streaks in my family must've passed me right by."

Briggs dug into a file and pulled out a glossy 8×10. "Did it look like this?" he asked.

"Yeah. Yeah, it did. Where'd you get that?"

Briggs shoved the Gypsy-murders casefile across the desk to him.

"This is too weird," Will said later that morning when he got back from court. He stared at the photograph of John Owczarek that Sam had dropped off on Briggs' desk along with the bio from the violinist's producer. "Bad—"

"Juju. I know. You recognize him?"

"Sure. It's Mr. I-need-that-money-you-know. His place got burned down the same night Romano Wood almost lost his head?"

"Bad choice of words," Briggs said with a grimace.

"So sue me." Will frowned, then tossed the picture on the desk.

"What're we going to do—run down a few of his friends and acquaintances?"

"I got the OK from the Inspector and put an APB out on one John Owczarek, aka Jim Cerinek. Now that we've got a taxpayer involved, not to mention three new deaths, he's gung ho to run with it again."

"So what else is new?" Will glanced at the photo, then looked thoughtfully at his partner. Various facts were being resorted inside his head and his eyes took on a distant look. "Well now we know he's a Gypsy, too. I just wonder what his game is?"

"I don't know," Briggs replied. "But we're going to find out. And the big question is: which is he, victim or our man?"

Will nodded. "He must tour the country doing gigs. That'd be a perfect set up for him. If we can tie him into a couple of other cities at the same time as the Gypsies there got killed . . ."

"And the house?"

"Maybe things were getting hot, so he burns it down to cover his tracks. . . ." Will shook his head. "Doesn't work. He hasn't got any scars."

"So maybe it was a mask Cleary saw."

"Maybe you're pushing too hard, Paddy."

The ghosts were a heavy weight on Briggs' shoulders. "Maybe," he said softly.

twenty-two

Jeff awoke from a restless sleep, troubled by unpleasant dreams. It was close on eleven and he was alone in Jackie Sim's bed for the second morning in a row. Bright sunlight came washing through the bedroom window, sparkling on the unicorn mobile, and he vaguely remembered Jackie coming in to tell him that she was heading off to work. Much clearer in his memory were the jagged shards of his dreams.

He'd relived that moment in Ola's porch, but this time the dead thing touched him, doughy hands grabbing his shoulders and pulling him down into a wet embrace from which he . . . stirred, turned over in the bed . . . saw Ola in a dark wood, surrounded by capering trees that were impossibly animate, her calico cat sitting on its haunches by a stump and playing a fiddle while singing in a low burry voice, and then something coming out from between the trees, malformed, a shadow that . . . he turned again, face pressed against the pillow and now . . . Jackie was running down a long corridor, clutching a package to her breast, and she opened a door to find him in her bed, threw the package at him and it fell open on the sheets, a severed head rolling onto his legs . . . his scream died soundlessly against the pillow . . . slept again . . . dreamless now . . . until the thing in Ola's cottage came reaching for him again and he finally . . . awoke. Safe.

He sat up, expecting the blood to start pounding in his temples again, but the headache had receded into a barely discernible buzz at the back of his head that was no louder than the whir of a fly's wings at the bedroom window as it tried to get through the glass. At least he had that much to be thankful for. The dresser mirror was right where it had been yesterday morning and last night when he'd gone to bed. He regarded his bruised features, touched the discolored skin gingerly. The swelling was going down a bit, but he still hurt like hell. A two-day growth of beard stubbled his cheek and chin, but there was no way he was going to run a razor over that tender flesh.

He swung his feet to the floor and stood experimentally. When the vertigo stayed away with the worst of yesterday's headache, he padded into the kitchen to put on water for coffee. He was still aching, but at least he knew now that he was going to live. There'd been times yesterday when he hadn't been all too sure of that, and last night . . . Weird dreams. Seeing that dead thing again . . .

Yesterday's experience bordered on the paranormal—something he'd only written about before, never encountered away from the pages that came out of his typewriter or from listening to things that Ola had recounted while they were researching their books. He

knew that what he'd seen on Ola's porch hadn't—*couldn't* have—
been real. Head injuries sometimes caused hallucinations—Dr. Mulley had warned him about it again yesterday—and he'd been under
a lot of stress, what with worrying about Ola and the beating he'd
received at the hands of the Gourlays, but none of that stopped a
small part of his mind from insisting that what he'd seen *had* been
real. It had been something dead that wasn't willing to give up its
hold on life. Something that wanted to take him down with it.

He shivered, staring at the dust motes dancing in the sunlight that
came in through the kitchen window. Something dead. . . . Except
Stan Gourlay wasn't dead, though Jeff wouldn't shed any tears if the
bastard was.

He got up when the kettle started to boil and mechanically set
about making his coffee, his thoughts a hundred miles away from
what he was doing. He was thinking about Ola now, how *different*
she was. It wasn't just her being an African here in the predomi-
nantly white Ottawa valley. Nor her herbal medicines and cures—
gathered from Wiccan, African, Gypsy and Lord knew what other
sources—or even the afterlife theories and philosophies like in
Beyond the Last Light, their third collaboration.

There was an otherworldliness about her sometimes, as though
she could see more and hear more than the people around her. He
thought about the way she spoke so seriously about the paranormal
and the things that came up when they were working on the
books. . . . Weird stuff that she always seemed to regret having spoken of afterward. She'd laugh and make a joke about it, saying
something like, "Of course we won't put anything that farfetched in
the book."

There was her cat Boboko, just sitting there, looking for all the
world as though he was listening to them in that way that only cats
can look. Or worse, as though he was understanding what they said.
Jeff shook his head, putting the image of Ola as witch out of his
head. He was starting to get a little carried away. Maybe he *should*
check himself into the hospital for a couple of days. First he was
having hallucinations, and now his thoughts were getting all twisted
around and crazy in his head.

He could almost see her, stirring some cauldron out in the moonlight, Boboko perched at her feet, the witch's familiar. They still had hoodoo men in Africa, didn't they? And hoodoo women, too. All these magics and remedies and cures she was so keen on. Gypsy stuff she'd learned about while traveling through Europe with her parents. Wiccan stuff that she'd picked up in the States. And what did he really know about her? Just what she'd told him, nothing that could be checked out. Ola Drake. Her name, Jeff realized, was all he had. All that he had in the way of cold hard facts anyway. He remembered his dream . . . the dark wood around her, the trees capering, the cat playing the fiddle and singing. . . .

What if the Gourlays *had* shown up at her place and she'd done . . . something to one of them, and then fled? But that had to be impossible. The Gourlays were a pair of bruisers, each one of them twice her size. They would've mopped up the floor with her—like they'd done with him outside of Tinkers. Unless . . . there was such a thing as . . . magic. And if she *was* a witch . . . an African hoodoo lady, a Wiccan priestess, a Gypsy witch . . .

Another chill traveled through him. What should he do? Should he even do anything? Christ, he was confused. The phone rang suddenly, lifting him a half inch from the chair. He stared at it blankly for a long moment—saw the shredded cord of the phone at Ola's place in his mind's eye—then lifted the receiver and brought it up to his ear.

"Hello?"

Jackie was behind the bar in Tinkers, talking to John Danning from *The Perth Courier* who was teasing her about taking in strays. It was just after twelve and the restaurant was almost empty—though that would change over the next few minutes as the lunch crowd started to come in. An old Eagles tape was playing on the sound system. When the front door opened, her gaze went to it automatically. Two dark-skinned men came in—one quite handsome, in a rugged way rather than pretty, and the other a lean shorter man with an incredible walrus mustache, the tips of which hung below his chin.

"Excuse me, John," she said as they took a table. John nodded and she plucked a couple of menus from beside the cash register and went over to their table. "Good afternoon," she said, laying the menus in front of them. "Can I get you something from the bar?"

The mustached man nodded and smiled. "Two drafts, please."

"Coming right up."

"Uh, miss?"

She turned, a questioning look in her eyes.

"I was wondering if Jeff Owen has been in yet today. I don't know him by sight, you see, but my friend here would like to meet him."

For no accountable reason, Jackie felt nervous. "Jeff?" she said. "What did you want to see him about?" She looked from the mustached man to his companion.

"We wanted to meet a friend of his. The lady he writes his books with."

"You mean Ola?" Stop fidgeting, she told herself.

The mustached man shrugged. "I'm not sure of her name, to be honest. I thought it was Rouge. Is it Ola Rouge?"

They must only know her from her books, Jackie thought. "I . . . I think I know where I can get hold of Jeff," she said.

"It's fairly important," the clean-shaven man said, speaking for the first time. "If we could meet Mr. Owen as soon as possible . . ."

"I'll call him right now." Oh, boy, she thought as she made her way back to the bar. What did these guys want? There was something so intense about them—especially the clean-shaven one. Before drawing their drafts, she went to the phone and dialed her home number. Glancing at the two men, she found them watching her. The mustached man looked away when her gaze alit on him, but the other man didn't even appear to realize he was staring at her. There was a distant, thoughtful look in his eyes. The phone rang once before Jeff picked it up.

"Jeff?"

"Hi, Jackie." Jeff balanced the receiver between his ear and shoulder and, picking up the phone, went to the counter to pour himself a coffee. "Listen, thanks a lot for nursing me through another night. I could get used to waking up in that room, you know."

"Jeff, there's a couple of guys in the restaurant who want to talk to you." She spoke quickly, ignoring the bantering tone in his voice. "They're looking for Ola."

"Oh, great. Are they cops?"

"No." There was a pause. "Jeff, is there more going on than you've told me?"

"If there is, I'm as much in the dark as you are. What do these guys look like?"

"Sort of . . . tough. Very dark complexions, like Ola, but they're not blacks. They're both wearing earrings and one of them's got a bandana around his neck. I don't think they're local, though the one with the mustache might have been in here before. I'm not sure."

"Did they say anything else?"

"No. They just want you to introduce them to Ola. They say it's important."

Jeff thought about Jackie's sketchy description, trying to place the men. "Are they old, young?"

"Late thirties, early forties. It's kind of hard to tell. They look like a couple of Gypsies," she added with a laugh.

Jeff didn't smile. Gypsies. When he thought about some of the things that went into the books he and Ola worked on . . . Maybe she wasn't all her jacket copy made her out to be. Her facial features had never looked that African to him in the first place, but he'd just put that down to what the hell did he know. Gypsies. Witches. A pattern that he didn't like was forming.

"Jackie, I'll be right down, okay?"

"Are you sure you're feeling up to it?"

"Oh, yeah. Fit as a fiddle, though maybe the varnish is just a little bit cracked in places."

"Shouldn't you maybe . . . I don't know . . . have someone come down with you? In case it gets, well, rough or something."

"Does it look like it could get rough?" Jeff asked, thinking this he didn't need.

"I suppose not."

"Just tell 'em I'll be down in half an hour or so, okay, Jackie? And don't worry. This time I'm not stepping outside with anybody. Not unless I've got a big stick."

"Okay."

Jeff replaced the receiver and glanced at his coffee. Shit. What the hell was *this* all about?

Jeff spotted the two men the moment he came in through the kitchen doors. The swinging doors closed behind him and he stood in the area where the waitresses prepared coffees, teas and desserts. Jackie came from behind the bar and hurried over to him.

"Those the guys?" he asked.

Jackie nodded.

"They do look kind of scruffy, don't they? Well, here goes nothing."

"Jeff?" Jackie caught his arm. "Be careful, okay?"

Jeff turned with a smile. The concern he saw in her eyes startled him—not because of what might happen with the two men, but because of what it told him of how she felt. Funny thing; he'd known Jackie for—how long? Was it five years now since she'd moved back to Perth? They'd taken in a couple of drive-ins, gone fishing together, and spent a lot of hours talking in Tinkers, but he'd never really thought of her as anything but a pal. It wasn't that he found her unattractive, for she wasn't. But he wasn't sure how to handle the intimacy he now saw in her eyes.

He laid his hand on hers, marveling at its warmth. Maybe something was changing in him too. "I'll be real careful," he said.

The two men looked up as he approached the table and he wondered what they were thinking. Two days stubble and the bruises didn't do much for his looks. He lowered himself gingerly into one of two vacant chair and found a smile to fit on his lips.

"Afternoon, gentlemen," he said. "I'm Jeff Owen. So what can I do for you?"

"My name is Tibo Williams," Tibo Lee said. "I live in the trailer park just outside of town on Highway 4."

"Oh, yeah. I know the place." He glanced at Tibo's smooth-shaven companion.

"I'm John—John Wood."

"John would like to meet the lady you write your books with," Tibo said. "I know where she lives, but we thought it would be more . . . proper if he was introduced to her by someone she knows."

"But I don't know either of you," Jeff pointed out.

"Yes, well . . ."

"What's all this about?"

There was a moment's silence, then Tibo asked: "You were in an accident?"

Jeff lifted a self-conscious finger to his cheek. "I had a little mis-understanding with a couple of the local yahoos. It's nothing seri-ous. Look, I've got things to do. Can we get to the point of this conversation? I know now who you say you are." He let that state-ment hang for a moment, just long enough for them to understand that he wasn't going to be taken in with their fake names, so why play around anymore? "So why don't you just tell me what it is you want with Ms. Rouge?"

"I'm not sure you would believe us," the man calling himself John Wood said. It wasn't quite the answer Jeff had been expecting. He glanced at the bar where Jackie was pretending to clean glasses, and felt his throat go dry. It wasn't at all the kind of answer he'd been expecting.

"Try me," he said.

"We . . . I'm looking for someone with a working knowledge of . . . magic. Gypsy magic." The clean-shaven man lifted his head, impaling Jeff with the intensity of his gaze. "Your friend, perhaps even you yourself, you know about this kind of thing, don't you? Tibo tells me you have written a number of books, some of which contain Gypsy lore. I need to know your sources. Do you make it all up? Or is it *real?*"

"Real?" Jeff swallowed dryly. The conversation was veering too close to the wild thoughts that had been running through his head this morning. He wished he had something to drink. "Depends on what you mean by real, I guess."

"Please. I'm not here to cause any trouble. But I *have* to know."

"Well, that sort of thing is more Ola's department. I just transcribe the material—pretty it up, that kind of thing."

"Could I speak to her, then? You're welcome to come along and keep me in line if you're afraid I have ulterior motives. But I must talk with her. I'm up against a blank wall and if I don't talk to someone I'll . . ." His shoulders lifted and fell as his voice trailed off.

"You'll what?"

"I don't know. Be back where I started, looking for something that probably doesn't even exist in the first place." He looked away, a troubled frown on his lips.

"Look," Jeff said. "If you could just tell me what the problem is . . ."

The man lifted his head suddenly, the intense gaze fixed on Jeff with a singular potency. "People are dying," he said. "My people. And not pleasantly. There is a *thing* out there . . . a monster . . ."

A cold rush of fear went up Jeff's spine. For a moment his vision blurred and instead of the restaurant, he was seeing the corpse in Ola's cottage rising from the floor, reaching for him. . . . He shut his eyes fiercely, willing it to go away. When he opened them again, both men were regarding him strangely. The clean-shaven man looked as though he regretted having said as much as he had—a look Jeff remembered from when Ola talked of things he knew she believed in, but didn't want him laughing at her about.

"I think I've made an error," the man said, mistaking the look on Jeff's face for disbelief. "This is a Gypsy matter. What can a *Gaje* know about Rom *draba?*"

The last words were said bitterly and Jeff wasn't sure what the man was talking about. He hesitated between telling them about Ola's disappearance and just letting them get up and walk out of here. Behind him the front door opened and the eyes of the two men sharing his table narrowed. Jeff turned enough in his seat to see who'd come in and recognized Craig Finlay, one of Perth's constables. He was a broad-shouldered bear of a man in his late thirties, well-liked in the community, tough but fair as the saying went.

"Heard about Wednesday night," he said to Jeff. "You want to press charges?"

Jeff shook his head and Craig sighed.

"Too bad," he said. "I'd love to put those suckers away for good. Well, hang in there, Jeff." He turned to the bar and sat on one of the stools. "Hey, Jackie. John. Do you know who owns that old Chev parked out front?"

Jeff had turned back to the table and saw the look that passed between the two men. Tibo's eyebrows rose questioningly. The other man gave a barely discernible shake of his head. It was their car, Jeff knew then. And they were uptight about Craig asking about it. When he put that down with the fact that they wanted to talk to Ola and the plain *weirdness* of the conversation they'd been having . . .

"I don't know whose it is," Jeff heard John Danning tell the constable. "You handing out parking tickets now, Craig?"

"Nope. Could you bring me a coffee, Jackie? I think I'll just sit here and rest a spell."

And watch who went to it, Jeff thought, completing the constable's unspoken sentence. He studied his companions. What were they guilty of? *People are dying,* the one man had said. *And not pleasantly.* . . . And they *were* Gypsies. So what did that make Ola? Not a Gypsy, but she knew people like this, didn't she? She had to have, somewhere along the line, to know so much about them. And now she was gone. *People are dying.* There was a chill hovering along his spine, but curiosity and worry for Ola got the better of him. He considered himself a good judge of character and foreign though these men seemed to be, there was a *need* about them—especially the clean-shaven one—that he felt he couldn't ignore with a clear conscience. And if it had *anything* to do with Ola's disappearance . . .

"You guys about finished those beers?" he asked, hoping his voice didn't sound too forcibly jovial and loud.

The two men exchanged glances. "Yes," Tibo said slowly.

"Well, maybe we'd better get back to work then. Those trees aren't going to come down by themselves." He gave a quick nod to the back of the restaurant and stood up. "I'm paying, okay? How much do we owe you, Jackie?" he added as he approached the bar.

"$4.50. Uh, Jeff . . ."

Craig glanced from Jeff to the two men rising from the table. "You going into the logging business, Jeff? What's the matter with your writing?"

"Writing's going fine, Craig. I'm just clearing out some bush from behind the house and John and Pat here are giving me a hand. What time are you working until, Jackie?"

"I'm off at seven."

"Keep the change. How about if I give you a call around six and maybe we'll have that dinner I promised you." Don't ask, he tried to tell her with his eyes, don't say a thing. Jackie looked puzzled, but she did her best to make like there was nothing going on.

"See what I told you?" John Danning said from down the bar. "You pick up a stray, Jackie, and they never go away—not until you take a broom to 'em."

Jackie nodded and found a smile. "This one I think I'll keep," she said. The look in her eyes was warm, if a bit worried, and it touched Jeff. He found his pulse quickening, and not simply from the lie he'd told Craig.

"Better watch what you say in public," he told her. "I just might hold you to it—and I've got witnesses. See you later. Take care, Craig . . . John." He led the way off through the kitchen and the two men followed him. When they were all standing outside the back door, he turned to regard them.

"Okay," he said. "Craig was looking for you. I know that and you know that, because that was your car, wasn't it?"

John Wood nodded. "Why are you helping us?"

"I think it's time we had a serious talk and that might be a little difficult to accomplish with Craig Finlay breathing down our necks."

"I don't understand. I appreciate the help you lent us back in there, but there's not really much for us to talk about. I told you back there that I've been wasting your time. The likelihood of you or your friend being able to help me was a remote one at best and—"

Jeff lifted his hand, cutting him off. "My friend's disappeared. When I went to her place yesterday, I saw . . . this. . . ." He was unable to finish. He didn't know these men at all and, what he'd seen . . . what *had* he seen anyway? "When you talk about people dying," he finished, "and then come looking for Ola and *she's* gone. . . ."

There was a moment's silence. John Wood sighed and turned to Tibo. "There's no need for you to come with us," he said. "It might be best if you went on home."

Tibo regarded Jeff, then shrugged. "As you wish, Boshengro."

"Thank you, Tibo."

The walrus mustache twitched as Tibo smiled. He nodded to Jeff, then strode off. Jeff watched him until he reached the end of the small lot behind Tinkers, then turned to the other man.

"What was that he called you?"

"Boshengro. It's a Romany word that means 'fellow who plays the fiddle.' I play the violin, you see. My name is Janfri la Yayal, Jeff. I don't tell many *Gaje* my true name."

"Then why are you telling me?"

"Because I think we need each other's help and we can't have lies, not even small ones between us."

"And *Gaje* means?"

"Anyone who is not a Rom—a Gypsy. Do you have some place we can go in case your friend—" he nodded over his shoulder to the restaurant "—decides to step out here?"

"I've been staying at Jackie's place—that's the waitress who phoned me for you—so we might as well go there. I live out aways and I'm not really sure *where* my car is." He touched his cheek. "I've been kept a little busy."

"Let's go," Janfri said.

Jeff nodded. And the first thing he'd do when he got there was call Jackie back at Tinkers so that she wouldn't be worrying. He led the way, glancing from time to time at his companion. He hoped he wasn't getting in way over his head, but he had a bad feeling that things were just starting to get weird.

twenty-three

Zach was making faces at her through the window, squinching up his face and sticking out his tongue. Ola tried not to laugh as she completed her call.

Gordon Webster's place had none of the lived-in practicality of Zach's home. It was so obviously a summer cottage, from the pre-sixties Zeller's furniture and linoleum floors; to the tacky fake wood paneling and the mounted bass above the brick mantel. But for all Zach's assurances—before he started to pull his faces—that there was no problem in using the phone here, she still felt nervous.

"I'm sorry. There is no service for that number."

The operator's voice startled her. She turned her back on the window so that she wouldn't inadvertently giggle. "Are you sure?" she asked. "Perhaps there's a new listing."

"What was the name again?"

"Owczarek. John Owczarek." She spelled it out. It was the third number she was trying, and the last contact she had for the Ottawa area. Of the first two numbers she'd called, one was a *Gaji* who told her that the Rom had all left Ottawa, while the second was an answering machine. She hadn't left a message at the beep. Where would she have them call her back?

"I'm afraid there's just that one listing," the operator said, "and there's no service for that number at the present time. If you'd like—"

"No. Thanks very much."

She set the receiver down, cutting the connection, and looked at the scrap of paper in her hand with its three names and telephone numbers. She didn't know any of these people. They were just con-

tacts where messages could be left. She had similar scraps in her wallet for major cities over most of North America, though the contacts
lived mostly on the coasts. The Rom rarely traveled through the
Bible-belt. Replacing the paper in her wallet, she went outside to
find Zach lounging on a deck chair. He looked up at her approach.

"Any luck?"

She shook her head.

"Bummer. But at least you tried."

"I suppose. I spoke to one woman who said that all the *kumpaniyi*
had left Ottawa, but she didn't know why." Ola's eyes were thoughtful.

"But we know."

"Yes. *Prikaza.*"

"And if they've all left then, like, they're safe—right?"

"I suppose." She left her thought unspoken: Until Mulengro
tracked them down.

Zach stood up and touched her arm. "C'mon," he said. "I want
to show you something." He led the way back to the shoreline
where his canoe was pulled up out of the water.

Mulengro walked steadily along the highway, eating up the miles
with a tireless pace. He wore a glamour of *draba* so that the motorists
passing him by each saw him as something different, something that
fit in for that time and that place. A jogger. A farm hand. An old
man out for his constitutional. A young boy pushing his bike. He
looked like anything but what he was—a tall Rom *drabarno,* with a
scarred face and pale-blue eyes that were not quite sane. The glamour would not withstand a close scrutiny. It merely allowed the
casual viewer to see what he expected to see walking along the two-
lane highway and sent his gaze on to other points of interest.

Gaje, Mulengro had realized long ago, saw only what they wished
to see, so that a small glamour such as he wore now was no great
effort for him to maintain. He could hold it firm with but a small
portion of his mind while he let the remainder of his magic forge
ahead. Each step brought him nearer to that bright flare of *draba* he
had first sensed while he was in Ottawa. He held its position firm in

his mind, keeping his pace steady. He could be patient. God's will was always done in the end.

As they approached the far side of the lake, Zach lifted his paddle from the water and let them drift shorewards. The reeds and cattails were thick here and the air was pleasantly heavy with marshy scents. In the bow of the canoe, Ola leaned forward. She caught a glimpse of movement from the corner of her eye and turned to see a small brown head, slick with water, disappear with a quick bobbing motion.

"Muskrat," Zach said quietly. He dipped the paddle back in and slowly propelled them through a break in the reeds. Here the water was stiller than on the lake. Lily pads lay in thick bunches, white flowers gleaming in the sunlight, the dark leaves glossy. Ola looked left and right as they moved silently through them. Everything was so quiet. So peaceful. Then she looked ahead and a small gasp escaped her throat.

In the shallows of the new inlet they'd entered, about a half-dozen long-legged heron were feeding. Their pickax bills dipped into the water, coming up with small fish or frogs, then their heads tilted back so that the catch could slide down their throats. Their blue and white feathers shimmered iridescently in the sunshine. At the far end of the inlet, where the marsh had claimed and killed some two dozen or so hardwoods, the birds had made their enormous nests of interwoven branches. By squinting, Ola could make out the fluffy gray feathers of the young.

Zach kept the canoe from drifting with the occasional back-stroke of his paddle and in silence the two of them drank in the sight. A half hour passed like a minute. Or like an entire day. Timeless. Then Zach sighed and back-paddled with a stronger stroke, turning the narrow craft. When they were back on the lake, Ola turned from the bow and smiled at him.

"Thank you," she said. Her eyes shone and the haunted look that had been in them was almost gone.

Zach grinned. "You're welcome," he said. He steered the canoe so that its course followed the shape of the shoreline, rather than heading straight out across the lake to his home. "Five minutes of watching those beauties," he added, "is worth all the lack of conveniences that living out here can bring. They're just too much, you know?"

"I could stay here forever."

"For sure," Zach said. "And you're welcome to stay as long as you want—though I should warn you, the winters get pretty cold."

"I don't mind the cold. I like walking in the woods, summer or winter. Just *being* in them and seeing everything. . . ." She knew she couldn't stay for more than a few days, little say forever, but it was a pleasant fantasy.

Zach chuckled. "You're a lady after my own heart, Ola. Better watch yourself, or you'll find me hanging out under your window some night with a fistful of posies in my hand and shuffling my feet. I might even bring a little fish along—just to keep that cat of yours quiet."

Ola smiled with him. Boboko had been sleeping in the sun when they'd left Zach's place, barely deigning to open one eye when she told him where they were going. She turned to say something to Zach, but suddenly buckled over, pressing her face against the bow of the canoe. There was a white fire shooting through her mind, burning. . . .

Noon came and the man in black paused on the roadside. His *mule* rose from all around him, their presence filling him with new strength. The weariness that had been steadily growing in him washed away and his *draba* shone inside him, replenished, strong again in the light of God. He flexed the magic as a weight lifter might his biceps when the muscles were loose after a workout. A smile flickered on his thin lips and he sent a quick spark of that power south and west of where he stood, sent it into the mind of the *drabarni* he stalked. The pain would make her sit up and understand what it was she faced if she stood up against him. It would warn her to make her peace with God, to take out and measure her sins, for soon she would stand in His judgment and an accounting would be due.

"I am coming," he whispered.

He set off once more, his *mule* streaming invisibly on all sides of him.

Zach brought the canoe to shore with a few quick strokes, afraid that Ola would overturn it with her misplaced weight and tumble in. As soon as the water was shallow enough, he clambered out and pulled her side of the canoe towards him.

"Ola?"

Her face was a mask of pain, the palms of her hands pressed tightly against her temples. She said something in Romany, the words coming out broken and tight. Zach patted her shoulder awkwardly, not knowing what he should do. If she was having some kind of an attack . . . He looked nervously around, wondering if this had something to do with the wizard that she was afraid of. Not that he'd be able to do anything about it if it did.

". . . coming," she muttered.

He leaned closer. "What's coming, Ola?"

She looked up then, her face clearing, hands dropping from where they'd been pressing so fiercely against her temples. The pain only remained in her eyes.

"Mulengro is," she said softly. "*Del!* He is so strong."

She could sit upright by herself now, so Zach brought the canoe closer to shore. Ola was shivering, though the day was warm. Looking around, Zach saw there was nothing he could put around her shoulders, so he set to work moving the canoe out once more, then climbed in and angled it across the lake to take the shortest route to his house. They didn't speak to each other again until they were safely inside.

Zach brought the teas out onto the porch and sat down in the rocker after handing Ola hers. The *drabarni* was staring moodily across the lake. When Zach cleared his throat, she turned, a wan smile playing on her lips.

"I'm nothing but trouble," she said.

Zach shook his head. "What happened out there?"

"He caught me off guard."

"The wizard?"

Ola nodded. "He's so strong. His power burned through my mind like . . . it was like someone stuck a knife in my head. That's what it felt like."

"He . . . he can do that? Like, attack you when he's not even near you?"

"Yes. But he can't really hurt me if I'm prepared for him. It's . . ." She searched for an analogy. "It's like hypnotism, I suppose. He can't really hurt me, but if he can convince my mind that he can, then it's the same thing as though he was standing right in front of me, with his hand on the hilt of a knife."

"What . . . what can we do to stop him?"

"God help us, Zach. I don't know. It's bad enough that he can command *mule* without us having to fear his sorcery as well. I can't stay here any longer. I'm just endangering you and this has nothing to do with you."

"Uh-uh. Like I said last night, you're going to need the vibes that are here just to be able to hold your own against him. We'll be all right. Everything's going to be copacetic."

"Zach, I appreciate your wanting to help me—I really do—but this is something so far beyond the realm of what you're familiar with. . . ." She sighed. For a long moment neither of them spoke. They stared across the lake, sipping their tea, not tasting it.

"Remember last night?" Zach said suddenly. "When we were talking about the manitous—the voices of the wind—and how I can sometimes hear what they're saying?" Ola nodded. "Well, right now they're saying that I can help you."

"Like they were singing 'Good Vibrations' last night?" Ola asked.

"I thought the vibes *were* pretty good last night."

"Yes. Yes, they were."

"This Mulengro, see, he's like a walking time-bomb, Ola. You talk about vibes—well, bad vibes spread a hell of a lot quicker than good ones do. I don't know why that is. But a guy like Mulengro— he's after your people, right now, dig? But the vibes don't stop there. He's killing Gypsies now. What's he going to kill next? The wind's telling me he's got to be stopped, right here and now, and it looks to me like it's up to us to do it 'cause no one else is stepping forward."

"But *what* will we do?"

"We'll think of something. The situation itself provides, you know?"

"This isn't a game, Zach. We can't go waltzing into it as if that's all it is."

"I know. But, like, we've got to go into it all the same."

"I don't have a choice," Ola said. "You do."

"I can't walk away from it. I'm into peace and flowers, Ola, don't get me wrong, but I'm not a pacifist. Someone's out to knock down what I believe in—I'm not going to stand by and watch them do it."

They said nothing for awhile then, each following a personal train of thought. The sound of scratching at the screen startled them. Ola looked over to see Boboko hanging from the screen with his claws.

"Do I have to go through this whole number," he asked, "or will you just let me in?"

Zach looked over and smiled. "It's hard to get used to in some ways," he said as Ola went to let the cat in. "I always did wonder what went on in their heads. They always seem so—"

"Hungry," Boboko interjected as he soft-stepped through the door. "Though we're inscrutable, too. But right now I'm hungry. My stomach's not as big as yours is, you see." He glanced from Ola to their host. "Has anyone given any thought to having some lunch?"

Zach and Ola looked at each other with exaggerated surprise, then they both began to laugh, the seriousness of their mood broken, the fears momentarily held at bay.

Boboko stalked off into the kitchen with his fur in a huff, muttering something about if there was any sense to be found in a creature that walked on two legs, he certainly hadn't seen any sign of it yet.

twenty-four

"Mr. Shaw? I'm Detective Sandler of the Ottawa Police Force and this is my partner, Detective-Sergeant Briggs. We'd like to ask you a few questions if you don't mind. May we come in?"

Tom regarded the two plainclothes policemen with a mixture of relief and the vague irrational fear that often touches civilians when they come into contact with an officer of the law. He knew why they were here. It was about John.

"Mr. Shaw?"

"What? Oh, yes. Please come on in. Can I get you something to drink?"

"So long as it's not alcoholic," Briggs said. He held up his pipe. "Do you mind if I smoke this?"

"No, no. Not at all. Coffee?"

"If it's no trouble."

"Not at all. Make yourselves comfortable while I put the kettle on."

The detectives entered the living room. Will settled on a low lounge chair while Briggs prowled slowly around the room, glancing at the art on the walls. There was an orderliness about the room that bothered him. Everything was too neat. There was too much open space. But when he compared it to his own place he had to admit there was something to say for this kind of designer look. For one thing, it'd keep you cleaning up after yourself, because if you invested this much money in a room you sure as hell wouldn't want to leave beer cans and last night's dirty dishes hanging around. This was the

kind of place Francine and her car salesman would be living in. . . .
He frowned, not wanting to think about her any more than his ghosts.

When Tom returned with the coffees balanced on a tray, he was accompanied by a striking woman. Even with her hair up in a loose bun and her paint-stained jeans and shirt, she was glamourous, Briggs thought.

"This is my wife Gillian," Tom said.

Will regarded her with interest, putting her name together with some of the art on the walls. "This *is* a pleasure," he said, standing up. "You know I almost bought your 'Traces of Spain' that was hanging in Den Art, but by the time I got the money together, it had already been sold. Now your stuff's right out of my price range. You do beautiful work."

"Thank you, Mr. . . . ?"

Tom made the introductions as he laid the coffee tray on the table before the couch. Gillian served them with a simple grace that raised more maudlin thoughts in Briggs. This must be what getting old meant, he thought. You just kept living with regrets and what-might-have-beens until . . . what? Where did it take you in the end?

"So, ah . . . how can I help you?" Tom asked.

Briggs put away his pipe and nodded to his partner. Will took out his notebook, opening it on his knee. "You've been working with John Owczarek recently, haven't you?" he asked.

"Yes. But I didn't just work with him—he was my friend as well. Look, can you tell me what this is all about? I haven't seen John since he lost his house—since it burned down. No one's seen him and I'm worried. Is he in some sort of trouble?"

"We were hoping that perhaps you could tell us."

"What do you mean?"

"Evidence points strongly to arson—your friend's house didn't burn down by itself. Now, normally our line of investigation is pretty clear-cut. We talk to the owner, look into the possibility of insurance fraud, potential enemies, that sort of thing, but since Mr. Owczarek wasn't even carrying any insurance on the place and—"

"It wasn't insured?"

"No."

"Oh, Jesus. He must've lost a bundle." Tom frowned and thought a moment. "Wait a second. If you're thinking that *he's* responsible, you're dead wrong. I was with him that whole evening. We were rehearsing at Doug's, then John and I walked back to his place together. We saw it burning and then . . ." His voice trailed off.

"And then, Mr. Shaw?"

A strange look touched Tom's features. "He looked at me and said, 'There is no John Owczarek,' and then he walked off."

There was a moment's silence, then Briggs leaned forward. "Can you think of any reason why he wouldn't step forward, Mr. Shaw? You'll have to admit that in normal circumstances the owner would make some attempt to contact us."

Tom nodded. He felt in a somewhat compromising situation. He'd considered John to be his friend and didn't want to get him into any more trouble than he obviously already was in—plain-clothes policemen didn't come visiting your friends and acquaintances unless the problem was serious—but on the other hand he wanted to help John. If he *was* in some kind of trouble. . . . But what did he really know about John in the first place? He glanced at Gillian and read the same look in her eyes that had been there last night when she told him that he had to do what he thought best when they'd talked about Tom's confusion. He could always count on her support, which was great, except that he didn't know what to do. There were levels of complexity rising out of John's disappearance that were totally beyond Tom's range of knowledge. Gypsies. Policemen. Arson. God knows what else.

"It's funny," he said finally. "I've been doing a lot of thinking about these things since John vanished as he did—about the way things are and what you really know about a person—and, well, I suppose it's my own naiveté that's been bothering me the most. I knew John for three years, and then suddenly I discovered I didn't know him at all." He told them about the woman he'd met on John's street and what she'd told him about the Gypsies, about how no one he'd contacted knew anything about John's whereabouts and, when questioned, had to admit that they didn't know all that much about him either. "The crazy thing is, he just didn't strike me as a secretive person. That's what's hardest to take. If you'd asked me about him two weeks ago, I would have told you that he's one of the most open people you could meet. But all the time there were all these secret layers. . . . I suppose I feel a little . . . I'm not sure. Betrayed."

Will nodded sympathetically as he took notes. "Do you know this woman's name?" he asked. "The neighbor?"

"No. But she lived right across the street from him. It was a red brick house with a white porch and wicker furniture. I don't know the number offhand, but . . ."

"That's okay. We can find it." Will glanced at Briggs who shrugged. "Well, I guess that's about it," he added, rising. "I'd like to thank you for your help, Mr. Shaw."

Tom nodded and stood as well. "Can you . . . can you tell me why you're looking for John? It's more than just the house, isn't it? But if he's in trouble and I could help . . . ?"

"I'm afraid we're not at liberty to tell you very much," Will said, "but if it'll set your mind at ease, it's mostly in connection with another case we're working on. And so far the evidence points more to Mr. Owczarek being a victim himself, rather than the perpetrator."

"I see. But if you do find him, could you . . . you know, tell him I'm here. That I'd like to help if I could."

"We can do that, Mr. Shaw. With pleasure. I hope he knows what a good friend you are."

Tom nodded. "Maybe. But maybe if I was such a good friend, I'd've known more about him. Been able to help him if he was in trouble. Maybe I wasn't there to talk to him when he needed someone."

"I'll tell you something, Mr. Shaw," Briggs said. "Gypsies aren't the same as you or me. They live in a very close-knit society and anyone who isn't a Gypsy doesn't rank very high in their estimation."

"I . . . I see."

"We'll be in touch, Mr. Shaw," Will said. "It was nice meeting you, Mrs. Shaw. I'll be looking forward to your next showing."

Gillian smiled and showed them the way to the door, leaving Tom standing in the living room, staring blankly at the mantel, his thoughts turned inward. Briggs paused at the front door and looked back at Tom.

"I guess maybe I shouldn't have said that," he said to Gillian. "That thing about Gypsies. I wasn't trying to upset him. I just thought it was something he should know. The way he's tearing himself up . . . There's nothing he could've done—not with a Gypsy. Believe me."

Gillian nodded. "He's upset," she said, "but I think it's always better to know the truth, don't you?"

"That's what our job is, ma'am. Trying to find the truth." Briggs hesitated a moment longer, but there was nothing more to say. He'd already said more than enough. "Thanks for the coffee, Mrs. Shaw."

When Gillian returned to the living room, Tom was sitting down, still pensive. She slipped onto the couch beside him and took his arm.

"I'm all right," Tom said. "I guess I had to hear that. It . . . explains a lot, doesn't it?"

Gillian nodded. "In a way. But even if that's how it is, it doesn't mean that John didn't care for you still in his own way."

"It's not the caring, or lack of it. It's just the . . . I don't know. All the secrecy. Never having *known*."

He leaned his head against hers, folding his arm around her shoulders. She snuggled close, offering him what comfort she could.

"Nice going, Mr. Sensitive," Will said as they got into the car.

"I just thought that he should know—that's all," Briggs replied, settling in his seat. "If you want to go around pointing fingers, save one for Sam. That was one hell of a job of investigating the neighbors he did. He's got an old gossip on the street who'll talk to anyone who stops long enough to pick their nose and what does *he* get out of her?"

"Maybe she doesn't like to talk to cops," Will said. "But at least we know now we can be pretty sure that Owczarek's a Gypsy—that makes the connection clearer."

"I *know* what his connection is," Briggs said. Before Will could reply, the radio squawked. Briggs took the call.

"No shit," Will said thoughtfully when the call was completed. "So he abandoned his car in Perth. What the hell is there in Perth?"

Briggs stared out the windshield. "Gypsies," he said softly. "What say we put our neigborhood gossip on a back burner and call that constable from headquarters, see what they've got in the way of Gypsies down around Perth?"

Will turned to Briggs. "Paddy, we don't *know* Owczarek's our man. He could be just a victim."

"*He's* not dead, Will."

"Not yet." Will turned the ignition and the car started with a cough of exhaust. "But maybe he's next."

Briggs shook his head. "I've got a gut feeling on this, Will."

"I'm the one that has gut feelings, Paddy. You never get 'em."

"So that's why I'm listening to this one. Owczarek's in this shit so deep it's coming out of his ears. He's not next. The only way he's connected to 'next' is that he's going to be wielding this *shuko* or leopard's paw club or whatever the hell it is that he's using to kill people."

Will put the car into gear and pulled away from the curb. "You're pushing," he said. "I'll admit he looks good. He's got the mobility . . . he's a Gypsy . . . but we need something more than what we've got right now to convince the Inspector."

"We'll get it."

The ghosts roiled in Briggs' mind, pushing, always pushing now. Somehow this case had set them all loose inside him, and he knew he'd get no peace until they brought the killer in—in pieces if they had to. Briggs didn't care. He just wanted this to be over.

twenty-five

Bob Gourlay was dreaming. He turned restlessly on the mattress, his hand between his legs, his mouth half-open, face nuzzled against the soiled pillow. He was dreaming about the big breasted girl who worked in the Becker's on Gore Street, that she was doing things to him that he'd only seen in the picture books that he and Stan bought over in Smiths Falls. The real hot books. He groaned, his hand moving faster. Her tongue was as long as a snake's in his dream and she could do tricks with it that made his testicles ache for release.

Outside the farmhouse, the traffic was light on Highway 2. It was just going on ten past twelve and the thing that had once been Stan Gourlay sat in the cab of the pickup, grinning with what was left of its mouth. It stared up at the farmhouse and hummed wetly through the flaps of skin.

> "A-huntin' we will go,
> a-huntin' we will go,
> hi-ho the fuckin' derry-o,
> a-huntin' we will go. . . ."

By twelve-thirty, the cab was empty. All that remained of its noontime visitor was a rotting smell that hung heavily in the air. In the farmhouse, Bob lay on his back, hand still, the pressure eased. He was still dreaming, but now he saw himself and his brother moving quietly—*real* quietly—through the woods and he had the .12-gauge in his hands, both hammers cocked. He smiled when he heard a cat meow.

twenty-six

Jeff remembered reading about the murders. Like most people, he was becoming inured to the endless parade of violence that touched the front pages of newspapers and videoed its way across the television screen at six and eleven o'clock each night. He'd been shocked—for about all of a minute or so—until he turned the page and read about something else. But now . . . When Janfri told him about the *mulo* of the first victim that had been seen walking down Scott Street in the company of a stranger in black, the thing he'd seen in Ola's cottage reared up in his mind's eye. He pushed it away, suppressing a shiver, and tried to concentrate on what Janfri was saying. But when the talk came to Old Lyuba and her name for the stranger, the image arose again.

What if there really were things that . . . didn't quite die? If, instead of hallucinating a few frames from a Roger Corman flick, he'd actually *seen* some half-dead creature lying there, reaching for him. . . .

What kept him from dismissing Janfri's story out of hand was the Gypsy's own obvious discomfort at accepting any of it as real. All it was was a collection of hints and macabre promises, fanned to a higher flame by the superstitious nature of the other Gypsies. And yet, even in the middle of the day, it was somehow easier to accept than to deny. When his own turn came, he told everything, from the beating the Gourlays had given him, to what he'd seen on Ola's porch, to the weird thoughts that had been filling his own head this morning. Ola as witch. Spirits that refused to die. Nonsense. Dreams. Unfortunately, Janfri didn't even smile.

"Is she a Gypsy?" Janfri asked when he was done.

"Ola? I didn't think so. But she knows a lot about your people— their remedies and lore—and she looks a lot like you—the same coloring, same kind of facial features. I never really thought about it before. I mean, she said she's an African and, while she doesn't really have African features, I never had any reason to question it. Why do you ask?"

"Because of the *drabarni* I'm looking for. She fits Lyuba's description better than anyone else I've run into so far."

Jeff shook his head. "I don't know." He got up from the kitchen table and filled the kettle again. "Where does all this leave us?" he asked as he set it on the stove.

Janfri looked thoughtful. "The only place we can begin," he said finally, "is with these Gourlays of yours."

Just mentioning their name made Jeff's bruises ache. "They're not going to tell us anything they don't want to," he said, "and I kind of doubt that we'll be able to beat it out of them."

Janfri shrugged. He was playing with a thin strip of cloth that was comprised of a number of short lengths knotted together. He ran his fingers over the knots, back and forth—like a nun with her rosary, Jeff thought.

"If they have your friend," the Gypsy said, "and they're not keeping her at their house, they can still lead us to her. We have only to follow them."

That was if Ola wasn't already dead, Jeff thought, but he refused to voice that thought and thereby give it more life than it already had in his own mind. "Do you want to go now?" he asked.

"No. I think it would be better if we waited until this evening. By now your Constable Finlay may have my description from the Ottawa Police. If he does, he'll be looking for both of us."

"What do the police want with you anyway?"

"What do they ever want with a Gypsy? My house burned down and I didn't report it. I knew the men who were killed. I gave a pair of plainclothesmen false ID. Take your choice—one or all of the above."

Jeff nodded. Follow the Gourlays. Tonight. Why wasn't he looking forward to this?

"I think you're flipping out," Jackie said when she got home. She gave Janfri a suspicious look and only nodded when Jeff introduced

her to him. "Craig was back just before I left—did you know that
he spent a good two hours in the restaurant this afternoon, just
watching that car? Well, when he came back he wanted to know if
you'd called, where you were. He was being very casual about it,
trying not to let on like it was anything important, but I could tell
he wanted to know badly." She looked at Janfri, not bothering to
hide her feelings. "Why are you hiding this guy? You don't know
anything about him. He could be a bank robber or a mass murderer
for all you know."

"Listen to me," Jeff said, "and then decide."

Jackie did. She was visibly upset, growing more so as the story
unfolded. Rather than listening straight through, she kept interrupting with questions or pointing out how flimsily everything hung
together.

"Now I know you're flipping out," she said when Jeff was done.
"You I don't know," she told Janfri, "but, Jeff. For God's sake. Listen
to what you're saying. How can you sit there and pretend that any
of it makes sense? Gypsies and witches and ghosts and God knows
what else."

"Jackie—"

"You know what I think? I think you took a good whack on the
head and it scrambled up your brains. And you," she added, turning
to Janfri. "I don't know what you're planning to get out of this, but
you should be ashamed of yourself at egging him on like this."

"What about the thing I saw at Ola's?"

Jackie tapped the side of her head. "The thing *you* saw—I didn't.
And I was right beside you, remember?"

"Well, what about Ola then?"

Jackie sighed and had to ask herself if Jeff's concern over the
black woman was really justified, or whether it was just her own
jealousy that was making small of it. She didn't like the idea of
being jealous, but she couldn't stop the feeling from coloring her
thinking. Not now, when there was a possibility of something happening between her and Jeff.

"Okay," she admitted. "Ola's just taking off doesn't make any
sense. But that still doesn't mean that there are mysterious men in

black running around trying to kill her—even if she *is* a Gypsy, which I doubt—nor that the Gourlays have kidnapped her. Right?"

Jeff nodded, willing to agree with that. Praying that it was true. "But what about the things that Janfri's told us?"

"I don't know Janfri from Adam," Jackie said, speaking as though the man wasn't even present. He bothered her with his dark good looks and that intense light in his eyes. "And even if half of what he says is true, that still doesn't mean it has any relevance to what we're talking about. I've talked to Ola, too, you know. All that magic mumbo jumbo's just for the books—I asked her about it once and that's what she told me. If she's a witch, Jeff, then I'm Stan Gourlay's sister." She paused for a breath and turned to Janfri. "You still haven't told me what you expect to get out of this," she said. "In fact you haven't said two words since we started talking about all of this."

Jeff sighed. He wished that Jackie wasn't acting so bitchy—it wasn't like her at all—but at the same time everything she said made sense as well. Made perfect sense, really, if it wasn't for what he'd seen and the *feeling* he had.

Janfri's fingers stilled their playing with the knotted cloth he held. "It doesn't really matter what you think, Miss Sim," he said. "Perhaps what Jeff hasn't made as clear as he should have is the fact that I'm not exactly comfortable with all this talk of magic and ghosts either. Unfortunately, I have an obligation—to an old woman, to my people—to do what I can. I can go ahead on my own and no longer interfere with your life, if that's what you wish. I have better things to do myself than go chasing after a woman who might or might not be a Gypsy, who might or might not be able to help me.

"What keeps me going is this one question I ask myself: What if it is all real? If it *is* real and I might have been able to do something about it but didn't, how could I live with myself? I realize that matters of honor are not so strictly upheld among the *Gaje* as they are among my people. But I am a Rom and so I will do what a true Rom would do. I will seek this woman because she might be able to help me. And if she is a Gypsy, then she is in danger as well, so I will try to help her. With or without Jeff's help. Or yours."

His gaze remained locked on hers the whole time he spoke, the potency of his dark eyes driving each point home. What if it *was* all true? she asked herself, wanting to laugh, but so long as he held her gaze, finding she couldn't. And even if it was just Ola being kidnapped by the Gourlays—never mind all the rest of it—shouldn't she want to help? Was she going to be that small-minded? Would she even want a relationship with someone if his heart belonged to someone else? She was beginning to feel, she realized, as though she was in the middle of a Harlequin Romance.

"So you're going to go to the Gourlays' place tonight and just . . . follow them?"

"One must begin somewhere," Janfri replied.

Jackie sighed. "Craig's going to have an eye out for your car, Jeff, and he's already impounded Janfri's, so I suppose we'll have to go in mine."

"You don't have to come too, Jackie," Jeff began, but she cut him off with an abrupt shake of her head.

"Maybe I've got something invested in this as well," she said. "I don't know Ola as well as you—but I still like her. I want to help. And I don't want to sit around here all night worrying about what's happening with you. If the Gourlays ever get hold of you out on a dark road somewhere . . ." She frowned, then forced a smile into place. "And besides. Maybe I'll get a firsthand look at all these magical goings-on."

"I hope not," Janfri said seriously.

Jackie nodded. "Yeah. Well, there's that, isn't there?"

There was a moment's silence. Janfri's fingers moved across the knotted cloth in his hands. Jeff and Jackie avoided each other's eyes, both wanting to say more than they could with a third person present, but relieved at the same time that they couldn't. After awhile, Jackie stood up.

"We'd better have something to eat before we go," she said. "Cheese and cuke sandwiches sound okay?"

The two men nodded. Jeff shifted in his chair, then got up to help her.

"I guess we should start out by checking The Zoo," he said, "see if their pickup's parked outside. Or maybe up at MacDonald's garage. Then we take a spin 'round their house. . . ."

Jackie nodded, cutting the bread with more force than was necessary to get the knife through the loaf. Janfri said nothing, letting his silence be agreement enough.

twenty-seven

Craig Finlay was a twelve-year veteran on the Perth Police Force. It was a job he liked and though it was limited in excitement, that suited him just fine. The big city could keep its murders and syndicates, its biker gangs, rapists, bank robberies, and just general bad craziness, thank you very much. The worst calls he got were civil disturbances like drunk & disorderly conduct, a few fights, some domestic squabbles. Occasionally he'd get called out to help the Ontario Provincial Police on a particularly messy highway accident, but that was rare. There was also the odd hunting accident, but nothing terminal, thank God, at least not since he'd joined the force back in the summer of '71.

It was going on six-thirty as he was leaving the police station. He paused by the cruiser. Going to be a nice night. Be even nicer if he hadn't bothered to take that call from Briggs. Detective-Sergeant Briggs. Let's keep those titles. Stomach in, shoulders out. Show your rank. Lucy hadn't been too happy that he'd be late for dinner—but he guessed she was used to it. Didn't like it—she never would and he didn't blame her because he didn't like it himself—but it came with the territory, even in a quiet town like Perth. Impounding Cerinek's car had been the high point of his day—until he'd talked to Patrick Briggs. He'd heard Briggs out patiently, then put in his own two cents worth. Not that it ever did any good. City Police, the OPP, the RCMP, they all figured small town police needed someone around to help them blow their noses, and all they were good for was doing the gopher work for the "real" cops, with smiles on their faces. But when you wanted something from them, like the time he'd called in to Ottawa to have them pick up Bradley Moulton a couple of months back, all he'd got from their dispatch was, "Shit, you think *you've* got problems?" The "hick" was left unsaid.

"Listen," he'd told Briggs. "Gypsies sort of left this area around the same time the automobile became popular, you know what I mean?"

"Cute. Real cute. Then how come you called in an abandoned car that was last seen driven by a Gypsy?"

"Hey, I called it in, right?"

"All I'm asking you to do is check up on any Gypsies in your area."

"Gypsies. Mendicants. Beggars. We kinda ran out of them all, Briggs. Mind you, we do get the odd hobo."

"So you've got nothing?"

"Zip." But then Craig remembered the two men who'd left Tinkers with Jeff Owen earlier in the afternoon. The guy with the walrus—hadn't he seen him around town over the summer? He closed his eyes, trying to remember.

"Yeah," Briggs said. "Well, thanks for your help. If things start to get messy down there in the next day or so, just remember I gave you fair warning."

"Sure. I'll keep you posted."

"You do that."

Briggs hung up with an abrupt click on his end and Craig slowly lowered the receiver into its cradle. Shit, he thought. Trailer camp on Highway 4. That's where he'd seen the guy before. He wasn't going to swear the old fellow was a Gypsy, but he had to go check it out, just in case. He picked up the phone again and dialed his home number.

"Lucy? Look, hon, I'm going to be a little late tonight. Yeah, I know, but . . ."

● ● ●

Craig eased the police cruiser up the rutted road that led to Jeff Owen's cabin. He parked in front of the two-story structure and got out, stretching his back muscles before walking up to the front door. He'd decided to check out a couple of things before he drove up to the trailer park. Calling in on Jackie had been the first thing, to see if she'd heard from Jeff. He'd done that as soon as he'd left the station. Now as he walked behind the cabin and saw the riot of vegetation that passed for Jeff's backyard, be began to get an uneasy feeling.

He liked Jeff. He was a decent guy. So what the hell was he doing getting himself involved with these guys? He was sure now that the clean-shaven one had been this Cerinek aka John something-or-other that the boys up in Ottawa were looking for, and it was plain from what he could see of the land behind Jeff's cabin that no one had been clearing out the bush here for a long, long time.

He headed for his car and drove back towards Perth. The light was steadily leaking from the sky, coming up hard on evening by the time he reached the turnoff to the trailer park. He wasn't really expecting to find either Cerinek, Jeff or the mustached man here, so he was somewhat surprised to find the latter sitting on the steps of a trailer, watching the cruiser's approach with expressionless eyes. Craig pulled up on the far side of the van and parked. Taking his cap from the seat beside him, he put it on and stepped outside.

"Nice evening, Mr. . . . ?"

"Fields," Tibo said. "William Fields. Call me Bill."

Craig smiled, nodded to the woman who was standing by a Coleman stove, smoking a pipe. Call him "Bill." Sure. Back at the restaurant his name had been Pat. "Saw you in Tinkers today," he said to Tibo. "Remember?"

Tibo nodded.

"How's that bush-clearing going?"

Tibo shrugged. "One day Jeff calls us in to work, the next day he changes his mind." He spat in the dirt beside the steps. "Wasted the whole day waiting for him to make up his mind."

Craig leaned against the hood of the cruiser, pushed his cap back from his forehead. "Comes from his being a writer," he said. "Never knew one that could make up his mind. Say, what happened to that friend of yours—what was his name again?"

"John Wood. He drove back up to Fallbrook. You just missed him."

"Yeah? Too bad. Some people were looking for him."

There was a moment's silence, then Tibo smiled. "That John. People are always looking for him. He's too handsome by half, I tell you! Was it a husband or someone he owes money to?"

"Neither. It was the police in Ottawa."

Foster Street was lined with parked cars as Jackie steered her Honda slowly down it. Jeff was beside her in the passenger's seat, while Jan-fri sat in the back. Jackie wasn't sure she liked having him behind her, but at the same time she didn't want him in the front with her either. She kept glancing in the rearview mirror to find his gaze meeting hers each time before she quickly slid hers away. They cruised the neighboring streets, right on Gore, left on Herriot and past the park, up north on Wilson. There was no sign of the Gourlays' pickup.

"Now what?" Jackie asked. She tried to keep the nervous quiver out of her voice, but couldn't stop gripping the steering wheel with tight fingers.

"Guess we'll have to try their house," Jeff said. "We can check out MacDonald's garage on the way."

Obediently, Jackie brought them back onto Gore Street and headed out of town.

As the shadows grew deeper, Mulengro drew strength from the thickening dark. His *mule* arose from the ground like low mists and trailed around his feet as he walked tirelessly along the highway. There was a humming in the scarred man's mind, a sense of urgency drawing him on. Twice more he'd mentally attacked the *drabarni* he sought, but she was prepared for him now and each attack was deflected. He would need physical contact with her now to defeat her. But then . . . what strength her *muli* would give him in his work. From the past he shaped a new future for the Rom and every strength was needed. He took what was *marhime* and cleansed it, using it to further his goal.

The doctors had told him that he embraced the past, rather than let it go, and it was for this reason that his condition did not improve. He clung too fiercely to the past and that was why he did not forget. But they were *Gaje* and what did they know? He had a destiny to fulfill and it was important that he did not forget the lessons that the past had taught him. God had given him work to do. The *mule* were his judgments and his executioners—the harbingers of doom to those who were *marhime,* as the *mule* themselves had been before they were cleansed in God's bright light. How could the doctors understand that?

The Nazis had called his people *Rassenverfolgle*—racially undesirable—and he could almost love them for the truth that they had inadvertently shown him, for all that they were *Gaje*. The Rom had become *marhime* in the eyes of God. That was why they suffered. That was the reason for their poverty, the reason they had first left their homeland to wander the world, the reason for their persecution. And that was the reason he must cleanse them in the eyes of God.

It was for him to prepare them for Romanestan—the land that God would surely give them for their own when they proved worthy of it. Mulengro cared nothing for *Gaje*. They could writhe in their own dirt for as long as they wished. They were not his people. But the Rom . . . oh, the Rom must learn. Even if they must die to learn. They might curse him now, but in the years to come, they would speak reverently of him and the thankless work he had done. The *swatura* told around the campfires would tell of his sacrifices. He would be remembered in all the years to come.

He walked on, his boot heels clicking against the asphalt, his *mule* misting about his feet. There were Rom near. Not many. Their souls called to him, but not with the same flare of power as did the soul of the *drabarni* he sought. His thin lips shaped what passed for a smile. She would serve him well. But first he would seek the measure of those Rom who, while not as powerful as her, were that much nearer.

Bob Gourlay sat on the front porch of the old farmhouse. He finished the remains of a sardine sandwich and washed it down with the last of his beer. Beside him lay Stan's rifle and his own .12-gauge, as well as a couple of boxes of spare shells. He crushed the beer can and tossed it into the weed jungle in the front yard. He'd woken with a headache behind his eyes and it hadn't gotten any better. It wouldn't get any better, he knew, not until they set some things to right.

"Say-hey, brother Bob. Sure wish I had a brew."

Bob started, turned slowly to find the thing that his brother had become sitting on the steps beside him. The sandwich and beer stirred uneasily in his stomach as he looked at the ruin of his brother's face. An odor of graveyard decay settled heavily on the air.

"I . . . I could get you one . . . Stan . . ."

The thing sighed wetly. "Can't drink, brother Bob. Can't do much of anythin', maybe, 'cept hurt."

"I cleaned your rifle."

Flaps of skin moved on the creature's face, shaping a rough parody of a grin. "Now that was right kind of you, little brother, but a gun won't be of much use to me, nossir." The thing stood up. "Come along now, brother Bob. We got business to attend to."

Bob scrambled to his feet.

"You just bring your old shotgun now. Time's a-wastin'."

Bob followed the shuffling monstrosity to the pickup, his eyes clogging with tears as the pounding in his head picked up its tempo. He slid into the driver's seat and bent his head over the steering wheel, took a deep breath and almost choked. The dead air in the cab was heavy with foulness—remnants of last night mixed with the fresh reek Stan brought into it when he took the passenger's seat.

"Don't crap out on me, little brother."

Bob shook his head, wincing at the pain the sudden movement brought. He fumbled with the ignition, turned the engine over, backed out onto the highway without even looking to see if there was any traffic coming.

"The lights, Bob."

"The . . . ? Oh, yeah."

Bob hit the switch and the pickup's headbeams stabbed the settling night. He stepped on the gas. The pickup lurched, smoothed out as he changed gears. He shot a glance at the thing beside him and lowered the window on his side. It wasn't like it was supposed to be, he thought. This thing might be his brother Stan, but it was still dead. He thought that he'd get used to it, but there was no way, no fucking way sir, he could ever get used to that thing. And yet if it was still his brother . . . what was left of his brother . . . and he still loved Stan and—Lord Jesus! If only his head would stop aching. If he could just think straight . . .

Jeff lowered the binoculars that Jackie had suggested they bring, his face pasty white. Half an hour ago they'd pulled over to the side of the highway about a quarter of a mile short of the Gourlay place, lights out, coasting to a stop with the engine dead. One by one they stepped out of the car and ran bent-backed along the ditch, squatting down when headlights warned them of oncoming vehicles. They moved steadily closer until they had a good view of the farmhouse, then took turns watching Bob Gourlay eat a sandwich and drink a couple of beers on the front porch, the binoculars bringing him up close. Bob sat there as time dragged by.

"What do you think he's doing, just sitting there?" Jackie had whispered after her first view. She passed the binoculars to Janfri, who received them with a silent nod.

"Waiting for Stan," Jeff guessed. "I don't know where *he* is, but that must be what Bob's doing. Waiting for his big brother." The binoculars came his way again and he took them, adjusting the focus slightly. "And I guess we just have to wait, too."

It was while Jeff had the glasses that Stan came shuffling out of the darkness. The sight of the thing woke an ache in Jeff's temples. He bit at his lip, a cold chill traveling through him.

"Jeff. What is it?"

Jeff slowly passed the binoculars to Jackie. Drops of sweat beaded his brow. "L-look," he said. The word came out like a frog's croak.

"It's kind of hard to see," Jackie said, peering through the glasses. "Looks like he's talking to himself." They only had the light coming from the hallway behind Bob to see him by—a weak light that left more in shadow than it illuminated.

"It . . . it's there!" Jeff said in a harsh whisper. "The thing from Ola's cottage!"

Jackie had been nervous ever since they'd left her apartment, but now she was getting scared. The hard fact hit her that maybe Jeff *was* flipping out. She swept the glasses back and forth across the porch, searching. All she could think of was that here she was spying on the Gourlays, which could be dangerous enough all on its own, with a potential crazy and some strange Gypsy on her hands.

"I don't see anyone else," she said slowly.

Jeff started to grab for the glasses, but Janfri's hand was there first, plucking them from Jackie's grip.

"Then that's it," Jeff said. He was shivering with his chill, his headache getting worse. He turned away from the house, crouched down against the embankment, and hugged his knees. "I've had it. I . . . I'm losing my grip. . . ."

Jackie hesitated, wanting to comfort him, but too scared to do it. What were you supposed to do in a situation like this? What if he got violent like he had back at Ola's? It'd lasted for only a second, but if that blow had connected . . .

"*O mulo,*" Janfri said softly. His voice was hard and confused all at the same time.

"What?" Jackie asked.

Janfri lowered the binoculars. When he turned to look at her, his eyes seemed to almost glow in the darkness. Oh, Jesus, Jackie thought. Don't let 'em both flip out on me.

"My uncle told me once," Janfri said, "that a person born between the halves of the day can see beyond this world."

"Are you saying that—"

"I was born between the night and the day," the Gypsy said in a sharp whisper, "and I see something on that porch that is not of this world. I don't want it to be there any more than you do, but I can't ignore the fact that it's there."

"You're just making it worse," Jackie began, but the sound of the Gourlays' pickup starting up cut off any further argument.

"I *must* follow them," Janfri said as the truck backed out of the driveway. "Will you lend me your car?"

Jeff caught his arm. "Did you *really* see something? Don't shit me now."

"Yes."

"Then I'm going too."

The pickup was backing onto the highway. The white glare of its back-up lights threw their faces into bold relief. The fear in Jeff's features and the haunted look in Janfri's eyes decided Jackie that they weren't putting her on. She glanced at the truck as the back-up lights died, then stood abruptly, her heart drumming in her chest.

"Let's go!" she cried.

She ran back to the Honda without waiting to hear their response.

"The police?" Tibo said. He exchanged a worried glance with Ursula.

"Look, Mr. Fields. I think it's time we stopped playing games, okay?" Craig moved away from the cruiser and stepped to where Tibo was sitting. He towered over the Gypsy. "Maybe you'd better come with me."

"But I've done nothing—I swear on my father's grave!"

"I'm not arresting you," Craig said. At least not until I talk to Briggs, he added to himself. That reminded him of the other thing the Ottawa detective had told him. "It's for your own protection," he began to add, then paused.

Something changed in the faces of the two Gypsies. Ursula's fingers went numb, dropping the ladle she was using to stir the stew she was cooking on the Coleman stove. She took a half-step back. Tibo started to rise from the steps, the whites of his eyes showing in the lantern light. Craig's hand went to his gun, then he realized that they weren't making a move against him. There was something behind him.

He turned, feeling a sudden cold draft on his neck, to see a black-clad figure stepping from the shadows. Wisps of fog wreathed his lower legs. The Gypsies' fear touched him like a palpable presence. His bowels went tight. Sweat started up in his armpits, soaking his shirt. At first he thought the stranger was wearing a mask, but when he stepped into the lantern light, Craig saw that it was a webwork of scar tissue on the man's upper cheeks that left that impression. There was an almost wolflike quality to his features . . . and a hunger in the man's eyes. Craig swallowed dryly.

"I'd like to see some ID," he said, hand tightening on the grip of his police-issue .38.

"Step aside, *shanglo,*" the stranger said. His voice went up Craig's spine like a rasping file rubbing against his bones. The menace emanating from him was like a physical blow. Jesus, Craig thought, realizing that the Fields weren't alone in being afraid. Feeling stupid, he found himself drawing his revolver.

"Hands on the car," he said, leveling the .38. "Let's *move!*"

The stranger regarded Craig for a long silent moment, a vague smile touching his lips. Craig cocked the hammer of his revolver with his thumb. The click sounded loud in the stillness. This was only the third time he'd drawn his weapon while on the job. He found himself incongruously thinking of the reports he'd have to fill out. Every time you pulled your piece you had to have a damn good reason, and it had to be in writing. And if the chief didn't think your reasons warranted—

Craig's flow of thought was cut off abruptly. The fog wreathing the man's legs was rising upward, moving between the man and himself, thickening, taking a humanoid shape. Craig stepped back, brought his left hand up to support his right wrist. The gun was a dead weight in his hands. His finger tightened on the trigger. The fog . . . it was . . . a man . . . three, four men . . .

He meant to pull the trigger. He *was* pulling it. But those insubstantial shadow-shapes tore into him before his brain could send the message to his finger. A hand like a vise gripped his shoulder, another his right arm. And they pulled. And there was a roar of pain flooding his head. Dumbly he watched his arm fall to the ground. Blood splattered his uniform. Red hot fires ran through him. Death came at the same time as he found his voice. Too late. Too late to do anything but die as the *mule* clawed open his chest cavity and scooped his organs out and onto the ground in front of him. He was dead before his body toppled to join them.

Tibo and Ursula were rooted where they stood. The *mule* moved towards them, drifting like smoke. There was no trace of blood on their gray taloned hands. No features in their empty faces.

"*Marhime*," Mulengro said softly, the word encompassing their crime and their fate all in one breath.

Tibo screamed as the *mule* touched him—a raw primal howl that carried across the fields behind them. Their trailer was the closest to the road. But the time their nearest neighbor came running up— Mrs. George Duncan, two hundred and ten pounds in a pair of Bermuda shorts and a tank top—there were only the three mutilated corpses lying in the lamplight. Mulengro and his *mule* were gone. Lisa Duncan's mindless wail of panic split the night's quiet like a siren.

Ola sat on the slope between Zach's cottage and the lakefront, her knees drawn up to her chin, her eyes on what she could see of the dark quiet water through the trees. Her hair hung down her back in a loose braid and she wore a light quilted jacket against the gathering coolness—a chill that came from inside her more than it did from the night air. When Boboko found her and climbed onto her lap, she stroked his fur with quick nervous movements.

"There's death in the air," Ola whispered, as though afraid that if she spoke too loudly there would be more.

"Not to mention too many spaced-out hippies," Boboko replied. His attempt at levity went unheard.

"I can *feel* him . . . drawing near."

Boboko remembered her vision. The coldness in her touched him as well now and he no longer felt able to joke.

"He must have seen me when he killed that old woman," Ola said. "Saw me watching from the shadows. And now he wants to kill me, too."

Boboko stirred uneasily in her lap. "Then we can't stay here," he said. "We've got to go."

"Go where? 'Mulengro,' the old woman called him. Where could we hide from one who controls the *mule* of the dead, Boboko?"

"You were strong in our old home."

"And weak now, so far from it, but I doubt I was ever strong enough to face this Mulengro. Yet face him I must."

Twice more today, after that first time on the lake, she'd felt the brush of Mulengro's thoughts against her mind—probing thoughts that measured her strengths, tested her for weaknesses. She could hold him at bay so long as there was distance between them. But he was coming closer. What would she do when she had to confront him physically? She would be no match for his power, his *mule*. . . .

Boboko moved his head against her hand, trying to reassure her. They sat quietly, listening to the night. A loon cried from the lake. From the cottage behind them they could hear Zach playing a dulcimer and singing Donovan's "Isle of Islay." The wind stirred the trees above them and Ola wondered what Zach would hear in its voice. But the wind, like the night, held its silence like a secret. After a while Ola pushed Boboko gently from her lap and stood, hugging her jacket close.

"Let's go in," she said.

Boboko regarded the dark forest surrounding Zach's lot for a long moment, then trotted to catch up with her before she went inside. He hated not being able to operate the door latch by himself and having to depend on Ola and Zach for his comings and goings.

"Turn around," Stan said when they reached Port Elmsley. "We're goin' the wrong way, little brother."

Bob pulled a U-turn at the intersection and pointed the pickup back in the same direction that they'd come.

"How . . . how do you know where we're goin' . . . Stan?"

"I just know, brother Bob. I can feel her in my head—like there's somethin' connectin' me to her. I'm hot-wired to her, yessir, and there's no way she can hide from me. Have yourself a brew, Bob. You're lookin' peak-ed."

"I . . . I'm not thirsty. Got a headache."

The thing beside him grinned obscenely. "Ann-tis-i-pay-shy-un—that's what it is, little brother. Keep that pedal to the floor. Time's a-wastin'."

The pickup shot forward, barreling down the highway. In the rearview mirror, if either Bob or Stan had bothered to look, a set of lights was still trailing behind them.

twenty-eight

The upper New York State night was quiet around the Hollis farm. Earl Hollis owned a hundred and twenty acres of rocky farmland off Highway 11 running northeast out of Malone. There was little travel on the dirt road leading out to his place. The nine touring cars of the Pataloeshti *kumpania* were probably the most traffic that the old road had seen since Billy-Bob's annual barbecue two weeks ago. The cars were now parked behind Earl's barn, out of sight of the road, and he was sitting outside Big George's tent sharing a mickey of brandy that the fat Gypsy had produced after dinner.

Earl liked Gypsies, liked the free work the *kumpaniyi* did for him whenever they were passing through; liked the music and the drinking around a fire till the birds' chorus started at first light; liked watching the young Gypsy women moving through the camp, though he knew better than to make a move on them. That kind of thing wasn't much up his line anymore—though he could still look. Clocking in at seventy-six last spring didn't make him much of a doer anymore.

He and Big George were just sitting in the firelight now, all talked out. He'd passed on what news he had from other Rom who'd passed through lately and listened gravely to Big George's story of the doings up across the border. Weird shit, he'd thought, puffing on his pipe. But that was the way things were around Gypsies. They were always caught up in the middle of something and it always made one hell of a tale. Not that he'd be shooting off his mouth to the likes of Billy-Bob or Old John Turner or any of his other neighbors about any of it. The thing that kept the Rom coming back to him was that he knew when to keep his mouth shut. And to whom. He liked the sense of importance that being a clearinghouse for Gypsy messages gave him. Hell, he didn't have much of anything else left, what with Meg dead four years now and the kids long gone.

He refilled his tin mug with a bottom of brandy and looked up as the tall Rom who'd been the last to arrive today walked up to the fire. This boy was all muscle, Earl thought. He was going to make a fine *rom baro* someday. You could see it in his build.

"*Sarishan,* Big George. Earl."

Big George nodded a greeting and indicated a stool. "Some brandy, Yojo?"

"You look like you could use it," Earl added as he handed over the bottle.

Yojo settled heavily on the stool and accepted the brandy with a nod of thanks. Fishing a small cup out of his jacket, he tipped the bottle, filling the cup halfway before returning the brandy to Earl. He took a gulp large enough to make his eyes burn. When the liquor settled warm in his stomach, he sighed.

"I wish Janfri was here," he said. "He shouldn't have stayed."

"O Boshbaro does what he pleases," Big George said. "That has always been his way."

"Not this time," Yojo said. "And I should have stayed with him."

"You have a family."

Yojo looked up, his eyes bright in the firelight. "I do, Big George. And here I am with them. But now I would ask you to care for them while I see to my other responsibility—the safety of my brother."

"What does Simza say?"

"That Janfri is my brother and I should be with him in his time of trouble."

"*Bater,*" Big George said. "I accept the responsibility of your *tsera,* Yojo. We will camp here for"— he glanced at Earl —"perhaps a week, then move on to Rommeville."

"It's okay by me," Earl said. "Stay as long as you like, boys."

Yojo finished his brandy and, thrusting the cup back into his pocket, stood. "Thank you, Big George. Stay with God."

Big George nodded. "Go with God, Yojo."

Earl and the *rom baro* watched the big Gypsy return to his tent. Thirty minutes later, his Lincoln was edging its way from the dirt road and onto Highway 11.

twenty-nine 29

Briggs stood outside the flood of lights that lit the area surrounding Tibo Lee's trailer. The night was awash with sound. Crickets. Bullfrogs from a creek out behind the trailer park. The murmur of reporters and onlookers behind the police barricades. He glanced to where Will was standing with some of the local police. The corpses were bagged and gone now, but there was still enough blood soaking the ground that you couldn't mistake this for anything but what it was: a homicide investigation.

Officially, this was out of their jurisdiction, but when the word reached Ottawa, the Inspector had sent them down to lend what aid they could on what had begun as "their case." It didn't make Briggs feel any better that they'd had Owczarek in their hands and just let him slip through. If they'd just taken the time to look in the trunk of his car . . . they would probably have found the leopard paw club that he was using on his victims. Or these *shuko* like MacDonald had shown them. Will thought he'd been pushing, but the evidence, circumstantial though most of it was, was pointing more and more to Owczarek.

He'd been in Ottawa when the other killings had taken place. He was a Gypsy himself. His house had been burned down and the symbol painted on its walls connected him to the murders. His car had been found abandoned in Perth—meaning the odds were good that he'd been here himself—and look what had happened. There was little doubt in Briggs' mind that Owczarek was their man. He'd killed Gypsies, two hookers, a wino, and now a cop. They'd had him and let him slip right through their fingers. Now the sucker was still out there somewhere and who knew where the hell he'd turn up next?

The man talking to Will by the trailer was Phillip Archambault, the OPP officer in charge of the case. Frederick Butler, Perth's Chief of Police, was standing with them. The case was out of Butler's jurisdiction as well, since the slaughter had taken place outside of the town limits, but Constable Finlay had been one of his men and who was going to tell Butler that his help wasn't wanted?

It was weird, Briggs thought, how something like this dissolved all the rivalry and friction between the various police forces. There were even a couple of horsemen here—being helpful, not lording it over the rest of them because they were federal, like they usually did. In different circumstances . . . It could be a kidnapping and everybody'd be screaming about jurisdiction, or a drug bust and they'd all be stepping on each other's toes, but as soon as a cop bought it, as soon as it was one of their own being taken away in the green bag, the rivalry vanished like it had never existed. It was kind of sad that it took something like this to bring them all together. They were all supposed to be working towards the same thing, after all. But Briggs knew himself how hard it was to take the RCMP when they were playing king shit on turd hill. And he hadn't exactly been easy on Finlay when he was talking to him this afternoon. Now Finlay was dead—his ghost joining the others inside Briggs—while Owczarek was running free.

Briggs sighed. He stuffed his cold pipe into his jacket and, hands in his pockets, wandered over to where Will stood to see how things were coming along.

"Hell," Archambault, the OPP officer was saying. "We don't even know if he *has* a vehicle. There haven't been any stolen cars reported and Finlay impounded Owczarek's Chev this afternoon—"

"I tell you, he's taken to the bush," Butler said. The Perth Chief of Police was a stocky man, balding and broad-faced. He'd been at a barbecue when the call came in and was still wearing an apron that said: "DON'T TELL ME HOW YOU WANT IT, *I'M* THE CHEF!" He looked, Briggs decided, like a man who wasn't about to take shit from anyone.

"Maybe he did," Archambault began, "but—"

"We need dogs to hunt the bastard down," Butler insisted, "and if you're not going to provide them, I know a lot of good men who will."

"Fred," Archambault said. "We've got enough problems without bringing civilians into it."

"Then do something! He was *my* man, for Christ's sake."

"And I'm damn sorry that he bought it, but I'm still not having some lynch mob out there beating the bush, ready to blow away anything that moves funny—do you understand?" Archambault immediately regretted snapping at the police chief. "Look, Fred. I'm sorry. We're all jumpy. We're going to nail this sucker—you've got my word on it—but let's just keep it in the family, okay? I'd just as soon see him blown away as brought to court and maybe get off—but we can't work it that way."

Briggs glanced back to the police barricades that kept a crowd of gawking onlookers at bay and was happy it was up. Wouldn't do to let the press get within earshot with this kind of shit going down. He caught Will's eye and nodded to have him come over to where he was standing.

"Doesn't look so good, does it?" he said.

Will sighed. "Well, they're trying, Paddy, but it's got everybody shook up. Christ, I thought the victims we had looked bad."

Briggs nodded, remembering. Owczarek had slaughtered them. "Any more word on the girl or this Owen fellow?" he asked.

Will shook his head. "Archambault's got an APB out on all three of them and his people are cruising the backroads, but shit, Paddy, have you seen a road map of this area? They could be anywhere—right out of the county by now—and no one would have spotted them. I don't think—"

Briggs held up his hand. "Hang on," he said as Archambault called him over. The OPP officer was a lean Frenchman, dark-haired and wiry. There was no trace of an accent when he spoke.

"Is this all you have on Owczarek?" he asked as Briggs stepped up. He held the slim file that Briggs and Will had brought down with them in his hand.

"What're you looking for?"

"Well, you say he's a concert violinist—but that doesn't tell me much. What I want to know is, has he had any experience in the woods? Can he handle weapons? Could he take to the bush and live off it for however long he needs to get away? You see what I'm getting at? I need more than just a name and what's in here. I need to know how he thinks."

Briggs nodded. He understood that need. The faceless man that had been haunting him had finally turned from the dark end of his mental street and shown his face—Owczarek's face.

"He's a Gypsy," Briggs said simply, "and that means we don't know anything about him except that we should expect him to be capable of anything. We can trace him back three years and all that comes up is clean living. We're still working at putting him in those other cities at the same time as the murders took place in them, but we've had trouble getting hold of his agent and her records."

"A Gypsy," Archambault repeated. "What the hell does that tell us?"

Briggs understood the frustration in the officer's voice and knew it wasn't directed at himself. "What it means," he said, "is that they're like chameleons—they can fit in anywhere. Will's been studying up on them and if you want to know whether Owczarek can survive out in the bush—even without bringing any supplies in with him—the answer's yes. If you want my advice, you'll get the dogs up here as soon as you can. Your witness only heard Constable Finlay's car, right?"

"Yeah. But that's not to say Owczarek didn't just park a vehicle down the road a-ways and head back to it over the fields after he finished here. He could've parked a mile away and by the time he reached it and started her up, this place would've been in such an uproar. . . ."

"The dogs'll tell us that, won't they?"

Archambault nodded. "Yeah. I've already put in a call for them. They'll be here in about twenty minutes or so." He paused, his gaze drawn to the blood-stained dirt. "Thing I don't understand is . . . Owczarek's not that big a guy, right? Duncan said his wife got here seconds after the first scream and he was right on her heels. The bodies were already torn up like you saw them and our boy was gone. If they've got their timing right, this boy's got to be fast. Strong as a fucking bear and *fast!*"

"Plus we've got two victims in Ottawa that we know he did something to, but they didn't have a mark on them."

Archambault frowned. "First you're telling me about leopard cults—now you're talking, what? Voodoo?"

"I never said it made any sense," Briggs said softly.

"Yeah. You never did," Archambault turned to his forensic team. "Are you just about finished here?"

Briggs returned to Will's side. He glanced at the Perth police chief. Butler was sitting on a lawn chair, hands cupping his chin, just staring off into the night. He's hurting bad, Briggs thought. And he's got one hell of a mad on. There were about a dozen other policemen around the trailer—in uniform and out—and anger was the predominant emotion. It crackled in the air like a physical presence. Owczarek was going to be lucky to survive the "resisting arrest" that'd be entered on his file when those boys got through with him. Briggs wasn't sure he wanted to be any part of that kind of thing until he remembered the victims. Red-eye Cleary. The hookers. Finlay. The other Gypsies. Their ghosts flitted like trapped bats through his thoughts, coloring the way he saw things.

"Are we sticking this out?" Will asked.

"I've got to," Briggs said. "I've got to see him brought in with my own two eyes. I don't want to read about it in the papers or in some report. I want to *know* he's finished." Because otherwise, he thought, the ghosts might never leave. . . .

Will nodded. "You know what scares me the most?"

"What?"

"The juju, Paddy. I've got the bad feeling that this guy's not even human."

Images of the dismembered corpses of Owczarek's latest victims floated into Briggs' mind, mingling with the ghosts of the other victims that had already taken up residence there. Owczarek. Even with a club like those cat cults used, or a *shuko* . . . The sheer ferocity of the man's attack . . . his strength . . . to leave them looking like that. . . . He suppressed a shiver of cold dread. And then there were the ones who had died, that he hadn't even touched. . . .

"Don't start," he said softly to his partner. "Don't even start me thinking along those lines."

He tried to turn his thoughts to a more pleasant line of thinking, but all he could see in his mind's eye was a dark street and Owczarek walking down it towards him. Around his neck he wore a necklace of tiny shrunken heads. They weren't all shriveled like the kind you'd see in a movie about head-hunters. They were just tiny heads, like Indian coups, hanging around his neck, and the one in the center, the one that was opening its eyes, had Briggs' own face. . . . He shook his head roughly, trying to dislodge the image.

"Paddy?" Will began.

"I'm okay. Let's go see if they've got any more coffee left."

He turned away from the scene of the murders and headed past the barricades. Will had a last look, then slowly followed. Both men ignored the microphones that were thrust into their faces by reporters, eager for a personal statement from the investigating officers.

thirty

Friday night in Lanark County.

In Tinkers, Toby Finnegan was finishing up his third set of the night. He put his fiddle away in its case and wandered over to the bar with his guitarist, Jessie Briton. She ordered a draft while he settled for a cup of tea. The restaurant was quiet tonight with less than fifteen people scattered at the various tables. Across the street in The Zoo the action was heavier, even if the Gourlays weren't there to add their usual bravado to the mayhem. The only person who missed them was one of the waitresses, Cathy Chambers, who thought Stan was a pretty funny guy, what with all his jokes and wisecracks. In the Perth Hotel, the Wide Acre Boys were in the middle of a laid-back version of "Your Cheatin' Heart," while the crowd at the Rideau Ferry Inn was talking over the piano that Hugh Tibbs played quietly in the corner, Tibbs letting his fingers walk over the black and white keys and thinking more about what he was going to do in the morning than about what he was playing.

Beyond the night spots, televisions flickered in living rooms, lights went out as the older folks went to bed, some hot-and-heavy back-seat loving was happening in laneways, and there was a significantly larger proportion of police vehicles patrolling the roads. Beyond the cottages and houses, the night life carried on as usual, ignorant of the affairs of men. Bats flitted in the dark air, hunting grasshoppers and moths. An owl fed on a fieldmouse, one claw holding the tiny corpse in place as its beak tore at the flesh. A fox stalked a nervous hare, a mole thrust a quivering nose out of the dark earth, looking for grubs, and mosquitos hunted anything with blood flowing through its veins.

On a dirt road, his black boots grey with the dust they scuffed up, Mulengro walked steadily, paradoxically aware yet oblivious to everything the night held. The mosquitos hummed around him, but did not alight, as though sensing a madness like poison in his veins. The mind of the *drabarni* he sought drew him on through the darkness. He saw her as a gold flare—now vague and flickering like *feux-follets* or the reflection of a cat's eyes, now a sparkling pulse like a tiny star in the distance, glittering like fool's fire. Her *draba* drew him. It would aid him in his work.

He thought of the *shanglo* who had tried to stop him from that work earlier this evening. The uniform had been too much like the uniforms of the guards in the hospital where the doctors prodded and pried him, filling him with *Gaje* drugs. He could hear their voices still sometimes, on nights like this, when the silence drew heavy across the woods. They had a hundred terms for his illness— an illness that he knew was caused only by the confinement and the drugs. When the *mule* freed him, the dark terrors fled. The madness was gone. He knew his work and he set about it sanely. As God brought the *mule* to him, so God had shown him what must be done that the Rom be freed of their *marhime,* that they would be loved in His eyes once more, as they had been before.

No, he was no longer mad. Not when he was finally free of the hospital and the last traces of the *Gaje* drugs had fled his system. Only the Rom who embraced their *marhime* were mad. And the *Gaje* who tried to stop him from his work.

In the beginning, in those first weeks of freedom, he'd thought the task set to him to be an easy one. The Nazis had done much of his work for him and not many of the Rom he first encountered needed cleansing. It was not until he left Europe, until he came to the Americas, that he understood the full scope of what he had undertaken. The Rom here had forsaken their *vurdon* for metal *Gaje* vehicles, had forsaken the old ways for those of a society that had no use for them.

He thought of the policeman again—the blond *shanglo* with his

gun. He knew the time would come when he would have to deal
with the *Gaje* as well—not to cleanse them, for they could never be
other than *marhime,* but to end their influence over the weaker Rom
who fell prey to the temptations that the *Gaje* offered them. Houses,
when all a Rom needed was the sky above his head. Cars, when a
horse-drawn *vurdon* moved as swiftly as any *phral* should rightfully
wish to travel. Oh, yes. The *Gaje* had so much to offer: glitter and
lights and drugs, a lack of morals, a lack of cleanliness.

His mouth tightened into a thin-lipped frown. The *mule* he had
would not be enough to complete his work for, with every Rom he
cleansed, a dozen more *marhime* arose in their place. He let his mind
taste again the *drabarni*'s potency. Her *muli* would be strong—
stronger than the *mule* he had serving him now. If he could seek out
other *drabarne* and use their strengths in his work, as he used the *mule*
he had already, as he used himself. . . .

He paused on the road. The *mule* gathered in a thick fog about his
calves. Before him stood a stiff-legged dog, ears laid back against the
sides of its head, lips drawn back in a soundless snarl, baring teeth.
The creature's fur was matted and hung with burrs and its body was
hungry-lean, gaunt ribs showing their ridges along its back. A second and a third drifted from the woods to either side of the road,
silent as the *mule* that writhed about Mulengro's legs. The man
smiled and held in check the *mule* that had begun to drift between
the threat of the feral dogs and himself. These were not Rom, nor
could he use their *mule,* if *mule* they had, but he could use them still.
He needed only their names.

Dogs that once were pets but have gone wild are an unexplained
biological phenomenon. Most are small packs of strays that gather
together simply to survive, growing bolder as their conquests multi-
ply. Others are pets deserted by cottagers during the week when
they return to the city to earn the money that allows them to spend
their weekends boating, fishing and, once in a while, wondering
what happened to the friendly family pooch. And in each pack of
feral dogs there can always be seen one or two sleek well-fed beasts
who obviously leave their homes to only periodically run with the
pack. Some of these might even return to their owners' porches in

the morning, spent from the night's exertions. But the pack that faced the man in black tonight was all feral.

As he watched, their number grew to seven. Lean and wary, they studied the lone man with his hungry eyes. There was game to run down in the forest and men were to be avoided at all costs—they learned that lesson far quicker than their domesticated brothers learned to fetch a paper and obey a sharply spoken "Sit" or "Stay"—but now something drew them from their normal haunts to seek the man in black who dared to walk alone along this dirt road that cut through their hunting ground, at this time of night, a time that belonged to them.

Mulengro took a step towards the pack leader, smiling as it sank into a crouch. The dog's snarl became audible, gained in volume. A red fire in the back of its brain told it to attack, but the victim was a man—to be feared—and the stink of fear that normally drove dogs wild was not on him. The remainder of the pack slunk to either side of Mulengro, enclosing him in a rough circle.

"I know you," he said to the pack leader, his voice dry and harsh. Unafraid.

Uncertainty flickered in the dog's eyes. It knew it should flee now, could not understand why it was here on this road, facing this hated man—letting the two-legged monster approach. . . .

Suddenly Mulengro was upon it. He caught it by the scruff of its neck and half lifted it from the ground so that its hind legs could get no purchase on the dirt road and its forepaws only scrabbled at the air. Mulengro held it at arm's length, grinning into its feral face. The rest of the pack hesitated between attacking and fleeing. They watched the *mule* taking shape, drifting between themselves and safety, between themselves and the man in black. Mulengro's grin broadened as the pack leader fought his grip.

"I do know you," he said. "All but your name."

His free hand snapped out, closing over the top of the dog's head, covering its eyes. He shut his gaze to the struggling creature and the night and let his mind touch the incoherent babble of the dog's panic and feral rage, sifting through and weighing the various facets of its being until he understood it and had its name. It was not a word in the sense of the languages that mankind used, but a sound that summed up the animal's essence. Mulengro spoke it aloud and the dog stopped its struggling. He took his hand from its eyes and it stared at him, losing its gaze in the pale-blue eyes that burned above Mulengro's scarred cheeks. The man in black loosened his grip and let the animal drop to the ground. It staggered, confusion reigning in its dim mind.

"You see," Mulengro said, his voice soft now, soothing. "We are much the same, you and I. We are both hunters. Death serves us; we do not serve death. And yet I think—" he voiced the sound that was the dog's name and it whined "—that you will serve me."

The pack leader moved, stiff-legged, hackles raised. Its hatred for the man-thing warred with its need to obey this being that knew its name. The power of names is a basic tenet of Gypsy *draba* as it is in many forms of magic—a concept the dog could only experience, not understand.

"You will hunt with me," Mulengro said. His eyes repeated the words in a language the creature could understand. "You will serve me." He voiced the name-sound a third time and the dog broke away. The *mule* withdrew, allowing the pack the freedom of the forest.

Mulengro smiled as he watched the dogs flee in amongst the trees. They would not go far. They were bound to him now, as his *mule* were, as the *drabarni* would be, as other *drabarne* would be. The humor quickened in him. From the darkness and the dead he would raise an army for God—an army of fallen angels. In time, *o Beng* himself might be fighting at Mulengro's side and all of heaven would laugh at the jest.

A long howl lifted from the forest, echoing low and chill in the still air. After a moment's pause it was answered. Howls tore from other feral throats. Mulengro nodded to himself as he followed the road again.

Rod Taylor stepped outside his cottage and lit a cigarette. The match flared, he took the smoke into his lungs, then shook the match out, grinding it under his heel. His wife Beth and their twelve-year-old daughter Lucy were both asleep inside the cottage. He stretched, then wandered down to the lake. The waters of Mill Pond lay like glass, undisturbed by boat or wind. Christ, it was a pretty sight. A moment like this made the five days slaving at the office each week worth it. No doubt about it.

The night was filled with familiar sounds—the frogs' chorus down by the creek where the water flowed from the pond over to Briton Bay, a loon on the lake, June bugs whirring, crickets chirruping. He loved it. Tomorrow he had some cleanup work to do around the cottage—trim a couple of trees, maybe clear out some of the brush up towards the Webster place, seeing how neat Gord kept his lot. But in the afternoon, he'd take Lucy out across the lake—Beth, too, if she wasn't planning on catching rays all day. Maybe they could have a picnic. Watch the herons.

He crouched by the water, snuffing his cigarette in it. It went out with a hiss. He squeezed it to make sure the ember was dead, then turned to go back to the cottage, the wet butt in the palm of his hand. He was right near the door when he heard it—the first long lonesome howl, silence, then a chorus of them. The frogs went still. The whole night stilled. A cold shiver traveled up his spine.

He stood silent, listening, wondering what the hell it had been. When it wasn't repeated, he finally went inside, locking the door behind him for no discernible reason except that he'd been a little spooked. He dumped his butt into the cast-iron stove. By the time he was crawling into bed beside Beth, he had to laugh at himself. It'd only been a bunch of farm dogs having a bit of a howl. What the hell had he been thinking? That there were wolves around the Pond? He smiled against the pillow and went to sleep.

thirty-one

"I feel like we're in a bad B-movie," Jeff said as they pulled over to the side of the road. They'd been following the Gourlays' pickup for the better part of two hours on a tour of the backroads that wound in a steady spiral down towards Portland. Jeff hoped that the Gourlays weren't just on a booze 'n' tour, or chasing the moon. He could remember doing that as a teenager, hitting the roads in his old man's Ford, taking any road that looked like it would take you in the direction of the moon, using up a lot of gas and more than a few six-packs in the process. The Honda's tank was getting low, its needle just touching a quarter full. They'd driven with the lights off and slow enough so that Jackie wouldn't have to use the brakes in case one of the Gourlays glanced in their rearview mirror and caught the telltale flicker of red behind them.

"Like we're going to hear the theme music to *Deliverance* start up any minute," Jeff added.

Jackie killed the engine. "I know what you mean."

"Well, better that than *Friday the 13th*. Where are we anyway?"

"We passed Scotch Point not too long ago. I think we're somewhere east of the Big Rideau."

"Lovely." Jeff was no longer running on adrenaline. He'd managed to put the vision of Stan Gourlay in the back of his head—at least temporarily. The fact that Janfri had seen the thing as well had done wonders for his morale. The two hours of following the pickup on the bumpy backroads had helped bring him down as well. The buzz was still there—a vague panic mixed with the irritation of his headache that had faded but still wasn't gone. But it wasn't until he lifted and focused the binoculars again that the cold sweat began to squeeze out of his pores once more. The adrenaline kicked in with a rush.

"What's he doing now?" Jackie asked.

Jeff noted her use of the singular. "Getting out of the truck."

Janfri touched Jeff's shoulder. "I want out," he said.

Jeff swallowed, lowered the glasses. He didn't like the idea of following Bob Gourlay and whatever the hell his brother had become through the bush, but he supposed at this point he really didn't have much choice. If they could lead him to Ola . . .

"Okay," he said. He got out and pulled the seat up for Janfri. The interior light bulb had been unscrewed so that its light wouldn't give them away. The Gypsy seemed none the worse for the long ride— not even stiff. He gave Jeff a gentle push out of the way and closed the door softly. Jackie stepped out onto the gravel on the driver's side.

"Now what?"

"We follow them," Janfri said. "Better lock up."

She nodded. Follow "them" where? she wondered. There was nothing out here, except for a few cottages that they'd passed further down the road, and at this time of year there'd be people up for the weekend at all of them. Not to mention the fact that she could only see one Gourlay. She leaned into the car, locked the passenger's door, then her own.

"They're already in the woods," Jeff said. "We're going to lose them if we don't hurry up." He was amazed at how calm his voice sounded. Inside his nerves were skittering like bugs trapped in a confined space.

Janfri led the way. When they reached the pickup, he stopped long enough to lift the hood and reach in. He tore the distributor cap off and held it up with a humorless smile. The wires hung from it like the legs of a spider. Jackie shivered and stepped closer to Jeff. The Gypsy tossed the cap into the brush and motioned them to follow him into the woods. The two exchanged nervous glances, then hurried to catch up to Janfri who was moving through the undergrowth with a silence that was unnerving.

Bob stumbled in his brother's wake, his head pounding, vision doubling. Branches slapped his face and arms. His T-shirt clung to his back and chest. His hand was sweaty where it gripped the shotgun. All he could hear were the sounds of his own passage through the brush. The dead thing he was following didn't make a sound. It drifted ahead of him, leaving a wake of fetid air that made Bob reel. He couldn't breathe through his nose anymore—not without gagging. His sardine and beer supper roiled acidly in his stomach. A root appeared suddenly in his path and he tripped on it, sprawling to the ground. Stan turned and a wave of graveyard air hit Bob like a fist. His stomach heaved and he retched up his supper.

"Now, little brother," the thing said. "Watcha go do that for?"

Bob couldn't lift his head. He took short ragged breaths through his mouth. "I'm sick, Stan," he mumbled. "Oh, Jesus. . . ." His vision spun like a carousel, his temples throbbing.

"You're sick? Well, ain't that a fuckin' shame. I'm *dead,* brother Bob, and you don't hear me whinin' 'bout it, do you?"

"You . . . you don't understand. . . ."

"You're wimpin' out on me, little brother. I understand *that.*"

The dead thing's face was inches from his own, flaps of skin hanging wetly from it.

"You're not my brother!" Bob roared. "You . . . you're dead! You're some fuckin' dead thing. No way you're real!"

"That's the black bitch talkin' in you, little brother. You're listenin' to that whore instead of me. She's gonna nail your fuckin' ass to the wall unless we get her. Unless we get 'em all. We're gonna be makin' the world a good place for honest folks like us Gourlays. You gonna argue with me, little brother? You gonna let me die for real and not do nothin' 'bout it? You gonna let people keep shittin' on the Gourlays when they should be kissin' *our* asses? We're special, brother Bob. That fuckin' whore killed me, but I *ain't* dead. You know any other man can say that?"

Bob backed away from the thing, his mind hovering on the brink of madness. The headache whined in his brain. The foul reek of the thing burned in his nostrils. Dead, dead, dead. Stan was dead. . . .

"Listen," the thing said in a soft wet whisper. There was a tone in its voice like a man might use with a skittish dog. "I'm not here to hurt you little brother. You got nothin' to fear from me. So I'm a little dead. So I don't look so pretty no more. I'm still your big brother. I still love you. I'm doing this for both of us. We're gonna kill that black whore so that she can't hurt *you,* little brother, and so that she can't kill me all the way. We're gonna fix it so that no one ever hurts us again. You believe me, don't you?"

Bob sniffled, nodding his head. His mind was numb. Paralyzed.

" 'Member the time Susie Crawford kicked you right in the balls, little brother? Who was it that tracked her down and got her up in the woods for you to stick the old one-two into her, huh? And she never talked, did she? And you wanna know *why* she never talked? 'Cause I told her I'd rip her pretty little eyes right out of her head if she did, that's why! And what 'bout the time the Runge boys had you down back of The Zoo? Who was it filled their asses with a shotgun load full of salt? 'Member how we tore out of there that night? Old Finlay came up to the house, but when he got us down to the station those Runge boys were just too scared to press charges. You 'member that?"

Bob nodded dully. "We . . . we sure showed 'em. . . ."

"You bet we did. And I was always lookin' out for you, little brother. Just like I'm doin' now."

"But I . . . I saw you dead. . . ."

"I *am* dead."

"It just makes my head hurt, Stan."

The thing looked up suddenly, its reply dying in the mangled cavity that passed for its mouth. Its gaze burned the forest behind Bob.

There was a branch poking Jackie in the stomach but she didn't dare move. She glanced at Jeff, his face a pale blur in the darkness. She thought she was going to die. Everything was just too weird. There was Bob Gourlay, huddled up against a tree, talking away, pausing as though he was listening to someone, then talking again. He'd cracked right up. But she didn't dare move because of the shotgun lying on the ground beside him. The starlight glinted from its metal barrel and drew her gaze, time and again. She glanced at Jeff once more, saw him go stiff. Beyond him, she could just barely make out Janfri reaching into his pocket.

"Little Jeffy Owen," the thing that had been Stan Gourlay said. "Best get your .12-gauge, brother Bob."

As Bob fumbled for the weapon, the thing rose from beside him and charged into the forest.

"Holy Jesus!" Jeff cried.

He lunged to his feet. Jackie started to turn towards him when something lifted her to her feet and slammed her against the trunk of a tree. Her breath went out of her in a whoosh and she saw bright spots dancing before her eyes. There was a stink in the air like meat gone bad. Her vision was a blur of tears and stars. Something had her by the throat. It was bruising her skin, cutting off her air, and she saw . . . she saw . . . The scream rose from deep inside her but couldn't pass through her throat. She clawed at the torso of the dead thing, but her fingers could find no purchase. There was nothing there, but she could feel it. She was choking on its stench. Choking from the bruising grip on her throat. Choking on fear—

The dead thing suddenly loosed her and howled. She collapsed into a sprawl as it turned from her, moaning with a weird high-pitched sound that scraped the nerves along her spine raw. It was the wetness of that sound . . . She hauled air into her lungs with great rasping gulps.

"*Kurav tu ando mul!*" Janfri cried. I defile your mouth! He brought another handful of salt, powdered garlic and red pepper out of his pocket. The dead thing howled again as the Gypsy flung the second handful of spices at it. Before they'd left Jackie's he'd emptied a couple of bottles from her spice rack into his pocket, thinking that if the old wives' tales were true and there were *mule,* then the old protections might work as well. The cloud of spices burned the *mulo,* tore away its resemblance to life so that it drifted apart like smoke. Janfri threw a third handful.

"You're hurtin' him!" Bob Gourlay roared. The thunder between his temples no longer held him in stasis. He lifted the shotgun to his shoulder and fired. Janfri ducked at the same moment and the tree branches just above his head exploded as the buckshot tore it apart. Bob lurched closer, bringing himself within a dozen feet of Janfri. Sweat was pouring from his brow, soaking his T-shirt. He drew aim again. Beside Janfri, Jeff's fingers closed on a short stick. He threw it with all the force he could muster. It struck Bob on the side of the head, just as he was firing the second barrel. The gun bucked against him, throwing him off his feet, the shot going wild. Then Janfri was upon him.

Janfri was strong, but adrenaline rushed through Bob like a brushfire. He tossed the Gypsy away from him and swung the barrel of the shotgun at Janfri's head. Janfri lifted an arm to protect himself. The barrel slapped against his hand, numbing the nerves in his palm. He tried to close his fingers around the weapon, but they wouldn't obey him. Bob tore the gun free from his limp grip and raised it for a killing blow. Then Jeff climbed on his back, wrestling the gun from his hands.

"He was dead!" Bob shouted, shrugging Jeff off. "He was already dead and you're still tryin' to hurt him!"

Jeff and Janfri backed away. There was no sign of Stan's *mulo*— just a disturbing sound like moaning that was drifting further and further away. Bob hesitated, hearing that sound. He wanted to hurt these men, needed to help his brother, wanted to kill them dead . . . kill everybody dead. . . . There was a jack-hammer pounding away between his temples and he suddenly turned and broke away, an inarticulate howl trailing behind him as the forest swallowed him. For long seconds, Jeff sucked in air. He shook from head to foot. Then he remembered Jackie. He bent beside her, touched her shoulder. She flinched, moaning at the touch.

"Please, God . . . no more. . . ."

"It's me," Jeff said. "Jackie?"

Her eyes went wide, taking him in, then she flung her arms around his neck, pulling him close. "It was real," she croaked. "God help us, it was *real!*"

Jeff held her, stroked her hair with a trembling hand. "They're gone," he said. His voice came out still panic-stricken rather than reassuring. He swallowed, his Adam's apple moving with difficulty because his throat was so dry. He tried again and his voice was firmer. "It's over, Jackie. They're gone."

Still standing, Janfri stared into the night. He slowly lifted his hand to his mouth and licked his palm. The mixture of salt, garlic and pepper fired his taste buds. His hand tingled as numbed nerves came back to life. The Gourlays were gone, he thought, but they would be back. He walked over to the shotgun and picked it up. Cracking it open, he let the two spent cartridges fall to the ground, then snapped the weapon shut. It was useless without ammunition. Good for nothing but a club.

He glanced at his companions. His own reaction to the events of the past few minutes was a wash of coldness that settled over him like a shroud. What Jackie had just come to understand, he had to accept as well: Against all his private beliefs, *mule* had proved to be real. Even after seeing Stan Gourlay join his brother back at their farmhouse he hadn't been entirely convinced that it wasn't some sort of trick. An illusion. But now he knew. *Mule* were real. And by that reckoning it meant that all that Old Lyuba had told him was true as well. There *was* a Mulengro. A man who controlled *mule* and slew Rom. The spices had sent the *mulo* away as the old tales had said they would, but the old tales said nothing about how to kill a ghost. How did one kill what was already dead?

"Where are we?" he asked his companions.

There was a moment's silence, then Jeff asked, "What?"

"I asked where are we?"

"I don't know. We're—Christ, what does it matter?"

Janfri crouched down so that his face was level with Jeff's. "I'll tell you why it matters. That thing was real. A *mulo*—a ghost. And that means I *have* to find your friend Ola now. If she has magic, I need it."

Jeff drew Jackie up and held her close to his side. "Magic?" he repeated numbly. "You . . . what was it you did to make the . . . thing take off?"

Janfri explained. "But it's only a preventive action—a protection. It doesn't kill the ghost. I have to know how they can be killed."

The idea seemed preposterous to Jeff. "They're already dead," he said. "You can't kill something that's already dead."

Janfri shook his head. "Lyuba told me—a *drabarni* knows how."

"You can't be serious? You're not going after them?"

"What else can we do? Who else can help us? Who would even believe us? Those two were going somewhere—perhaps to where they have your friend held captive—and we must get to her before they do. So where are we? What's near here?"

"Nothing. We're in the middle of a Conservation Area. There's nothing around here."

"Maybe they have a cabin or a hunting lodge hidden away?" Janfri suggested.

"No way. There're hikers coming up through here all the time. Somebody would've spotted it."

"There has to be something."

Jackie lifted her head from Jeff's shoulder. "The Pond," she said. "Mill Pond's just north of here somewhere. There are a few cottages on it."

"Can you show me where they are?"

"I . . . I'm not really sure."

Jeff shook his head. "This is crazy," he said. "We don't even know that they *have* Ola."

"But what if they do?"

Jeff looked from the Gypsy to Jackie. He couldn't see either of their features very clearly, but he could read the determination in Janfri's voice and felt Jackie's muscles tense up against his side.

"We have to do something," she said. It cost her almost all the remnants of her tattered courage to say that, Jeff knew, which was more than he could say for himself. He didn't think he could go on. He was more afraid of confronting dead Stan Gourlay again than of anything he'd ever had to face before. But if Jackie could go on, and Janfri could . . . The Gypsy was a cold fish and maybe he was used to this kind of thing for all his protestations to the contrary. Just look at how he'd known what to use against the . . . the thing. But

Jackie was an ordinary person, like he was. And if she could do it . . .

He got to his feet and helped Jackie up. "Okay," he said to Janfri. "We'll go on."

The Gypsy nodded, hefting the shotgun. He thought a moment. "You can lead us right to these cottages?" he asked.

Jeff and Jackie exchanged glances. Her hand found his. "Well, it would be easier by the road," she said. "There's a windmill where you turn off and then just a track going into the bush . . ."

"I remember the windmill," Janfri said. He looked northward, then back to his companions. "So let's get back to the car and go in by the road."

"But—"

"We might lose some time," Janfri said quickly, forestalling the argument, "but on the other hand, if we get lost wandering around out here in the bush where neither of you are completely sure of what's where, we'll lose even more." He left unsaid the worry he had that the police might have put together the fact that he was with Jeff, and therefore with Jackie. If they were seriously looking for him, they'd discover the connection quickly enough and he didn't want the car sitting by the road, pointing the way they'd gone. It would be a very simple matter to track them down with dogs once they knew where they'd taken to the bush.

"Makes sense," Jeff said. "Can the Honda handle the road in?"

"It has before," Jackie said. "Ellen Lynch rented a cottage there two summers ago and I used to drive in to visit her."

"Then it's settled," Janfri said. He knew the way back to the car—his sense of direction had always been good—but, once he pointed the way they had to go, he fell in behind the pair. He took the shotgun with him. With any luck, there might be shells for it in the pickup.

Thinking of the Gourlays brought a frown to his lips. The *mulo* of Stan Gourlay troubled him far beyond the existence of *mule*. The dead man wasn't a Gypsy. So why had his *mulo* not gone on to wherever it was that the spirits of the *Gaje* dead went? Perhaps Jeff's friend Ola would know. The muscles between his shoulders tightened. He was beginning to believe that this Ola *was* the *drabarni* that

Lyuba had told him about, though he couldn't have said why. It was just a feeling that he had, akin to the instinct that had prompted him to fill his pocket with *baXt* spices before leaving Jackie's apartment.

Ola might or might not be a Gypsy, but he sensed there was something like magic about her. He wasn't sure that he was looking forward to meeting her. Now that he knew *mule* existed, the old superstitious awe concerning *drabarne* arose in him. If *mule* were real, then so was magic. It wasn't a comforting thought. Not when he recalled Old Lyuba and what she'd told him. Not when he remembered his house burning and the *marhime patrin* on its wall. For it meant he was marked by something that could reach beyond the grave and he doubted that all the salt in the world would keep Mulengro from him.

thirty-two

Mulengro paused, his *mule* thickening around his legs. He stared at the *patrin* carved into the fencepost by the road. It was familiar, but unexpected. It was an old *patrin,* judging by its wear, that told him Rom could find a welcome at this farm. Their horses could be watered, their *vurdon* parked in the fields about the farm. Mulengro frowned as he looked up the lane to the dark farm buildings and shook his head. This was a *Gaje* holding and not a place for Rom. What Rom needed, they could take. It was mingling with *Gaje* that had brought God's wrath down upon them in the first place. And though the *patrin* was old, though the Rom that had carved it into the wood were probably dead and gone now a dozen years, and though the owners of the farm itself had probably changed over the years . . . It made no difference.

He approached the fencepost, *draba* fires gleaming in his pale eyes. Laying his hand against the *patrin,* he closed his eyes and called up heat. The wood smoked where his palm lay against it. When he drew back his hand, the old *patrin* was eliminated, replaced by the symbol of *marhime*. The smell of burnt wood was strong in the air. A thin smile touched his lips as he called a name into the night.

His *mule* shivered in anticipation as the lean shapes of feral dogs slunk from the undergrowth. Mulengro pointed in the direction of the farm. The pack leader hesitated until it felt the full force of the man's pale gaze on him, then trotted up the lane, followed by the rest of its pack. Mulengro fell in behind them, his *mule* drifting to either side of him. A dog began to bark in the farmyard ahead of them.

The Lennox Farm was set back from the road on a low hill just a stone's throw from the North Burgess/South Elmsley Township Line in Leeds County. It was a two-story fieldstone structure, built around the turn of the century by Duncan Lennox. Behind it still stood the original cabin built by his great grandfather Martin Lennox in 1816—a time when the veterans of the Scottish Regiments that fought in the War of 1812 were encouraged to settle in the region as a means of keeping able-bodied fighting men in the area of the Rideau Waterway for strategic purposes. Martin Lennox had been a captain in the Glengarry Light Infantry Regiment of Fencibles at the time and received a grant of eight hundred acres. By the late sixties, his descendant Gerald Lennox was still working the farm, but its acreage had dwindled to one hundred sixty, much of which had reverted to bush.

On Friday night, Gerald Lennox went to bed after the late CBC news and was asleep before his head hit the pillow. Less than an hour later, the sound of his German shepherd's barking woke him. He sat up, startled, head still thick with sleep.

"What is it, Gerald?" his wife asked. Sheila sat up beside him, one hand tightening on the bedclothes as she listened to the dog barking.

"Don't know," Gerald said. "Sounds like Gillie's got something treed." He stepped out of bed and put on his trousers, slipping the bands of his suspenders over his bare shoulders. As he put on his work boots, Sheila called to him.

"You be careful now."

Gillie was barking up a storm. Gerald nodded and plucked his shotgun from the corner and checked its load. He snapped it shut, then paused. The dog's barking had turned into a low growl that curdled his blood.

"Jesus," he muttered.

"You be careful," Sheila repeated.

"Don't nag."

He was halfway down the stairs when a chorus of growls broke out. He heard heavy bodies moving on the porch, the scratching of claws on wood. A howl of pain. He took the rest of the stairs two at a time and ran for the porch door, his workboots clomping. When he snapped on the porch light and flung the door open, the first thing he saw was Gillie lying in a pool of his own blood right by the steps.

"Jesus H. Christ," Gerald breathed.

He pushed the screen door open with the toe of his boot and stepped cautiously outside, the shotgun moving in a slow arc in front of him. The night was silent. He looked slowly around, then knelt beside Gillie, reached out to touch the bloody fur with a nervous hand. Something struck him in the small of the back and he was bowled over, falling down the steps. He heard the snap of a dog's jaws—loud in his ear. A thick waft of canine breath touched him.

He rolled down the steps, bringing up the shotgun, turned. A slavering dog stood at the top of the stairs, staring at him with blood-hungry eyes. His finger tightened on the trigger and the shotgun boomed, blowing the animal apart. He drew back the hammer spur for the second barrel but never had a chance to aim. The pack was all over him and the second barrel emptied its load into the roof of the porch, exploding shingles and wood with its blast.

"Gerald!" Sheila screamed from the bedroom.

She flung aside the bedclothes and ran for the stairs. The night was filled with growls and the wet sound of the dogs tearing at flesh. She got as far as the end of the hall, then froze as a wild-eyed dog stared at her through the screen door. Her fist went up to her mouth and she flinched as it threw itself at the screen. The flimsy barrier tore and the dog was half through, its claws scraping on the door frame as it fought for purchase.

"No. . . ." Sheila mumbled as she backed away. "Please, God, no. . . ."

The dog was through, followed by a second. Their nails clicked on the floor. Their muzzles were wet with blood and saliva. Sheila turned and bolted. The first dog caught her by the back of her calf, bit through the muscle, hamstringing her. When she fell in a wailing sprawl, the second dog's jaws closed on her throat.

The pack leader sniffed at the remains of the man, the scent of blood firing its brain. It peered towards the house, blinking in the bright porch light. Padding up the stairs, it put its nose to the corpse of the slain pack member. It growled, low in its throat, then turned and barked. Two dogs emerged from the house. Three more crowded near, coming from private investigations along the side of the house. They were only six now, the pack leader registered. It shook its muzzle, spraying drops of blood onto the dusty driveway. It barked again, then turned to face the silent figure in black who regarded it with an unblinking gaze.

The fresh blood burned in the pack leader's brain. It longed to throw itself at the still figure—hated man-thing—but Mulengro's gaze froze it in its place. He held out a hand and the dog, against its will, approached. Mulengro stroked the dirty fur.

"You did well," he said.

He turned and set off down the lane, his thoughts turned once more to the *drabarni* he sought. The dogs trailed along behind in a ragged line, fearful of the *mule,* of the fearless stranger, but more afraid of what their new master would do if they did not obey him. He would get more of these beasts, Mulengro thought. There would be a use for them in the days to come.

Behind, on the porch, the air grew heavy with the sound of flies.

thirty-three

Bob ran, trying to follow the fading sound of his brother's painful howling. His side stitched with pain and he was sobbing. He should've listened to Stan—didn't matter what he looked like or how dead he was. The side of his head was bruised from where Jeff had hit him with the stick, and his headache was a throbbing fire. He should've listened. All anybody ever wanted to do was hurt the Gourlays—weren't no one that loved 'em.

Trees reared up in his path and he bounced off more of them than he avoided. "Stan!" he cried as the faint sound he followed led him deeper and deeper into the bush. "Stan! Don't leave me!"

He didn't know how his brother could have survived death, or what exactly it was that he had now become, but he sure as hell knew one thing wasn't gonna change: The world was gonna fuck the Gourlays over and it was never gonna stop, not unless they did somethin' 'bout it themselves.

"Stan! It's me, Stan! Don't leave me. Oh, shit, don't leave me. . . ."

The ground was getting marshy underfoot. He ran full tilt into a half-dead oak and stumbled face first into a stand of rushes and stagnant water. The blades of the leaves whipped his face and he choked as he swallowed some of the water. Turning over, he gasped like a beached whale. His head drummed. He clawed his way to his feet and stood still, trying to hear beyond the rough sound of his own breathing. There was nothing. No more sound. Nothing left of Stan for him to follow. He stumbled on.

"You killed him," he mumbled, seeing Jeff Owen's face in his mind. "You fucker. You killed him and he was already dead!"

He hit a piece of higher ground and sprawled full-length in the dirt and brush, deep sobs wracking him. He was all alone now. Even being with that dead thing that his brother had become was better than being all alone. Now he had nothing. . . .

• • •

Janfri knew something was wrong as they approached the road. He stopped just inside the edge of the forest and started to call out a warning to his companions, but he was too late. A search beam stabbed the night, pinning Jeff and Jackie in its glare.

"Hold it right there!" a voice cried through a bullhorn. "This is the police. We have you covered. Hands on your heads now. Let's *move!*"

The police. Janfri faded back into the forest and ran for the Gourlays' pickup, the shotgun heavy in his hands. At the driver's door, he threw a quick thanks to whatever God was watching over him that the window was open. He couldn't have chanced opening the door and letting the interior light give him away. He could hear the police still calling their orders and turned to see Jeff and Jackie moving slowly across the field, hands on their heads. Putting a foot on the running board, he hauled himself up and leaned in through the window. There was no box of shells sitting on the dash like he'd hoped there would be. He was about to lower himself down again when he caught a brief glint of a casing on the floor.

He hopped down and laid the shotgun on the ground. Jeff and Jackie were almost at the policemen's car. One officer stood behind the light, handgun drawn. The other was moving carefully to one side, covering them with his own weapon while staying out of his partner's field of fire.

"Hands on the car!" the man behind the lights commanded. He no longer used the bullhorn.

Janfri went up, through the window, and dragged himself into the cab of the pickup. Twisting around, he felt with his hand along the floor. One, two . . . four altogether. He smiled grimly. He wouldn't really need more than one, unless the *shangle* called his bluff. He went back out the window and caught up the shotgun. Keeping an eye on the scene unfolding down the road, he quickly crossed the open stretch of road. On the far side, he hunched down, broke the shotgun open and inserted two of the cartridges. Then he moved through the bush until he was behind the man operating the light.

"Please," he heard Jeff say. "You're making some kind of mistake. . . ."

"Not half as bad as the one you made, asshole. Now shut up and get your hands on the roof of the car." He kept his gun on them, hand steady, unwavering. His partner moved in to shake them down for weapons. "You have the right to remain silent," he said and proceeded to read them their rights. Janfri waited until the other officer had holstered his handgun and was patting Jeff's legs, before he slipped from the brush. He moved like a ghost across the road. The first inkling that either policeman had that something was wrong was when the double barrels of the shotgun pressed into the small of the speaking officer's back. His voice cut off in mid-sentence and Janfri cocked the hammers of the shotgun in the silence.

"Don't move," he said softly. "Don't even breathe. You," he called to the other man whose hand was inching to his holster, "stand up and get into the light." He pushed the shotgun harder against the first officer's back. "Lay your gun on the hood of the car." He could feel the man's tension as he weighed his options.

"Look, mister," the policeman began. "You're making a big mistake. You're not going to get away with this. We've got enough men—"

"Let me worry about that," Janfri snapped. "The gun."

Slowly the officer laid his weapon on the hood of the car.

"Jeff. Get the other one's weapon. Come *on!*"

Jeff blinked in the glare of the searchlight. He couldn't see the Gypsy. All he knew was that this was going from bad to worse. "We can't do this," he told Janfri. "This is nuts." He glanced at Jackie. Her face was drawn and pale—as much from the bright light on her face as from her shock.

"I . . . I told you," she said. "He's crazy."

Jeff nodded. Never mind the fact that they'd just seen a dead man walking through the woods and Janfri had saved them. These were *cops*. And neither he nor Jackie really knew anything about the Gypsy except that he was wanted by the police. He wanted to argue, but he wasn't sure what Janfri was going to do. He sounded like he was capable of anything right now. Except . . . Jeff watched the

Gypsy herd the officer into the light. The shotgun—it wasn't loaded.

"You haven't got any ammunition!" he blurted.

Before either policeman could react, Janfri shoved the officer he was herding forward and pointed the shotgun down the road. The blast of one barrel loosing its load boomed in the night air. The weapon swung back to cover the two officers.

"It wasn't before," Janfri said grimly, "but it is now." He regarded the policeman. "I've one shot left. Either of you want to play hero?"

They both shook their heads. The one with the holstered weapon gingerly removed his gun from his holster using the tips of his thumb and index finger. He held it out.

"Collect it," Janfri told Jeff.

Numbly, Jeff did what he was told.

"Now lie down," Janfri ordered the policemen. "Face down. Jeff, find something to tie them up with—use the cord from their radio or their belts if you have to."

"This is insane," Jeff told him. He stared at the gun in his hand, but the brief thought running through his mind didn't make any more sense. There was no way he could use that thing—not even to stop this madness. He put it down on the hood of the cruiser like it was a hot coal. "These are cops," he said, turning back to Janfri. "They put you in jail for shit like this."

One of the officers hadn't lain down yet. He turned, on his hands and knees, and tried again.

"He's right," he told Janfri, keeping his voice reasonable. "You're calling the shots now, but you're just making things worse in the long run."

"Tell them what you want with us," Janfri said. He knew from the way that they'd dealt with Jeff and Jackie earlier that something else had happened. "Go on."

The officer tried to judge the man behind the shotgun. He didn't know what to say. He didn't want to set him off, because he didn't want to die, but . . .

"Look," he said, still keeping his voice calm. "We don't have to talk about it. You know and we know, so—"

"Tell them!" Janfri wasn't sure what lie they were going to come up with, but he wanted it out in the open so that he'd have a better idea of what they were up against.

"Please," Jackie said. She started to move forward, but Jeff caught her arm, keeping her out of the Gypsy's range of fire.

The policeman nodded dully. "All right," he said. "You want to hear me say it? What's it going to do—make you feel good, hearing it? Are you planning to blow us away like you did Finlay and the Gypsies?"

"Finlay?" Jeff said. "Craig Finlay? What are you talking about?"

"I'm talking about Constable Finlay being killed earlier this evening—by your friend here and maybe you too. Were you in on it? Did you get your rocks off doing it? Is it giving you a hard-on hearing me tell you? Guess it's not so easy to get the kind of high your kind are usually looking for, being out here in the bush. It hasn't had time to make the front pages yet."

Craig was dead? Killed earlier this evening? Jeff shook his head, unable to understand what he was being told. Craig was dead and they thought that Janfri had done it? That he and Jackie had helped him?

"Oh, Jesus," he said. He was going to be sick.

"What do you want now?" the officer asked him. "Do you want me to tell you about the rest of the people your friend butchered? Like maybe—"

"Shut up!" Jeff cried. "Just shut up! There's no way he could have killed anyone. We were with him all night."

"Oh, sure. And I guess—"

"That's enough," Janfri said. "On the ground and keep your mouth shut. Do you see what I mean?" he asked Jeff. "*Now* will you tie them up? We want to get across the border before it gets light and we're just wasting time now."

"Across the border?" Jeff asked. "You mean to the States? We can't do that."

"Where else can we go?" Janfri demanded. "Come *on*, Jeff. Tie them up."

Jeff started to say something else, but Jackie tugged at his arm. He nodded and went to the cruiser, then thought about their handcuffs.

"Sure," Janfri said when Jeff mentioned them. "But make sure they haven't got any keys on them."

He didn't lay the shotgun down until both men were tied up—first with their hands cuffed together behind their backs, one man's left to the other's right, and then with the cord from the radio in their cruiser. When Jeff and Jackie were finished, the two men were sitting on their knees, backs to each other, trussed like a pair of game birds.

"You won't get away with this," the first officer repeated. "I'm going to personally hunt you down, Gypsy—all the way to Mexico if that's what it's going to take."

Janfri shook his head. "Once we're across the border, you're never going to even see our tracks, friend." He shook his head as the man began to speak again. "Open your mouth one more time and I'll gag you as well."

The policeman said nothing, though his eyes spoke volumes.

"Okay," Janfri said, collecting the shotgun and handguns, as well as a high-powered rifle that was in the police cruiser. After shutting down the searchbeam, he led the way to Jackie's Honda, waited for her to open the door with her key. Her hand shook so badly that he cradled the weapons, took the key from her and helped her get into the back with Jeff. Laying the handguns on the passenger's seat, with the rifle and shotgun on the floor, he got in behind the wheel and shut the door. A shudder touched him and he laid his head against the steering wheel, waiting for the reaction to leave him. One wrong move back there . . .

"Janfri?" Jeff asked. "Are you all right?"

He took a long breath, exhaled it slowly, sat up. "I think so."

"You wouldn't really have shot either of those men—would you have?"

The Gypsy shook his head. "I couldn't have. I don't have any real fight with them—not the kind of fight that would make me want to shoot them, at any rate."

Jeff held Jackie close, relieved at Janfri's reaction to what had just happened, but somehow more frightened as well. It was good to know that Janfri *wasn't* crazy, but now that he was beginning to understand more of what they were up against, he didn't want to lose the small comfort of having someone in charge who seemed to know what he was doing. Because everything was going wrong. Ola's disappearance, the Gourlays, the dead thing in the woods. . . . Now the police were after them and Craig Finlay was dead.

"What're we going to do?" he asked aloud.

"Disappear," Janfri said. His voice sounded firmer now.

"In the States?" Jackie asked.

The Gypsy shook his head. "I just said that in the hopes that it will throw them off a little. I doubt that it'll do much good, but at least it will spread them a little thinner."

"Then what *are* we going to do?"

Janfri turned to look at them. "We're going to Mill Pond," he said. "We'll hide the car in the bush up there and try to find your friend Ola before anyone else finds us." He faced front again and started the car. Left unsaid was his fear that Ola wasn't going to be where they could find her. "Which way do we go?" he asked instead.

"You have to turn the car around first," Jackie said. She was almost resigned to her new fate. It was funny. She'd been looking for some direction in her life, something to plan for for the future. But now, in just a few short hours, she wasn't even sure she had a future anymore. If the thing in the woods didn't get them—she was trying hard not to think of this Mulengro and *his* ghosts that Janfri had mentioned—they were probably going to get shot down by the police. Their options were so narrowed now that they weren't even worth thinking about anymore.

"Turn here," she said as the windmill came up on their left.

Janfri took the turn and slowed the car to a crawl on the rough track of a road that led by a house and a mowed field behind it, then headed off into the forest.

"I wish . . ." she began, then let her voice trail off.

Jeff held her closer and she leaned her head on his shoulder. "What do you wish?" he asked.

"It doesn't matter," she replied. "I was going to say I wish that this had never happened, but I guess we all feel that way. I suppose all there's left to wish for is that we make it through, you know?"

Jeff nodded. In the front seat, Janfri said nothing. The hopelessness in Jackie's voice did nothing to bolster his own lack of optimism as to what the next few hours held for them. He tried to concentrate on the track as it wound through the forest.

thirty-four

Ola couldn't relax. She moved back and forth across Zach's living room, fidgeting whenever she did sit down. She was standing now, looking out at the dark lake through the window, one finger idly touching the half-finished dulcimer that lay on the low worktable in front of her. Boboko watched her through slitted eyes from a worn throw rug by the cast-iron stove. Zach sat in his favorite reading chair, a book lying open on his lap, his gaze shifting from the page he'd read ten times already to the stiff back of his guest.

The wood grain seemed to breathe under Ola's fingertip. She could almost feel the tree that the wood had come from if she opened herself enough, but then she would remember . . . Mulengro . . . out there in the night . . . seeking her . . . coming for her . . . and she'd close her mind from accepting any external impressions. Or at least she would try to. The night outside was so quiet. Silent with menace. *Prikaza*. Bad luck rode the wind and called her name.

"There's, like, nothing much you can do," Zach said softly. "Sit down, Ola. Ease up. You're just bad-vibing yourself."

"Can't."

"Won't," Boboko muttered.

Ola shot him a look, then sighed. It wasn't Boboko's fault. She moved away from the worktable, away from the silent night beyond the window, and curled up on the sofa.

"I can't see my own future, you know," she said suddenly. Zach said nothing, using her own Gypsy patience against her until she went on. "I've never wanted to see my own future," she added finally. "But now . . . tonight . . . I know he's coming, Zach. He's out there, waiting for me, coming for me, and I can't even use my *dook* to see if I'll survive."

"Everything's going to be copacetic," Zach said. "Unless you keep psyching yourself out."

"I can't help it. There's just too much bad luck in the air."

Earlier they'd heard dogs howling. Zach had smiled away her nervousness. "It's just some farm dogs hooting it up," he told her, but Ola had felt Mulengro's presence in that eerie sound—just as she felt it in the silence now. It seemed inescapable. She couldn't shake the fear that her fate lay in Mulengro's hands . . . and that it was inescapable as well.

Zach laid his book on the floor. "There was this old guy that used to live down the road," he said. "He told me, 'When you meet the devil, you can't waste time being scared. You got to just spit in his eye!' This Mulengro—he's your devil, Ola, and unless you stop being afraid of him, he's going to have the battle half won already. Do you know what I mean?"

She nodded. "We call him *o Beng*," she said.

"What's the devil?" Boboko wanted to know. The sound of the word, the way Zach said it, intrigued him.

"Well, if you're a Christian," Zach said, "you see him as a fallen angel. According to—" He broke off. "Did you hear that?"

Ola shook her head, but then the sound was repeated—a distant coughing like the backfire from a car.

"Shotgun," Zach said. "Some redneck's out in the woods with a gun."

Ola shivered and hugged her knees, goose bumps lifting on the skin of her forearms. She was so on edge that everything was making her nervous. For a long moment the three of them sat quietly, waiting for yet another repetition of the sound.

"Some say that the devil's like a big old ugly black dog," Zach said finally, looking at Boboko. "There's a little piece of him in every one of us—a place where it's dark and our fears grow, where anger comes roaring up and bad vibes hang out. And the thing we've got to do in this life is to, like, keep that darkness down and not let it creep up and take us over. That's how you get an evil man, you know. He doesn't come from a bad family, or a bad street or a bad part of town. He comes from somebody who wasn't strong enough to hold back the darkness, or was too lazy to, or just plain didn't care. I think they freak me out the most—the ones that don't care."

Boboko rather doubted that he had even the smallest part of a dog inside him, black or otherwise, but he was trying to stay on his best behavior because Ola was upset enough without adding to her worries. He still wasn't sure he cared that much for Dr. Rainbow, but his initial impressions had been greatly tempered by the day spent in his company.

"That doesn't apply to everything in this world," Ola said. "There are places and things that are evil simply because that's what they are."

"Maybe, maybe not," Zach replied. "Take yourself, now. With all you went through as a kid . . . if the liberals are right, you'd be an embittered evil woman, just looking for ways to get back at everyone who hassled you."

"I *am* bitter."

"But not evil."

Ola sighed. "I don't know what I am sometimes, Zach. I can't fit in with the *Gaje* world—it simply goes against everything I believe in—but I'm not welcome to live amongst my own people. I don't want to be alone all my life."

"I can dig that," Zach said. "But, look. We haven't known each other for more than a day or so but, like, I think we're getting along pretty good. At least the vibes are right from this side of the room. There must be more folks out there in the world that you could be tight with."

"I suppose."

Ola didn't understand what it was about her host that let her open up to him the way she did. It had to have something to do with the fact that he had the *sight* as well—his own kind of *dook*. And in a way, though she wasn't sure that he would admit it, he was as much an outcast as she was. He was a refugee from a lost era, a hippie in a time when caring for yourself was more important than caring for other people or the world around you. Most of his peers had forsaken their beads and their long hair to become executives and businessmen, while he remained an anachronism, living alone on an out-of-the-way lake, with only the voices he heard on the wind for company. Did he have any friends?

"Don't you get lonely?" she asked.

"Sometimes. I've got a few friends that'll drop by from time to time, but most of the people I used to know just got tired of waiting for me to grow out of all this, you know? Like there was something wrong with being what I am." His gaze met hers and he smiled sadly. "I know all about not fitting in, Ola."

Silence fell between them again. They were both misfits, Ola thought. When Zach picked up his book again, she swung her legs to the floor.

"Can I borrow your canoe?" she asked.

"Sure. You want company?"

Ola shook her head. "I just want to float out on the water for a while and think."

"I know the feeling." He hesitated, wanting to add, "Be careful," but he didn't want her thinking along those lines if she wasn't already.

Ola fetched her jacket. "Don't wait up," she said. "I don't know how long I'll be."

"Take your time," Zach said as he followed her to the door.

"You don't mind me going off on my own like this?"

"Hey, everybody needs their own space sometimes, you know?"

Ola nodded and lifted her hand in a wave. "Stay out of trouble, Boboko," she called to the cat.

Zach lifted a hand in return and watched her vanish into the darkness that lay thick below the hill. He stood there for a long moment, just staring. For the first time in all the years that he'd lived here, night fears arose in him. The darkness beyond the lights of the cottage no longer seemed peaceful. Its secret blackness had taken on a malevolent edge that sent chills traveling up his spine. He thought of calling to Ola—afraid for her now—but didn't want to intrude on her privacy. He was just blowing things out of proportion, he told himself. Except he heard a mutter on the wind, a whisper that brought last night's dream reeling back into his head. Dory playing his flute and the ghosts spilling out, riding the music.

Zach shivered, feeling as though he'd stepped into the middle of an episode of *The Twilight Zone*. He started to turn back inside, then paused. He thought he heard something else—something more substantial than the wind. For a moment the sound was so alien that a claw of fear crawled up his spine, then he placed it and laughed at the turn his imagination had taken. It was only a car. But what was it doing out here at this time of night?

The Honda made its way up the steep incline. When it reached the top, Janfri let it coast to a stop. They were still driving with the lights out. On the right he could see darkened cottages.

"Now what?" he asked.

Jackie leaned forward, resting her arms on the front seat. Her face was very close to the Gypsy's. When she spoke, it was in a whisper, as though she was afraid the night outside the car would hear and do something to stop them.

"There're a few cottages here—about six, I think. If we keep going straight ahead, we'll reach a 'Y' in the road. The righthand turn takes us to the last cottage where this hippie named Dr. Rainbow lives year-round. The lefthand turn goes on into the Conservation Area and then just sort of fades out. We could drive up there as far as the car can go and hide it in the bush. After that . . ."

"We look for Ola," Janfri said. He put the car into first and
inched it forward again.

Zach put on a fringed buckskin jacket and, picking up a flashlight,
started for the door.

"Where are *you* going?" Boboko asked.

"There's someone in a car out there and I want to check it out.
Someone was shooting out there earlier—I heard two shots, and
maybe a third a little later on. If it's that same damn fool, I want to
get his plate numbers and call the OPP."

Boboko looked around the cottage, frowning. "I'm going with
you."

"Suit yourself."

Zach held the door open and Boboko slipped out ahead of him,
every sense alert. "Why did you bring the light?" the cat asked.

"In case it's just someone who got lost or something."

"And how are we going to know which it is?"

"Guess we'll have to cross that bridge when we come to it. Now
if we're done rapping . . ." He could hear the car still, heading into
the Conservation Area.

"I don't know," Jeff said. Janfri had squeezed the Honda into a stand
of cedars and was now trying to erase the marks of its passage by
pulling the flattened grass upright once more. "If they come looking
for us with a helicopter, they'll spot it awfully fast."

"We'll cover it with brush. Are you going to give me a hand?"

"Yeah. Sure. What about the guns?"

"We'll leave them in the car—cover them up."

"There's a blanket in the back," Jackie said.

All three of them worked nervously, expecting a search-light's
beam to trap them again at any moment. Janfri snapped off cedar
boughs where the breaks were unlikely to be noticed and passed
them to Jeff and Jackie, who laid them on the car.

"The most important thing," the Gypsy said, "is to make sure there's no metal exposed that the sun can catch. It doesn't matter if the boughs get discolored. From the air it'll just look like a patch of brown."

Jeff grunted in reply. His muscles were still stiff and he was sore from his ordeal with the Gourlays two nights ago. Tonight's exertions hadn't helped.

"Have you been giving any more thought as to where we might find your friend?" Janfri asked.

"Maybe she knows someone in one of the cottages," Jackie said.

Jeff shook his head. "She would have mentioned it before. I'm just afraid that the Gourlays have got her tied up in the bush somewhere. We're never going to find her then."

"We'll just have to try," Janfri said. "How's it going?"

"We need a few more boughs."

Zach drew out of earshot and hunched down on the ground. "What do you think?" he whispered to Boboko. "Are they Ola's friends?"

"The blond-haired man is Jeff Owen," Boboko replied. "I don't know the others."

"They think the Gourlays kidnapped her?"

"Who knows what humans think?" Boboko replied wearily.

"Well, this Owen guy, he's, like, her friend, right?"

"I suppose."

"Well, I guess I'd better go talk to them. Wonder why the hell they're hiding their car."

"Why do humans do anything?" Boboko asked in return, but Zach was already up and moving, acting as though he hadn't heard him. Boboko sighed. He tried to remember what it was like to have things be peaceful, but couldn't. The cottage in Rideau Ferry seemed to be just a dim memory now. With a shake of his head, he padded after his companion. He reached Zach just as the man was stepping out from between the trees.

· · ·

When the last bough was in place, Jackie sat down on the grass. "So now what do we do?" she asked.

Jeff came to sit beside her while Janfri remained inside the shadow of the cedars, almost invisible. The starlight made the faces of his companions look paler than they already were.

"I think we should check the cottages first," he said.

"How?" Jeff asked.

"Well, we could start by—"

"Halooo, the car!"

The voice came from about fifteen feet away. Jeff and Jackie froze while Janfri melted further back into the trees.

"Janfri!" Jackie cried, recognizing the voice. It was Dr. Rainbow. She and Ellen had visited him a few times the summer Ellen had her cottage on the Pond. He was a bit of a space cadet, but harmless. If the Gypsy tried to hurt him . . .

"One of you folks Jeff Owen?" Zach asked. He stepped closer and Jackie noticed the cat by his feet.

"I am," Jeff said. He saw the cat as well. In the dark, it looked like Ola's.

"Well, I'm Dr. Rainbow."

"Hello, Zach," Jackie said, standing up. "Remember me?"

Zach moved closer. "Far out! You're Jackie, right? Ellen's friend? How's it going? Are you still working at Tinkers?" Jackie nodded. "What're you guys doing out here at this time of night? You haven't been, like, doing any shooting, have you?"

"We, ah . . ."

"I heard some of what you were saying. You're looking for Ola, right? I suppose you know she's in a bit of a hassle. . . ."

Boboko tracked the Gypsy as he moved through the woods, circling behind them while Zach spoke. He was impressed with the human's quiet movement. But while it might fool Zach, it certainly didn't hide the man's presence from him. He moved closer to Jeff and Jackie, a grin of anticipation touching his jaws.

"Why don't you tell your friend to stop skulking around in the woods," he said.

The shock on their faces was everything that Boboko could have hoped for. He couldn't understand why Ola hadn't let him do this before.

"Jesus!" Jeff said. The word came out almost like a moan.

"The cat . . ." Jackie began shaking her head. She felt as though the entire fabric of the world was coming unseamed all in one big rush.

"That's Boboko," Zach said matter-of-factly, enjoying their reaction as well.

"But . . ." Jeff began.

"Maybe you should, like, tell your friend that we're not here to hurt anyone."

Janfri stepped out of the trees behind Zach, his eyes narrow with suspicion, their gaze fixed on the cat. *Mule* he was prepared to accept, and even *draba,* but a talking animal . . . ? It had to be a trick.

"Well, look who's here," Boboko said. He took in the gold earrings and the knotted *diklo* about Janfri's throat, the dark complexion that was so similar to Ola's. *"San tu Rom?"* he asked. Are you a Gypsy?

Janfri took a stunned step back.

"I don't—I *can't* believe this," Jeff muttered. "It's just too weird. . . ." He touched his temple with a nervous finger, massaging the skin. His headache was back, droning like flies behind his eyes.

"Maybe you'd all better come back to my place," Zach said. "Ola's not there right now, but we're expecting her soon. Why don't you bring the car as well?"

"We can't," Jackie began. "That is . . ."

"If it's a long story, let's save it for over tea—okay?"

Still watching the cat, Janfri collected himself. Fine, he thought. If Ola was a Gypsy *drabarni,* why shouldn't she have a talking cat? A familiar. At this point he had to be ready to accept anything, he supposed, no matter how insane it seemed. He took a steadying breath.

"Do you have any cinder blocks at your cottage?" he asked.

"For sure. What do you need them for?"

They found out when they reached Zach's place. Out of view of the lake and the track, Janfri removed the wheels of the Honda, one by one, replacing each with a cinder block. The Honda was a '77 model with enough rust that, once the plates were removed and it was up on blocks, could conceivably pass for any of the hundreds of similar junked cars one could find in backyards and farmyards throughout southern Ontario and up in Quebec. They were as much a part of the scenery as stone farmhouses and roadside vegetable stands.

"What do you think?" Janfri asked when they were done.

Zach admired the work with a critical eye. "Far out," he said. He regarded the Gypsy thoughtfully for a long moment. The man wasn't wearing black and he was with Ola's friends, so he had to be okay. He just hoped Ola wasn't going to freak out when she saw him. "Needs a couple of finishing touches," he added, finally turning his attention back to the car.

He moved forward and wound down all the windows. Then he removed the bolt from the lower hinge of the passenger's door and left it ajar. It hung down at an awkward angle. Standing near Jeff, Jackie regarded her car with dismay. It looked like it was ready for the scrap heap.

"Well, that was the general idea, wasn't it?" Zach asked with a grin when she mentioned it. He glanced around at them, letting his gaze linger longest on Janfri again. "So who're we putting the show on for?"

"Maybe we could tell you that story over the tea you offered us," the Gypsy replied.

"Maybe we could have something to eat as well," Boboko said. He was sitting on the hood of Zach's VW, from where he'd watched the proceedings with the increasing opinion that there *was* no sense to be found anywhere when one came right down to it. Zach's new guests still regarded the cat with a mixture of fear and awe, but the luthier just laughed.

"Maybe we will," he said.

thirty-five

Yojo's eyes narrowed when he spotted the flashing red lights of the OPP cruiser on the highway ahead of him. He fought down his initial impulse to turn right around and flee. Instead he pulled over to the side of the road and waited for the *shanglo* to come to the car. He was glad now that he'd taken the time to change into a new suit before leaving the Hollis farm. It had seen him through Customs without any trouble and might just help him now.

"What's the problem, officer?" he asked as the policeman leaned over his window.

The constable shone a flashlight into the rear of the car and said, "We're just doing a routine check. Could I see your driver's license and registration please?"

Yojo pulled out his wallet and removed the two pieces of identification, handing them to the constable. The man shone his light onto them.

"I'll be right back," he said and went over to the cruiser. He handed the ID to his partner and stood leaning against the car, regarding Yojo's vehicle. After a moment or so, he returned to Yojo's window.

"Everything seems to be in order, Mr. Greenly." He passed the license and registration over to Yojo. "Tell me, are you going far?"

Yojo shook his head. "To tell you the truth, officer, I've been on the road all day and I'm rather beat. I was hoping to find a motel somewhere along here where I could get a room."

"Well, you're a couple of miles from Rideau Ferry. There's a motel this side of the bridge and the Inn's right across the narrows. You should be able to get a room at either one of them, though I wouldn't hold my breath if you wanted something to eat as well."

Yojo grinned. "I ate a few hours back. Just a couple of miles you said?"

"That's right. Stay on the highway and you can't miss them."

"Thanks very much, officer."

"My pleasure, Mr. Greenly."

Yojo waited until the constable had crossed to the side of the road before he pulled out and drove slowly by the police cruiser. He let out a long inheld breath and dried his sweaty palms one by one on the legs of his trousers. A routine check, was it? Not likely. He was less than ten miles from Perth, where Janfri had said he was going yesterday afternoon. The nervousness that had been steadily growing in Yojo took on a new urgency. Something was very wrong here and he was afraid for his brother. The road block worried him. If the *shangle* were mobilized to such an extent, it was going to make finding Janfri all that much more difficult. If he was even in the area still . . .

Yojo tapped the steering wheel. No. Janfri was near. He could *feel* his *prala*'s nearness. He would stop at the motel or the Inn and take a room, just as he'd said he would. He needed an hour or two of rest. His shoulders and back were stiff from all the driving he'd done today. But then he had to try to find Janfri. He didn't know how he would go about it, but he had to find him. He could taste omens in the night. Bad luck riding the wind. He *had* to find Janfri, before the man in black found them.

thirty-six

"Gin." Will laid his cards on the desk—four aces and three queens. Sighing, Briggs spread out his own hand. "Guess you needed that Queen of Hearts," Will said, looking at his partner's cards. "Let's see now. A penny a point, and you're down another fifteen with that last beautiful hand. . . . Looks like you owe me $7.85, Paddy. Want to keep playing?"

"Double or nothing?" Briggs tried.

Will laughed. "Sure. Why not?"

Archambault, the OPP officer in charge of the case, had brought them back to the OPP station just outside of Perth on Highway 7 where they'd spent most of the evening going over various aspects of the different killings with Archambault while they waited for something to break. Neither Will nor Briggs were expecting much as the time wound steadily closer to twelve. By now they figured Owczarek was out of the province—if not out of the country itself. Though you never could tell with the crazies.

Briggs took the cards and started to shuffle them. "Cut?" he asked, offering the pack to his partner when he was done.

"Quit stalling," Will said. "Just deal them out and weep." He collected the cards one by one as they were dealt and held them out in a fan in his hand. Briggs studied his own hand and tried to hold back a smile. He had four face cards and three of them were jacks. When Will discarded his extra card, Briggs took the top card from the pack. Both men looked up when Phillip Archambault came into the room.

"This the kind of policework you handle up in Ottawa?" he asked. His face was haggard, but he smiled to take the sting from his words.

"Dogs pick up anything?" Briggs asked.

"Nope. They lost the scent at the Lower Rideau. Looks like Owczarek took to the highway and there's been enough traffic on it by now that the dogs'll never pick up his trail again."

"He's gone," Will said.

Archambault's eyebrows lifted. "Oh, yeah? You *know?*" He lowered himself wearily into the chair behind the desk.

"Just a feeling. Would *you* stick around?"

"How the hell would I know *what* he'd do? I don't think like him and I don't go around killing people for kicks either."

Will laid his cards down on the desk, no longer interested in playing. "There's that."

Archambault rubbed his temples and glanced at the clock. "We're planning to take out the 'copter in the morning. You boys sticking it out?"

Briggs nodded. "We were off-duty as of eleven tonight and we've got nothing planned for the weekend."

"Well, I appreciate your help."

"We haven't really done anything yet."

"You will. Tomorrow we're going to start beating the bush behind the Rideau. Do some door-to-door with the cottages and houses. You up for that?" He looked beyond the Ottawa detectives to where one of his men stood in the doorway. "What do you have, Tweedie?"

"We can't raise Car Seven."

"Shit. Who's in it?"

"Carson and Walsh."

"And there's *nothing?*" Archambault frowned, more worried about the two men than about what Briggs or Will might be thinking of his department's inefficiency. His men knew they were supposed to call in *every* time they left their car. There was no hotdogging in his outfit. That might work in one of the *Dirty Harry* movies, but it sure didn't cut any ice with him.

"Where were they the last time they called in?"

Paul Tweedie shrugged. "Turning off 15 towards Scotch Point."

"Shit!" Archambault was out of his chair and looking at the area map pinned to his wall. He stabbed his finger on the turnoff when Briggs and Will joined him by the map.

"That puts them . . . ?" Will asked.

"Right where Owczarek could be." Archambault turned to Tweedie. "Who've we got in the area?"

"Car Three's manning a roadblock at the Lombardy turnoff."

Archambault thought a moment, then decided. "Get them into the area."

"Right."

"And I don't even want them picking their noses without first calling in!" As Tweedie left, Archambault regarded the two Ottawa detectives. "I'm taking a car down—you want in?"

Briggs thought regretfully of his three jacks as he nodded.

"Okay. Let's go. You boys carrying handguns?"

Briggs pulled back his jacket to show his shoulder holster. Will merely nodded. He had a .38 Smith & Wesson in a clip-on holster on his belt.

"Well, I'm breaking out rifles for all three of us."

The two detectives exchanged glances, then followed Archambault out of the office.

"Sure gets dark out here," Will said. He was sitting in the back seat of the unmarked car with Briggs on his left. They each had a high-powered rifle, stocks on the floor, hands on the barrels to keep the weapons from being jostled. Archambault was in the front with their driver, a young constable named Keith Jackson.

"We call it the country," Archambault said. "Turn here," he added to Jackson as they passed the motel a couple of miles beyond Lombardy.

"Shortcut?" Briggs asked. All he could see outside the windows now were forest and fields.

"Just an alternate route. We're going to have to check all of these roads until we find Car Seven."

"Lot of country," Briggs said, thinking of the map. He didn't like the feel of the rifle in his hands. Didn't like all of this open country without houses or streetlights. You needed to be a cowboy to be a cop out here. He was surprised they didn't still use horses.

"We've got that," Archambault said. "We've even got a few pockets of real wilderness, not to mention some heavy-duty marshes. I hope you brought your waders."

"Our what?"

"Waders. Wellington boots. They're what we wear when we go into the marshes."

Will looked down at his shoes. They'd cost him $74 and were only three weeks old. "Great," he said.

"What's that?" Briggs asked, pointing ahead and to their left where a bright spotlight lit up a farmyard.

"Lennox place. Wonder why Gerald's up? Slow down," he added to the driver as they neared the end of the driveway. The glare of the spotlight looked unnatural after all the dark countryside they'd

been driving through. Briggs leaned close to the window to have a
look. The ghosts in his mind were crowding him and an uneasy feeling started up in the pit of his stomach. Before he could say anything, Jackson stepped on the brakes and all four men jerked
forward, then back.

"What the hell?" Archambault began.

But Briggs and the others had seen it too. There was something
lying in the yard. Jackson backed up and aimed the car up the
laneway.

"Oh, Jesus," Archambault muttered as they all saw the body
sprawled out in the dirt. There was a dead dog with its entrails
spilled out lying beyond it on the stairs and a huge hole in the screen
of the door. Archambault was out of the car almost before it came to
a stop. "Call it in," he ordered over his shoulder.

Briggs and Will disembarked. They had their rifles at the ready,
gazes raking the darkness beyond the bright pool of light in the
farmyard.

"Jesus, Jesus, Jesus," Archambault mumbled.

Leaving Will to keep watch, Briggs crossed the yard to where the
OPP officer was standing over the body. It wasn't a pretty sight. If
anything, it was in worse shape than the ones they'd found in the
trailer park.

"Did you know him?" he asked Archambault quietly.

"Yeah. I knew him. Shit. I don't even want to go into the house."

"I'll go."

Briggs mounted the stairs carefully, avoiding the corpse of the
dog. There were already flies thick on it. A swarm arose as he moved
by it, disturbed by his passage. There was a second dog lying further
down the porch that looked as if it had taken a point-blank blast
from a shotgun. Briggs looked from the dog on the stairs to the second one, marking the differences. The second dog, from what was
left of it, was lean and mangy, with burrs stuck in the matted fur,
while the one on the stairs looked like it had been healthier . . .
before something ripped its guts out. The ghosts stirred uneasily
inside him, but he pushed them back. Whatever had hit this place, it
hadn't been the man they were looking for.

He was standing beside the door now. Easing it open with the barrel of his rifle, he stepped quickly inside, the weapon leveled. He found himself in a short hallway with a living room running off it to the left. There were stairs on the right. The hallway continued back towards the kitchen and that was where he found the second body. This one looked like it had been mauled by a bear. Its face was all chewed up, white cheek bones poking through the shredded facial flesh. Blood pooled, thick and congealing, on the wooden floor beneath the body. His stomach gave a lurch and he was glad to look away at Archambault's approach.

"So they got Sheila, too," Archambault said. His voice was level now. Hard.

Briggs nodded. "Let's go on outside," he said. He took Archambault's arm and led him back down the hallway. "It was some kind of wild dogs, wasn't it?" he asked. "Have you had this kind of a problem before?" He kept his tone professional.

"Feral dogs? Yeah. Sometimes cottagers leave their pets behind and they go wild. You might get three or four of them running together in a small pack. They'll run down small game, sometimes something bigger like deer, or the odd cow, that kind of thing. But that's rare. And . . . and never anything like this." His voice was starting to get a little frayed again.

The ghosts kept up their push inside Briggs' head as he led the way out of the house. He tried to ignore them, but when he reached the yard, he saw something in Will's face and their clamor erupted inside him with a new intensity.

"What's up?" he asked.

Will motioned with his head. Briggs shot a glance at Archambault, then followed his partner down the lane. When they left the lit farmyard, Will flicked on a flashlight and played its beam across the dirt laneway in front of them.

"I came down here—just checking things out, you know?—and I don't know what made me look over here, but . . . well, have a look for yourself."

They had reached the end of the land. Will aimed the beam of light at a fencepost and Briggs felt his chest constrict.

"Oh, Jesus," he said. He stared at the *marhime patrin,* not wanting to accept that it was there. The ghosts whined in his head, demanding their retribution.

"He was here," Will said softly.

"But . . ." Briggs turned to look at the farm behind them. "Why?"

"There was another symbol under this one—an older one. See it? The new one was burnt on top of it."

"Those people were killed by dogs," Briggs said, indicating the farm. "There's one of those dogs lying there on the porch, cut in two by buckshot. There's no way Owczarek could have been responsible for this."

"Juju," Will said grimly. "That's what it's all coming down to, Paddy. Ritual killings and medicine murder. This guy's dangerous, Paddy. Like he invented the word. His juju's the real stuff."

Briggs blinked away the accusing faces of Red-eye Cleary, Tracy Hilborn and the other victims. They seemed to stare at him from out of the darkness.

"If dogs killed those people back there," Will said, "then he's running them, Paddy. I don't know how, but he's running them."

"You know what we're going to sound like, don't you?"

Will nodded. "But we've got to show this to Archambault."

Briggs turned away from the fencepost. "Yeah," he said. "But what are we going to tell them? Christ, I don't even know what to think myself!"

Archambault looked up as they returned to the farmyard. Gerald Lennox's body had been covered by a blanket and the OPP officer was leaning wearily against the hood of their car.

"We called it in," he told them. "Dispatch reported that Tanner and Price—the men in Car Three—found Car Seven. It was up near the turnoff to the Conservation Area—that's just up the road from here. Constables Carson and Walsh were tied up by two men and a woman. One of the men answers Owczarek's description."

"The other two?"

"Walsh said he recognized Jackie Sim—the woman who works in Tinkers. The other man must have been Jeff Owen."

"How long ago did your men have their run in with them?"

"Hour—hour and a half ago. Why?"

Briggs glanced at Will, wondering how long ago the murders here had taken place. If they could fit a timetable to Owczarek's movements it might make their own conclusions sound a little more reasonable. In the end, he just sighed.

"We've got something to show you," he said, "and you're not going to like it."

thirty-seven

The starlight was bright on the lake, giving its surface a magical silvery sheen. The water was still as glass, except for where the bow of the canoe broke the water and the dip and lift of Ola's paddle. The wind with its bad omens and muttering stayed behind in the trees on shore. Out on the lake, Ola drew the paddle from the water and laid it across the sides of the canoe. The craft drifted in silence, quiet as a thought. Ola no longer felt the touch of Mulengro's shadow in the night. Instead, the still water eased the anxiety inside her. She would still have to confront him—the murderer, the *drabarno,* the black dog that he was. Her personal devil. But the panic that had been welling up inside her all day had drained away. Zach was right. There was a purity, a power in this lake, and she was drawing it inside her, using it to replenish her lost strengths, using it to banish her fears.

If she turned, she could see the pale yellow lights of Zach's cottage behind her. Some of the other cottagers were up now, too. She saw lights in at least two more buildings. But she turned away from them to look ahead, to the marsh and the nesting ground of the herons, to the peace. It was there, waiting for her. It was all around her. Mulengro would come, but that was still in the future. If one lived in fear of what was to come, one lost what could be gained in the here and now.

She dipped her paddle into the water once more and slowly moved the canoe towards the shore. The reeds and bullrushes grew larger as she approached. The wind had returned and it rattled the dried stalks against one another. She let the canoe float in amongst them while she drifted in a trancelike state.

She remembered her father and her mother and the roads of Europe. The *vurdon* rolling along a dusty backroad. She was a young girl, squeezed between her parents, allowed to hold the reins sometimes and feeling proud when she did, enjoying the love that flowed between her parents. Loiza Faher was a bear of a man with surprisingly gentle hands. She could remember the warmth in his eyes and his humor like an overflowing ale-keg. And her mother Pika was different then, too. Younger, slimmer. Quick-tongued and happy. It was easier to recall her father as he'd been than her mother. Memories of Pika were dragged down by the slums of Toronto and the frail woman lying on a cot in an unfurnished room—the skin almost luminescent it was stretched so tautly across her bones, the eyes dull and sad with their own lost memories.

When death took Loiza into the land of shadows, it stole the future from the Fahers. Pika took sick and never recovered, while Ola, barely thirteen and trying to cope with the fearful changes in her body and mind, held herself to blame for her mother's death. There should have been *something* that she could have done instead of cowering in a corner, cursing the *draba* that filled her with its penetrating *sight* so that she could *see* the disease eat away at her mother. And the bleeding that came to her like a pronouncement from God that she was evil. . . . What good was womanhood or magic, when there was so much pain in the world? The *draba*. Medicine and magic. What had either done to save her mother? The *draba* was as much of a curse as the menstrual cramps and bleeding were. More, rather, for the *draba* was with her for every hour of every day. . . .

Ola sighed. She reached out and ran a finger along the smooth long leaf of a bullrush and wondered what had brought that old guilt to the fore tonight. It stole away the peace as surely as the man in black could. Why was it that happiness was so frail, so easily laid aside, while anger and sorrow and fear were so strong? She shivered, feeling Mulengro's voice in the wind, his *mule,* his danger. . . . Dipping the paddle into the water, she returned to the open water of the lake, trying to recapture the well-being that her memories had chased away, but it was gone now. The lake's surface was no longer calm. The night was no longer safe. With long hard strokes of the paddle, she made her way back to Zach's waterfront.

She beached the canoe and turned towards the cottage. There was something in the air and she wasn't sure what it was. A difference. She was tired and disappointed at losing her moment of peace, so the slope leading up from the lake to the cottage seemed steeper than ever. As she neared the building, nervous fears skittered more strongly inside her and she couldn't understand why. It wasn't just the night, or the knowledge that every passing moment brought Mulengro that much closer to her. She sidled up to a window, peered in, and then she knew what her *dook* had been warning her about.

Shock froze her. She saw Jeff first, then Jackie. What were *they* doing here? And then her gaze rested on the dark-haired man sitting alone by the kitchen table, his face in profile to her. Her heart skipped a beat. Mulengro! she thought, then chided herself. No. It was another Rom—not the man in black. This Gypsy had no scars and, now that she looked more closely, she realized he seemed familiar because she'd seen him before—in a vision. His house had burned down. . . .

She pushed away from the window and leaned wearily with her back to the wall of the cottage. She was of half a mind to simply take to the woods and hide there until everything was over. Mulengro. The man she'd killed in Rideau Ferry and his brother. The police. All the troubles. But it wasn't that easy. She didn't know about the police, but Bob Gourlay would still be looking for her. And Mulengro . . . he would come for her no matter where she hid. What she needed to do was make preparations. There were herbs to be readied for use against Mulengro's *mule* and a night on a soft bed in Zach's guest room was far more appealing than a night spent sleeping in the forest. It would be more comfortable. And safer.

She drew in a long breath. Jeff was her friend—as much as any *Gajo* could be—and she'd always liked Jackie. The Gypsy was an unknown factor, but as he was in their company, surely that said something for him? And Mulengro *had* attacked him as well. Burned his home. She stirred finally and moved to the door. Her palm was damp on the doorknob and she turned it quickly. The four humans in the room looked up sharply as she stepped inside. By the stove, Boboko opened one eye and a Cheshire cat's smile touched his mouth.

"Hello, Ola," he said.

Janfri regarded the woman standing in the door with undisguised interest. She was younger than he'd expected her to be. A striking woman. She would command a high bridal price—if a man could be found that she'd be willing to marry. He judged her proud, by the way she stood in the doorway, by the quiet control that lay in her eyes. The strength that was in her drew his gaze like a magnet.

"We've got visitors," Zach said unnecessarily.

Ola nodded. "So I see." Janfri noted the veiling of her eyes. The strengths were hidden in their depths now, but he remembered what he'd seen. Young though the woman was, she had the air of a *drabarni* about her, and she was unmistakably of Gypsy blood. She turned to look at Jeff. "Why are you here, Jeff?" she asked. "Jackie?"

"It's a long story," Jeff replied. "A long *weird* story. Are you okay, Ola?"

Ola shrugged. Her gaze shifted to Janfri, the wariness plain. "And who are you, you Romany *chal?*

"*Sarishan, drabarni,*" Janfri said softly, rising to his feet. "My name is Janfri la Yayal le Pataloeshti, *hay kiro?*" And yours?

"Ola Faher. You don't look like one of Big George's people."

"I am Lowara. My brother Yojo married into Big George's *kumpania* and I, too, once had a wife with them." Ola nodded. She hadn't thought he was a Coppersmith. "And you?" Janfri added. "Who are your people? Was your mother's name Pika?"

"It was. But I have no people," Ola replied with a faint bitterness, "save that all Rom are my people. In a time of trouble, when *prikaza* rides the wind, then the Rom will come to me. But in times of good fortune, when the *baXt* is strong . . ." She let her voice trail off. A moment's silence touched the room and she sighed. *"Droboy tune Romale,"* she added, giving him greeting. *"Devlesa avilan."* It is God who brought you.

"Devlesa araklum tume," Janfri replied. It is with God we have found you. "I would offer you the guest cup, but this is not my *tsera.*"

Zach got up and went to put on the water, catching enough to realize that they'd all be wanting more tea. Ola sat wearily at the table across from Janfri. Jeff and Jackie drew up chairs. When Boboko came up onto her lap, she scratched him idly behind the ears, wondering how his speaking was being taken by the two *Gaje* and Janfri.

"Where did you go?" Boboko asked. Ola had to smile as she watched the skin around three pairs of eyes tighten at the cat's voice.

"Just across the lake. I was thinking."

"You think too much sometimes."

"I know." She looked from Jeff to Jackie, expectantly. Jeff cleared his throat.

"I guess you want that story now," he said.

Ola nodded. "You look like you've been in a fight."

"It was all one-sided," Jeff said. "It started with the Gourlays— the two guys that attacked you at the Ferry. They *did* attack you, didn't they?"

Ola paled. "Yes," she said softly. How much did they know?

Jeff nodded sympathetically. "Yeah, well, no one believed me when I told them I'd seen Stan's ghost, or whatever the hell he's become since he died, you see, at least not until . . ."

Ola let the story wash over her without interrupting. She smiled at Zach, thanking him for the tea he handed her, but otherwise kept her attention fixed on each speaker with a singularity that bordered on obsessiveness. She was using her *dook* to weigh their words. Janfri's tale made her sit forward, cupping her chin with her hands, the weight of her head supported by her elbows. When he related his conversation with Old Lyuba and spoke of her dying that same night, she remembered what she'd *seen*—the *mule,* Mulengro—and was about to speak, then decided to let him finish first. When all three had completed their tales she finally sat back, rubbing at her temples. Silence stretched uncomfortably.

"The *mulo,*" she said then. "The ghost of Stan Gourlay . . . it's still in the woods near us?"

"*And* his brother," Jeff said, "though he's not dead. Or at least I don't think he is. He's sure whacked right out of it, though. Janfri did something to the ghost that made it sort of come apart. . . ."

"*BaXt* spices," Janfri explained. "Salt and pepper, some garlic powder . . ."

Ola nodded. It was simple, but effective. A preventative, mostly, but it had done the job. It was much harder to send a *mulo* on to the land of shadows. First it must listen to you, truly *listen.* All ties that held it to this world must be broken; it must be forgiven. . . . She was curious about Janfri, though not surprised that she'd been carrying his name and phone number about in her wallet for the past few years. Fate had a way of tying threads together or, as the *Gaje* would say, it was a small world. She'd also heard of him from Big George's people that she'd met from time to time—but only as o Boshbaro, the Big Fiddle. From his own story, it seemed as though he still only half believed what had been happening to him. But at the same time he'd known enough to prepare in case the impossible became reality. When she asked him how he'd known to do that much, he shrugged.

"I heard as many of the *swatura* around the campfires of my uncle's *kumpania* as did any Rom," he replied.

Another silence followed, broken this time by Jeff. "All this time," he said, struggling for the words. "It's all been real, hasn't it? These magics—all this stuff we've been writing about . . . ?"

"Yes."

"Why didn't you tell me?"

"Would you have believed? Besides, you're a *Gajo,* Jeff. There is Gypsy *draba* that is for Gypsies alone."

"But . . . you could have shown me *some* of it, couldn't you? I'd believe what I saw. I mean, just so I'd *know*. And the cat . . . Boboko. How long has he been able to talk?"

Ola smiled. "Sometimes I think for too long." Boboko sank his claws lightly into her leg, then retracted them.

"And now," Janfri said. "I think it's perhaps your turn to tell what you know, *drabarni*."

Ola shrugged. "The things that I could tell you would mean nothing to you. You have seen *mule* and been witness to odd occurrences, but what does it really mean to you?"

"Try us," Janfri said.

For a moment Ola concentrated. When her pack came floating through the air from the guest room, Jeff and Jackie stirred uncomfortably at the table.

"Jesus," Jeff said. "Do you have to do that?"

"I'm making a point," Ola told him. "If you can't accept such a simple thing as this—" she plucked the pack from the air and set it down on the floor by her chair "—then how can you expect to understand what I have to tell you?"

"But . . . Never mind. Go ahead. We're listening."

So Ola told them about Mulengro and his *draba,* about his *mule*. She could see that for all that they'd experienced tonight, they still found it too hard to accept. Jeff and Jackie were openly skeptical. Zach, who'd already heard it before and believed, merely nodded encouragingly to her as she spoke. Janfri appeared to hover between the two camps—willing to believe, but not sure that he could.

"And that's it," Ola said, finishing. From the pack beside her she drew out a small wooden bowl and a leather water-skin.

"This *draba,*" Janfri asked. "You can only control what you *know?*"

Ola nodded as she poured water from the skin into the bowl. "And it takes time. I've been staying with Zach for only a day or so. Because I still don't *know* his things, I could no more control something of his with my *dook* than might any of you with your thoughts."

"And yet the things that you brought with you . . . ?"

"They are mine to use."

"What are you doing now?" Jeff asked, indicating the bowl.

Ola sighed. There was a tone in his voice that she had no patience for. "I think you should go back," she said. "You and Jackie. This doesn't really concern you. I appreciate your wanting to help me—and also for what you've done so far—but this is too far over your heads."

"You haven't been listening, have you?" Jeff said. "We can't just 'go back'—thanks to our Gypsy friend here. We've probably got the police looking for us right across the country."

"I'm sorry," Ola said.

Janfri shot a dark look at Jeff, then regarded Ola. "I had no choice," he explained. "The *shangle* were not prepared to listen to me—only to lock me away."

"You didn't even try to explain," Jeff said.

Jackie touched his arm. "Don't make things more difficult," she said softly. She was having a very hard time accepting what was happening and she didn't want to make it worse by having them fight amongst themselves. The way she saw it was that they had to pool their resources together to survive. She could almost feel those dead hands at her throat again. . . .

"It's not just myself that I'm worried about," Jeff said.

Jackie swallowed dryly, forcing the memory away. "I know," she said. "But I'm a big girl now, Jeff. None of us asked to get mixed up in this, but now that we're in it, why don't we just try to work together, okay?" She turned her attention to Ola and Janfri. "I'm not sure how much I can believe of what you've told us. I know what *I* saw, what I felt. . . ." She shook her head slowly, trying to frame what she wanted to say. "It's just that witches and wizards and—" she indicated Ola's pack "—all of this is a little too much to take, you know? That doesn't mean I won't help. I just—I don't know what I'm trying to say. We'll help where we can and try to stay out of your way."

Ola closed her hand on Jackie's. "Thank you," she said.

Jackie shrugged. All she wanted was for them to survive.

"What *are* you going to do with that bowl?" Janfri asked, bringing the conversation back to the question that had originally started off the argument.

"Farseeing," she replied. "I want to find out if there are any other Gypsies in the area besides ourselves. I'd rather have Mulengro drawn to us than to someone unprepared for him. There will be no more deaths—save his."

Janfri nodded. No more deaths. Like Lyuba's. Like Tibo and Ursula's.

Ola bent over the bowl and let her eyes go unfocused. Her hands cupped either side of the bowl. For a long moment she sat like that, stillness spreading out from her so that not a person at the table felt they should even breathe. When Ola lifted her thumbs and dipped them in the water, every gaze was on her and the bowl. The water rippled as she agitated it. Then she held her thumbs still against the sides of the bowl, leaving them in the water so that there was direct contact between the *draba* she would make and her *dook*. The water stilled and the clear liquid grew smoky. An image formed in the gray, clearing to a photographic sharpness. Jackie drew in a sharp breath.

"That's the motel in Rideau Ferry," she said.

Like a camera zooming in, the perspective drew nearer to the building, in through a window, to show a man sleeping on a bed. The image of his face filled the bowl. Now it was Janfri's turn to recognize what Ola's farseeing had shown them.

"Yojo!" he cried. He looked quickly to Jackie. "Where is this place? How far is it?"

Jackie drew back at the intensity in the Gypsy's eyes, frightened again. He could be so fierce. "It . . . it's not that far," she began.

Ola withdrew her thumbs from the bowl and the image vanished. The water was simply water once more. She dried her thumbs on her shirt.

"Tu prala?" she asked Janfri. Your brother?

"Uva." Yes.

"He is the only one close enough to be in danger."

Janfri stared into the bowl, trying to will the image to return.

"He was supposed to be with his family, with Big George's *kumpa-nia*. He must have come back. I have to go to him."

"Are you crazy?" Jeff demanded. "There're going to be cops everywhere—looking for you. Not to mention the fact that the Gourlays are still out there. *And* this Mulengro . . ."

"Can you find the *drabarno* with your magic?" Janfri asked.

Ola shook her head. "I don't dare. I'm too tired. If he was to sense my searching for him . . ."

"Tomorrow will be soon enough," Janfri agreed. "Especially if there are no other Rom in the area. But I have to go to Yojo."

"My car's not going to be much help," Jackie said. "It wouldn't take all that long to put the wheels back on, I suppose, but the police are sure to be looking for it." She glanced at Zach. "What about yours?"

"I've got a better idea," he said. "I'll just go down to Gord's place and, like, phone the motel. I'll tell Janfri's brother how to get here and he can drive himself. That way no one's got to go out."

"He won't be using his own name," Janfri said.

"What one will he be using?"

"You could try Greenly or Cerinek." Those were the two names Yojo had told him he'd be using before he'd left. For Yojo's sake, Janfri hoped he'd stuck with Greenly. The police would be looking for Cerineks as well.

"I'll go make that call now," Zach said.

Ola looked worriedly at him. "It's late."

"Hey, it's no hassle. Gord owes me a few favors. I just have to think up a good story to make it worth his while getting out of bed so late." He grinned. "Everything's copacetic." He glanced at Janfri. "What name should I give this Yojo fellow?"

"Janfri."

"You got it," Zach said.

The door closed behind him. Ola sagged in her chair, utterly spent. She *had* to get some sleep. She let her eyes close, but the silence in the room was growing uncomfortable again. The vibes were tense, as Zach would have put it. Why was it that most *Gaje* needed to hear the sound of their own voice? she wondered.

"What is that thing?" Jeff asked suddenly.

Ola opened her eyes to glance at Janfri. The object in question was a strip of knotted cloth that the Gypsy was running between his fingers, back and forth, like a rosary.

"It's a *mulengi dori,*" she answered for Janfri. "A dead man's string."

"A what?"

"It's used to measure the size of a dead man for his coffin. It's very good luck to carry one and it can be used to . . . to do things."

"What sorts of things?" Jackie asked.

Ola shrugged. "It depends. Mostly it's just for luck. Was that used to measure your father's coffin?" she asked Janfri.

He shook his head. "It was for my uncle's. My father and mother were killed by the Nazis."

Jackie blanched.

"Jesus," Jeff said. "Like in the camps?"

"No. They never made it to the camps. They were burned alive. They took us—the children of the *kumpania*—and penned us up like cattle. Yojo and I escaped with the help of the man who became our uncle. I have never heard from the others . . . the other children that went in with us."

"I thought Yojo was your brother."

"He is. Not my brother by blood, but my brother all the same."

Janfri's eyes grew clouded and the two *Gaje* didn't press him for any more details. Like most North Americans of their generation, the death camps weren't a reality that they could truly understand. As Janfri thrust the *mulengri dori* into his pocket, he caught Ola's thoughtful gaze from across the table and slowly shook his head. He didn't think he'd call on his uncle—no matter how bad things got. There were enough *mule* abroad in the countryside as it was.

"You should get some rest, *drabarni,*" he said. "Tomorrow you will need all your strengths."

Ola nodded. "But Zach . . ."

"I will wait up for him. It's for my sake that he went on this errand."

"Bater." She glanced at Jeff and Jackie. "You should try to get

some sleep as well. There's an extra bed in the room I'm using, Jackie, if you want to try it. It's not very big, but it's a bed."

"I'll take it," she said. "I'm dead on my feet."

"You can have the couch," Janfri told Jeff.

Jeff hesitated, then decided he was too tired to argue, and besides, he didn't really relish sitting up alone with Janfri.

"Jeff?"

He turned to see Ola and Jackie about to go down the short hall that led to the guest room. It was Ola who had spoken.

"Thank you—for all you did and tried to do," she said.

"That's okay," he replied. "Sleep well, Ola. Jackie."

Five minutes later the cottage was as quiet as though everyone had been asleep for hours. Janfri poured himself a cup of cold tea and sipped it slowly. He could just see the top of Boboko's head on the other side of the table. The cat was lying on the chair that Ola had vacated.

"So what do you know?" he asked softly.

The cat opened one eye and regarded the Gypsy thoughtfully. "Secrets," he said in a knowing voice. "And you?"

"Little enough, it seems."

The cat gave a shrug of its calico shoulders and settled down, closing its eyes again. Janfri glanced at the door, wondering what was taking Zach so long. He hoped Yojo wasn't using still a third name and that he would believe the message Zach gave him. How long would it take Yojo to reach this place? God, he hated waiting. He smiled at himself. That came from too much time spent among the *Gaje*, for a *phral*'s patience lasted forever.

The smile left his face as he thought about that. How much of a true Rom was he, anyway? Why did he always reach into the *Gaje* world? Surely he could be satisfied with what the Romany life could give him? He sighed, liking the present turn of his thoughts even less than having to think about Mulengro and the trouble the man in black brought with him. At least Mulengro could be fought. The dichotomy inside himself couldn't be dealt with as easily. He glanced at the door again. Where *was* Zach?

thirty-eight

The vixen was a russet shadow as she padded into the field. Hunting had been poor. There was something in the air tonight that made her prey too wary to be caught, something that caused a constant prickle of uneasiness to travel through her as well. She paused at the border of forest and field. The wrongness was more pronounced here. She stared ahead, nostrils quivering as she drew in the scents of the night. But the wind was behind her, sending her own scent into the field, and she had only her eyes and her ears to rely on. The wrongness . . .

Her ears twitched. She saw nothing but a field of low-hanging fog. Her own track was on the ground, for she was following the same trail home to her den that she'd taken on the night's hunting. She took a few careful steps into the field, paused again. The fog drifted around her. Suddenly, too nervous to brave the fog-covered field, she turned to flee the way she'd come. Too late.

Dogs rose from the grass all around her—lean, feral hounds, gaunt and wild-eyed. Whichever way she moved, they closed the circle against her. Stiff-legged, the dogs edged in towards her. She turned one way, then another. Then she saw the tall shape step near—the hated man-smell on it. It towered over the dogs like a gaunt scarecrow's shadow.

"No, no," Mulengro said softly to the dogs. "This is not our enemy."

The stiff-legged forms hesitated, confused.

"Men are *marhime*," he said. "Not this poor frightened thing. Let her go."

The pack leader snarled, lips baring its teeth. Mulengro spoke its name and the dog backed away.

"There, there," the man in black said to the vixen. "You have nothing to fear from us, pretty little one." The fog had gathered

from throughout the field to wreathe about him. It thickened into
manlike shapes when the fox snarled at their master. "Go with
God," Mulengro murmured, stepping back from the panicked animal. He shooed the dogs away from it. "We have other prey to
hunt," he told them.

He led the way into the forest, his *mule* thick about him, the dogs
following in a ragged line. In the field, the vixen stood trembling.
When Mulengro glanced back, he saw the fox finally flee and he
nodded to himself. A soft misting rain began to fall.

"We have other prey," he repeated softly.

thirty-nine

Sleeplessness burned behind Briggs' eyes. He and Will were sitting
in Archambault's car, watching the proceedings in the Lennox farmyard. Briggs had his door open and was sitting with his feet on the
ground. His pipe was between his teeth, smoldering. The bowl was
down to its last dregs of tobacco and starting to taste bitter so he
finally tapped it empty against his shoe and stowed it away.

There were men all over the farmyard—photographers, forensic
people, off-duty police. A light drizzle had started up. It was no
more than a fine mist of rain, but it effectively cut off their chances
of using dogs to track either Owczarek or the feral pack that had hit
the Lennox farm earlier tonight. Briggs' ghosts were quieter now, as
though the drizzle that had washed away their hopes of using the
dogs had washed them away as well. He felt empty and tired. With
the toe of his shoe he drew the *marhime patrin* in the dirt, stared at it,
then slowly scuffed it over.

"If Owczarek's not running those dogs," Will said suddenly,
"then he's on the run himself."

Briggs nodded. "I thought of that myself. The two men he tied
up . . ."

"That's just it," Will said. "He looked good for a while there, but he doesn't feel right anymore. Why didn't he just kill those patrolmen when he had them dead to rights? Why just tie them up and leave them where we could find them?"

"If he's our boy, he's nuts anyway. So who can figure him?"

"Or maybe he's just scared."

"Maybe," Briggs was willing to admit.

"Thing is, we can explain the bodies that got torn up," Will said, thinking aloud. "There's the *shuko* MacDonald showed us . . . the leopard paw clubs, that sort of thing. But this . . ." He nodded towards the farmhouse. "And the bodies we've got without a mark on them, like Cleary and Carol Wesley's. . . ."

"Cooper said Cleary had internal bruising on his heart," Briggs said.

Will nodded. "Something really wicked's going down, Paddy. When we finally come up against whatever the hell it is that's behind all of this, I just hope we can take it down with bullets."

"Oh, we'll take him down," Briggs said. "Whatever he is, we'll take him down."

Before Will could say anything more, Archambault and his driver showed up. The OPP officer had rings under his eyes and he was moving slowly. The lean frame was tight with tension.

"We're finished here," he said as he slid wearily into the front passenger's seat. He leaned over the back of the seat to regard the two men. "We're taking out a chopper in the morning and we'll coordinate it with a ground search using the dogs. We've got enough scent so that if we run across their trail, we'll pick them up."

If the drizzle lets up, Briggs thought, but he nodded expressionlessly, swung his legs into the car, and closed his door. Jackson started up the engine and backed slowly out of the farmyard. As the car passed the ambulance, Briggs stared at the men loading the victims into the back of it. His ghosts returned, and there were more of them now. He saw the ravaged features of the old farmer and his wife in amongst the other dead faces. The car pulled away and he leaned back in his seat, closing his eyes, trying to get rid of the images. The weariness was still burning behind his eyes, but he wasn't sleepy anymore. He was so beat that he'd come out on the other side of being tired. Beside him, Will whistled tunelessly between his teeth.

forty

Things weren't copacetic at all, Zach thought as he left his cottage, and the way they were shaping up, they wouldn't be copacetic for a long time. The vibes just weren't right anymore. For the first time in longer than he could remember, the simple short hike down to Gord's place had him scared silly by the time he reached his neighbor's door. He missed the friendly murmur in the wind. Tonight it seemed to mutter in the trees. He felt abandoned. The thin misting rain that was coming down merely added to his melancholy. He would have put it all down to paranoia, but paranoia was based on delusion and irrationality. The hassle here was that the bad vibes were more than just vibes. They were real.

Zach figured himself as a pretty up-front sort of a guy. He got laughed at a lot and had lost most of his friends because of the way he lived and what he believed. But he knew that the friends that he'd lost hadn't really been friends or they would have just accepted him for what he was. But it still hurt that they were gone and he missed them. He missed hanging out and just rapping, jam sessions that lasted all night in rooms thick with cigarette and Mary Jane smoke, having people relate to him like he was a person not a joke.

Okay, he could handle not having all that anymore, because he had his space here, the lake and the land, the wind to talk to him, the odd person that came by and took the time to look beyond the image. He kept that image because it still seemed important to him. As it had been back in the sixties. It made a statement. And that statement could still be made, perhaps even stronger, in the eighties. When you plugged into what was happening in the world—Iran,

Iraq, Ireland, Israel, unemployment, the economy, the Sandinistas, cruise missiles, acid rain. . . . Christ, the list just went on forever. How could anyone believe that peace and flowers wasn't the *only* way to go?

He had his little corner of heaven, playing at being a modern Thoreau of sorts on his own pond, and he'd given up trying to change anybody else a long time ago.

But now the purity of the land, of the spring-fed waters, was going bad. The wind didn't murmur, it muttered. And the darkness, instead of being invigorating and peaceful, was downright spooky. He didn't blame Ola for it. The vibes he got from her were all mellow. He got a kick out of the cat and the backpack floating through the air and all the other stuff. Magic. Zach felt like a kid in a candy store with what Ola'd brought with her. But the trouble was, you got the bad with the good.

He'd always believed in the good shit. That trees and animals and the wind could talk. You just had to be tuned to their wavelength. And this thing about names and their power that Ola had told him about—hell, it made perfect sense. Once you *knew* something, knew its essence, you could talk to it, move it, relate to it on a deeper level. So why the hell did some pig like this Mulengro have to step in and blow it all?

Mulengro. He made everything go sour. Zach could *feel* him in the wind, in the dark . . . just waiting. And it scared the shit out of him. It wasn't the possibility of immediate physical danger that scared him so much as what was going to happen to his space. Mulengro was going to pollute the good vibes so badly that the forest might as well be a parking lot. With that small stir of what Ola called the *dook* that he had, he could *see* it happening and it just made him want to die.

"There's no way you can get away from it, man," Tamber had told him when the band broke up. They'd been like brothers in Raggle Taggle—Dory and Tamber and himself. But then Dory ODed and Tamber dropped in—as opposed to the way they'd all dropped out years before—and Zach was the only one of them left. Tamber was using the name his parents had given him now. Tom

Hodgell. It had no soul to it, that name. Not like Tamber did. But it sure as hell fit the man Tamber had become, living in New England and working as a salesman for a chocolate bar distributor. Chocolate bars!

"No matter where you go," he'd told Zach, "the world's going to find you."

"I'm not hiding from the world," Zach had tried to explain. "I'm trying to find the real world. You can't tell me it's out there, Tamber. Not after all we've been through together. It's here. By this lake. Or it's gone forever."

Tamber had shaken his head. "We were kids, Zach, and we had a good time, you know? But it's time to grow up. You go hide yourself away in some little woodlands commune and all you're going to do is stagnate, man. You want to grow? You want to find the real world? Then stop pretending it's still 1967 and plug into what's happening now!"

Zach knew what was happening now. He just didn't want any part of it—didn't want any part of the negative side of it, at least. He wasn't hiding. He was just filtering what he took in and making sure he never let the glitter blind him. What he had here wasn't for everyone, but it was all he wanted. And now it was threatened by Mulengro and, win or lose against the sorcerer, things just weren't going to be the same again. It was like Tamber had promised him that last time they'd been together: The world had found him. Found his space. And in the shape of Mulengro and his horrors, it was going to steal it all away.

He sighed and wiped his face dry of the misting rain that mingled with his tears. He'd reached Gord's door and had to get his head straight before he went in. He took a deep breath to steady himself, then rapped on the door. When there was still no reply by the fourth knock, he tried the doorknob and found it turned under his hand. He hesitated then, his melancholy vanishing under a wave of cold fear. Why was there no reply? Gord's car was in the lane and he was a light sleeper. He hesitated there, listening to the mutter of the wind in the trees, then slowly swung the door open and stepped inside.

"Gord?" he called softly. "Hey, Gord!"

He found the wall switch and flicked it. The ceiling light came on, flooding the room with light. The back door facing the lake stood ajar. Zach crossed the room and called outside, but there was still no reply. Just the wind and the sound of water dripping. He stood there for a long moment, listening, then he turned back inside the cottage. A quick search showed him that the place was empty.

Where had Gord gone? The vibes were not good. Moving quickly now, Zach dug out the phone book, found the number for the motel, and dialed it. Leaning against the wall that the phone hung from, he listened to it ring at the other end, feeling more nervous with every passing moment. A sleepy voice finally answered.

"Sorry to get you up," Zach said into the receiver, "but, like, do you have a Mr. Cerinek or a Mr. Greenly staying with you? Sure, I can hold. . . ." His throat was all dry, his palms damp. It was funny how fear could bring out such opposite reactions. "You do?" he said when the motel manager came back on the line. "Can you call his room for me? Well, sure I know what time it is but, like, this is important, man. Okay, okay. Would you just do it. No, it can't wait. Yeah, I'll hold."

It was another endless minute before a cautious voice came on the line. "Yes?"

"Hello, Greenly?" Zach asked. "You don't know me, but I've got a message for you from your brother Janfri. If you've got a pencil, I'll give you the directions to get to my place where he's staying. He wants you to come right away." As he spoke, Zach stared around the empty cottage, the pinprickle of nervousness never leaving the nape of his neck where it had lodged when he first came in through the door.

Janfri stepped outside and eased the door closed so that it wouldn't slam and wake up the sleepers inside. The night was quiet, but because the area was unfamiliar to him, he wasn't sure if it was too quiet or not. The faint drizzle that was coming down would help muffle the usual rustlings and murmurs of the forest. He ambled across the lawn in back of the cottage and looked up the hill to where the driveway led off, enjoying the misty rain that wet his face. He wondered if he should have a look to see what was keeping Zach, then decided to sit down on a swing and try to relax instead. He was too wound up—with good reason, perhaps—and it wasn't the best way to face a problem such as this.

He concentrated on the stillness, tried to let it take the place of the endless swirl of conversation inside him. He was thinking of this, and answering with that, and replying to yet another—just like a *Gajo*. They never stopped talking—not even when their mouths were closed— and he was too much like them.

His night vision sharpened as his eyes adjusted to the darkness. He'd lived in cities too long, that much was clear. A Rom needed the night around him, like this, not walls. The sky above, cloudy with a mist of rain like tonight, or lit by stars, not diffused by streetlights and neon signs. He drew the *mulengi dori* from his pocket and traced the familiar knots with his fingers. They were like these knots—he and Ola and the others. All part of a dead man's string. And it would be the measure of their strength that would fit the coffin for Mulengro. It was a curious notion and gave him a sense of disquiet. If they were knots, then which one of them would have to be untied?

Sweet dead one, let the noose about to be tied around my neck be undone. . . .

He put the *mulengi dori* away and stood up. The swing moved back and forth behind him, the length of its arc shortening until it was motionless again. He started up the driveway, topped the hill. The track disappeared into the darkness and there was still no sign of Ola's friend. He thought he saw something move far down the track—a low quick shape. Fox maybe? Or a dog? He stood there watching for a few minutes longer, but whatever it had been was gone now. He turned then and went back down the hill to the cottage. As soon as he left the hilltop, there was movement on the track again.

· · ·

Zach cradled the phone. He looked out the window, not much relishing the idea of the walk back to his own place. Not that it was all that far or anything. It was just that he could feel *things* out there beyond the glass panes that separated him from the night. Ghosts. Bad vibes. Danger. He remembered the story Janfri had told him and looked for some salt and pepper, emptied out a couple of small shakers into a napkin and put it in his pocket. Then he went through the kitchen drawers looking for a flashlight.

He thought it'd be better it he hung around until Janfri's friend showed up and would ride back with him. If Yojo missed the turn to his place—which was easy enough to do in the dark—he'd find himself bogged down in the Conservation Area. Meanwhile, he would scout around a bit outside. Perhaps Gord had fallen down somewhere in the bush and hurt himself; he could be lying out there somewhere, unconscious.

Zach turned off the lights in the cottage and went outside, playing the beam of the flashlight on the lawn around the cottage. The wet grass glimmered in its light. He heard something behind the cottage and moved around the building, the flashlight's beam stabbing the darkness. When it caught and reflected a pair of eyes, low to the ground, Zach thought he'd shit his pants. He backed up as whatever it was began to growl.

forty-one

"Hey, Briggs?"

They were back at the OPP headquarters on Highway 7. Briggs and Will were sitting in Archambault's office finishing off a couple of ham and cheese sandwiches. They were both wearing ill-fitting bush clothes that Archambault had dragged up from somewhere for them—jeans, plaid shirts, police-issue windbreakers and heavy-duty boots. Briggs looked up at the sound of his name to see one of the

RCMP officers who had been present at the trailer park standing in the doorway. His name was Jack Killens.

"Yo!" Briggs said.

"I ran that check through for you," Killens said, stepping into the room. "The Stateside boys don't have anything but I turned up something interesting when I ran an international check on Gypsies with Interpol."

He laid a folder on the desk and took Archambault's chair. Briggs flipped the file open and looked at the fuzzy 8 × 10 B&W blowup that was on top.

"Who's this?"

"Guy's name is Josef Wells. He was an inmate at a psycho ward in a place called Hôpital St. Marie in Strasbourg, France."

"What's with the scars?"

"It's in the file. *Lupus vulgaris*—a skin disease that leaves heavy scarring."

"I'll say. Looks like a mask. Gives him a kind of wolfish look."

Killens smiled. "That's why they call it *lupus*."

"What was wrong with him?" Will asked.

"He was a survivor of the Dachau camp—if you can call it surviving. He never recovered completely."

"What do you mean?"

Killens shrugged. "Look, this isn't in the file, but I know a man who survived the camps and what he's told me about them isn't pretty. This guy's in his fifties now and he still wakes up screaming some nights, thinking he's back there, that he's never getting out. The file doesn't make it really clear what happened to Wells. They just say he couldn't adjust back to the real world, you know? I mean, he was just a fucking kid when he went in—nine-years-old. And they worked him over in there. The Americans brought him back to France when they liberated Dachau. Nobody else wanted him. The French didn't want him either, but he ended up just getting dumped on them. The kid was bad news. Had visions. He was violent and was kept under sedation most of the time. And he was in that psycho ward since the end of the war."

"Jesus."

"Yeah. Tell me about it. Anyway, he busted out about a year ago and they've been looking for him ever since. The trouble is, with Gypsies—"

"You don't have to tell me about Gypsies," Briggs said. "They're nothing but trouble. And if they want to disappear, they're gone."

"What's he got to do with Owczarek?" Will asked.

"Nothing—that I know of. You asked about Gypsies, this came up, so I pulled it for you. The thing that made me sit up when I read the file is, that when he was in St. Marie, he talked a lot about having to cleanse his people, even if it meant killing them."

Briggs stared down at the picture. "Cleanse his people?"

"Yeah. He told the doctors that the reason the Nazis were killing his people was because they weren't clean anymore. That the Nazis were doing God's work and nobody should have stopped them."

"So now he's doing it," Will said softly.

"I don't know," Killens said. "It's a long way from Strasburg to Canada. And with a guy that looks like that—not to mention that his elevator doesn't go all the way to the top floor—he'd be kind of hard to miss, don't you think?"

"But he *is* a Gypsy," Briggs said. "And they *haven't* picked him up yet—have they?"

"No."

"What about Gypsies getting murdered over there? Was there anything on that?"

"If there was, I couldn't get it. The only reason I picked up on this Wells guy was because they have a bulletin out on him across Europe—at all the border patrols and that kind of thing."

Will took the picture and studied it. The man looking back at him from the photo was a very scary looking guy.

"This is one we owe you, Jack," Briggs said.

"Yeah, well if you pick him up, you can mention my name. But if you don't, you never heard of me, understand? The brass doesn't much like us using our connections to help out the local boys—though that's not official either. Word gets out, my ass is in a sling. Unless you pick him up."

Briggs nodded. "I never heard of you, Jack."

"So long as we've got that understood." He arose from behind the desk and headed for the door. "Don't leave that file hanging around, okay?"

"I won't." When he was gone, Briggs turned to his partner. "What do you think?"

"I don't know, Paddy. I don't see a connection with Owczarek. But then again, maybe there isn't one."

"I've been thinking of that too. Gypsies—you push them and they just melt away. We probably just scared Owczarek off, coming down too hard."

Will nodded, his gaze still on the picture. "Or maybe someone else did," he said. When he looked at the man's wolfish features, he kept seeing the bodies they'd found at the Lennox farm. Feral dogs and juju. He shook his head. It was too weird. But he couldn't shake the feeling that they were all connected. There was that damn symbol on the fencepost. . . .

"I still want Owczarek," Briggs said softly. He too studied the picture. He tried that face on the mental picture he had of the man they were looking for and found that it fit better than Owczarek's had. The ghosts stirred inside him, as though they agreed. "There's a connection," he added. "There has to be. The way Owczarek's running—it can't just be Gypsy reticence."

"Maybe he's not running from something so much as at something," Will offered.

"There's that," Briggs admitted, though he had trouble picturing Owczarek and himself on the same side. "Guess we'll find the answer to that when we catch up with him."

Will nodded. "Are we sharing this with Archambault?" he asked, indicating the file.

Briggs sighed heavily. "I don't see that we've got much choice. It's his manpower we're going to be using tomorrow."

"I'd rather we just took a car out on our own," Will said. "We can work with them, but I'm not real big on having Archambault's boys stumbling over our feet."

Briggs found a tired smile and fit it to his lips. "Seems to me you're always the one who's warning me about hotdogging."

Will shrugged. "This one's almost personal, Paddy, and we're so far out of our own jurisdiction anyway. . . ."

Briggs closed the file. "Maybe we'll play it close for another day," he said. "I'll talk to Archambault about letting us check out the area where Owczarek was last seen on our own. There's a lot of country out there and he's already got his hands full trying to coordinate things. Could be he'll be happy to get *us* out of *his* hair."

"I've got a feeling about that area," Will said. "We're getting so close to him now I can almost taste it."

The ghosts stirred inside Briggs again, a swirl of dead faces that demanded retribution.

"Christ, I hope so," he said.

42
forty-two

Yojo cradled the handset and sat down on the bed, staring at the phone. Who was this *Gajo?* He had known Yojo's name and Janfri's, as well as the names Yojo was traveling under. How could he know these things? How could he know where Yojo would be staying, that he was returning, when even Janfri didn't know these things? It smacked of the supernatural to the big Gypsy and a nervous twitch cat-pawed its way up his spine. The *Gajo's* instructions had been clear—Yojo had memorized them as he could read and write only with great difficulty. But what would he find at the end of them? Janfri or the man in black?

He stood abruptly and plucked his small traveling bag from the top of the dresser. He left the door to the room unlocked, with the key on the dresser, and went out to his car. Tossing the bag into the back seat, he backed out of the parking space, turned, and nosed the Lincoln towards the highway. Left on 15, the *Gajo* had said, until he saw the Conservation Area sign, then he was to take the road there on the right. Yojo pulled out onto the highway and floored the gas pedal. The big Lincoln growled as it picked up speed.

I am coming, *prala,* he told the night behind his windshield, the darkness beyond the light thrown by his headbeams. I am coming.

Janfri started up the hill a second time, plainly worried now. Zach had been gone too long. But when he reached its crest and looked down the track, there was still no one coming. He had half-decided to go looking for their host, when he realized that he should at least leave word with the others as to where he was going. He could tell the cat. He shook his head at the mystery, no, the sheer absurdity, of a talking cat, and was turning away, when he paused. He'd caught movement out of the corner of his eye again. A low shape, fox or dog, moving further down the track, out of sight now. He thought of *mule.* Back in the cottage there was a talking cat and a bowl of water that could show images of things happening miles away. And he had seen for himself, grappled with, the ghost of a dead man. *Draba.* The night was alive with magic.

He thought he heard something moving in the brush to his left, but when he turned his head, the sound stopped and he could see nothing. He backed slowly down the hill. There was more movement, on either side. Something stalked him. He caught a quick glimpse of a low canine shape, heard a growl. Dogs? Did Mulengro have dogs to hunt them with as well? His hands opened and closed at his sides. He had nothing. No weapon. Only the *baXt* spices in his pockets, but he doubted that they would be effective against anything living. There was also his *mulengi dori,* but even if it could help him he didn't think there was much wisdom in calling up another *mulo.*

The furtive sounds drew nearer. From the corners of his eyes he could see lean shapes sidling closer, but when he turned, all motion stopped in the direction he looked and the dogs melted into the darkness. Then the sounds would begin again, from behind him. He spun in a circle, glaring at the shadowed forest that surrounded Zach's lot. For a long moment silence hung heavy in the air. He turned again and bolted for the cottage. The silence was swallowed by a chorus of snarls.

• • •

It was a dog, Zach realized as he backed away. And it was pissed off. Thing to do was show it he wasn't afraid. Send out the good vibes. Right. Sure. And meanwhile he was shaking in his boots. He let the beam of his flashlight move towards the animal again, then gagged when he saw what the dog was standing over. Gord Webster lay on the ground with his throat torn open.

"Oh, Jesus," Zach mumbled.

It was rabid. It had to be rabid. The dog began to move forward on stiff legs, still growling. Zach's gaze darted left and right, but there was nowhere to run to. The flashlight trembled in his hand as he continued to slowly back away.

They were all over her, a pack of wild dogs with the smell of the marsh in their fur, rank and stinking. They held her motionless with their weight, claws digging into her skin, feral eyes grinning at her helplessness. Whenever she tried to fight their weight, jaws would snap inches from her face. They were playing with her. Her throat was too constricted to scream, her body trapped. Saliva dripped hot on her skin. The pack leader lunged at her, at her neck. She tried to twist her head, but couldn't, and the jaws—

Ola awoke, drenched in sweat. She lay silent, testing the air with adrenaline-charged senses. Just a dream, she told herself. That was all it had been. But then she heard the growling outside.

She slipped out of bed, the long flannel shirt that she wore as a nightgown sticking unpleasantly to her skin. That sound. . . . She glanced at the other bed, but Jackie was sleeping. Out into the hall. There was still a light on by the kitchen table. But when she got there she saw only Boboko sitting up, ears cocked. Her gaze swept the living room to find Jeff sprawled on the couch, asleep. Where were Zach and Janfri?

"That sound . . . ?"

This time she spoke the words aloud. She hurried barefoot across the kitchen to the door. Boboko followed, fur bristling. As the growls broke into a chorus of snarling, she jerked the door open.

• • •

Zach flung the flashlight at the dog as it lunged for him and ran for the nearest tree. The makeshift weapon struck the animal a glancing blow, breaking the impetus of its attack. It stumbled and fell, recovered quickly. Zach ran, but he knew he wasn't going to make the tree. He turned to face the dog, aimed a kick at it. It dodged the blow, came in from another side.

"Leave me alone!" Zach cried.

He was utterly panic-stricken. Instinct alone lifted his arm as the dog went for his throat. The jaws closed on his arm. The weight of the animal knocked him down with the dog on top. It loosed its grip on his arm and snapped at his face. He grabbed its throat with both hands and held it at bay. The forepaws scrabbled for purchase, tearing at his buckskin jacket. He thought he heard a car on the road leading in to the cottages. That'd be Janfri's friend, some part of his mind below the panic reasoned. But Yojo was going to come too late because his arms were already getting weaker and the dog renewed its attack with a frenzy. The wet fur began to slip in his grip.

The time for pretense was past. Lean feral shapes exploded from the forest to cut Janfri off from the cottage. One on his left, two on the right, with at least one more closing in from behind. He wasn't going to make it. He shot a glance at Jackie's Honda, but he was too far from it to reach the weapons that they'd hidden in it. His only hope was to try to barrel through the ones that were between him and the cottage. Twenty paces. God in heaven, surely he could cover that distance before they had him?

A dog hit him in the center of the back and he went sprawling. He rolled, half rose, smashed a fist against the jaw of the first dog as it attacked him, teeth snapping inches from his own face, then threw himself toward Zach's rock garden. His scrabbling hands closed around a stone, but before he could use it, two more of the dogs were on him and the stone was knocked from his hand. He flailed at the animals, trying to protect his face and throat. Jaws closed on one arm, the weight of the animal pulling the protection away from him. As another shot forward, he lowered his head abruptly, skull meeting skull with a jar that stunned him. Then the door to the cottage burst open.

The Lincoln's headlights caught the struggling pair in the driveway and Yojo slammed on the brakes. Without even thinking of what he was doing, the big Gypsy leapt from the car and ran for them. Before either Zach or the dog were aware of his presence, Yojo grabbed the dog by the scruff of its neck and flung it bodily across the lawn. The dog landed in a tumble, bewildered and yelped with confusion. It scrambled to its feet, shaking its head. The feral eyes sought its new attacker, locked its gaze on the big man.

For a long moment they stared each other down, the rain misting about them, then the dog began to circle the man. Zach sat up, shaking like a leaf. His gaze went from the dog to his rescuer. The big Gypsy flicked open a pocket knife with a six-inch blade and grinned mirthlessly as he waited for the dog's attack.

Ola's nightsight allowed her to grasp the situation in an instant. She focused her will and stepped aside as her backpack came whirring from out of the cottage. It struck the two dogs on top of Janfri and sent them sprawling, strewing her belongings across the wet lawn with the impact. A pair of jeans arose and wrapped themselves about another dog's head, blinding it as it pulled the dog away from the Gypsy. Janfri began to crawl towards Ola as a barrage of shirts, underwear and a long pleated skirt clouded the air, confusing the animals.

"We need a gun!" she cried to Janfri as he stumbled to his feet.

He nodded, eyes wide as he stared at the animated clothing. *Draba.* Madness. He hobbled to the Honda. As he made his way, the dogs tore at the clothing, shredding it. One broke free and lunged after Janfri, but the canvas backpack slapped it away. Another struggled out of the constricting folds of Ola's skirt. Boboko hissed, throwing himself upon its back, claws digging in. The dog howled and rolled, dislodging the cat. Before its jaws could close on him, the backpack came whistling through the air, striking the dog with enough force to knock it off its feet.

"Janfri!" Ola cried, willing him to hurry.

The dogs were breaking free and she couldn't hold them. He was taking too long.

Zach watched numbly as the dog charged them. He couldn't believe that his companion was going to try to stop it with only a knife. The dog was a mangy breed—half Collie, half German shepherd. Lean and wasted looking, but strong. Zach had already discovered how strong and fast it was. He threw himself to one side as the animal attacked, but Yojo stepped forward to meet it.

The big man moved deceptively swiftly for his size. One hand shot out and caught the dog by the scruff of its neck, the other drew the blade of his knife across its jugular. Blood sprayed from the severed arteries and the body flopped in the Gypsy's grip, the knife gash widening into a huge bloody grin. Yojo dropped the animal to the wet ground where it twitched as the last of its life bled from it. When he turned to Zach, the luthier backed away, shaking his head, stunned at the night's events. His glasses hung from his ear and fell as he moved. He plucked them up with trembling fingers, wiped the rain from his face. At that moment, the big man with his bloody knife looked like he was ready to finish him off next.

"Who are you?" the Gypsy demanded.

Janfri cursed his leg as he half hobbled, half dragged the limb across the lawn to the car. It had twisted under him when he fell. Nothing was broken so far as he could tell—he wouldn't be using it at all if it was broken, now would he?—but it wouldn't bear his weight. When he reached the car he almost fell against it, using it for support as he fumbled at the open door, trying to get the seat up so that he could climb into the back and get to the weapons.

He bumped his leg as he squeezed into the back. Closing his mind to the pain, his fingers found the rifle behind the seat and dragged it out. It seemed to take forever before he was leaning weakly against the outside of the car once more. He lifted the rifle and aimed, finger tightening on the trigger. The backlash just about took off his shoulder and the boom of the big rifle deafened him for a moment. The shot was a clean miss, but it froze the dogs. He worked the bolt on the rifle and another cartridge clicked into place.

Zach held a hand up defensively. "I . . . my name's Dr. Rainbow— Zach. I called you, remember?"

Yojo regarded him steadily, then toed the corpse of the dog. Zach watched, his Adam's apple bobbing as he tried to swallow. His throat was dry and raw. When the Gypsy spoke again, he started.

"How did you know my name?" Yojo demanded. "How did you know where I was?"

"Don't . . . don't get crazy or nothing," Zach began. "Janfri—"

The sound of a gunshot boomed in the night air.

"Oh, shit," Zach said. "That came from my place."

Yojo stepped close. "*Where* is Janfri?"

Zach lifted a hand that was still shaking and pointed in the direction that the gunshot had come from.

As Janfri lifted the rifle to his shoulder once more, the dogs withdrew. One minute they were in full attack, now the lawn was empty except for the contents of Ola's backpack that were strewn wetly across it. Gaze raking the forest, Janfri hobbled back to the door of the cottage. He saw Boboko rising from where he'd fallen, fur still bristling, tail puffed out to twice its normal size. Ola leaned weakly against the door frame. The woods were silent. Still favoring his leg,

Janfri made his way to the door. Jeff and Jackie appeared in the doorway, Jeff carrying a wrought-iron poker.

"What . . . what's going on?" he asked in a low voice.

"Jeff," Janfri said. "Would you get a box of salt and that string of garlic that's hanging up in the kitchen?"

Jeff stood staring at Ola's belongings scattered across the yard. He'd arrived too late to actually see the dogs, but he'd heard them snarling and growling.

"Jeff?"

He turned to Janfri. "What? Oh, yeah. Sure." He passed the poker to Jackie who accepted it gingerly.

"What happened?" Jackie asked. She didn't think the night was ever going to end. It was just getting weirder and weirder. . . .

"It was dogs," Ola said. She looked around, counting heads as Jeff returned. "Where's Zach?" she asked.

"He hasn't come back yet," Janfri replied. He took the garlic and salt from Jeff and added it to the small amount he still had in his pockets. "That's why I was outside—I was looking to see if I could find him."

Ola rubbed her forehead with a weary hand. She was beginning to feel a chill, standing out here in her damp nightshirt. The day would probably be warm again, unless the drizzle kept up, but right now she was cold, and not just from the temperature.

"We have to go look for him," she said. She couldn't bear the thought of anything happening to Zach. When Janfri nodded in agreement, she seemed to register what he was putting into his pockets for the first time. "Those won't do anything against the dogs," she said.

"I know. I just thought . . . he must have sent them. And if he's near . . ."

Ola understood what he meant. She didn't want to voice Mulengro's name either, in case the mere speaking of it would call him to them. Jeff had gone to the car and was returning with the rest of the guns, his mouth set in an expression of distaste.

"Look," Jackie said suddenly, pointing to the top of the hill where the driveway vanished. Fog was wreathing there, low to the ground. The lean shapes of the feral dogs moved in amongst it.

"Come, then," Yojo said. He caught Zach by the arm and hauled him to his feet. Leaving Zach to totter uncertainly, the Gypsy knelt, cleaned his knife on the wet grass and put it away. When he rose; he steered Zach towards the car. "Show me the way," he said.

"There's a man . . . a dead man back there. . . ."

Yojo glanced over his shoulder in the direction that Zach had indicated. "We must see to the living first, before we bury the dead."

"But . . ."

Zach stopped protesting as they reached the car. He got numbly into the passenger's side. He felt the car shift on its springs under the weight of the Gypsy. Then they were in motion and he closed his eyes, fighting down the nausea that roiled inside him. All he could see was that one brief glimpse he'd had of Gord's body, the torn flesh and the wild-eyed dog standing over it.

The fog thickened and moved unnaturally, tendrils moving to either side of the road like the weaving arms of an octopus. The dogs stalked back and forth, filling the air with deep-chested growls. Below by the cottage, Ola and the others watched with growing horror. The fog took manlike shapes and Ola recognized the *mule* for what they were. When Mulengro finally appeared, standing at the top of the hill and looking down at them, Ola's fear tightened like a hand squeezing her heart.

They had no defense against this creature. Salt or other *baXt* spices would not repel him as they did his *mule*. Even in the dark and with the distance between them, she could see the mocking look in his pale eyes, the smile that touched his lips. The potency of his power brushed against her mind, chilling her.

"Oh, Jesus," Jeff murmured. He drew close to Jackie, the weaponry in his arms just so much useless metal. Janfri came over to him, moving slowly to favor his leg. He took the pistols and thrust them into his belt, the rifle in his hands once more as he turned. He left the shotgun for Jeff.

"You can't kill him with that," Ola said. She *knew*. Her *dook* let her feel the strength of Mulengro's *draba*. It rose from him like a wind and staggered her.

"He's a man," Janfri said, bringing the rifle to his shoulder. "And a man can die."

"He's a *drabarno*," she said. "Only *draba*, or fire, or the *mule* he controls can kill him."

Janfri didn't reply. He aimed carefully, braced himself for the recoil, and squeezed the trigger. The backlash of the shot stung his shoulder and almost turned him around. But his gaze remained on the man in black. He saw a *mulo* move between Mulengro and the bullet. The crack of the rifle was deafening, but Mulengro didn't fall.

"I had him in my sights!" Janfri cried. "I shot him!"

"The *mulo* swallowed your bullet," Ola said dully.

And now they were moving down the hill. Not Mulengro, nor the dogs, but the *mule,* creeping down the slope, a slow and deadly flow of fog that took, here the shape of an arm, there a head, were lost again in the roil of the smokelike cloud as it flowed down, were visible again. Janfri fired once more, but on the crest of the hill, a *mulo* swallowed his second bullet. He threw down the rifle, dug the salt and garlic from his pocket, and went hobbling forward to meet the *mule*.

He heard the sound of a car, but did not turn his attention from the *mule*. He held the box ready, prepared to strew them with the salt. The garlic was upraised in his other hand. Only Ola's gaze didn't follow him, nor the approach of the *mule*. So she was the only one to see Mulengro turn when he was suddenly outlined in the headbeams of the approaching car.

"Who's that?" Zach cried.

The Lincoln's headlights caught a figure as they turned the last corner before the straight stretch that led to his cottage. Zach had filled Yojo in as much as he could on the short drive from Webster's cottage. Beside him the big Gypsy stiffened.

"Mulengro," he said softly.

He stomped on the gas pedal and the rear wheels of the Lincoln tore at the rough road and sod, seeking purchase on the wet ground. Zach shivered as they went barreling down the drive. It was almost dawn. He'd been praying that it was over for the night. That the gunshot had been a false alarm. That he could just collapse on his bed when he got home and let everyone else handle this weird stuff, because he was too tired and too scared for any of it. Instead he was going to die. Because the Gypsy didn't know what lay on the other side of the man in black, the man whose eyes caught the headbeams' lights and reflected them back like a cat's might when he turned.

The drop was too steep, Zach thought. They might run down this Mulengro fellow, but they'd probably end up in the middle of his cottage at the same time. But he didn't plan to argue with the big Gypsy again. He just closed his eyes.

Janfri flung the garlic into the thick of the *mule,* then swept the box in front of them, spraying an arc of salt that cut them in two. A weird hissing sound arose from the *mule.* On the crest of the hill, one of the dogs howled at the sound. The *mule* roiled back from Janfri as he swung the box a second time. A third time, and it was empty. He was at the bottom of the hill now, moving forward through the wet grass in a limping shuffle. Tossing the empty salt box aside, he drew one of the handguns and aimed at the man in black.

He squeezed the trigger, but the hammer fell on an empty chamber. Before he could fire again, he heard someone screaming behind him, and then the night was filled with a terrible roaring. Suddenly Mulengro was no longer there on the crest of the hill. He'd vanished into the forest like one of his *mule* while Yojo's Lincoln lifted from the top of the slope like some mechanical dragon, its headbeams the metal monster's glaring eyes.

Janfri froze for a fraction of a second, then threw himself to one side. The car left the ground. For one moment it was airborne, all four wheels off the ground. Time seemed to slow down, to not move at all. The Lincoln was suspended in the air for ages, just floating there. Then it hit the ground with a thunderous crash. At the front of the cottage, Ola and the others scattered. The car skidded, bounced once, then slewed to one side as Yojo fought the wheel. It came sideways at the cottage, wheels tearing huge gouges in the grass and wet ground. Ola saw one of her skirts get entangled in a wheel. It could have been her. . . . Then she hit the ground at the same time as the car slammed broadside into the cottage.

She could feel the impact from where she lay. The ground shook. The cottage trembled, but held, losing only the small porch over its front door. The car's engine sputtered, then stalled. There was a dull roaring in Ola's ears. She got slowly to her feet, staring at the car, then swung her gaze to where Mulengro had been standing. The crest of the hill was empty now. Even the dogs were gone. Through the overcast haze of the misting rain, the eastern horizon was lightening. Looking back at the car, she saw a big man with a walrus mustache emerge from the driver's side. He turned back to the car and helped a gangly figure out.

"Oh, Zach!" Ola cried as she ran up to where Yojo was supporting the luthier. He was dirty with mud and his jacket was ripped. His hair was plastered against his head and he favored the arm that the dog had gripped with its jaws. Only the buckskin of his jacket had saved him from being hurt worse. He was still badly shaken from his ordeal.

"No way," he said slowly to Yojo, "I'm *ever* going to hitch a ride with you again!"

Yojo smiled briefly then handed Zach over into Ola's care. He looked for his *prala,* saw Janfri climbing the hill. He followed, reaching Janfri at the same time as Janfri topped the hill. They looked at each other, then around themselves.

"Quite an entrance," Janfri said finally. Yojo shrugged. It was growing steadily brighter and the rain had completely let up now.

Janfri looked down at the gun in his hand, then thrust it into his belt. Mulengro was gone, for now.

"I thought you were going with Big George," Janfri added.

"I did. But Simza and I decided my place is here with you."

Janfri was tired and sore. As he looked at Yojo, his eyes misted. "I'm glad you came, *prala*," he said.

Yojo made no reply. He looked down at the ground between them, his face paling. Janfri followed his gaze and saw it then, too. A *patrin* scratched into the dirt. *Marhime*. The symbol was cut deep into the wet ground.

"He had no time to make that mark," Janfri said. "No time. . . ."

Yojo put his arm around Janfri's shoulders to lead him back down to the cottage. He'd had the man in black in sight the whole time that the car was roaring towards him and hadn't seen him make the *patrin* either. It would take time to cut it so deep. And it hadn't been made long ago. But still . . .

"Perhaps he made it earlier," Yojo said.

"*Uva*," Janfri agreed. "That must be what he did." He leaned against Yojo, gaining strength from his *prala*'s presence.

"Come," Yojo said and led the way down the slope.

Halfway down, Janfri paused to look at the destruction that the night had left on Zach's property. The Lincoln was close by the house, the small porch over the door folded over it. Ola's clothing and other belongings were scattered across the yard. There were raw gouges in the grass where the wheels of the car had torn up the muddy sod.

The others were waiting for them by the Lincoln—as motley looking a crew as he could imagine, knowing that he looked no better himself. They were all in varying stages of dress, muddy and wet. But at least they were alive. They had survived the night. Ola was standing by the hood of the car with Boboko in her arms and Zach leaning wearily against the car beside her. Jeff had gathered the various guns, including the revolver that Janfri had dropped while trying to escape the airborne car. Jackie was trying to salvage some of Ola's clothes that weren't too torn and muddy.

"Who's your friend?" Boboko asked Janfri as he and Yojo drew near. Yojo took a quick step back and stared at the cat with a stunned expression. The others, almost used to it by now, smiled wearily.

"His name is Yojo," Janfri said.

Yojo looked from Ola to the cat. "You . . . found your *drabarni,*" he said softly to Janfri.

"Or she found me. Perhaps we should go inside."

They trooped alongside the house to the back porch and went in. Finding seats where they could, they settled down to put their stories together while Zach and Jackie made breakfast. Outside, the drizzle began to come down once more.

forty-three

Earl Hollis sat on his front porch and watched the Rom arrive. They came in beat-up limousines and touring cars, Cadillacs, Lincolns, Plymouths, Chryslers, Chevys. There was no hiding the Gypsy presence on the farm any longer. Tents had sprung up all over his fields. The cars choked his land and yard and were lined up along the road down to the highway. By the time the last one arrived around midnight, he'd counted thirty-eight of them.

He sat and watched them come, drinking canned beer and smoking his pipe, rocking back and forth in his old wicker rocker. Big George had asked him to stay in the house tonight and, watching all these Rom arrive, Earl was happy to do just that. No matter how well-liked he was, he was still a *Gajo* and these Rom looked grim tonight. He didn't know what had called them all together and figured he didn't really want to know. Big George or one of the other *rom bare* would tell him if he needed to know.

At that moment Big George was sitting in front of his tent. Tshaya kept a big pot with sweetened tea on the fire, doling out the guest cups as each car unloaded its occupants. Representatives from most of the major *kumpaniyi* in New England, Quebec and Ontario were present here. What troubled Big George was that he hadn't summoned them and those Rom that he had asked had simply shrugged and said the word had gone out that they should come and so here they were. By now there were over two hundred and fifty Romany *chal* and *chi* gathered, young and old, but it wasn't until the last car arrived that Big George understood who had put out the word.

The old woman was called Pivli Gozzle, the Widow of Goose Hill. She was a thin old *drabarni*, with a man's features. Some said that she was over a hundred years old. Others insisted that she'd come with the first Rom when they'd left their homeland and lived in one guise or another ever since. She wore a cloak of raven feathers that gleamed with a blue-black sheen in the light of the kerosene lamps and hung from her shoulders to her ankles. On her head was a wide-brimmed hat, shading her dark eyes, and her hair was white and thick, hanging in braids to her waist, stark like beams of moonlight in a dark wood. She was an English Lowara and because she was a *drabarni*, black was not considered *prikaza* for her.

She came to Big George's fire, flanked on either side by two strapping lads. Big George stood at their approach and offered the old woman his chair. Pivli's teeth gleamed white as she grinned and accepted the seat as though it was her due.

"*Sarishan, rom baro* Luluvo," she said. "I have come to see the northern *dilo* for myself." Big George frowned when she called him a fool, but said nothing. She was old and she was a *drabarni*. She could say such a thing.

"*Devlesa avilan,*" he replied. It is God who brought you.

"Perhaps."

As though her arrival was a signal, the gossiping Rom drifted from all parts of the swelled encampment and stood or sat in silence in as close a circle about Big George's tent as their numbers would allow. Pivli looked idly at the sea of Rom faces.

"I miss the features of your fiddler, Boshengro," she remarked. "And his brother Yojo."

Big George sighed. Now he knew why she had come.

"The danger that they face," she said before he could speak, "they face for all Rom. I have felt the presence of the *drabarno* and his *mule* before, but he has always been like smoke—here and then gone before I could find him. But now . . . now . . ." Her voice trailed off. The listening Rom were as silent as an inheld breath and waited. A hunting barn owl hooted as it crossed a nearby field. Here and there, heads lifted uneasily.

"We must help them," Pivli said. She stood and her cloak shivered as the breeze touched its feathers. "We are Rom. We have only each other. There will always be *mule* in the night and at noon. Martiya will walk the darkness forever and the unwary must see to their luck to stay free of that night spirit's touch. So it will be until Moshto's eldest son no longer creates the world anew. It is the way of things and cannot be changed. But this *drabarno* . . . he must be dealt with."

Again she let the silence grow thick. She looked into the faces of the nearest Rom, looked from face to face, met their dark eyes with her own dark gaze, her cloak shimmering in the lamplight.

"And this is how we will do it," she said.

Part Three

Czardas

Stanki nashti tshi arak enpe manushen shai.
                              —Romany saying

[Mountains do not meet but people do.]

I'm a freeborn man of the travelling people,
got no fixed abode,
with nomads I am numbered,
country lanes and byways,
were always my ways,
I never fancied being lumbered.
                    —from "The Travelling People"
                    by Ewan MacColl

forty-four

The dawn woke Bob Gourlay.

He rolled over and stared into the lightening sky, bewildered by his surroundings and cursing the fact that for some reason he was soaked to the skin. His face and arms were swollen with mosquito bites. He sat up weakly and the events of the previous night spilled through him in a confusing tumble. It was difficult for him to sort out what had been real and what had been imagined. What *had* to have been imagined.

He scratched at his arm and looked slowly around himself, blinking the misting rain from his eyes. He'd gone crazy was what had happened. He nodded slowly. Stan was dead. Jeff Owen's black whore had killed him and he owed the both of them for that. But . . . He blinked away the cascade of images. Stan coming to him with half his face hanging from him . . . the black woman forcing him from her house with some kind of weird *power* . . . her talking cat. . . . None of that had been real. It couldn't have been.

He got to his feet. The headache was finally gone—that had to have been what was driving him. The pain in his head and the grief. But he was okay now. Sure. He was bruised and sore—probably ran into more than one tree in his wild flight last night—but he was going to be okay. As okay as he could be on his own . . . alone. . . .

"Oh, Stan. Why'd you have to go and die on me?"

The marsh swallowed his words and gave him nothing in return. He half expected to see that ruined face peering back at him from between the reeds and willows, whispering a wet "say-hey," but the morning lay still around him except for the steady drip of the rain. His clothes hung limply on him. The wind was cool in gusts, rattling the reeds quietly against each other. Cattails with their brown bobbin tops stirred with a slow movement as the breeze touched them. Christ, he thought, rubbing at his face. He had to get out of here.

He wasn't all that sure exactly where "here" was. He looked around, trying to pick a direction to take. Didn't much matter, he supposed, whether he was stuck out here in the middle of a swamp in the rain, or back at home. Nothing was going to change. Stan would still be dead, while he . . . he didn't know what he was going to do. Get back at Jeff Owen and his woman—that was for sure. But afterwards?

He couldn't imagine life without Stan. Maybe he just shouldn't be trying to make any plans right now, he thought as he chose a direction. First he had to get to someplace dry. He sank to his ankles in the shallow water and muck as soon as he left the hillock where he'd collapsed last night. The mud pulled at his feet as he tugged them free each step, making a wet sucking noise. If he tried to think too much right now, he'd just get that headache back and Christ knew what he'd do—or where he'd find himself. Like where the hell was he right now? He remembered driving last night—a lot of driving. So where was the pickup?

Muttering to himself, he plunged on. He cursed the drizzle, cursed even louder when he found himself back on the hillock and realized that he'd been walking in a circle. No more fucking around, he told himself. He had to get out of here. He started off again.

forty-five

Zach stared numbly at the spot where he'd seen Gord Webster's corpse last night. There was nothing there now. Not a sign that a dead man had been lying there, his neck spewing blood all over the ground. He pushed wet hair back from his face and shook his head, confused.

"It was, like, lying right here," he said to Janfri and Yojo who'd come with him to collect the body.

"Perhaps you only thought you saw it," Janfri offered. "It was dark and there was a lot going on."

"I *saw* it! It was as real as that dog." He pointed to the body of the animal that Yojo had dispatched last night. The big Gypsy knelt down and studied the ground where Webster's corpse had lain. He fingered the grass here and there and looked towards the woods.

"There was something here, *prala,*" he said to Janfri. "It was dragged into the forest."

"Those other dogs," Zach said. "They must've dragged it off. We've got to get that body. We can't just leave him to the dogs."

"Too dangerous," Yojo said, standing. "Mulengro is out there waiting for us. He might not have his *mule* at the moment, but with those dogs . . ."

Janfri nodded in agreement. "Yojo is right, Zach. It'll be noon before we know it and we have to prepare for Mulengro. His *mule* will walk for half an hour at noon. We must be ready for him."

It didn't seem fitting somehow, Zach thought, but he nodded wearily. The Gypsies were right. They could look for Gord's body after—if there was an after. He led the way back to his own place, the drizzle fitting his depression. The two Gypsies followed after him, Janfri still favoring his injured leg, though the limp was not nearly as pronounced as it had been last night. When they reached the cottage, Zach went inside while Janfri and Yojo set about shifting the Lincoln from the front of the house. It required a fair amount of digging, for the tires had ploughed deep holes for themselves in the soft wet dirt. While they were working on it, Ola joined them. Yojo was still in awe of her, but Janfri nodded in a friendly fashion as he wedged a plank under one of the rear tires.

"Try it now," he called to Yojo.

He stood aside as the Lincoln coughed into life. The wheels spun, digging deeper, and Janfri called a halt to force the board in further. He moved to where Ola was standing as Yojo tried again.

"We must do something with the *Gaje*," he said. "They can't help us against Mulengro."

"And what can *we* do against him?" Ola asked.

Janfri shrugged and moved over to the car, putting his shoulder to the trunk. He braced himself with most of his weight on his good leg. Yojo rocked the car until the wheel finally grabbed the board. The car surged out of the ruts, spitting the board behind it and narrowly missing Janfri.

"Where are they now?" he asked. He returned to where Ola was standing, rubbing the dirt from his hands, seeming blithely unaware at how close he had come to almost losing his legs. Ola sighed. Romany *chal* would never change. There was always a swagger to everything they did—an attitude that, while it could irritate her, she realized she'd missed as well. Not that the *chi* were any different—especially the younger girls.

"Jackie and Jeff are sleeping in my room," she said and had to smile at how after only a couple of days the guest room had become "hers." She lowered her voice when Yojo shut off the Lincoln's engine and she no longer had to talk above it. "And Zach's out on the back porch. This has been very hard on him. He's a gentle man. Evil and violence don't become him."

"They become none of us," Janfri replied, "though some of us can adjust more quickly to what must be done than the others. We must send them home."

"And Zach? This is his home."

"True. Is there nowhere he can go until this is over . . . one way or another?"

Ola shook her head. "He has the right to remain and defend what is his."

"*Bater*," Janfri murmured. "And we must plan—against Mulengro, against his *mule*, against his dogs."

"It is like a *paramitsha*," Yojo said as he joined them. *Paramitsha* were fairy tales. Like the *darane swatura*, they were stories told for fun rather than the *swatura* that chronicled the history of the Rom. "*Drabarne* and wild dogs. Next we will see *o kesali* flitting between the trees. Remember Nonoka used to tell us about them? The forest fairies . . . And there were *o nivasi* in the water, *o phuvus* who lived underground, and *o urme* who decided the fates of men—Rom and *Gaje* alike."

"Nonoka was our uncle," Janfri explained to Ola. He smiled suddenly. "When I think of our troubles, I remember something else he used to say to us. He'd catch us up to our ears in mischief and sit us down, saying: 'All Rom lead two successive lives. In the first you have the chance to live as you want, making all the mistakes you can possibly make. The second life is to correct and avoid the mistakes you made in the first.' "

Yojo grinned, anticipating the punchline.

"And?" Ola asked, leaving herself open.

"He would nod and regard us sagely," Janfri said, "and then tell us: 'Unfortunately, this happens to be your second life.' "

Yojo roared and slapped Janfri on his back, staggering him. "He is our *nano* reborn, is Janfri," he told Ola with pride.

"It's good to remember one's family," Ola said. She had to smile as well, seeing the affection that passed between her two companions, but she couldn't help comparing their adolescence with her own. When her family lived in Europe, she'd been just a little girl. But of her teenage years . . . All she had by way of memories was poverty and hardship, it seemed. Her mother dying alone and without friend or kin to speed her passage to the land of shadows, except for a frightened young girl. Ola would never be as poor as her mother had been—that much she had taken from the *Gaje*—but she would die alone.

"I must be by myself for a while," she said. "To think. To plan."

"Not alone," Janfri said.

Yojo touched his brother's arm. "She is a *drabarni*," he said softly. "As such, she knows how to fend for herself."

I am too much by myself, Ola thought, but she nodded. "I won't go far," she said.

"But Mulengro . . ."

"He will be without his *mule* until noon—and I will be back before then."

"And his dogs?"

"I must think," Ola explained, "and I can't do it with everyone here, clouding my thoughts with their presence."

"*Bater,*" Janfri said finally. "And when you return—we will farsee Mulengro's presence, *uva?*"

"We will try."

"*Arakav tut,*" Yojo said. Take care.

"I will."

Yojo waited until Ola had entered the forest before turning to Janfri. "We should take stock of our weapons," he said.

Janfri's gaze turned from the forest to meet Yojo's.

Rod Taylor had been up by seven, but even rising that early he still woke to find his daughter Lucy awake and reading a Piers Anthony *Xanth* novel in the living room. She was wearing a pink T-shirt and cut off jeans, her head a tangle of uncombed corn-yellow curls.

"Don't you ever sleep?" Rod asked her.

Lucy shook her head. "I'm part elf," she said, "and elves never sleep."

"Except when they do," he warned her, "it's for a hundred years."

"How do you know that?"

"I read it somewhere."

"I'll bet you made it up."

Rod grinned at her. He loved the way she could put on a pout. In fact, he loved everything about his daughter. She was twelve and a half years old now and—thank Christ—wasn't showing any signs of entering that "difficult" stage that everyone insisted all teenagers did.

"I'll tell you what," he said. "If you make me some coffee while I'm shaving, I'll take you out fishing with me today."

Lucy gave him a withering look. "You *already* promised to take me."

"Okay. So give your dad a break. How about some coffee?"

She laid down her book with an exaggerated sigh. "Okay. Are you going to wake Mom?"

"I'm still working on waking myself."

As he headed for the bathroom, Lucy called after him: "Do the fish bite better or worse when it's raining?"

Rod stuck his head out of the bathroom doorway. "It's raining? I thought it was just my eyes adjusting to this ungodly hour of the morning."

Lucy studied the back lawn through the kitchen window as she filled the kettle. "It's definitely raining," she pronounced. As she was about to turn away, she caught a glimpse of movement from the corner of her eye. "Hey, Dad!" she called. "Come look at this."

Face full of lather, Rod dutifully made his way to the kitchen and looked out to see a mangy dog sniffing along the edge of their vegetable garden.

"Poor thing looks like it's starving," Lucy said. "Can I give it some of the leftover chicken?"

Rod started to nod, then he remembered last night, the smoke he'd had by the lake and the eerie howling he'd heard that had given him the willies. Looking at this dog now, he knew an unreasoning fear. He put an arm around his daughter's shoulders—she was really getting tall, one part of his mind noted—and was afraid for her, for his wife, for himself, and couldn't explain it.

"I don't want you going outside while it's there," he told Lucy.

"Oh, come *on*, Dad."

"No. I'm serious. That dog looks wild. It could be rabid for all we know."

"That dog," Lucy said, "looks like its having trouble keeping its head up."

"Please. Just do what I asked, okay, honey? Why don't you put the kettle on and wake your mother."

"Oh, all right. But I think you're being silly."

"Humor me, would you?"

Rod returned to the bathroom, wishing he'd never let Beth talk him into getting rid of his shotgun. That damned dog out there *looked* harmless, but he couldn't shake the creepy feeling he'd had seeing it out there. The distant howling he'd heard last night was just too real—too unsettling—for him to feel safe.

Ola paused as soon as the cottage was out of sight. She sat down where she was in a dry spot under an old pine and leaned back against its fat bole. The bark pinched at her hair as she moved her head. The scent of the tree was thick in the air, combined with the wet smell of the forest. She'd only told Janfri and Yojo a half truth. She didn't want to get away to plan, so much as to be alone for a moment. She was unused to having crowds of people around her. She couldn't think with them so near, crowding her thoughts.

"Hiding?"

She looked over to see Boboko soft-stepping across the wet ground. He lifted each foot and set it down fastidiously, a small frown on his expressive features.

"Not from you," she said.

He covered the final distance between them and settled gratefully in her lap. "Well, that's good to hear," he said. "When I saw you creeping off a few minutes ago I thought you were abandoning me."

"Never." She played with his damp fur. "And besides, there's no running away now."

"Mulengro," Boboko said, rubbing his head against her hand.

She nodded. Closing her eyes, she could see the *drabarno*'s scarred features as clearly as though he stood before her.

"Romany *drabarne* don't war," she said. "Not against each other."

"They do now."

"*Uva.*"

"How can he be killed?" the cat asked.

"The same way as any Rom or *Gaje,* but they only stay dead if they're killed in a certain way."

"And what way is that?"

Ola sighed. "I have only stories to go by, Boboko. In the old *swatura* evil *drabarne* could only be killed by *mule,* by fire . . . or by *draba* itself. By the will of one magician contesting against the other."

"Mulengro is too strong for you," Boboko said. He made a statement of it, not a question.

Ola nodded.

"And he controls the *mule.* . . ."

Ola nodded again. "Which leaves—"

"Only fire," Boboko finished.

Ola sighed and stared out into the forest. "He won't stand meekly by and let us set a torch to him," she said.

"If we find him during the day . . . when he is without his *mule* . . ."

Ola's fingers tightened in Boboko's fur. "I don't think I could do it," she said. "I don't think it's in me to so coldly destroy him—even though he's a murderer."

"If I could hold a torch . . ." Boboko began. His voice trailed off and he stood up in Ola's lap, fur bristling.

"Boboko? What is—"

Ola's voice broke up as she saw what had roused him. Twenty yards away, one of the dogs stood regarding them. Its wet fur was matted with burrs and mud, and its tongue lolled from the side of its mouth. It seemed to grin at them. The eyes were shining with a feral light. Ola reached slowly for the nearest piece of wood and stood with it held between the dog and herself. The wood was rotten and would probably fall apart when she swung it. But it was all she had.

Lucy turned from the window to where her parents were sitting, drinking coffee. She frowned as her father lit up a cigarette, but didn't say anything. It was a pointless argument; they'd been through it before.

"I haven't seen Cujo for about ten minutes now," she said, grinning as her father winced at the name, "so can I go out?"

"Lucy, why do you want to go out? It's raining. You haven't had any breakfast, and your father says that it's dangerous."

"I want to see Zach. He said he'd show me how to make a whistle out of a reed this weekend."

"Well, at least have some breakfast first."

"Okay." She slid into her seat and heaped a bowl with cornflakes.

"I thought we were going fishing," Rod said.

Lucy shrugged as she poured milk over her cereal. "I didn't think you wanted to go anymore." She glanced at him. "I thought maybe you'd be afraid that the Loch Ness Monster's taken up swimming in the Pond."

"Okay, okay," Rod said. "I give up. Rain or no rain, rabid dogs or no rabid dogs—finish up your breakfast and we'll take the boat out."

Lucy grinned. "All *right*. Can we see the herons, too?"

Rod met his wife's gaze and smiled. "Why not?" he said.

forty-six

The unmarked car carried the two Ottawa detectives down Highway 15. They were looking for the turnoff to the Conservation Area and talking over the case. Even though they had the file on Josef Wells and, with his scars and proven craziness, he looked like their best bet so far, they still wanted to question Owczarek. The Gypsy might be innocent of murder, but he was up to his neck in something and both Briggs and Will were sure it had a connection with their case. With the rain continuing today, Archambault had been happy to have their help and assigned them to the area they'd wanted without question. That suited the two men. Neither of them believed that Owczarek had left the county, little say the country. He was holed up in the backwoods somewhere and they were going to find him.

"Heads up," Will said, pointing ahead.

But Briggs had already seen them. He took his foot off the gas pedal and eased down on the brake. Whatever they'd been expecting to find out here, this wasn't it. Three black touring cars, dirty with mud, were parked on the roadside right beside the turnoff they'd been looking for. There was also an OPP cruiser parked by them.

The two officers from the cruiser were talking to a small crowd of what had to be Gypsies. In fact, Briggs realized as he pulled over to the side of the road, he was sure he recognized one of the women as being Big George Luluvo's wife.

Will glanced at his partner with a questioning look. Briggs shrugged and turned off the engine. "Only one way to find out," he said.

One of the OPP officers met them as they approached, nodding when Briggs showed him his badge.

"Paddy Briggs, right? I'm Jim Gilhuly. Phillip told me you'd be in the area."

"Nice to meet you, Jim. What've you got here?"

"Blown radiator. We were just seeing if they wanted us to call a tow truck in from Portland, but they're planning to fix it themselves. One of them's got a load of welding gear in the trunk of his car."

"You tell them about the dogs?" Will asked. Archambault had asked them to keep the information concerning the *marhime patrin* and the fact that a man could be controlling the dogs to themselves. A general bulletin about the threat of the dogs had been released to the press and a public warning was in effect.

"Yeah. They offered to help us hunt them down. A couple of the old-timers are from Hungary and said they've had experience with that kind of thing."

"I'll bet," Briggs said. "How's the hunt going?"

"Last I heard, the 'copter hadn't spotted them, but that's to be expected with this weather. A farmer claims he spotted some dogs running in a pack up around Bass Lake, so most of the men are in that area."

"What's the country like up that way?"

"Bush and field. Gets marshy up near the lake. There're a lot of places those dogs could hide out."

"You think they're that smart?" Will asked.

"Hell, there's no telling with dogs. You ever hunt fox?" When Will shook his head, the constable shrugged. "People think dogs are stupid, but my old man used to hunt fox with them and there weren't many tricks old Reynard could come up with that they didn't work out pretty damn quick. I figure they're going to lie low. Really makes you think, though, doesn't it? I wonder what the hell set those dogs off."

"I guess that's something we'll never know," Briggs said. "Do you mind if we talk to these people?"

"Go ahead. Still hunting Gypsies, are you?"

Briggs shook his head. "I'm not sure. All I know is I'm after someone who's killing them and it looks like it's one of their own. . . ."

"Well, if you nail the fucker who killed Finlay, save a piece of him for us, you hear?"

Briggs nodded. He moved to where a number of Gypsies, ignoring the drizzle, had already set up folding lawn chairs and were cooking on Coleman stoves. He aimed for a huge man who had to weigh over three hundred pounds. Beside him was a tough-looking old woman with eyes so bright they almost seemed luminous and features that reminded Briggs of a horse. The woman he'd recognized as Big George's wife was now standing at the Coleman stove making tea.

"Big George?" Briggs asked the large man. When he nodded, Briggs produced his badge for the second time. "I'd like to talk to you about a couple of men who are members of your company."

"*Kumpania,*" Will corrected him. The old woman regarded Will with interest.

"Whatever," Briggs said.

"We are no longer in your jurisdiction," Big George said.

"Do you want me to ask those OPP boys to arrest you? I'm sure we can think up something to hold you on—long enough to have you transferred to Ottawa."

"I am guilty of no crime," Big George said. "We have stopped here only because of a problem with one of our cars. You have no right to treat us as criminals."

Will saw the red flush start up his partner's neck and laid a hand on Briggs' arm. He didn't like the way this was going.

"Let me talk to him," he said when Briggs turned to him. Briggs frowned, then nodded, and Will hunched down, resting his weight on his ankles. He had to look up now to speak to the seated Gypsy, and he could see the man visibly relax. "We're after the same thing you are," he said. "Someone's killing your people and it's our job to find him."

"This is a matter between Gypsies," Big George said.

Will shook his head. "Murder is police business, Mr. Luluvo. And this isn't a Gypsy matter anymore—not since an officer of the law was killed last night."

Big George glanced at the old woman. He had been told of Tibo and Ursula's deaths, but not of this third.

"I think you wish to speak to me," the old woman said.

"And your name is, ma'am?"

"You may call me Pivli Gozzle."

Will nodded. She was a cool one all right. He could call her that, but that was no promise that it was really her name.

"My name's Will Sandler, ma'am," he said slowly, "and I'm a detective with the Ottawa Police Force."

Pivli frowned at him, eyes flashing. "There is no need to treat me as a child, *shanglo,* simply because I am old."

"You're right. I'm sorry."

The frown eased and the white teeth showed as Pivli grinned. She might be old, Will thought, but she still had all her teeth. They were too crooked to be a dental fixture—unless the dentist who'd put them in had been drunk, or stoned, or both.

"These two men you are looking for," she asked. "Who are they? Why do you want them?"

"One goes by the name of John Owczarek—he's a violinist."

Pivli glanced at Big George. "Boshengro?" The *rom baro* nodded. "And the other?" she asked, turning back to Will.

Will consulted his notebook. "Yojo Kore," He explained that they had met Owczarek at Yojo's house, but not known who he was at the time. Since then, the two men—along with the rest of the Gypsy community in Ottawa—had vanished. Until now.

"But they are not murderers, are they?"

"I'm afraid we believe they're involved, ma'am—how much, we're not sure of at this time."

"Why?" Pivli asked. "Because they are Rom? Because they do not follow the prescribed way of the *Gaje,* therefore they must be guilty of something?"

"It's not that cut and dried, ma'am, and I think you know that. Kore we're only interested in because of his association with Owczarek, and as for Owczarek . . . His house was burned down recently, yet he never reported it. Is that how an honest man acts? He's been seen in this area—he abandoned his car in Perth—and to be honest, we do have outstanding charges laid against him and two of his—" he hesitated, looking for the word she'd used, then settled on "—non-Gypsy companions."

"And what is it that he is accused of?"

"Assault on two police officers. A weapons charge. Theft of firearms."

Pivli's gaze never left his face as he spoke. The intensity of that gaze made him uneasy. There was something in those eyes that told him he was making a fool of himself, but he didn't know how. Beside him, Briggs shifted from foot to foot, plainly impatient.

"This isn't getting us anywhere, Will," Briggs said. He left unsaid, but understood, that the less said to the Gypsies, the better.

"The one you call Owczarek is not the one you truly seek," the old woman said.

Will held up his hand to forestall Briggs. "What can you tell us?" he asked.

"I know who it is that you truly seek," she replied.

Briggs knelt down beside Will, the knee of his jeans on the wet gravel.

"Who is it?" Will asked. He wanted to hear how she'd name the killer before he told her what they had.

"I have no name. But I have *seen* him."

"Where?"

"You must understand," Pivli said. "This is a thing that even the Rom are not comfortable with. They will listen to me, but I am not always welcome in their *tsera*—their tents."

"What do you mean?"

"I am a *drabarni,*" she said simply. At his blank look, she smiled wickedly. "You would call me a witch or a medicine woman, *shanglo*. I know the murderer, for I have *seen* him in visions. He, too, works the *draba*. Black is his hair and black are his clothes, and his face is scarred, giving him the look of a wolf."

"Oh, Jesus," Briggs said wearily.

Will shook his head. "Wait a minute, Paddy. Did you *listen* to what she just said?"

"Mumbo jumbo's all I heard."

"The scars?"

Briggs regarded the old woman through narrowed eyes. He drew a folded picture from his pocket and opened it up to show her. A gnarled finger stabbed the photo, almost knocking it from his hands.

"That is him," she hissed.

"And you don't know his name?"

She turned her gaze to Will. There was a hard murderous look in their depths. "If I knew his name," she said, "his true name . . . I would be able to kill him."

"Josef Wells," Will said.

Pivli studied the picture, tasting the name, then slowly shook her head. "It is a name he might be known by, but not his true name."

Briggs stood abruptly and stuffed the photo back into his pocket. "What is it with you people anyway?" he demanded. "What's the big secret? You hide behind a dozen aliases, creep around the country like a pack of dogs—when you're not nesting like rats in the worst part of a city. . . . Don't you have any pride? Don't you get a little tired of all these fucking games?"

He was suddenly aware that he and Will were encircled by a ring of dark-faced Gypsies. He looked past them to where the two OPP officers stood. The mood of the Gypsies was turning ugly and they looked on with mounting alarm. The tableau held for long tense moments. Everyone, it seemed, waited for how the old woman would react.

"We have pride," she said firmly. "We are Rom. Our ways are different from yours, so do not seek to judge us by your rules. You speak of poverty—and we are poor, but by choice, and only in regards to worldly possessions. But we are rich in ways you could not imagine, *shanglo*. I see you, your soul stunted because you will not give it room to breathe, because you want one thing, but always seek another. We are wretches in your eyes, yet we are happy. We are content with what we are. Can you say the same?"

The woman's words hit too close to home for Briggs. Content? Happy? He couldn't even pretend he was either. He just went through the motions. Pivli reached out and touched his arm, smiling wanly.

"You are what you are," she said, "as we are what we are. Let it be so." Briggs found himself nodding. "There is a message for you," she added suddenly.

"What?"

She pointed to the OPP cruiser at the same time as the radio squawked inside the car. Jim Gilhuly bent in through the window and hooked the microphone free, then looked over to Briggs. "It's for you!" he called to Briggs.

Will and Briggs exchanged glances. There was something happening here, Briggs thought, and he didn't understand it. He didn't know if he wanted to understand it. He turned and made for the OPP cruiser, the Gypsies parting to let him go by, closing their ranks once more when he'd gone by.

"And what of you, black man?" Pivli asked Will. "Do you question our way of life as well?"

Will shook his head. "I'm curious," he said, "but I figure you've got the right to live however you want—just so long as you don't break any laws or hurt people. I've been reading about Gypsies. . . ." His voice trailed off at Pivli's grin.

"Books," she said. "What do books know? We have no books, nor need for them. A book traps words so that they can no longer change, so that the tale must always remain the same. The Rom are not like your books. We adapt. We change."

"And yet you still stay the same."

"Just so. That is the secret, black man. Think on it."

"But—"

"The man you seek is in there," Pivli said, motioning to the forest behind her with a jerk of her head. "Chase him if you must, but know this: He will be slain by a Rom, or not at all."

"Is that why you're here?"

"To see justice done—*that* is why we came, *shanglo*. For no other reason." She half turned her chair so that she could view the forest. "It will end in there," she said. "We are here to see that it does end, that the evil does not escape its fate." She turned back to look at Will. "You do not understand—but you will, if you enter those woods."

Will started to ask her what she meant, but then Briggs called to him from the OPP cruiser. He stood up and nodded gravely to the old woman.

"Thank you for what you've told me," he said, adding to himself: little enough though it was.

"Listen with more than your ears," Pivli told him. "See with more than your eyes. There is a whole realm hidden to you otherwise."

"I'll try to keep that in mind."

He turned and the Gypsies opened a way for him.

"God go with you!" Pivli called after him.

Will hesitated a step, then kept walking. He glanced at the men and women he passed. Their faces were shiny and damp from the drizzle, their clothes wet. They were all grim looking, dark-haired, with secrets in their eyes, though not one of them was so commanding, so unnerving as the old woman had been. Juju. He tried to put the eerie feeling aside.

"What's up?" he asked as he reached the car.

"That was Archambault passing on a message," Briggs said. "They're all over the place."

"Gypsies?"

Briggs nodded. " 'Copter did a count on them—forty cars in all."

"But what are they doing?"

"Same as this bunch. Each group that Archambault's men approached had engine trouble of one kind or another and they're just fixing it. Mostly they're just hanging around . . . waiting."

"So what does he want to do?"

"Nothing," Briggs said disgustedly. "So far they haven't broken any laws. He's going to check out that sighting at Bass Lake, but he wants us to keep in touch—close touch. No, and I quote, 'hotdogging,' end of quote."

"What *are* we going to do?"

Briggs turned to look down the road that led towards the Conservation Area. "The Gypsy bands have pretty well sewn up this area back here—like they're trying to hold something in. I guess we're going in to find out who or what it is."

"There's no figuring some folks," Jim Gilhuly said, coming up to them. He looked back at the Gypsies. "Well, if they don't want any help, it's no skin off my nose. Are you guys going in?" He made a motion with his thumb down the road Briggs and Will had just been studying. Briggs nodded. "Need any help?" Gilhuly asked. "Because if not, we've got a patrol to finish."

"You go on," Briggs said. "We'll call in if something comes up."

The OPP officer nodded, then got into the cruiser. His partner was already behind the wheel. When Gilhuly shut his door, the car pulled out onto the highway. Briggs' gaze followed it down the road, then he glanced at the Gypsies. They stood in a silent knot, staring back at the two detectives. Inside him, Briggs' ghosts stirred, then were still.

"Well, let's go see what's down this road," Briggs said.

Will could still feel the old Gypsy woman's eyes on him, but he didn't look back. "You driving?" he asked.

"Sure."

They headed back to their own car.

forty-seven

"Go back to the cottage!" Boboko hissed.

He didn't look back as he moved slowly forward to confront the dog on his own. The animal was four times his size and its grin widened as it watched Ola's small protector approach.

"Boboko, no!"

Beyond the first dog, Ola saw a second and third move out of the undergrowth, their fur wet and matted. Like the first, they were lean and gaunt, with feral eyes and grinning jaws. Boboko crouched down low about a half-dozen paces from the first dog, just the tip of his tail twitching. Before they could engage, Ola ran forward with a curse and threw her makeshift club. The dog dodged it easily and leapt at Boboko at the same time as the other two dogs exploded into motion.

Ola saw Boboko throw himself at the first dog's throat, then kicked off her shoes. At her command, they lifted into the air, batting the first dog, throwing it off balance. Boboko hooked a claw in its left eye, blinding it before he was thrown off.

The dog howled and broke free. But the other two were closing in. One snapped at Boboko, missed, turned abruptly. Its paws scrabbled on the wet ground, spraying needles as it attacked again. The second ignored Ola's airborne shoes and launched itself at her.

She lifted her arms to fend it off, knowing as she did that it was a futile gesture. Time seemed to slow down as the dog attacked. Its forepaws left the ground, its jaws gaped. Just before the dog hit her, smashing her back against the tree with the force of its rush, there came a sound like an explosion, Then the dog knocked the breath out of her and she tumbled to the ground, its weight upon her.

"What the hell was that?" Rod asked, pausing on his way to the boat with a couple of life preservers and his tackle box in hand. He looked in the direction of Zach's cottage from where the sound had come.

"It sounded like a gunshot!" Lucy cried, recognizing the sound from a thousand TV shows. She dropped the pair of fishing rods she was carrying and started for the woods.

"Lucy!" her father roared.

She stopped in her tracks and turned. "Zach doesn't have a gun, dad."

"And what did you think you were going to do?" Worry put iron into Rod's voice. Ever since that no-account dog had appeared in the yard this morning, he'd been on edge.

"But, Dad. Zach could be hurt."

"You just stay here," he said. He set down his own load and headed for the bush that separated Gordon Webster's place from their own.

"Where's your father going?" Beth asked as she came out onto the back porch.

Lucy turned from the woods. "Someone's shooting up at Zach's place and Dad's gone to see what's going on."

"Shooting?"

Lucy nodded. "It sounded like an explosion, it was so loud!"

"Well, I don't know what he thinks he's going to do if there is trouble. Honestly. Sometimes I wonder what he . . ." Beth's voice trailed off as she saw her husband reappear from amongst the trees. She lifted a hand to her mouth at the look on his face. Under the fine sheen of water that the drizzle had put on it, his face was white. "Rod . . . ?" she began, stepping down from the porch. "My God, what is it?"

"St-stay where you are," he told her. "Lucy, go into the cottage with your mother."

"Dad?"

"Do what I say!" Rod could feel the shakes hit him. He needed a cigarette. He needed a stiff drink. Jesus. He closed his eyes, but the image wouldn't go away. A half-dozen yards into the forest he'd come upon Gord's body, torn apart by Christ knew what. Half-eaten. . . . A tremor went through him and then he stood stock-still. From around the corner of the cottage he saw the lean shape of a feral dog step out onto the lawn.

Bob Gourlay lifted his head. Gunshot. He turned slowly, allowing for the echo of the sound in the forest as he homed in on it. He had a sudden flash of himself leaving the house last night, carrying . . . carrying his old 12-gauge. His hands opened and closed at his side.

He sure as fuck didn't have that gun with him now. But someone was firing one out here in the bush. He started off in a lumbering trot in the direction he thought the sound had come from. Someone was shooting a 12-gauge, sure as shit, and he'd lay ten-to-one the gun they were firing was his, yessir.

He held an arm before his face to fend off the wet slapping branches and barreled his way through the trees. Memories were starting to jog into place as he ran. He remembered seeing Jeff Owen here in the bush. Jeff Owen, one of the waitresses from Tinkers, and another guy. He shook his head as an image of Stan intruded on that memory. That couldn't be right. Stan couldn't have been there, 'cause Stan was dead. But he could *see* Stan goin' for the girl and he remembered—

He broke into a clearing suddenly and came to an abrupt halt. There was a man with his back to him across the clearing. A man all in black. At his side a wild-looking dog lifted its head and turned towards Bob. The man turned then as well, following the gaze of the dog until his pale eyes studied Bob. Bob took a half step back and swallowed thickly. For no reason he could understand, he was scared shitless. Again his hands opened and closed, looking for the 12-gauge that he didn't have anymore.

The drizzle was getting into his eyes and he blinked rapidly to clear them. Beyond the stranger he could make out neat rows of Scotch pine, planted rows, and he knew where he was. The marsh he'd been in had to be the one running off Mill Pond, right between the Pond and the Big Rideau. This'd be the Conservation Area. He seemed to remember parking the truck not all that far from here. He and Stan'd been—Scratch that. Stan was dead. He'd been . . . what the fuck *had* he been doing?

His head started to hurt—sharp little pains behind his temples. Don't think, he told himself. He tried to smile at the stranger who stood motionlessly staring at him. The dog was on its feet. Bob looked down at his hands and saw they were trembling. He swallowed quickly.

"Hey, mister," he began.

"Kill him," the stranger said to the dog and turned away.

As the dog left the man's side, Bob turned and bolted into the bush.

The dog's blood was all over Ola as she tried to push it from her. It mixed with the rain, slicking her hands. The animal's glazed eyes stared into hers as she clawed madly at its wet fur, but she didn't realize the dog was dead until its weight was suddenly lifted from her. She looked up into Janfri's worried features.

"Are you all right?" he asked as he helped her to her feet.

"There were others. . . ."

"They scattered when I killed this one. I would have fired sooner, but this buckshot spreads wide very quickly and you were in my line of fire."

"*Misto kedast tute,*" Ola said. You did well. "Thank you." She stared down at the dead beast, then looked quickly across the field. "Boboko . . . ?" she began, remembering her last sight of the cat. One of the dogs had been bearing down on him. . . .

A mirthless smile touched Janfri's lips. "Treed," he said, nodding with his head.

Ola pulled free of Janfri's support and walked gingerly to where the calico tom was perched in the lower boughs of a pine. Lifting her arms, she could just reach him. "Are you all right?" she asked as she cradled him in her arms.

For once Boboko looked serious. He nodded, seemed about to speak, then his ears flattened against his head as he looked beyond Ola. Janfri lifted the shotgun he was carrying, but the lean shape was lost from his sight before he could squeeze the trigger.

"We should get back," he said. "I only have one shell left in this."

Ola nodded numbly, still shaken by her close call, and let him lead her back to Zach's cottage.

Briggs pulled the car over to the side of the road and came to a stop behind the parked pickup truck. The two men sat in the car for a long moment, watching the woods as the wipers went slowly back and forth, then they got out. Will drew his revolver from its belt holster and held it down by his leg.

"Did Archambault say who belongs to that truck?" he asked.

Briggs nodded. "Some local yahoo by the name of Stan Gourlay. He was going to check up on him when this dog-pack shit came down."

They drifted easily over to the pickup, alert for anything out of the ordinary. While Will kept his attention on their surroundings, Briggs opened the door on the driver's side and peered in. He stepped back, wrinkling his nose.

"Christ, what a smell!"

Will glanced at him. "Smells a little like roses?"

"More like something died in here. Even with the windows open all night. I was wondering why this Gourlay fellow abandoned it, but now I think I know." He moved to the front of the truck and raised the hood.

"Maybe he had engine trouble?" Will offered.

"Maybe someone made engine trouble for him. Take a look at this."

Will joined him and peered under the hood. Someone had removed the distributor cap and been none too gentle about it.

"Doesn't fit," Will said. "It feels like there's a connection between this and Owczarek, but it doesn't fit."

Briggs nodded uneasily. His ghosts were stirring inside him. Presences. Faces. The dead, waiting for him to *do* something. Shaking his head, he looked towards the woods.

"Maybe we should go in a ways," he said. "See if we can find something the local boys missed. We've got the daylight on our side now."

Will smiled without humor. "Not to mention the weather." He replaced his revolver in its holster and accepted one of the rain-slickers that Briggs fetched from the car. Moving slowly, the two men entered the woods.

The dog started for Rod, then caught sight of Lucy—frozen in place in the middle of the lawn—and changed direction.

"Jesus, no!" Rod roared.

He moved like he'd never moved before, angling across the lawn in a desperate attempt to make it to the dog before it reached his daughter. He heard his wife's mindless wail of terror, the rasping snarl of the dog, the wheeze in his own chest. Please, God, he prayed. But there wasn't going to be time. He wasn't going to make it. The dog launched itself at Lucy, but the wet ground slid under its paws and it went sprawling. Before it could rise, Rod was on it, hammering at it with his fists. He could hear himself shouting over and over, "Kill you, fucker kill you. . . ." as he pounded away, but it was like he was listening to someone else.

The dog turned with a stomach-wrenching snarl, its jaws snapping in his face. He tried to get a grip on the wet fur to keep the teeth from his neck, but he couldn't get a hold. He saw Beth snatch Lucy up and back slowly towards the cottage, then the jaws were at his throat and he knew only a hot fire of pain that dissolved into black.

Zach stood in the misting rain, watching the lake, trying not to think about the gunshot he'd heard from the direction that Janfri had taken. His body was tight with tension. There were bad vibes everywhere, lying thick and uncomfortable in the wet air. He'd thought maybe the drizzle would clear his head. Instead he was just getting wet.

He could hear Yojo inside the cottage, explaining the gunshot to Jeff and Jackie, thought of going back inside, but he wasn't interested in being around strangers just now. Ola was okay, but the others . . . he didn't have anything against them. But it seemed like the trouble hadn't started until they'd shown up.

He was still trying to make up his mind as to what he was going to do when he heard a woman's scream. He glanced quickly to the woods where Janfri had disappeared. That cry had come from the Taylors' place. He thought of Beth Taylor and little Lucy, of the dog that had killed Gord, then took off towards their cottage, looking for something he could use as a weapon as he ran.

He heard Yojo call to him from his own place. Ignoring the Gypsy, he plunged into the forest.

The dog snapped at Bob's ankles. He tried to dodge its jaws, slipped on the wet ground and went sprawling. The dog lunged at him as he lifted his arm to protect his throat, teeth closing on his forearm. Sucker wasn't all that big, he thought just before the pain went through him. He hit the dog between the eyes with a meaty fist, half stunning it. The grip loosened on his arm and he hit the dog again. Before it could rise, he was on his feet. He jumped on the animal, landing on its chest. His weight was enough to do the job. The dog's ribcage collapsed with a satisfying crunch under his boots. Breathing heavily through his mouth, Bob stared at the animal.

"Teach you, you fucker," he muttered and kicked the dog in the head. "I'll teach you. Mess with a Gourlay and *this* is what you get."

He continued to kick the animal until the life died in its eyes. Then nursing his arm against his chest, he stumbled off through the forest. The whole fucking world'd gone apeshit . . . ever since Stan died. Jeff Owen's little black whore had one fuck of a lot to answer for, yessir.

"Baby, baby, baby," Beth crooned, holding Lucy tightly.

She backed up slowly, stunned gaze riveted on the monster that had killed her husband. Her mind was locked in a circle of shock, playing and replaying the last moment of his life in an endless loop. Not until the dog lifted its bloody jaws from her husband's corpse, did she stumble the last few steps onto the porch and into the house, dragging Lucy in with her. A second dog swaggered out of the woods and the two animals regarded the house. Moaning, Beth fumbled with the door, shut it. Her fingers were like stiff fat dowels and wouldn't seem to work as she tried to work the bolt on the door.

"Da-daddy. . . ." Lucy mumbled in a tiny voice, trying to push her mother from the door. "We have . . . to get . . . daddy. . . ."

Tears streamed down Beth's cheeks as she finally shot the bolt home. When the first thump resounded against the door, she slid slowly to the floor and held Lucy in a suffocating grip.

"The *Gajo* Zach ran off," Yojo told Janfri as he was helping Ola into the cottage. Yojo stared at Ola's blood-covered clothing. Behind him, Jeff and Jackie hovered uncertainly, not sure what to do.

"It's the dog's blood," Janfri said. "Not hers."

Ola freed herself from his arm. "Where did Zach go?" she asked.

Yojo shrugged and pointed east.

"I have to go after him."

"No, *drabarni,*" Yojo said. "I will go for you."

Jeff looked at his watch. "Ah . . . look," he began. "It's going on eleven-thirty. Didn't you say something about these . . . ah . . . ghosts . . ."

Yojo nodded grimly. "Yet the man gave us hospitality when we needed it. Would you leave him to the *mule* and Mulengro's dogs?" He picked up the rifle that they'd taken from the OPP cruiser as he spoke.

Jeff shook his head. "No. I just thought . . . we had to make plans or something."

"Then this is the plan," Yojo said. "I will go after Zach while you remain here and prepare for Mulengro's attack, *uva?*"

There was a long moment of silence, then Jackie moved to Ola's side. "C'mon," she said. "I'll bet you could use a change of clothes."

Ola nodded. The shock was wearing off. She set Boboko down on the table and followed the dark-haired girl to the guest room they were sharing.

"Take one of the pistols with you," Janfri told Yojo.

The big Gypsy shook his head. "This will be enough," he said, patting the rifle. "For the dogs at least." His glance moved between Janfri and the *Gajo.* He hoped Jeff would hold up. He didn't know *Gaje* the way his brother did. He could never understand them. His gaze moved to the cat who was watching him through slitted eyes.

"*Arakav tut,*" Boboko said softly. Watch out for yourself.

Yojo started, still not used to an animal that could speak like a man—like a Romany man yet. Then he nodded. "I will," he said. His bulk was in the doorway, briefly outlined as he searched the lawn for more of the pack, then he was gone.

The only thing Briggs could think of as he heard something come crashing through the brush towards them was bears. Great big bears hungry for man-meat. He stopped, glanced at Will who'd already drawn his revolver, then looked around for a tree big enough to climb. Not that he was even sure he could climb a tree fast enough, considering the shape he was in. He brought his own gun out from under his slicker.

Without needing to speak, the two men moved apart so as not to provide a single target for whatever was coming their way. Briggs raised his gun, finger taking up the slack on the trigger. When the man came stumbling into sight, he almost fired. Then his training took over. He put his piece away and approached the man while Will kept him covered.

Christ, he thought as he moved closer. This guy's been through the mill. Blood all over his arm and the front of his shirt, hair matted and slicked against his head, face streaked with mud. Looking at the man's arm, he had a sudden flash of standing in an Ottawa alleyway, looking down at a man whose forearm was torn up from trying to keep something from ripping out his throat. . . . Briggs' ghosts moved restlessly inside him.

The man stopped suddenly as he caught sight of them. His eyes filled with wariness and he looked like he was going to bolt.

"Okay," Briggs said soothingly. "Take it easy. No one's going to hurt you. We're police officers. . . ."

"Dogs," Bob Gourlay said, holding out his bleeding arm. "A dog got me. Fuck, it hurts." The wariness never left his eyes. He was playing for time. He didn't know what these cops were doin' here—couldn't even recognize 'em, for Christ's sake, and he thought he knew all those boys—but he wasn't about to mess around with them. Not when one of them was holdin' a gun, and there was a madman back in the woods siccing dogs on him. If these guys were lookin' for him . . . well, right now a jail cell looked like a slice of heaven, yessir.

"It's okay," Briggs repeated. "Let's have a look at that arm."

Mulengro stood amongst the pines looking down at Zach's cottage. He watched the big Gypsy move slowly into the forest towards the other cottages where his dogs were hunting. By his side two more of the lean rangy animals whined, watching Yojo disappear amongst the trees. Mulengro smiled. Noon was fast approaching. In a short while his *mule* would be with him and he would finish them all, Rom and *Gaje* alike. Until then, he could be patient.

His original pack had been joined by other dogs—easily summoned now. The first pack leader was dead—slain by the big Gypsy—and Mulengro had taken the place of that leader in the animals' dim minds. Once he learned the resonance that bound the dogs to him, it was child's play to summon more. His pack numbered a dozen now. They were mostly other feral beasts, but one or two were domesticated animals that had gone wild when he called them. They were better fed and stronger than his original pack, better suited to his purposes for all that burrs and the mud and rain in the forest had lent their coats the same bedraggled appearance as the feral ones.

The pair at his side were still uneasy, eager to hunt with their brothers, confused as to why they were forced to remain with this strange pack leader that walked on two legs, smelled like a two-legs, but bound them to him all the same. Mulengro kept his control firm. He meant to cleanse this entire area of Rom and *Gaje,* but the need to do God's work had not clouded his own sensibilities. Without his *mule,* he was not as protected. There were limits to his *draba*—as any Romany magic-worker knew. These two must protect his person . . . until noon. After the half hour following the noon, there would be nothing in the immediate vicinity for him to be protected from. He would rest then, in the deep woods, rest and wait for night to come. And then . . .

Mulengro smiled. He was not unaware of Pivli Gozzle and the gathering of the Rom. For interfering with him, with God's work, they were all *marhime*. He would cleanse them all. And one day the Rom that survived would bless him for what he had done.

Zach leaned weakly against the tree, staring down at Gord's corpse. His stomach roiled with sour acid. The axe he'd picked up at Gord's cottage trembled in his hand. He didn't think he could go on. It wasn't that he was scared—though he was so scared that he wasn't sure his legs would hold him for even one more step. It was just that everything seemed finished now. The purity of the lake was gone and it wasn't going to come back. The bad vibes were just too strong. Wild dogs. Ghosts. And the dead. . . .

He heard the snarls that came from the direction of the Taylors' cottage then and knew there was one other thing left. There was still the living.

He held the axe handle so tightly that his knuckles went white. Pushing away from the tree, he headed for the Taylors' cottage, his wet pony tail slapping his back as he ran, face slick with tears and rain. The first thing he saw as he came out onto their lawn was Rod's corpse. There were two or three dogs worrying at it, muzzles red when they lifted them from their grisly feast. Beyond them were more, scrabbling at the door to the cottage. For one long moment Zach froze, then anger went through him like a flare of white searing heat.

He charged the dogs around Rod's corpse, axe swinging. They came at him from two sides, snarling. The axe connected with the foremost of the two coming in at him from the right, almost taking the animal's head off. Blood sprayed and he lost his balance from the force of the blow. Then the lone dog that came in from the left struck his back and he went sprawling on the wet grass.

Yojo stepped out of the woods at the same time as Zach killed the first dog with his axe. The Gypsy brought the rifle to his shoulder and fired, killing the animal that had knocked the luthier to the ground. The third dog veered from Zach and charged Yojo, but Yojo already had another round ready for it. His second shot stopped the dog in its tracks, bowling it over. He worked the action once more and stepped in close. The dog twitched, then lay still. Yojo brought the muzzle of his gun up to fire at the two animals by the cottage door but they were already bolting for the woods and offered a poor target. Lowering the rifle, he hurried to Zach's side.

"Th-that's . . . two I . . . owe you," Zach mumbled. Yojo shrugged and helped him to his feet.

"We must get back to the others," the Gypsy said. "The noon draws too close."

"There's . . ." Zach's gaze found Rod's corpse. He looked quickly away. "There are people in the cottage. We've got to take 'em back with us, man."

Yojo nodded. "Fetch them. But hurry. We will take their *mobile*—their car. And, Zach," he added. "Look for salt and other *baXt* spices. We will need them before the day is done."

Zach swallowed. "Yeah. Gotcha." He wiped the rain from his face, checked his breast pocket to make sure that his glasses were still there and in one piece, and started for the cottage. Yojo made a quick study of the yard, then went to the Taylors' car.

"Did you see anyone back in there?" Briggs asked as he took a look at Bob's arm. "Anybody at all?"

Bob thought about the man in black but before he could speak, all three of them heard the sharp crack of gunfire echoing through the woods.

"What the hell was that?" Briggs asked.

"Rifle," Will replied.

Bob nodded. It sure wasn't the shotgun he'd heard earlier. He saw the look that passed between the two detectives.

"Look," he said. "If you guys want to check that out, I don't mind taggin' along."

"But your arm . . . ?"

"If you've got something to wrap around it, I'll be okay."

Briggs glanced at Will, who nodded. "Okay," Briggs said. He opened his slicker and tore a strip from the bottom of his shirt. "But you stay out of our way, you hear?"

"The last thing I want is trouble," Bob said as he held out his arm. "Yessir." He grimaced as Briggs wrapped the make-shift bandage around his wound. The pain from it was nothing like the pounding in his temples.

"That's it," Briggs said as he tied it off. "Let's go."

"I can see them," Boboko said from the windowsill where he was perched. "Three, maybe four of them, just at the edge of the trees."

Janfri and Jeff stepped over to the window, the Gypsy holding one of the .38's they'd taken from the OPP patrolmen.

"They're probably all around the cottage," Jeff said.

"They're waiting," Janfri added in a soft voice. "Waiting for Mulengro's *mule* and noon."

Jeff shivered and turned from the window, but the Gypsy and Boboko remained where they were, watching.

The dogs heard the three men coming through the woods before the man in black did and whined eagerly.

"Not yet, not yet," Mulengro said. He drifted back amongst the trees when he spotted them, moving as silently as one of his *mule*, until he was out of the man's view. The dogs followed him, bound to his will. "But soon," the scarred Gypsy told them.

The dirt track took Briggs and Will by surprise.

"I thought it was all bush around here," Briggs said.

Bob had been expecting it. "There's a little lake just down here a ways," he told them. "Got a handful of cottages on it."

"Maybe we can find someone with a first aid kit," Briggs said as he led the way down the track. "Then we can get that arm of yours properly looked after."

Bob shrugged. "Don't know if I want to go callin' on someone who's shootin' off a gun as big as the one we just heard." It took all his self-control to keep his voice casual around the cops. His head hurt like it was on fire and he could feel something building up in the air like an electric charge. His vision was blurring, more from the pain in his temples than from the light rain, and he had the weirdest sensation that Stan was going to step out of the woods at just any minute, a wet "say-hey" coming from his mangled lips. Jesus, he thought. It's startin' again. The crazy shit. . . .

They'd reached the top of the hill where the track led down to Zach's cottage.

"Nice looking place," Will said.

Briggs grinned. "Hippie heaven," he said, then froze. His ghosts were moving through his mind again, setting the hairs at the nape of his neck on end.

"What's the matt—" Will began, then he saw them too. A couple of lean dog shapes had been at the end of the forest to the right of the cottage and melted quickly back into the undergrowth. Both detectives drew their revolvers.

"Let's get down there," Briggs said stiffly. He started down the incline and called out as they neared the cottage. "Halooo, the house! Don't shoot! We're police and we're here to help you!"

It was no wonder, he thought, that they'd heard some gunfire. Archambault and his men were in the wrong neck of the woods looking for those dogs.

Zach sat in the front seat beside Yojo, dividing his attention between the muddy road and their two passengers in the back. Beth Taylor hadn't said a word since he'd kicked in the door and led her and Lucy to the car. Her eyes had a glazed look to them. Zach knew they were both suffering from shock, but he didn't know what to do about it. He'd covered them with a blanket because he'd heard that you were supposed to keep shock victims warm, but it didn't seem to have done much good. They were just huddled together on the back seat, white-faced and spooky-looking. If he could just do *something*.

"The *drabarni* will help them," Yojo said, not taking his gaze from the road. The track was narrow and the driving was treacherous on its mud-slicked surface.

Zach nodded. He hoped Ola could help him as well. He was feeling pretty numb, too.

The drive today was a far cry from the wild trip last night, but somehow, Zach felt more nervous now than he had then. He glanced at the clock set in the dashboard. Eleven fifty-nine. Oh, Jesus. As if the dogs hadn't been bad enough.

Janfri stared numbly out the window as the three men approached. He didn't need Briggs' identification to tell him that they were police. He recognized two of them as the Ottawa detectives who had questioned him on Yojo's doorstep. As for the third man . . .

"Oh, Christ," Jeff said, standing behind the Gypsy once more. "We're fucked. The cops *and* Bob Gourlay."

"Don't panic!" Janfri said harshly.

"Don't panic? Jesus *Christ!* What're you talking about? If you think I'm—"

Janfri turned, lifting the revolver. "You're going to do exactly what I say, do you understand me, Jeff?"

There was a stranger looking out of the Gypsy's eyes again. Jeff nodded numbly. "Su-sure, Janfri. No . . . no problem."

"Boboko. Get Ola."

The cat nodded and jumped down from the sill. Janfri moved quickly to the kitchen table, thrusting the revolver into his belt. He picked up the shotgun and motioned for Jeff to go to the door.

"Open it," he said, "and then stand back."

Jeff nodded nervously. "Jesus, you're not going to—"

"Do it!"

As Jeff moved towards the door, Janfri shot a quick glance out the window. It was hard to tell with the drizzle, but he thought he could see misty shapes taking form at the top of the hill.

"J-Janfri?" Jeff asked, his hand on the door knob.

Janfri nodded and moved in front of the door, aiming the shotgun at the center of it. "Open it," he said.

forty-eight

Jackie ushered Ola into the small spare bedroom in Zach's cottage. The gray drizzle outside made the room seem gloomy, but when Jackie went to flick on the overhead light, Ola touched her arm and shook her head. Jackie drew back, startled at the touch. She was afraid for Ola—but afraid of her as well. The *drabarni* looked frighteningly intense—as Janfri could. Jackie thought of a talking cat and objects that moved without a hand upon them and for a moment she saw the blood on the Gypsy's clothes as belonging not to some dog that had died on top of her, but as the result of some cabalistic ceremony. She shuddered, was afraid that Ola had seen the fear in her, could read her thoughts, but the *drabarni* was no longer paying attention to her. She stood in front of the mirror, staring at her own reflection.

"O-Ola . . . ?" Jackie said.

Ola stared into the mirror. There was blood, stark against the white of her blouse, and smears of mud and grass; her hair was a wild tangle and her eyes held fear now in their depths. The drawn features of the reflection's face no longer seemed familiar. She felt Mulengro's presence drawing near like a discordant note in a familiar melody. She wanted to look away from the changing features in the mirror, but her gaze was trapped. Scar tissue formed under the reflection's eyes, the eyes became another's. They were pale eyes and held a fanatic's gaze. Mulengro watched her from the mirror—his image replacing her own reflection completely. Madness stared back at her from those eyes, a madness made all the more terrifying by its obvious belief in its own sanity.

No, she told the image.

Wolflike, the image smiled with sadness. *It is God's work I do, drabarni. Do not fight what must be.*

No. If she could not tear her gaze away, then she would will another's image to shape on the mirror's surface. Mulengro's features wavered.

There can be no escape, she heard him say, but his voice seemed more distant.

She bent her will to the task. *Be gone, be gone, be gone. . . .* The image rippled, like a heat mirage, then grew stronger once more. *Be gone, be gone. . . .* Ola concentrated harder. Again the image wavered. A vein throbbed at her temple and she could feel the beginning of a headache start up behind her eyes. Mulengro became no more than a shadow on the mirror, a vagueness that threatened the borders of her thoughts, but for the moment he was ousted from her mind. She knew the moment's freedom wouldn't last. He was stronger than she, his *draba* more potent. She reached for another Gypsy mind to help her—for Janfri, or Yojo—but when the ether gave up the bolstering strength she needed, the mirror reflected another face back to her. Pivli Gozzle looked back at her from its surface.

Help me, Ola thought to the image.

The old woman in the reflection seemed to be looking directly into her own eyes. For a moment there was no distance between them, and Mulengro's presence was banished.

This is your task, pen, Pivli replied. *I will help as I can, but I have seen that it will be you and your companions that will cleanse us of this evil . . . or it will not be cleansed at all.*

Give me at least his name.

It did not seem odd to Ola at that moment that Pivli Gozzle should be communicating with her. The last time she'd seen the old woman had been in Rommeville and she had no reason to suppose Pivli should be anywhere else. But as their minds reached across the distance separating their bodies, Ola understood that the old *drabarni* was very near. She was near and there were other Rom . . . a great many Rom nearby. . . .

His name I do not have, the old woman replied. *I can only give you my own, sister, and it is Magda Chikno.*

Mine is—

Do not speak of it, pen, *lest he hear you.*

But you . . .

I am an old woman now, sister. Martiya and o Beng already know my name, so why not let him know it as well? If you fail in this task, it will make no difference in the end that he knows it or not.

Why must this task fall to me?

The old woman shrugged. *Is there ever a choice in such matters?* Her image began to waver. *You spend your strength needlessly, farspeaking to me, when you could be using it to fight him,* pen. *God be with you.*

No. Don't go! Ola concentrated, to no avail. The image was almost gone and Mulengro's presence could be felt once more, buffeting her mind. Behind her eyes, the pain was a stabbing wound. *Magda,* she thought then. *Magda Chikno.* The power of the old woman's name brought her image back onto the surface of the mirror. *He is too strong for me, old mother. Even without his mule . . . he is too strong. . . .*

Are you not a Rom? Outwit him, sister, if you cannot stand against him.

But his ghosts . . .

Call up your own ghosts to deal with his.

Ola shook her head. *I have no ghosts.*

We all have ghosts, pen.

He controls the mule—not I.

There are ghosts and there are ghosts, Pivli replied. *You know the ghosts of the dead, those lost mule who haunt the night. Fearsome are they, but not nearly so fearsome as the ghost that springs from the mind of the living. Sinister and vile thoughts—anger, hatred, vengeance, bloodlust—they are strong enough to send such a mulo forth from a man's mind and into the world of the living. Those mule exist only to destroy.*

Ola shivered. *I could never call up such a monstrous thing.*

Just so. And so you must call the dead to help you against this Mulengro, pen.

But . . . Ola began and got no further.

There was a disturbance in the ether. The old woman's image shimmered and was gone. For a long stunned moment Ola stared at the mirror. It reflected nothing, threw no image back, either of herself, or those she could lay on it with the power of her *draba*. She tore her gaze from its black surface to stare about the room, and then she knew. Mulengro's time had come. The noon was upon him and his *mule* walked the earth once more.

She felt the power of Mulengro's mind battering at her thoughts, increasing the pain that already throbbed between her temples. She heard shouts from the front of the cottage, but could not make out what was being said. She felt the *mule* gathering and approaching the cottage. She sensed Mulengro's nearness, felt the hot breath of his dogs on her neck. Her fearful gaze fell upon Jackie's pale features.

"I have no ghosts," Ola said bleakly.

Jackie shook her head, backing towards the door. Her gaze caught movement behind Ola, a misting shape that was creeping in between the cracks in the frame of the window, and she froze. Ola turned slowly. A face took shape in the mist, grew more solid. The blood drained from Ola's cheeks.

"Say-hey," Stan said wetly through his ruined mouth. "What've we got here?"

Pivli sighed, staring at the forest through the misting rain. She'd wanted to tell Ola that she *was* here to help, but couldn't take the chance that Mulengro would learn more than he should. She had felt him listening in. His power was all that she had feared it to be, and more. But she could do nothing now—not without the night. Only in the night, when Martiya roamed, could they deal with him. Otherwise he would simply rise again. The half hour of freedom that *mule* had at noon was not long enough to do what must be done. So they must wait.

Let Mulengro think that the Rom had gathered to box him in. But when the night came, when he had his *mule* gathered at his side and his strengths at their full potency, he would discover why the

Rom had come. Each trunk of the Gypsies' cars was filled with bags of salt, strings of garlic, packages of black pepper and red, and other herbs and spices. They would scatter his *mule* to the four winds and the *drabarno* himself . . . he they would deal with as only the Rom knew how to deal justice.

So they must wait. And pray that Ola and her companions survived this noon assault.

"A half hour," she muttered. Big George looked up from where he sat under a broad umbrella and stirred nervously. Her bright eyes looked up and pinned the *rom baro* with their fierceness. "Is it so long?" she demanded.

Big George shook his head quickly, not at all certain as to what the old woman was speaking of. Pivli nodded to herself and looked down at the muddy ground between her feet. And if they could not rescue Ola and her companions tonight, they could at least avenge them. Water ran in rivulets down her cheeks and not all of it was rain.

forty-nine

Briggs took in the ruined porch and the deep ruts in the lawn in front of the cottage. Looked, he thought, like someone had been hotrodding it and plowed right into the front of the place. He glanced to his left, saw Yojo's Lincoln. He thought of Big George and those long black cars that his Gypsies had parked alongside the road, but before he could remark on the car to Will, the front door of the cottage swung open and he saw a dark-haired man standing there, the twin barrels of a shotgun pointed in their direction. He recognized Janfri immediately.

"Drop it!" the Gypsy ordered as Briggs started to bring up his gun. "And stay close to each other," he added as Will instinctively began to move to one side to make a separate target.

Briggs hesitated, staring at the shotgun. At this range . . .

He started to lower his hand, but then Bob Gourlay hit him from behind and was trying to wrest the gun from his hand.

Boboko reached the doorway of the spare bedroom as Stan Gourlay's *mulo* moved across the room to prevent Jackie from running off. The *mulo* struck her across the face and then pushed her against Ola. The two women stumbled and Stan looked down at the cat.

"Well, shit," he said. "Looks like it's old home week, yessir."

Boboko launched himself at the *mulo*'s leg and passed straight through it. He landed in a startled tumble beyond the ghost, chilled by the misty touch of it.

"It's easy," Stan said conversationally, "once you get the hang of it. I can touch you, you little fucker, but you can't lay a paw on me." He kicked at the cat. Boboko moved a fraction too slow and took a bruising blow on one hip that swung him about and knocked him against the wall.

"No!" Ola cried, moving past Jackie to confront the *mulo*.

Stan's grin was a lopsided leer. "When I'm finished with you," he told her, "there just isn't goin' to be enough left for sloppy seconds, nosir." He grasped the *drabarni* and threw her to the bed. "See, I'm kinda curious," he said as he stood over her. "I'm wonderin'. Can I still get it up when I'm dead, or not?"

Jackie came at him from the side and he punched her in the stomach. As she doubled over, he hit her across the face again and shoved her to the floor.

"You gotta wait your turn," he said. "Me an' the little lady here got us some unfinished business, don't we?"

The bedsprings sagged under his weight and his corpse-reek attacked Ola's nostrils. The ruined face bent low towards her.

"I'm learnin' real fast," Stan told her. " 'Bout the salt and that kinda shit. See, I know you ain't got any on you, little lady, so there's dick-all you can do to me. You or—" he turned as Boboko came at him once more, a meaty fist striking the cat in midair, knocking the animal to the floor "—your little cat."

When he turned back to her, Ola took a quick breath through her mouth and tried to steady the fear, the rage, the sense of helplessness that had turned her muscles to water. She understood now what she must do. Before the *mulo* could touch her, she reached up with her gaze and caught his eyes.

"Te aves yertime mander tai te yertil tut o Del," she said, willing herself to believe what she said. I forgive you and may God forgive you too.

The *mulo* shivered, like a ripple running across a still pool.

"Shut up!" Stan roared, not understanding the meaning of what she said, only knowing that it hurt him. "Shut the fuck up!" He slapped her across the mouth. Her teeth cut her lips and blood sprayed across the side of her face and the bedsheet. Before he could hit her again, she repeated the words, *believing* them fiercely.

Stan Gourlay's *mulo* moaned.

When Bob saw the Gypsy standing in the doorway with the shotgun in his hand—*his* fucking shotgun, for Christ's sake!—the pain in his head exploded and he lunged forward. He fought Briggs for the detective's handgun, but pain lanced up his arm from where the dog had bitten him. Before he could break free, Will stepped in close and hit him in the kidney with the butt of his own revolver. As the big man stumbled, Will pushed him and he went sprawling in a muddy rut.

Will expected to hear the shotgun's blast at any moment, to feel the pellets tear into him. He turned quickly, aiming his gun at the door. He saw that Paddy had the Gypsy covered as well. He glanced at the Gypsy's emotionless features. The shotgun was still pointed at them. The way he and Paddy were standing, the Gypsy could take out the both of them.

"Easy," Will said softly. "Just take it easy, Mr. Owczarek or whoever it is that you are. You pull that trigger and you're not going to solve anything. Either my partner or I'll get off at least one shot and we won't miss. So why don't you lay that thing down and nobody'll get hurt."

Janfri smiled without humor. "Will you tell that to the dead?" he asked.

Briggs started, feeling his own ghosts stirring inside him. They had a standoff for the moment, but with a psycho like this guy obviously was, Christ knew how long it would last. He wondered if Owczarek and Wells were working together.

"What do you mean?" Will asked, keeping his voice reasonable.

Briggs nodded to himself. That's it, Will. Humor him. Just until we can turn this thing around on him.

"The dead rise behind you," Janfri said.

Jesus, Briggs thought. He was being so matter-of-fact about it. What the hell went on inside the head of a guy like this? He might not be the scarred Josef Wells' partner, but he was right out of the loony bin all the same. Briggs could feel his partner's tension. The .38 was slick in his own rain-wet hand. He stared at the Gypsy and for all the world wanted to turn around to see the nonexistent ghosts he was talking about. Ghosts. Maybe Owczarek had them in his head the same way that Briggs did. Then he heard the growling, remembered the dogs—

He turned suddenly. The movement startled Will. As Briggs turned, Will moved a quick step to one side, weapon still leveled at Janfri, but he'd heard the dogs, too, and at last he had to look as well. The shotgun boomed and Will turned in time to see a dog blown apart by its blast not a half-dozen feet from where he stood. And there were more. He fired at the nearest. And then he saw . . . His mouth went slack as he saw the fog-draped shapes moving down the hill, gliding, the rain going right through them. . . .

Briggs' weapon sounded as well. Two quick shots. Then the detectives were backing towards the door. The remaining dogs held off their charge. Four of them were down. But there were others. And those things. . . . Will remembered the hookers' statements, and Red-eye Cleary's . . . fog . . . a man in black. . . . He looked up to the top of the hill and saw the black-clad figure staring down at them. A hand grabbed his arm and hauled him into the cottage.

"Oh, Jesus," he mumbled. "What the hell *are* those things?"

Janfri pushed him away from the door. He dropped the shotgun and hefted a bag of rock salt that Zach used on the heavy ice in the wintertime.

"They are the dead," he told the policeman as he moved towards the door. "And this is all we have against them."

Will glanced at his partner. Paddy looked as ashen-faced as he felt.

"But . . ." Will began. They can't exist, he wanted to say. They can't be real. He turned back to the door in time to see Janfri being bowled over by Bob Gourlay and the bag of rock salt flying from his hands. A dog rushed in after the big man, bounding over their struggling bodies. Briggs fired and the animal was knocked aside by the force of the bullet. Then the doorway filled with fog.

"You are dead," Ola said, "and this world is no longer yours. The land of shadows calls to you. I forgive you and free you, *mulo*."

"No," Stan moaned. He tried to hit her, but his hand no longer had substance. He could feel himself drifting apart, as he had when Janfri had thrown the *baXt* spices on him the night before, but now his essence was being sucked away . . . out of the world itself. . . .

"You are free, dead man," Ola said, rising from the bed.

Stan's *mulo* backed away from her, afraid of touching her. Contact would finish him, he thought.

"No," he told her. "I'm not dead!"

A strange radiance filled Ola. She knew she hated this man, but the man who'd earned her enmity was dead. He no longer existed. This was only a *mulo*. A lost soul that needed her to guide it away from the world of the living, that required her forgiveness to be free. And that forgiveness she could freely give. Mulengro's *mule* were his responsibility and nothing she could do or say would send them on to the land of shadows. But this ghost . . . it existed because she had slain its body. This *mulo* she could banish from the world of the living.

"I forgive you," she said yet again. "Be free, dead man. There is nothing to hold you here anymore."

The radiance spun out of her and touched the *mulo,* glittering upon its fading shape like winter sun on frost. She heard neither the gunfire from the front of the cottage, nor the small sounds that Jackie made as she huddled in a corner of the room. Her entire essence was focused on the *mulo* of Stan Gourlay. Its shape dissolved into ragged tatters of mist, then they too drifted apart, were gone. The last awareness she had of the ghost was a diminishing wail that she could hear only with her inner witch senses. Then it too was gone.

She stumbled to the floor and leaned against the bed. Her hand drifted to touch Boboko's hurt body. The cat's glazing gaze met hers weakly. She bowed her head over the small animal. She was weak, so weak. Stretched so thin. But before the radiance could leave her completely, she fed it into the cat and spoke his secret name. Then she collapsed against the bed, her head lying slack upon the sheets, no longer feeling the pain in her mouth, in her temples. Unconsciousness swept it all away.

Jackie rose slowly from the floor to look at her.

"Ola . . . ?" she said.

Before she could touch the *drabarni,* a rough sound at the window drew her gaze. A huge German shepherd, muzzle smeared with mud, threw itself against the window. The force of its blow shattered the glass pane, but the screen held, pushing the animal back to the ground.

"Please, God," Jackie said hoarsely. "Let it *end!*"

As the dog attacked the screen again, she stumbled to her feet and grabbed hold of a chair. She swung it at the animal as it came through the torn screen.

Grappling with Janfri, Bob felt his brother's *mulo* leave the world for good. There had been a bond between the two Gourlays, as strong as that between twins, and it was through that bond that Bob felt Stan slipping away. The pain in his head was a white-heat sear that burned him to the bone. An inarticulate cry escaped his throat. Gone for good. Stan. Gone forever. He fought Janfri with a new strength, as though killing the Gypsy would somehow ease the pain, the loss, but his arm betrayed him. The dog's bite had stolen the strength from it. And Stan . . . slipping away. . . .

Janfri, fighting for breath, bit down suddenly on Bob's wound. The new pain slackened the larger man's muscles long enough for Janfri to wriggle out of his bear grip. It fired a burning in Bob's head so that he couldn't see anymore. He felt Stan go . . . lost forever . . . gone to wherever the dead go. . . . Moaning, he pushed himself up from the floor, away from Janfri. The pain made him dizzy.

"St-Stan. . . ." he stuttered, flailing his arms. Turning, he fled through the door, straight into the first of Mulengro's *mule*. The ghostly shape was suddenly solid—a black shadow come to life. Its head was like some bizarre cross between a panther and a wolf. It swiped at Bob with taloned paws and tore the man's chest cavity open.

"Oh, Jesus!" Briggs cried.

He fired at the creature, but his bullets had no effect upon it. Bob Gourlay's torn body tumbled to the floor, severed veins still pumping blood. The *mulo* moved over it, towards them. Others thickened in the doorway. Then from the floor, Janfri threw a handful of rock salt at the creatures. They howled as the crystals struck them, tearing ragged holes in their bodies. In a moment, Jeff was on his knees beside the Gypsy, scrabbling for the precious substance. They both threw the crystals at the creatures as quickly as they could scoop them up into their hands. The *mule* retreated from the onslaught, moaning deep and eerily.

Briggs and Will stared, frozen in place by the impossibility of what they were seeing. It wasn't until the dog came through the window that either of them roused themselves. The animal was a rangy mongrel that looked like a cross between a German shepherd and a Doberman. Its pelt was wet with rain and its own blood as it charged across the shards of glass littering the floor. The detectives fired at the same time, the combined blasts of their handguns booming in the confines of the cottage. The force of the shots flipped the big dog over onto its back where it lay twitching until Briggs fired another round into it.

Will moved to the window, followed by Janfri, a scoop of rock salt in either hand. They could see the man in black, halfway down the hill now. Three or four dogs ran back and forth between him and the cottage. Fog hung low across the lawn. Shapes rose and fell in it, twisting sinuously like a clutch of snakes that had been disturbed.

"Oh, Christ!" Will said as the nose of a station wagon appeared at the crest of the hill.

"Yojo!" Janfri cried and ran for the door.

Jackie's panic flooded her with adrenaline and a false strength. She swung the chair and hit the dog alongside its head and shoulders, breaking its lunge. Before it had a chance to rise, she hit it again, driving the chair against it with all the force she could muster. She heard something snap and wasn't sure if it was a rung of the chair or the dog's bones. As she lifted the chair a third time, she saw the dog still coming for her, but its body had a strange twist to it. It snapped its jaws and dragged itself towards her by its forelegs. Its hind legs didn't appear to be working properly. Its spine, she thought numbly. She must have snapped its spine.

She struck the animal again, then slowly backed from it, the chair slipping from her hands. The dog lay still and she collapsed to her knees, gaze going to the window. Rain was coming in, coming down with a little more force than it had before. It splattered on the sill. She glanced at the dog. Its glazed eyes regarded her with reproach. She shivered and looked away, body trembling, then started to circle around the dying animal, making for where Ola lay. Motion caught her eye and drew her gaze to the window again. Fog was thickening there.

"No," she moaned. "No . . . more. . . ."

The fog began to take the shape of a grotesque apish monstrosity that was clambering through the broken window. Jackie screamed.

• • •

The car was already over the crest of the hill before Yojo saw the *mule* and their master. He hesitated, then realized it was too late to throw the station wagon into reverse and back up the incline. It was too steep and with the speed he was already going. . . . Flooring the gas pedal, he stared between the slapping windshield wipers, aiming for the figure in black. The wagon slewed when it hit the mud at the bottom of the hill. Yojo tromped the brake and fought the wheel, muscles bunching under his shirt. Beside him, Zach braced himself. The man in black dodged and suddenly the fog was all over the car. The men inside heard the sound of metal tearing as the *mule* clawed at the vehicle, then they hit Yojo's Lincoln with a thundering crash. The long rear end of the station wagon smashed into the driver's side of the Lincoln, bringing the wagon to an abrupt halt.

Yojo shook his head to clear it. He could see nothing but the gray fog against the windows. Something struck the windshield and a spiderweb pattern appeared on the glass.

"The *mule*," Yojo said. He turned to Zach, but his long-haired companion was as much at a loss as he was. Zach had been so freaked at the state he'd found Beth and Lucy in that he hadn't remembered Yojo telling him to get what salt and *baXt* spices he could from the Taylors' cottage. By the time he remembered, they were halfway to his own place. They should have gone back, he thought now. But it was too late. They were dead if they stepped out of the car. Dead if they remained. They had nothing to stop the *mule*.

Briggs heard a woman scream from the back of the cottage. He started for the hallway, hesitated, then thrust his .38 into its holster and scooped up a double handful of the rock salt. He didn't know what the hell these things were, or why something like salt could drive them off, but he wasn't about to stand around asking questions just now. Time enough for that later. If there was a later. His ghosts whined between his temples as he hurried down the short hall.

. . .

Janfri was out the door and a dozen steps from the cottage when the station wagon slid into the Lincoln with a crash of crunched metal and shattering glass. The *mule* wavered when they saw him coming. A few left the car to drift towards him while the remainder hammered at the car, trying to break in through the windows. The remainder clawed at the roof and the scream of tearing metal was sharp in the air. Janfri flung his first handful of rock salt at the nearest *mule,* then charged through the opening he'd made for himself. When he reached the passenger's door, he heaved the second handful in a wide arc. The *mule* came apart where the crystals struck them. Janfri fumbled with the door handle. He had to get Yojo and the others out of the car—fast. The *mule* were already thickening, regrouping to attack. The door popped open and he grabbed Zach's shoulder, hauling him out of the car.

"Yojo!" he called inside. "Move!"

But a quick glance at the *mule* told him that they weren't going to make it. The *mule* were recovering too quickly. He made a split-second decision and pushed Zach towards the cottage.

"Run!" he commanded, then turned back to the car.

"The Taylors!" Zach cried. "You've got to get—"

Tearing metal screeched in the air as the *mule* tore open the car on the far side, ripping the door right off of its hinges. Zach stumbled against Jeff, who appeared out of the rain like a ghost, what remained of the bag of rock salt in his hand. The two men immediately began to pitch the crystals at the churning foggy mass of *mule* as Yojo emerged from the car, carrying Lucy. Once the big Gypsy was out, Janfri plunged inside the station wagon, trying to get the remaining woman out, but she fought his grip.

"Rod!" she wailed. "They've got Rod and . . . and Lucy. . . . Please, God, don't let them . . . hurt her. . . ."

Janfri lost his grip on the woman as the *mule* on the far side of the car tore her from his hands. He backed quickly away as long taloned paws swept towards him. Only a spray of salt flung from behind him gave him enough time to work free of the car. Janfri tried to concentrate on getting back to the cottage, but all he could see was the *Gaji*'s face as the *mule* tore into her.

"*Bostaris!*" he roared at Mulengro. Bastard. There were too many deaths. Mulengro owed the living too much. . . .

Jeff grabbed his arm and propelled him towards the cottage. A pair of dogs appeared out of the rain, which was coming down stronger every moment. Will dropped the first with a shot from his revolver, but the second was upon Jeff before the detective could fire again. The blond-haired man went down, losing the bag of salt as he tried to keep the animal's jaws from his throat. The *mule* swept over him. By the time Will killed the second dog, Jeff's head lay at an awkward angle and the *mule* were tearing at his body.

Janfri turned, too late to do anything but see Jeff die. Howling, he recovered the rock salt and ran at the creatures, spraying the crystals in a wide arc before him. The *mule* withdrew as the salt gouged tatters from their shapes. The low unearthly moaning began again, deepening as Janfri charged them, whipping the remainder of the crystals at them. Then the Gypsy saw, through the rain and the veil that his rage had thrown across his eyes, Mulengro standing in amongst the trees beyond the lawn, his black clothing merging with their shadows. Dropping the empty bag at his feet, Janfri dragged his handgun from his belt and leveled it at the scar-faced man.

Briggs took in the situation at a glance. Ola was lying half-across the bed, unconscious. The dying dog was sprawled on the floor between the bed and the window. Jackie was on her knees, staring at the monstrosity that was coming in through the window. For one long second, the detective paused, numbed by what he was seeing, his mind refusing to accept the data that his eyes were sending to it. Then he crossed the room in a rush and threw most of the salt into the unformed features of the *mulo*. The effect of the crystals was instantaneous. The salt tore ragged holes in the creature. It lost its shape, became a tattered shroud of mist that moaned with its pain. When Briggs threw the remainder of the salt through the window, the *mulo* came apart and only the rain was there, forcing its way in.

The detective pulled Jackie to her feet and started for the door, then bent down to lift Ola. The *drabarni* was lighter than he'd expected, her head lolling against his chest. On the floor, Boboko lifted his head weakly. Briggs met the animal's stare. He wasn't sure if the cat was Ola's pet or one of the sorcerer's creatures, but it didn't really matter. He didn't have the time to haul cats out of the room as well.

"D-don't . . . wait . . . for me. . . ." Boboko managed.

Briggs almost fell over himself getting out of the room.

Janfri pulled the trigger. The .38 bucked in his hand, but he recovered quickly and moved forward, the weapon leveled for his next shot. He searched the woods with his gaze, but he couldn't see the *drabarno* anymore. He went as far as the first trees, moving in a careful stalk, but Mulengro was gone. Backing slowly from the trees, he turned to chance a quick glance at Zach's cottage. He ended up simply staring, no longer caring what came at him from out of the forest.

He saw the woman he'd been unable to save, lying half-in, half-out of the back door of the station wagon. Beyond the car he saw the corpses of dogs and Jeff's body. So many dead. By the door lay Bob Gourlay's corpse.

The gun slipped from Janfri's fingers and hit the wet ground with a dull slap. The rain was coming down harder than ever. His hair was plastered to the sides of his head. His clothes were soaked through. He fell slowly to his knees. So many dead. And for what? So that they could live only to struggle again tonight? Mulengro's half hour at noon was over—that was the only reason he and his creatures had retreated. But they would be back. What would they do when the dark man returned? Throw salt again at his ghosts that couldn't be killed a second time? Try to kill the *drabarno* who was so untouchable he might as well be a *mulo* himself?

He stared at the ground, plucked the .38 from the muddy grass and turned it over in his hands. A *Gaje* weapon. It was useless against *mule*. They needed Rom weapons against such monsters, but the

Rom had no weapons of their own. Nothing save for their wits. What could cleverness do against such enemies? He started as Yojo appeared suddenly in front of him.

"Come, *prala,*" the big Gypsy said. "It is over for now." He helped Janfri to his feet and took the handgun from his limp fingers.

"Until tonight," Janfri said bitterly.

"Until tonight," Yojo agreed.

Neither man spoke again as they crossed the battlefield of Zach's lawn.

fifty

OPP officer Phillip Archambault climbed wearily into his car and sank back into the seat. He turned his head to regard his driver.

"Anything new?"

Keith Jackson nodded. "Got a couple of sightings."

"Where?"

"Tay Marsh, for starters. Pete Timmons and some of his crowd claim they chased the pack up from the Bevridge Locks. The other sighting was down by McLean's Bay—across from McVeety's Island."

Archambault sighed. He stared through the windshield that was kept clear by the monotonously steady back and forth slap of the wipers. "If this damn rain would just let up. . . ." He closed his eyes for a moment. "Any word on our two big city dicks?"

"Gilhuly called in a while before noon. Said they were heading down into the Mill Pond area."

"Good. That'll keep 'em out of our hair. Now if we could just—"

A crack of thunder rolled across the sky, sounding directly above them. Both men started, then grinned sheepishly at each other. Archambault sat up, rubbing at his temples. Christ, he was tired. He stared at the rain, cursing it. If they could just get the 'copter up again, they'd probably have run those dogs down hours ago.

"Let's head down to McLean's," he said and reached for the radio microphone to give his orders to the other cars. He thought about the slain Perth constable, Craig Finlay, and about the bodies at the Lennox farm. He thought about the Gypsies that were infiltrating the area—up to shit, no doubt, and if he had the manpower right now, he'd be running them out again just as quickly as they came in. He thought about Briggs and his partner. There was something a little strange about Briggs—like he was wired on something. Trying too hard.

Archambault shook his head as the car coughed into life and Jackson pulled out onto the road. Pushing away the turmoil of thoughts, Archambault spoke into the microphone. The one thought he couldn't avoid was, what if the dogs hit another place before they ran them down?

Pivli Gozzle called brusquely for a cup of tea that was brought to her by Big George's wife Tshaya. The half hour when the *mule* could haunt at noon was over, and Ola and most of her companions had survived. Pivli sipped at her tea, ignoring Tshaya, Big George and the others. She was weary from her farseeing, and sickened by what she had *seen*. Mulengro *had* to be stopped. And tonight. . . . She nodded to herself, staring out at the rain-drenched fields. She herself was dry, for Big George had rigged an umbrella to her chair. But out there, in the wet woods. Tonight. They would deal with the *drabarno* who shamed their race. Until then they could only wait some more.

Remembering what she'd so recently *seen*, the old woman's lean frame shivered. *Prikaza* rode the wind today, come to earth on the back of the rain. The bad luck was everywhere. She prayed that it could be turned aside.

fifty-one

After what they had been witness to, it was impossible for Briggs and Will not to accept the Gypsies' stories at face value. It went against everything they knew about the workings of the world, but the supporting evidence was overwhelming. The fact that it neatly explained the murders in Ottawa that the two detectives had been investigating certainly helped, but nothing brought it all into focus as much as the bizarre assault they had been victims to along with the Gypsies that very noon.

The detectives were working with Yojo, clearing out Zach's toolshed-cum-guest-cabin. It was smaller and therefore, Janfri explained, more easily defended. All three men were soaked to the skin as they removed Zach's decade-or-so build up of tools, old furniture and other paraphernalia from the cabin and out onto the lawn. It looked to Briggs, with the rain splattering against it and the various objects piled in a a haphazard heap, like the tail end of an unsuccessful yard sale. He sighed as he set down the remains of a wicker rocker and wiped the rain from his face. A moment later his skin was glistening again. He glanced over to the cottage to see Zach approaching with an armload of supplies.

Briggs grimaced as he picked out the box of salt and string of garlic that lay on top. It was like they were up against vampires or something equally fictional. But then he remembered the *mule* and was glad that they had *something* to hold them off. They were going to need anything they could get.

"How's the kid?" he asked as he followed Zach into the cabin.

The luthier was drawn and haggard. Dark rings hung under his eyes and he moved like a sleepwalker. He'd lost his glasses and the whole world had a slightly out-of-focus look to it for him, which hadn't been helped by the events of the past few hours.

"She's finally sleeping," he said as he put his burden down, "on the back porch. Jackie's lying down there, too."

"She's taking it pretty hard," Briggs said.

Zach thought about Jeff and regarded the detective wearily. "Aren't we all, man?"

Briggs nodded. "Yeah. Look. I'm sorry. I didn't mean—"

"That's okay. Fucking world's going down the drain and, like, what've we got left now anyway?" Zach glanced at Yojo. "Want to give me a hand with some more of this stuff?"

"Whatever I can do to help," the big Gypsy replied.

Briggs watched the two men crossing the lawn, then turned back to Will.

"We've got to get out of here," Will said. "Get some help."

"You figure we can make it through the woods with those dogs just waiting for us?" Briggs replied.

Will shook his head. "But, Paddy. We just squeaked through by the skin of our teeth this afternoon. How the hell are we going to make it through a whole night?"

"Owczarek's got some ideas."

"Which he's not sharing."

"The way I see it, he's planning to go one-on-one with this Mulengro guy."

"Then he's a dead man, Paddy, and where does that leave the rest of us?" Will sat down on a stool and stared at his partner. "I just can't believe this shit, you know? I mean, I know what I saw when we were fighting them off, but it just doesn't feel real. When juju starts stepping out into the real world . . . I just don't know, Paddy."

"Oh, it's real all right." Briggs settled down on the floor and leaned his back against the wall. He dug his pipe out of his pocket and chewed on the stem. He remembered something Ola had told them. Some old woman had given her advice. They had to raise their own ghosts against Mulengro's. He thought about the memories he had that wouldn't go away. The faces of the dead. What he called *his* ghosts. The two hookers and Red-eye, the Gypsies, the Perth constable and the old couple on the farm. . . . He wanted to lay those ghosts to rest. But somehow he didn't think Ola was talking about that kind of ghost. Not when they had real ones to contend with.

"One of us should make a try for the car," Will said, going back to his argument.

Briggs shook his head. "The cars aren't running and you wouldn't make it on foot, Will. You know that."

Both the Lincoln and the station wagon that had belonged to the Taylors were out of commission, and Mulengro or his *mule* had sabotaged Jackie and Zach's cars.

"Maybe Archambault will send someone in looking for us," Will said.

"We better hope he doesn't. It's bad enough we're here, twiddling our thumbs. Do you want half the local OPP taken out in a battle with a bunch of dead things? I say we leave it to the Gypsies— Owczarek and Ola seem to know what they're about. We'll just hang in as back up, Will."

"Changed your tune about Gypsies awfully fast."

Briggs thought about the *mule*. "You don't call this trouble?" he asked softly. The two men sat silently until Briggs rose wearily to his feet. He snagged a string of garlic from the pile of goods that Zach had brought in. Owczarek said they should hang them above each of the two windows and around the door. Then there was the salt and other spices. . . . "Want to give me a hand with this stuff?" he asked.

Will frowned, but rose to help him.

Ola and Janfri watched the lake from Zach's back porch. Ola was in the rocker and Janfri had dragged a chair out from the kitchen. Lucy Taylor lay sleeping in a nest of blankets that Ola had made for her in a corner of the porch, while Jackie had finally fallen asleep on the sofa. A herb tea that Ola had brewed for them allowed them to sleep where the shock and loss that filled them gave no respite. Neither of the Gypsies tried to think of the three bodies that lay in Zach's spare bedroom.

"You know what frightens me the most?" Janfri said suddenly. Ola looked at him, stroking a strangely quiet Boboko on her lap, but Janfri never took his gaze from the rain-soaked view of the lake. The downpour sounded like the sizzling of something cooking in a frying pan.

"What?"

Janfri turned finally, his eyes as haunted as Ola knew her own to be. "That he's right. Mulengro. That we *are marhime* and perhaps deserve his judgment."

Ola nodded. The thought had come to her as well.

"Ever since Yojo and I landed in Rommeville," Janfri said, "I've not been the same, not been the Rom I was. I tried. When Pesha—my wife—when she was still alive. But when she died because I lacked the money needed for her medicine, I vowed never to be poor again. I stepped then into that half-world between *Gaje* ways and those of our own people, taking from each, giving to each, but never truly a part of either. If we have God's blessing, as the *swatura* say we do, to live as we do, taking what we need from the *Gaje* but never letting them *touch* us . . . If that is true, then I have sinned.

"I have friends in the *Gaje* world—friends I might have been even closer to than I was, except that I didn't dare to. I couldn't face losing my place in the *kumpania* for all that it could only offer me poverty and a hard life. I wasn't brave enough to dare that, yet I was distanced from it as well. On the one hand I would see my *Gaje* companions and know they were as good as any Rom, but then I would see the value they placed on always *possessing* things and I would look again at the Rom and see their poverty as something that bound them to each other. Hardship, yes, but a hardship that knit them into a strong unit with which to face the rest of the world. And then I would think . . ." He paused, sighed. "I don't know what I would think."

Janfri's words frightened Ola. They paralleled her own feelings too closely. She thought of her own vows when her mother died, of the ties she had with the *Gaje*. . . . Jeff Owen's dead features swam up in her mind and she pushed them fiercely away. If she let her grief rise now, it would drown her. But this confusion was so over-whelming. . . .

She and Janfri were like mirrors of one another. Caught between the two worlds. And if that *was* a sin in the eyes of God, then perhaps—it could not be!—but perhaps Mulengro's cause *was* just. That which was *marhime* needed cleansing. It was a basic tenet of Rom belief. But need the cleansing be so final? It depended, she thought fearfully, on how deeply the *marhime* ran. When she thought of the Rom she knew now and compared them to those she'd known when her family traveled in Europe and Asia, they were greatly changed. They had strayed, perhaps too far, from what a Rom should be. Unchanging, fiercely so in some ways, but irrevoca-bly altered in so many others.

"Is he right?" Janfri asked softly. "*Are* we unfit?"

Ola had no answer. She was as startled as Janfri when Boboko spoke from her lap.

"You are *dile*—fools the both of you."

Ola's hand stilled on the cat's back and Janfri stared down at him.

"Mulengro's *dook* is speaking in you now," Boboko said. "His *prikaza* turns your thoughts from what you know to be true. Cus-toms and beliefs are important, but you both worry so much about what you are—Rom or *Gaje, marhime* or not—that you lose sight of what is important: who *you* are. If all the Rom in the world allow Mulengro to kill them, what does that mean? That he was right, or that they were fools? Think on that, rather than letting Mulengro's lies think for you."

Neither of the humans replied for a long time. They watched the rain fall on the lake and listened to its voice on the roof above them. Ola fiddled with Boboko's fur and Janfri counted the knots of his *mulengi dori*.

"We will fight him," Ola said then. "I have no answers, but Boboko is right in this much: The choice is ours. And I choose to fight him. If it is God's will that I die, if He decides that I am *marhime,* then I will die at Mulengro's hand. But I will not surren-der to him. I have no answers, but I reserve the right to seek them on my own, not accept them from a murderer's hand."

"And is not murder," Janfri asked softly, "*marhime* itself?"

Boboko grinned fiercely at him.

"*Bater,*" Janfri said. So be it. He thrust the dead man's string into his pocket and rose from his chair. "I must prepare for the murderer and his *mule.*"

Ola said nothing as Janfri left the room. She stroked Boboko's fur. He'd used up two of his lives in almost as many days. Scratching under his ear, she asked, "How are you so wise now?"

Boboko purred, but made no reply.

Briggs watched Janfri siphon the gas from the various cars in Zach's yard, filling a couple of jerry cans that he and Will had only recently added to the growing junk pile on the lawn.

"Now what's he up to?" he wondered aloud.

"The woman—Ola," Will said. "Didn't she say something about fire doing a number on a . . . a sorcerer?"

Yojo joined the two detectives at the window of the cabin and worriedly watched Janfri go about his work. His *prala* had been strangely reticent, ever since this trouble with Mulengro began, and he ached for him. He knew Janfri meant to call on their dead uncle, but who was to say Nonoka would come? Surely he was in the land of shadows, beyond the call of men? And what was one ghost to do against Mulengro's many *mule? Mule* that were not only spirits of the dead but also—if the old *drabarni* Pivli Gozzle was to be believed—creations of Mulengro's own hatred. Such a thing Yojo found difficult to understand. A ghost was a ghost. Either a spirit of the dead, or it was not a ghost. How could it be otherwise? Bad enough it was to learn that *mule* were real and not just stories. But to know that a man's hatred could create such things as well. . . .

"Well," Briggs was saying. "He can sure as hell start quite a blaze with all that gas."

Will nodded. "Thing I wonder is, how's he planning to get Mulengro to step into it?"

"Molotov cocktail?"

"Hard to say. You saw what those . . . those *mule* could do with a bullet. Swallowed them whole. What's to say they can't do the same with a fire bomb?"

"Christ," Briggs replied. "How should I know?"

Yojo listened to the detectives and nodded to himself. What was his *prala* planning? He watched awhile longer, then went back to helping Zach set the simple wards that would keep them safe from Mulengro's creatures. The long wet day was steadily draining away. Soon the night would be here and with it, the *mule* and their master. As he poured salt along the edges of the window frames, Yojo continued to worry at the puzzle of what Janfri and Ola had planned. They did not want to share it, they had said, lest Mulengro steal it from the unwary minds of those untrained to protect their thoughts. But since when had Janfri become a *drabarno*?

What Yojo feared was that Janfri's plan entailed too much danger for him to share it with the rest of them. The big Gypsy vowed then and there, that no matter what, when the night came, he would be at his brother's side. Those in the cabin would be safe. But he would go with Janfri to take their battle to the enemy. That would be the best way. This was a matter for Rom. The enemy was one of their own, so they must deal with him themselves. He only wished he knew how they were supposed to do this thing.

fifty-two

The rain did not let up. When the guest cabin was as prepared as they could make it, they gathered in the main room of Zach's cottage, studiously ignoring the hallway that led to the spare bedroom where the dead were laid out. They were a quiet group, forcing themselves to eat, for they knew they would need all their strengths for the coming night. But they had little appetite. Zach was the first to rise from the table. He laid his dirty dishes in the sink and puttered around with them a bit, then finally strode out onto the porch.

He could feel the night approaching. There was an oppressiveness in the air that had nothing to do with the day long rain.

The past few days had left their mark on him. Staring out at the lake, listening to the rain, he searched himself for feelings, for some reaction, but found only numbness inside—the same numbness that had let him get through the day. That disturbed him more than the thought of what they'd be facing tonight. He should be feeling *something,* but there was only emptiness inside. He heard footsteps behind him and turned to find that Ola had joined him.

"I'm sorry," she said. "I never wanted to bring any of this onto you . . . onto anyone."

"It wasn't your fault."

Ola sighed. "If I hadn't come here, none of this would have touched you."

"But then I'd never have known you and Boboko," Zach said. "I know it's only been a couple of days, but it seems like it was a lot longer, you know? The vibes were right—even with the boogyman knocking on our door."

His simple forgiveness hurt Ola almost more than the anger she felt he was justified to feel towards her. She'd destroyed the peace of his lake. His sanctuary. He was still alive—not like Jeff lying cold and stiffening in the spare room—but perhaps that wasn't a blessing. Zach had been a man untouched by darkness. A kind soul—truly a Dr. Rainbow. Now *o Beng* had a foothold in his soul and he would never see the world the same again. She wanted to speak, to somehow convey her understanding of the hurt he was feeling, but there weren't words adequate enough.

"It's time," she said finally.

He nodded. "Guess so. I can *feel* the night coming down on us." As he started to rejoin the others, Ola laid a hand on his arm.

"We're going to find a way to get Yojo up to the cabin. Will you keep him there? Perhaps the *shangle* could help you?"

"What're you and Janfri planning?"

"We are going to raise our own dead," she said.

Zach shook his head. "You're not staying in here? Ola, we took everything up to the cabin, the salt and—"

"We do what must be done," Ola said firmly. "Don't worry, Zach. Neither of us are martyrs. It's just that we don't want to have to divide our attention between Mulengro and the safety of you and the others."

"But if you couldn't stop him before—"

"Promise me you'll stay in the cabin—and that you'll see that the others remain there as well."

"Ola, you're just going to die."

"Promise me."

She repeated the words fiercely, eyes flashing. Zach remembered that she was a *drabarni,* that she had power where the rest of them didn't.

"Trust me," she added softly.

He nodded. "I just don't want to see you hurt."

"We'll be careful, Zach. I promise you that."

"Okay. I'll try to keep them inside."

"If you break the wards, if the *mule* gain even the smallest foothold, you will all die. Remember that. Think of the child."

Lucy. Parents dead. Zach nodded. She'd suffered enough.

"You see?" Ola said. "You have responsibilities as well."

"I guess . . ."

"Come. The night's almost upon us. We must move quickly now." She smiled with a sureness that she didn't feel, but it was enough to wake a faint reply on Zach's lips. "Let's go," she said and led the way back to the others.

Pivli Gozzle arose from her chair and went to Big George's car. From the back seat she took her feathered cloak and threw it over her shoulders. The rain glistened on it, ran from the feathers in streams. Big George stared at her. With the black cloak and her wide-brimmed hat pulled low, she appeared to be the Angel of Death herself.

"It is time," Pivli said.

Big George shivered, but nodded. He opened the trunk of his car and began to unload the bags of salt and other spices that the *drabarni* had prepared for them at the Hollis farm. The other Gypsies followed suit. Soon they were following the old woman down the road, laden with their sacks and bags, the rain coming steadily down on them. Pivli nodded to herself as she led the way. She did not need her *dook* to *see* that the other groups of Gypsies were doing the same. She could *feel* them moving into the woods with her, coming into them from all sides. They would meet by the shores of a small lake where Ola Faher and her companions made their stand against Mulengro.

Tonight would see an end to the scarred man in black who claimed he did God's work. Pivli spat on the wet ground. God did His own work, as every Rom knew. He did it, or it did not need to be done. The affairs of men, *Gaje* and Rom alike, were their own while they lived. It was only when they stepped beyond life, into the land of shadows, that God made his judgments. Tonight they would send Mulengro to God's court. She grinned fiercely. The murderer would have nothing to fear if in his life he had been the holy man he claimed to be.

Zach walked by Jackie's side, leading the way to the cabin. The night was settling fast over the land and he could *feel* the *mule* stirring on the wind. Yojo was behind him, carrying Lucy. The two policemen followed him, with Janfri and Ola bringing up the rear. When Yojo entered the cabin, Ola and Janfri exchanged glances. Janfri nodded and the two of them moved quickly across the lawn, back to the cottage. Briggs closed the door of the cabin and bolted it, then drew his gun. He stood to one side as Will checked to make sure the garlic strings were in place along the door frame and then began to lay a line of the last of their salt along the bottom of the door.

While Yojo lay Lucy down on a pile of blankets, Zach lit a kerosene lamp. The big Gypsy straightened up and looked around. When he realized that Janfri and Ola were missing, he started for the door. Briggs' .38 brought him up short and his eyes narrowed into dangerous slits.

"Step aside, *shanglo,*" he said quietly.

"Can't," Briggs replied.

Yojo took a half step forward and Zach cried out: "Don't!"

"That is my brother out there," Yojo said, turning to him.

Zach nodded. "And if you go out there, you'll kill him." He glanced at Briggs, relieved that the policeman had agreed to help out with this. There was no way he could have stopped Yojo on his own.

Yojo shook his head. "I want to help him—not hurt him."

"Look," Briggs said. "Zach here explained it to us. So long as we're safe up here, they don't have to divide their attention between us and this Mulengro fellow. If we're running around out there with them . . . All it takes is a split second to lose your attention—and that's something they can't afford. Now I don't like hiding up here any more than you do, but neither you nor we've got the skills those two have. Right or wrong, we're playing it their way."

"Janfri is not a *drabarno,*" Yojo said. He looked from the detectives to Zach. "He has no magic—nothing to protect himself against the *mule.* He will *die* out there!"

Will pointed out the window to where a fog was rolling down the hill through the rain. "We open that door now," he said, "and we're all dead, mister."

Yojo's hands opened and closed at his side as he stared helplessly at the approaching *mule.* For one long moment Briggs was sure the big Gypsy was going to jump him. But before he could work out what he'd do if Yojo did—because there was no way he was going to pull the trigger—Yojo's shoulders sagged and he turned away to sit beside Lucy and Jackie.

Briggs let out a breath that he hadn't been aware of holding and turned to the window again, grateful that the Gypsy hadn't called his bluff. His own ghosts stirred as he watched the *mule* come rolling down the hill like a thick mist. Looking at them, remembering the assault at noon, he wondered at the wisdom of letting the other two stay out there. What the hell could they do against this kind of madness?

"Christ," Will said softly. "I hope this place holds."

Briggs nodded. But he was more concerned about the man and woman out there with the *mule* at this moment, than he was about their own safety. He'd seen what the salt could do to the *mule*. It did a pretty good number on them. But Owczarek and the woman— what did they have to protect themselves?

Mulengro stood at the top of the hill and watched his *mule* move down. He had only four dogs left—and only one of them was a member of the original pack. But he did not foresee needing them. His *mule* would be enough. Tonight . . . ah, tonight. He could sense the other Gypsies moving towards him, but they would be too late to do anything to help the two that were waiting for him in the cottage below. Tonight the blood would flow like God's rain fell, and the world would be cleansed of a great blight of *marhime* as surely as the rain cleansed the earth. Anticipation brought a thin smile to his lips and he started down the hill towards the cottage.

Boboko was waiting for Janfri and Ola when they returned to the cottage.

"They are coming," he said.

Janfri nodded, turning to Ola. "Now?" he asked. He pulled the *mulengi dori* from his pocket and held it between them. Looking at that worn strip of knotted cloth, he wondered at the wisdom of putting their faith in such a little thing.

"Now," Ola agreed. "We will do as the old tales say we must do." Janfri began to hand the cloth to her, but she shook her head. "This is a thing you must do, not I. We will call your uncle, Janfri. If he answers at all, it will be because you called him."

Janfri stared at the cloth. "One *mulo* . . . against all of Mulengro's. . . ."

"They're at the top of the hill," Boboko said from the window. "If you've got anything planned, you'd better do it now."

Janfri nodded. He knew what the tales said. Undo a knot and call the dead to him. A simple thing. Surely it was too simple? "Isn't there some sort of a ceremony?" he asked Ola. "It seems too simple a thing."

They had been through all this before. "Salt is a simple thing as well," she replied.

"Do it, Rom!" Boboko called. "Do it, or flee."

Janfri shot a glance at the cat, then worked at the knot with his finger, loosening it, feeling foolish. "Nonoka Kejako," he said. "*Nano*. Oh, sweet dead one, let the noose about to be tied about my neck be undone. Answer my call, *nano*." His gaze met Ola's, questioningly. She nodded assurance.

"Can't you feel it?" she asked softly. Her *dook* could feel the night stir with more than Mulengro's *mule*.

Janfri felt nothing, only the room growing a little colder. Boboko hopped down from the windowsill, accepted the *mulengi dori* from him, then padded off through the open door in the back porch with the knotted cloth hanging from his mouth. The charm was complete, but to keep its luck, Boboko went to throw the dead man's string into running water. They'd all agreed earlier that they needed every ounce of *baXt* they could get. The night was full of enough *prikaza* and ill omens.

Neither Janfri nor Ola watched him go. They faced the front of the cottage. The room was growing steadily chillier. Ola reached for Janfri's hand. When Mulengro's *mule* began to drift in through the open door and broken windows, the creatures found the pair of them standing in the middle of the cottage's main room, waiting. Ola's *dook* buzzed between her temples. She gripped Janfri's hand more tightly as he increased the pressure of his own grip. The *mule* were inside, but from the floorboards at the Gypsies' feet, thin drifts of mist were rising.

Janfri, a voice as cold as the grave whispered, echoing in the room. Janfri started, recognizing his uncle's voice. But the *mulo* that spoke was not alone. Other shapes drifted out of the floorboards to stand between the two Gypsies and Mulengro's *mule*.

Boshengro, a voice Janfri knew to be Old Lyuba's said.

Ola let go of Janfri's hand. They had their own *mule* now. It was time for her to do her part. She backed away onto the porch, outside to where Janfri had stored the jerry cans of gasoline. She shivered as the cold rain hit her. Manhandling the first can, she sloshed the gasoline along the back of the porch, on the wooden walls and alongside the cottage.

Forgive us Zach, she thought as she worked. If we survive this night, we will build you another cottage—as God is my witness, we will.

When the can was empty, she returned for the second and went inside, spilling its contents on the inside of the porch. The last of the gasoline she kept to fill the small bowl that she'd used the day before for her farseeing. She searched for Mulengro with her *dook* and could feel him approaching, step by step. Withdrawing from actual contact with his mind, she crouched down to wait for his arrival. Her back was to the porch door. She stared at the *mule*—both Mulengro's and their own—that drifted like smoke between Janfri and the front door. Her ears were filled with the sound of the rain. She wasn't aware of the dog behind her until it growled, low in its chest.

"There he is," Will said.

The others, except for Lucy and Jackie, crowded the window to have a look at the man in black. Briggs gripped the windowsill. His mind rocked with a sudden flood of pain. His ghosts roiled between his temples, crying for vengeance, but he couldn't do a thing.

"I count three dogs," Zach said.

"Four," Will said. "I just saw one head around to the back porch."

Yojo stood behind the three men, towering over them, silent.

"They . . . they weren't, like, expecting the dogs," Zach said. "I mean, we should have figured on them, but we didn't, did we?"

There was a long tense silence.

"We've got to help them."

The men turned, startled at Jackie's voice. She hadn't spoken more than a couple of words since the attack at noon.

"She's right," Briggs said.

Will shook his head. "No way, Paddy. You said it yourself. They've got a plan. If we go down there, we could be fucking it up."

The faces of Mulengro's victims swam in Briggs' mind. Red-eye and the hookers. The Gypsies that he hadn't even known when they were alive.

"I've got to go," he said.

"Paddy—"

"I'm pulling rank, Will. I'm going out there and you're staying. Just make sure you get all this salt and crap back in place once the door's closed behind me."

"I am going with you," Yojo said.

Briggs regarded the big Gypsy and nodded. "You're on. Let's go."

Before anyone could raise another protest, Yojo was at the door, drawing the bolt.

"Paddy . . ." Will began.

"Hold the fort, okay, Will? Don't worry about us. Yojo and I are just going to take on the dogs. We're not going to play heroes."

Yojo nodded. "There are no heroes," he said. "Only fools—or men who have no choice."

The two men slipped out and Zach closed the door behind them, bolting it. Will helped him rearrange the line of salt so that it was the same as Ola had shown them—covering the entire space between the floor and the bottom of the door. When Zach stood up, he saw that Jackie had taken their place at the window. The look on her face reminded him of Ola. There was no mercy in it. Not for the man in black.

Janfri could smell the gasoline that Ola was splashing on the porch but he didn't turn around. He stared at the swirl of misty shapes that were taking form in front of him. His head was filled with voices that he knew—voices of the dead. His aunt's. His parents'. His wife's. They had all come. The formed a wall between Mulengro's *mule* and himself.

"Devlesa avilan," Janfri murmured. It is God who brought you.

His head rang as ghostly whispers filled his mind with the traditional reply: *Devlesa araklam tume.* It is with God that we found you.

Mulengro's *mule* surged forward, but the spirits of Janfri's dead would not let them pass. The air hummed with an eerie sound as the *mule* struggled. Janfri could feel the hairs at the nape of his neck stand on end. The mists thickened, roiling in the confined space, until the struggle took the *mule* outside. Janfri let out a breath. His head rang with the weird sound of the ghostly battle. He was about to turn to look at Ola, to make certain that she was ready, when movement in the doorway caught his eye. He froze and stared into the scarred face of Mulengro. A pair of dogs, fur matted and dripping, crowded the doorway by the dark man's legs. Mulengro smiled.

"You are a clever Rom," he said mockingly, "but not clever enough. Have you become a *drabarno* now as well? For you will need *draba* if you wish to stand against me."

Janfri remained silent and began to sidle to one side of the room. Mulengro stepped inside, still smiling. He moved slowly forward and Janfri prayed that Ola was ready to throw her gasoline. His hand was in his pocket, fingers wrapped around the Zippo lighter that he'd found in one of Zach's kitchen drawers. He was worried about the dogs—how could they have been so stupid as to forget the dogs?— but their plan could still work. Mulengro need only move a little deeper into the cottage. Far enough from the door. Then Ola would throw the gasoline onto Mulengro with her *draba* and he would throw the lighter. . . .

It was a simple plan. Too simple, he'd feared. But they had managed to raise their ghosts as Ola's friend Pivli had said they must. With that success . . . He waited until Mulengro glanced at his dogs and stole his own quick glance to the porch where Ola was waiting in the shadows. He looked back quickly—quickly enough so that

Mulengro hadn't caught the movement of his eyes—and set his face into a hard mask, refusing to betray the dismay that ran through him. When he'd looked to the porch, Ola hadn't been there.

Ola moved without thinking. She threw the bowl of gasoline directly into the dog's face. It struck the animal's eyes and went into its open mouth, choking and blinding it. Breaking the bowl on the floor, she lunged forward, using one of the shards as a makeshift knife. She overextended herself at the same moment as the dog was frantically shaking its head and fell over it, landing outside. The dog turned instinctively and bowled her over as she started to rise. She slid on the mud, down the steep incline that ran from the back of the cottage towards the lake.

The dog came after her—driven by its need to obey Mulengro above its personal pain—but before it reached her, a small calico shape launched itself at the dog and landed on its head. Boboko raked down with his hind paws, tearing out one eye. The dog howled, swinging its head frantically as it tried to dislodge the cat. Boboko's hind legs churned, cutting strips of flesh from the dog's face and blinding its other eye. Not until the dog fled howling did Boboko drop from his perch. The cat stumbled, regained his balance quickly.

"Janfri!" Ola cried and began to scramble back up the muddy incline. He was alone in the cottage with Mulengro, without her there to complete their plan.

She caught hold of a thin-boled birch and used it as leverage to get over the worst of the muddy slope. Then she saw the second dog, standing guard between herself and the porch door, and she knew that Janfri was on his own.

The Gypsies moved like *mule* themselves as they hurried through the dripping forest. Big George silently cursed the old *drabarni* that led them on at an ever quickening pace. The speed neither slowed her nor seemed to tire her.

"Hurry!" Pivli hissed from ahead. "Are you Rom, or *Gaje* weakened from the easy life?"

They were Rom weakened from the easy life, Big George thought, but he stepped up his pace.

Somehow, Janfri thought, he had known it would come to this. From that first moment when he'd seen his *tsera* aflame, when he'd watched it burn down and seen the *marhime patrin* painted on its wall, he had known his life would never be the same again. He began to slowly back onto the porch, the gasoline reek thick in his nostrils, his fingers tight around the lighter.

"You are not the only one that God speaks to," he told Mulengro. "He has spoken to me as well. He has told me that you are not His hand of justice, but *o Beng*'s offal. That at night you suck at *o Beng*'s penis as a babe might at its mother's breast."

Mulengro's face contorted, the scars drawing tightly under his eyes.

"For that you will die slowly," he said.

Janfri grinned. The barbs had scored. Mulengro was moving forward, following him onto the porch, not stopping to smell the gasoline that choked the air, not bothering to listen to his *dook* that must be warning him of the danger.

"Is it not true?" Janfri mocked. "That when God numbers His mistakes, you are the first He counts? He told me of your birth. Did you think you were a Rom? He told me that you were hatched from the shit of the *Gaje*."

Mulengro charged him, his *draba* forgotten. Janfri pulled the lighter from his pocket. He was ready now. It no longer mattered that he lived between the worlds of the Rom and the *Gaje*. It did not matter how he lived. Only how he died.

Janfri thumbed open the Zippo and, as he reached for the man in black with his free hand, he turned the metal wheel against the flint. The spark ignited the gas fumes and the porch exploded.

• • •

The blast of the explosion knocked Ola from her feet and threw her to the bottom of the hill. She landed hard, knocking the breath out of her. She moaned as she clawed herself to her hands and knees and stared at the roaring inferno above her. The flames leapt high, hissing as the rain struck them; all around her were burning boards and the heavy reek of the fire.

"Oh, Janfri," she whispered and buried her face in the wet grass.

"Janfri!" Yojo roared as he tried to make his way up to the burning building.

Briggs tackled him, refusing to let go.

"You can't do anything!" he shouted in the big Gypsy's ear. "For God's sake, man! There's nothing you can do!"

"My brother," Yojo moaned. "Let me go to my brother. . . ."

Briggs tightened his hold. There were tears in his eyes. He didn't know this Owczarek. He was just a Gypsy. But the ghosts inside him were quiet now, and as he watched the building burn he knew that Janfri had done what he was sure he wouldn't have had the courage to do himself. He let the tears fall and held onto Yojo, refusing to let another pay the awful price that Owczarek had.

"It's over now," he said softly, his mouth close to Yojo's ear.

It took a long time before Yojo lay still, sobbing quietly with his face pressed against the wet earth.

Pivli Gozzle stepped from the forest into the clearing around the burning cottage. She had seen the explosion. And with her *dook,* she had *seen* what had caused it.

"We are too late," she said in a voice suddenly weighted with weariness. She felt her years as she had not felt them before.

Big George stared at the burning building, eyes wide with shock. "Too late?" he repeated numbly.

"Too late to save Boshengro. But there is still that final task to complete. The reason that we came." Pivli turned to the *rom baro.* "Give me that sack you carry."

Silently, Big George handed it over. The lawn around them was filling with Gypsies. They stood as quietly as he did in the rain, watching the old woman in her feathered cloak draw near the inferno. She approached the cottage and, reaching into the sack, threw salt and other *baXt* spices into the flames.

"You accepted the name of Mulengro while you lived," she cried, raising her voice above the roar of the flames. "I need no name to command you now that you are dead. Come to me, *mulo,* o bitter dead one. Come to me and hear what the Widow of Goose Hill has to say to you."

What came out of the burning cottage was a ghostly shape, tattered like a torn funeral shawl.

"What do you want of me, old woman?" the apparition demanded.

The Rom grew more quiet still and stood closer to one another. Zach and the others came out of the guest cabin to stare speechlessly at the Gypsies, at the old woman and the thing she confronted.

"You can do nothing to me now, old woman," Mulengro's *mulo* said.

Pivli laughed, harsh and bitterly. "And you have done so much! Murderer! I would spit on you, but you are nothing now. You are dead and the land of shadows calls you. We will revile your memory, but we forgive you."

"No!" the apparition roared. "I will not go!"

"We forgive you." Pivli turned to the gathered Rom. "Is that not so, you Romany *chal* and *chi?* Do we not forgive this murderer? Will we not send him on to the land of shadows where he can trouble the living no more?"

"No! NO!" Mulengro cried.

But the Rom had listened well to the old woman before they left the Hollis farm. They moved forward by ones and twos, throwing handfuls of *baXt* spices into the flames. They *believed* their forgiveness as they had believed nothing else before.

"Bater," Pivli said. "You see?"

"No. . . ." Mulengro moaned. But his shape was already drifting apart.

"We are the *kris* of all the Rom tonight, murderer. You have our judgment. You are *marhime*. You will never be spoken of again. But we will forgive you—now and forever more. Be GONE!"

The wind and rain blew apart the *mulo,* and it was gone. For long moments only the hiss and splatter of the fire and rain could be heard. Then another shape emerged from the fire.

"And I?" it asked in Janfri's voice, grown hollow and distant, for it, too, was a *mulo.* "Am I forgiven too?"

Pivli regarded the apparition with tears in her old eyes. "There was nothing to forgive, Boshengro. You were always *o phral* in our eyes."

For a moment, those who knew Janfri saw his features in the misty shape of his *mulo.* A trace of a smile touched its lips.

"A true Rom," it repeated. "*Bater.* Tell my *prala* Yojo . . . I loved him well."

"I will," Pivli said. "I will do this thing, as God is my witness."

She bowed her head. When she lifted her gaze, the *mulo* was gone.

The old woman turned and slowly made her way alongside the cottage to where her *dook* told her Ola was. There were still *mule* loose in the night—those Janfri had called to him, but they would return soon to the land of shadows, and those of Mulengro's, but they no longer had his madness driving them on. Pivli vowed to remain in these woods until the last of them was gone. But for now . . . for tonight . . . by the grace of God, it was over.

Epilogue

Akana mukav tut le Devlasa.
—Romany saying
[I leave you now to God.]

The autumn was gone and so was the long winter that had followed it. Spring was in the air and Leeds County was green with the joy of it. Ola had the taxi drop her off at the windmill on the Scotch Point Road. She shouldered her knapsack and walked along the dirt track, her mind filling with memories with each step she took. The ghosts were still here, but they were only the ghosts of her mind—memories, not the *mule* that she had fought with the others last summer, the summer that Janfri la Yayal and Jeff Owen had died.

When she reached the crest of the hill, she paused. Zach's land lay just beyond it. A few more steps and she would see it. She could hear a hammer. The sound was clear in the still air. It was still too early for the cottagers to start coming up. She thought again of her choice, of why she was here, of what it meant to her, as a Rom and as a human being. A sad smile touched her lips as she remembered Boboko's advice on that terrible night. What was important was what *she* was—not how she fit into either *Gaje* or Rom society. She smiled. She'd missed Boboko. Both his wisdom and his humor.

She took a quick breath and took those last few steps, then looked down. The new cottage was only a foundation and a webwork of two-by-four frames, but she could see by its lines that it was going to be even lovelier than the old place. She could see Zach, stripped to the waist, hair tied back, bandana around his head and granny glasses perched on his nose. He was hammering away, oblivious to her presence, but a small calico head looked up right away. Ola's smile widened. Boboko's *dook* had probably told him she was coming before she even got out of the taxi. She saw the cat say something to Zach and the luthier straightened, shading his eyes as he looked in her direction. She held her breath. Only when he smiled and waved did she start down.

There was an awkward silence after she'd laid her knapsack down. She ruffled Boboko's fur and looked at Zach.

"You're looking well," she said finally.

"You too."

"How's Lucy?"

Zach shrugged, a shadow touching his eyes. "Haven't seen her, though she writes. She's staying with an aunt and uncle out west, around Calgary. She says she doesn't like it too much—it's too, like, flat, you know?"

"And Jackie? Do you hear from her?"

"Not since—you know. Folks up at Tinkers say she moved down to New England somewhere. Better vibes. I see that detective once in a while—Paddy Briggs. Remember him? He was the older one. He drops by just to, like, see how things are going. He brought a friend of Janfri's up the first time, a musician. He'd been working on an album with Janfri and he left me a tape of their demos for it. It's rough—but beautiful, you know?"

"And how are things going with you, Zach?"

She looked at the frame of the cottage, then turned so that she could see the guest cabin that he'd been living in until the cottage was rebuilt.

"They're going," Zach said.

Another awkward silence followed.

"There's . . . no one chasing me this time," Ola said.

"Hey. I never said—"

"I know." She smiled. "Are you still looking for a partner?"

"You mean it? You're going to stay?"

She nodded.

"Oh, wow. No shit?"

"No shit."

They both grinned. Ola thrust out her hand. "Partners?"

He took her hand. "You bet."

Boboko yawned and stood up on the plank that he'd been lying on. "Well, now that we've got that settled," he said, "how's about some lunch?"

"What do you think?" Zach asked.

"Sounds lovely."

Zach headed off to the cabin with Boboko trailing in his wake, but Ola stood for a moment, looking at the lake, remembering. The water was still. The reeds on the far shore beyond which the herons nested were still brown, but the trees on the hills above the marsh were a perfect shade of green. She knew they were all gone, the *mule,* but for a moment she imagined she could hear a fiddle playing, softly, as though from a great distance away. She smiled. Glancing at her knapsack, she willed it into the air and headed over to the cabin where Zach and Boboko were waiting for her. The knapsack bobbed in the air behind her.

"You're going to have to teach me how you do that," Zach said.

Ola laughed. "Only if you teach me how to be a carpenter and whatever else I'll need to be to help get this place in shape. I want to build it *with* you, not watch you do it."

"I think I'm getting the better part of the deal."

Ola shook her head. "I don't think so," she said. Her voice was soft and happy.

"Lunch?" Boboko piped up hopefully.

Ola let the knapsack swoop down at him.

Afterword

Romanies have fascinated me for a great many years, not just because of their Romantic image, but because they represent a living embodiment of the Trickster—whether it be the Puck of the British Isles, or Old Man Coyote of our Native Peoples. What appears amoral about them is, in fact, merely a completely different viewpoint. Perhaps, by exchanging their horse-drawn caravans for Caddys, and their tents for tenements, they don't hold the same appeal for as many people as they did in the early part of this century. But for me, their continued coexistence with, but refusal to assimiliate into, Western society merely enhances their romance.

Being a *Gajo* I doubt very much that I've been able to do more than scratch the surface in regards to Rom beliefs and customs, but I hope that any Gypsy reading this book will understand that I tried my best to present them in an honest light and tell a good story at the same time. To the rest of you *Gaje* out there, I hope this book will interest you in the Rom enough to seek out some more factual books on them—particularly books written by Romanies, rather than just about them.

And for those of you whose interests include music, the Ewan MacColl songs quoted as epigraphs come from a radio ballad that he wrote for the BBC in England, along with Peggy Seeger and Charles Parker. It was called "The Travelling People" and a recording was available in the late sixties from Argo Records (catalogue # DA 133). The song by Robin Williamson (who's as much a Trickster as he is a bard) comes from his LP, *A Glint at the Kindling* (Flying Fish, FF 096).

Addendum to Afterword

And now as I write this, it's eighteen years on.

Ewan MacCol passed away in 1989 and his voice—both the songs he wrote and his singing—is much missed. Robin Williamson is still gypsying around the world, telling his stories and playing his music. The world is much changed and there blows a wind in certain literary quarters that frowns upon something called cultural appropriation, by which is usually meant white authors mining the cultures of minorities for their own profit and gain while the voices of writers from those same minority cultures go unheard.

I understand their discouragement. It must be so frustrating to see your culture represented in somebody else's book—perhaps wrongly, perhaps hitting a best-seller list and making all kinds of money for its author—while your own work goes mostly unread because it seems only small literary presses will take a chance on something that is (mistakenly) perceived as not capable of grabbing a viable enough market share to make a larger-scale publication commercially viable.

But I don't think that censuring the white authors is the answer. We should rather be presenting a united front and promoting each other's work.

I come from a mostly white Western cultural background—at least I was brought up that way. My mother's Dutch, my father was born in Sumatra of a mix of Dutch, Spanish, and Japanese blood. Does this mean that my literary palette can only be composed of characters with that same genetic background? By such logic, I couldn't even have completely white characters in my writing, little say women, blacks, Native Americans . . . or Gypsies.

And let's not even get into the fields of fantasy and science fiction. I mean, when was the last time you read a book written by an elf, a wizard, an android, a Martian?

No, we can't limit our palette—that's the death of good writing.

But we can make sure that we approach cultural and sexual differences with respect when we write about them. We have to do our research. If we can, we might even run the material by someone from that different culture—not to be politically correct, but for the sake of veracity. Nothing is worse than the uninformed author; all they do is spread stereotypes and, often, outright lies.

And as I mentioned above, we can support our brother and sister authors whose work comes from a less mainstream perspective. We can and should promote their writing. We can and should be buying and reading those books ourselves, because if those voices aren't heard, we're not only doing those writers a disservice but we're doing literature a disservice as well. Instead of tearing down the white literary establishment, let's work to turn it into a rainbow. My life has been greatly enriched by reading the books of writers such as Thomas King, Sherman Alexie, Susan Power, Toni Morrison, Lisa Jones, Ronald Lee, Manfri Frederick Wood, Sandra Cisneros, Evelyn Lau, William Wu, Leslie Marmon Silko, Robert Rodi, Sarah Schulman, Jeanette Winterson, Dorothy Allison . . . the list could go on for pages. These are simply a few that come immediately to mind.

Some have already been embraced by the literary establishment; others aren't but should be. The point is, let's not simply lionize the Shakespeares and Dickenses; let's not forget the other voices. But let's not censure each other as well. You can learn as much from reading a white author writing about the black experience as you can from reading a black author writing about it. You don't learn the same thing, but both are worthy of our attention.

Let the criteria be good writing—books that inform and enlighten us while they tell a story—not the source of the writing. And if that makes me sound naïve, so be it. But I'll continue to read as widely as I can, and I'll be enriched by it. And I'll continue to use as large a character palette in my writing as the story requires, because I can't do otherwise and still maintain my integrity to my work.

—Charles de Lint
Fall 2003

Glossary

[NOTE: Romany is not usually written down, so opinions about the pronunciation, spelling and sometimes the meanings of words vary in different parts of the world.]

arakav tut—take care; watch out
ashen Devlesa—may you remain with God

bater—so be it
baXt—good luck (the "X" is pronounced like the "ch" in loch)
Beng, o—the Devil
Bi kashtesko merel i yag.—Without wood the fire would die.
boshbaro—big fiddle
boshengro—literally "fellow who plays the fiddle"
bostaris—bastard
bozur—the money-switching game

chal—man
chao—tea brewed with sugar and served over fruit
che chorobia—what vagaries; how odd; how unusual
chi—woman
czardas—a musical finale; illogical in a musical sense; pure emotion

darane swatura—stories told for fun
Devlesa araklam tume—It is with God that we found you
Devlesa avilan—It is God who brought you
diklo—traditional Rom scarf
dilo (f. dili; pl. dile)—fool

dook—abbreviation of "dukkerin;" means variously "the luck," "the sight" or "the magic"

draba—magic; medicine

drabarni (m.*drabarno;* pl. *drabarne*)—one who works with medicine or magic

droboy tune Romale—traditional Rom greeting

dukkerin—fortune-telling

Feri ando payi sitsholpe le nayuas.—It was in the water that one learned to swim.

Gaje (adj. & pl. noun; m. *Gajo;* f. *Gaji*)—non-Gypsy

Gaje si dilo—The non-Gypsy is a fool

Hay kiro?—And yours?

kesali—forest fairies

khanamik—father of groom or bride

kris—group of elders; collected will of the Rom

kumpania (pl. *kumpaniyi*)—a group of Rom traveling or living together in a community

Kurav tu ando mul.—I defile your mouth.

marhime—ceremonially defiled; unclean

Martiya—the night spirit; the Angel of Death

Mek len te han muro kar.—Let them eat my penis.

Misto kedast tute—You did well.

mobile—vehicle; car

Moshto—The God of Life; has three sons

mulengi dori—dead man's string

mulo (f. *muli;* pl. *mule*)—ghost; spirit of a dead Rom

na may kharunde kai tshi khal tut—Not to scratch where it did not itch.

nano—uncle

natsia (pl. *natsiyi*)—tribe

nivasi—water fairies

paramitsha—fairy tales

patrin—information symbol

patteran—signs the Rom leave behind for other Rom that might take the same trail

pen—sister

perdal l paya—beyond the waters (European Rom expression meaning North America)

phral—a true Rom

phuri dai—wise woman

phuvus—underground fairies

pivli—widow

pliashka—bridal brandy offered as gift to bride's father

pomana—wake

prala—brother

prikaza—bad luck; misfortune

rom baro (f. *rom bari;* pl. *rom bare*)—the leader of a *kumpania;* literally "big Gypsy" or "important Gypsy"

Rommeville—Rom name for New York City

Royal Town—Rom name for London, England

San tu Rom?—Are you a Gypsy?

sarishan—how do you do; traditional Rom greeting

shanglo (f. *shangli;* pl. *shangle*)—police

swato (pl. *swatura*)—stories told to chronicle the history of the Rom and keep it alive

Te aves yertime mander tai te yertil tut o Del.—I forgive you and may God forgive you.

te merav—may I die if

Te xal o rako lengo gortiano.—May the crabs (cancer) eat their gullets.

tsera—tent; household

Tshatshimo Romano.—The truth is expressed in Romany.

Tu prala?—Your brother?

urme—fairies or evil spirits believed to be responsible for the fates of men

uva—yes

vadni ratsa—the wild goose of Rom legend
vurdon—wagon

World's Fair Worker—corruption of "Welfare Worker"

Yekka buliasa nashti beshes pe done grastende.—With one behind you cannot sit on two horses.